Praise for the novels of
New York Times bestselling author

SUSAN KRINARD

"Animal lovers as well as romance readers and those who enjoy stories about mystical creatures and what happens when their world collides with ours will all find Krinard's book impossible to put down."
—*Booklist* on *Lord of the Beasts*

"A poignant tale of redemption."
—*Booklist* on *To Tame a Wolf*

"A master of atmosphere and description."
—*Library Journal*

"Susan Krinard was born to write romance."
—*New York Times* bestselling author Amanda Quick

"Magical, mystical, and moving...fans will be delighted."
—*Booklist* on *The Forest Lord*

"A darkly magical story of love, betrayal, and redemption....
Krinard is a bestselling, highly regarded writer who is deservedly carving out a niche in the romance arena."
—*Library Journal* on *The Forest Lord*

"With riveting dialogue and passionate characters, Ms. Krinard exemplifies her exceptional knack for creating an extraordinary story of love, strength, courage and compassion."
—*Romantic Times BOOKreviews* on *Secret of the Wolf*

Also available from

Susan Krinard

and HQN Books

Come the Night
Dark of the Moon
Chasing Midnight
Lord of the Beasts
To Tame a Wolf

**Available from Susan Krinard
and LUNA Books**

Shield of the Sky
Hammer of the Earth

**Watch for the latest paranormal romance from
Susan Krinard and HQN Books**

Lord of Sin

Coming in fall 2009

SUSAN KRINARD
Lord of Legends

HQN™

Recycling programs
for this product may
not exist in your area.

ISBN-13: 978-0-373-77365-7
ISBN-10:   0-373-77365-X

LORD OF LEGENDS

www.HQNBooks.com

Printed in U.S.A.

Dear Reader,

Of all the mythological creatures that have sprung from man's imagination, none has been more beloved than the unicorn.

Nearly every culture in the world has its unicorn. The ancient Greeks were convinced that the unicorn, which they called the monoceros, made its home in India. The Chinese had the qilin, a peaceful beast that could walk on water and harmed no creature save sinners. Sometimes depicted with a dragon's head, a deer's body, a horse's hooves and a lion's tail, the qilin most often made its appearance during the reigns of benevolent rulers, and was considered the king of all "hairy beasts." Similarly, the Japanese kirin was a creature of good luck and paramount among all living creatures.

In medieval Europe, the unicorn was a part of Christian symbolism and tales of courtly love. He represented fidelity, purity and nobility. He was fierce but gentle, wild and proud, but easily tamed by a virgin maid. His horn could become a deadly weapon or neutralize poison. In the famous "Hunt of the Unicorn" tapestries, he is brought low by a virgin and wounded by hunters, but in the end becomes a contented captive, chained by a golden collar to a pomegranate tree…a symbol of fertility.

The unicorn has continued to inspire stories, novels, art and music even today. He cannot be destroyed by the cynical pragmatism of our modern world. But he remains elusive, mysterious, invisible to our mortal eyes.

But what if a unicorn returned to our world from the Faerie realm where he had taken refuge from the hounds and spears of men? What if he were cast out in human form, compelled to accept a new body, imprisonment…and the aid of a beautiful virgin determined to "save" this strange man from a seemingly terrible fate?

Lord of Legends was based on these ideas. I hope you enjoy Ash and Mariah's journey as much as I enjoyed creating it.

Susan Krinard

Lord of Legends

Now I will believe
That there are unicorns...
—William Shakespeare,
The Tempest

PROLOGUE

New York City, 1883

"MAMA? Mama!"

Portia Marron looked at Mariah the same way she had for the past week, her eyes slightly glazed and unfocused, as if she could no longer see the real world.

But the world as Mariah knew it hadn't been real to her mother for many years. Portia saw one much more beautiful, inhabited by wondrous creatures who sometimes crossed the barriers in her mind to whisper in her ear.

"Mama," Mariah said again, squeezing the frail hand. "Please come back."

Briefly, the faded blue eyes cleared. "Is that my little girl?" Portia asked in the croak of a voice seldom used. "Now, now. Don't you fret none."

Mariah looked away. Mama had relapsed so far that she was living in the distant past, when Papa had still been working on the railroad with his own hands and muscle, and Mama had been a rancher's daughter.

Papa had tried to put that past far behind him. He'd done his best to buy his way into New York society, but his efforts had proved largely futile. Wealthy as he was, he was still one of the nouveau riche, without an ancient family name to open the gates.

Not that Mama had cared. In fact, it had always seemed that

the harder Papa pushed his family to enter a society that rejected them, the deeper Mama retreated into her realms of fantasy.

Mariah patted the withered flesh stretched over the hills of blue veins. "Yes, Mama," she said. "Everything will be all right."

The brief moment of coherence left Mama's eyes. "Do you hear them?" she asked dreamily. "They're louder now. They're calling me."

It took all Mariah's control not to squeeze too tight before she released Mama's hand. "Not yet, Mama. They don't want you yet."

"But they sing so beautifully. Can't you hear?" Mrs. Marron rolled her head on the down pillow. "So sweet. You *must* hear them, my darling. They will be coming for you, too."

Mariah shuddered, knowing her mother wouldn't see. "Perhaps someday, Mama."

"Someday," Portia sighed, releasing her breath too slowly. Then she turned her head toward Mariah, and a strange ferocity took hold of her gaunt face.

"Don't let those doctors take me back," she said. "Promise me, Merry. Promise me you won't let them take me."

Sickness surged in Mariah's throat. "No, Mama. I won't."

"Promise!"

"I promise." She sketched a pattern across her chest just as she'd done as a little girl. "Cross my heart and hope to die."

Mrs. Marron relaxed, the tension draining from her body. "You're a good girl, Merry. Always have been. You never cared about them snooty harpies. The best of them ain't as good as you." She smiled again. "You remember when you was little, and I read you them fairy stories? How you loved them."

"Yes, Mama." She *had* loved them: fairy tales and all the romantic adventure stories about lost princes and hidden treasures. She'd half believed they were true. Not anymore.

Mama felt across the sheets for Mariah's hand. "Don't

give up, Merry," she said. "Sometimes the good things seem far away. Good things like love. But it'll find you, my girl. Sooner or later, you'll have to believe in something you can't see."

That was the old Mama. The one who had been less and less in evidence as the months and years passed. The one who never would have survived in the asylum if not for her invisible companions.

The one Mariah missed so terribly.

She leaned over to kiss Mama's cheek. "You should sleep now," she said. "When you wake, I'll bring you a nice cup of tea and a few of Cook's fresh biscuits."

"Biscuits." Mama slipped away again. "I wonder if they have biscuits there. I'll have to ask…." She closed her eyes and almost immediately sank into a deep sleep.

Mariah's legs were trembling as she rose from the chair beside the bed. All her efforts had gone for nothing. She had been the one to insist that Mama be brought home, so she could care for her. But she'd failed. She was certain that Mama was dying for no other reason than that she wanted to go to that other place.

A place that wasn't heaven. It wasn't even hell. It didn't exist at all and never had.

Mariah trudged down the stairs, hardly bothering to lift her skirts above the floor. The idea of dressing for dinner was repellent to her, but Papa would insist. He would not abandon the life he'd fought so hard to achieve, not even with death so close in the house.

"Miss Marron?"

Ives bowed slightly, always proper, as only an English butler could be. "Mr. Marron requests your presence in his office."

"Yes, Ives. I shall be there presently."

"Very good, miss." Ives bowed again, passed her and continued up the stairs. Mariah wondered if Papa had sent him to check on Mama. He still loved the woman he'd married, though in truth she'd left him long ago.

Mariah continued on to the office and knocked on the door. Papa let her in, chomping furiously on an unlit cigar. His big bear paws hung in the air, as if he didn't know whether he ought to embrace her or fend her away.

"Well, sit down," he said, gesturing toward a chair. "I've something to discuss with you."

She sat and smoothed her skirts, reminded again of how much she detested the new fashion of large, projecting bustles.

Papa cleared his throat. She sat up straighter. He still wanted her to be the proper lady, even when no one was there to see or care.

"You know your mother and I had always planned for you to have an advantageous marriage," Papa began, sinking heavily into his leather chair. "You asked that we put off such discussions while…while your mother was indisposed. But it is now clear that she will not recover as we had hoped."

"She needs more time," Mariah said, knowing that she was lying to herself as much as to him. "Please, Papa. Be patient just a while longer."

"No." He stubbed out his cigar and leaned heavily on the ebony desk. "No more waiting, Merry. It's time and past that you were married."

To someone who will take me before I begin showing the same signs as Mama, Mariah added silently. If such a person existed.

"You may wonder if I have someone specific in mind," he rushed on. "There is a fresh crop of English gentlemen arriving this season, and you will be meeting all of them."

Impoverished gentlemen, he meant. "Viscounts" and "earls" and assorted "sirs" who were in desperate need of a wealthy wife, even if she *were* American.

Mariah didn't have to ask why Papa wanted her out of New York. Away from the influence of her crazy mother. Away from the gossip. He wanted to secure her future, her security…and, above all, her sanity. But there were some things the human will, however indomitable, could not overcome.

"I don't wish to leave New York," she said, meeting his gaze. "Not so long as Mama needs me."

"You've spent enough time in asylums," he said harshly. "You can't make your mother any better, there or here." He pinched the bridge of his nose. "She wants your happiness. You know that, Merry." His commanding tone became persuasive, almost gentle. "You'd make her happiest in these… last days by marrying well and starting on the road to having your own family."

Mariah pressed her palms to her hot cheeks. She wanted children. She wanted them badly. But if she should inherit the madness that had claimed her mother and her mother's mother before her…

Papa was blinded by the hope that she would be different. He still intended to see that she climbed to the heights of society, high enough to sneer at the snobbish "old money" of New York. And the surest way of achieving his goal was by trading money for a title.

As if that would make a difference.

I don't need it, Papa. Oh, I can ape the manners of a fine lady, but I don't belong among them. I've been by myself too long. All I want is a quiet life. Then, if anything goes wrong…

"I can't, Papa. You know I can't."

"I know you *can.*" He was all brute force now, the man who had brought the New York Stock Exchange to its knees more than once, and in spite of herself, she quailed. "You *will.* And you'll begin next week, when the Viscount Ainscough arrives." He turned his back on her. "Mrs. Abercrombie is throwing a ball for him. She has invited you."

Mariah wondered how Papa had wangled such an invitation. Perhaps Mr. Abercrombie hoped to encourage a substantial investment from Mr. Marron and had prevailed upon his wife to accept the former pariah.

"—you'll be wearing a new gown and looking like a queen," Papa was saying.

"I don't need more gowns, Papa."

"You will from now on. A new one for every concert, soirée, breakfast and party during the Season."

Mariah rose and walked to the window, looking out over Central Park. Leaves were turning and beginning to fall. Mrs. Abercrombie's ball was only the beginning. Soon the Season would be in full bloom, and she would be in the thick of it, as if Mama didn't exist.

"I know it's difficult for you, sweetheart," Papa said, coming up behind her and laying his broad hand on her shoulder. "But you'll carry on. You're stronger than…"

Stronger than your mother. You won't hear voices. You'll behave normally. You won't ever end up in a… "Promise that you won't send Mama back to the asylum," she said.

He looked at her with that shrewd, hard gaze. "Are you trying to bargain with me, Merry?"

"Keep her here. Let me see her between engagements, and I'll become whatever you want me to be."

His shoulders sagged. "I don't want to send her back. I only want what's best." He seemed to shrink to the size of an ordinary man. "I agree."

All the air rushed out of Mariah's lungs. "Thank you, Papa."

He waved his hand, dismissing her words, and returned to his desk. "The ivory gown from Worth just arrived from Paris," he said, as if they had never discussed anything more important than her wardrobe. "You'll wear that one to the ball. We'll have to use a few local couturiers until the rest arrive."

"Yes, Papa." Mariah drew her finger across the window-pane, watching her breath condense on the glass. "How many Englishmen do you suppose I'll have to choose from?"

"I imagine you'll snag a duke, Merry. How could any man resist you?"

And what about love? Wasn't she as unlikely to find that with an English lord as with anyone in New York? Was there a man anywhere who didn't want her only for her money?

Papa would use every means necessary to quash any current gossip about the state of Mrs. Marron's sanity, of course. Sufficient wealth could buy almost everything. Everything but what really mattered.

Mariah walked to the door. "I'd best get ready for dinner, Papa."

"You do that. Wear that little pink frock, the one with the lace at the bottom. Bring some cheer to the table."

She nodded, left the office and climbed the stairs, acknowledging the nurse who was just leaving Mama's suite. As she entered her room, she wondered if she might possibly escape marriage entirely. Papa thought her beautiful, but she knew that to be untrue. She was, in fact, a nobody. She had a considerable allowance of her own. Perhaps she could bribe the noblemen to leave her alone. Then Papa would have to give up, and she could find a way to be with Mama until the end.

But things didn't work out as she'd planned. Halfway through the Season she met the dashing Earl of Donnington, already wealthy in his own right, and fell in love. He wanted a quiet, unassuming wife who would be content to remain at his estate in Cambridgeshire while he pursued his own interests; she could think of no better arrangement.

A few months later, Mama died. Mariah insisted on the full period of mourning, but Donnington waited patiently. A year later, she was on a steamer bound for England and the marriage her father had so wanted for her. The end of one life and the beginning of another.

And she never heard a single voice in her head.

CHAPTER ONE

Cambridgeshire, 1885

IT HAD BEEN no marriage at all.

Mariah crossed the well-groomed park as she had done every day for the past few months, her walking boots leaving a damp trail in the grass. Tall trees stood alone or in small clusters, strewn about the park in a seemingly random pattern that belied the perfect organization of the estate.

Donbridge. It was hers now. Or should have been.

No one will ever know what happened that night.

The maids had blushed and giggled behind their hands the next morning when she had descended from her room into the grim, dark hall with its mounted animal heads and pelts on display. She had run the gauntlet of glassy, staring eyes, letting nothing show on her face.

They didn't know. Neither did Vivian, the dowager Lady Donnington, for all her barely veiled barbs. Giles had left too soon...suspiciously soon. But no one would believe that the lord of Donbridge had failed to claim his husbandly rights.

Was it me? Did he sense something wrong?

She broke off the familiar thought and walked more quickly, lifting her skirts above the dew-soaked lawn. She was the Countess of Donnington, whether or not she had a right to be. And she would play the part. It was all she had, now that Mama was gone and Papa believed her safely disposed in a highly advantageous marriage.

Lady Donnington. In name only.

A bird called tentatively from a nearby tree. Mariah turned abruptly and set off toward the small mere, neatly oblong and graced by a spurting marble fountain. One of the several follies, vaguely Georgian in striking contrast to the Old English manor house, stood to one side of the mere. It had been built in the rotunda style, patterned after a Greek temple, with white fluted columns, a domed roof and an open portico, welcoming anyone who might chance by.

A man stood near the folly…a shadowy, bent figure she could not remember ever having seen before. *One of the groundskeepers,* she thought.

But there was something very odd about him, about the way he started when he saw her and went loping off like a three-legged dog. *A poacher. A gypsy.* Either way, someone who ought not to be on the estate.

Mariah hesitated and then continued toward the folly. The man scuttled into the shrubbery and disappeared. Mariah paused beside the folly, considered her lack of defenses and thought better of further pursuit.

As she debated returning to the manor, a large flock of birds flew up from the lakeshore in a swirl of wings. She shaded her eyes with one hand to watch them fly, though they didn't go far. What seemed peculiar to her was that the birds were not all of one type, but a mixture of what the English called robins, blackbirds and thrushes.

She noticed at once that the folly seemed to have attracted an unusual variety of wildlife. She caught sight of a pair of foxes, several rabbits and a doughty badger. The fact that the rabbits had apparently remained safe from the foxes was remarkable in itself, but that all should be congregating so near the folly aroused an interest in Mariah that she had not felt since Giles had left.

Kneeling at the foot of the marble steps, she held out her hands. The rabbits came close enough to sniff her fingers. The badger snuffled and grunted, but didn't run away. The foxes merely watched, half-hidden in the foliage. Mariah heard a faint sound and glanced up at the folly. The animals melted into the grass as she stood, shook out the hem of her walking skirt and mounted the steps.

The sound did not come again, but Mariah felt something pulling her, tugging at her body, whispering in her soul. Not a voice, precisely, but—

Her heart stopped, and so did her feet. *You're imagining things. That's all it is.*

Perhaps it *would* be best to go back. At least she could find solace in the old favorite books she'd begun to read again, and the servants would leave her alone.

But then she would have to endure her mother-in-law's sour, suspicious glances. *You drove him away,* the dowager's eyes accused. *What is wrong with you?*

She dismissed the thought and continued up to the portico. There were no more unexpected animal visitors. The area was utterly silent. Even the birds across the mere seemed to stand still and watch her.

The nape of her neck prickling, Mariah walked between the columns and listened. It wasn't only her imagination; she *could* hear something. Something inside the small, round building, beyond the door that led to the interior.

She tested the door. It wouldn't budge. She walked completely around the rotunda, finding not a single window or additional door. Air, she supposed, must enter the building from the cupola above, but the place was so inaccessible that she might almost have guessed that it had been built to hide a secret…a secret somebody didn't want anyone else to find.

Perhaps this was where her prodigal husband stored the vast quantity of guns he must need to shoot the plethora of game he so proudly displayed on every available wall of the house.

But why should he hide them? He was certainly not ashamed of his bloody pastime, of which she'd been so ignorant when she'd accompanied him to England.

Defying the doubts that had haunted her since Giles's departure, she searched the portico and then the general area around the folly. Impulse prompted her to look under several large, decoratively placed stones.

The key was under the smallest of them. She flourished it with an all-too-fleeting sense of triumph, walked back up the stairs and slipped the key in the lock.

The door opened with a groan. Directly inside was a small antechamber with a single chair and a second door. The room smelled of mice.

That was what you heard, she thought to herself. But she also detected the scent of stale food. Someone had eaten in here, sitting on that rickety chair. Perhaps even that man she'd seen loitering about the place with such a suspicious air.

But why?

She stood facing the inner door, wondering if the key would fit that lock, as well.

Leave well enough alone, she told herself. But she couldn't. She walked slowly to the door and tried the key.

It worked. Though the lock grated terribly and gave way only with the greatest effort on her part, the door opened.

The smell rolled over her like the heavy wetness of a New York summer afternoon. A body left unwashed, the stale-food odor and something else she couldn't quite define. She was already backing away when she saw the prisoner.

He crouched at the back of the cell, behind the heavy bars that crossed the semicircular room from one wall to the other.

The first thing Mariah noticed was his eyes…black, as black as her husband's but twice as brilliant, like the darkest of diamonds. They were even more striking when contrasted with the prisoner's pale hair, true silver without a trace of gray. And the face…

It didn't match the silver hair. Not in the least. In fact, it looked very much like Lord Donnington's. Too much.

She backed away another step. *I'm seeing things. Just like Mama. I'm…*

With a movement too swift for her to follow, the prisoner leaped across the cell and crashed into the bars. His strong, white teeth were bared, his eyes crazed with rage and despair. He rattled his cage frantically, never taking his gaze from hers.

Mariah retreated no farther. She was not imagining *this*. Whoever this man might be, he was being held captive in a cell so small that no matter how he had begun, he must surely have been driven insane. A violent captive who, should he escape, might strangle her on the spot.

A madman.

Her mouth too dry for speech, Mariah stood very still and forced herself to remain calm. The man's body was all whipcord muscle; the tendons stood out on his neck as he clutched the bars, and his broad shoulders strained with tension. He wore only a scrap of cloth around his hips, barely covering a part of him that must have been quite impressively large. Papa, for all his talk of her "starting a family," would have been shocked to learn that she knew about such matters, and had since she first visited Mama in the asylum at the age of fourteen.

The prisoner must have noticed the direction of her gaze, because his silent snarl turned into an expression she could only describe as "waiting."

"I beg your pardon," she said, knowing how ridiculous the words sounded even as she spoke them. "May I ask…do you know who you are?"

Anyone else might have laughed at so foolish a question. But Mariah knew the mad often had no idea of their own identities. She had seen many examples of severe amnesia and far worse afflictions at the asylum.

The prisoner tossed back his wild, pale mane and closed his mouth. It was a fine mouth above a strong chin, identical to Donnington's in almost every way. Only his hair and his pale skin distinguished him from the Earl of Donnington.

Surely they are related. The prospect made the situation that much more horrible.

"*My* name," she said, summoning up her courage, "is Mariah."

He cocked his head as if he found something fascinating in her pronouncement. But when he opened his mouth as if to answer, only a faint moan escaped.

It was all Mariah could do not to run. *Perhaps he's mute. Or worse.*

"It's all right," she said, feeling she was speaking more to a beast than a man. "No one will hurt you."

His face suggested that he might have laughed had he been able. Instead, he continued to stare at her, and her heart began to pound uncomfortably.

"I want to help you," she said, the words out of her mouth before she could stop them.

The man's expression lost any suggestion of mirth. He touched his lips and shook his head.

He understands me, Mariah thought, relief rushing through her. *He isn't a half-wit. He understands.*

Self-consciousness froze her in place. He was looking at her with the same intent purpose as she had looked at him…studying her clothing, her face, her figure.

She swallowed, walked back through the door, picked up the chair and carried it into the inner chamber. She placed it as far from the cage as she could and sat down. It creaked as she settled, only a little noisier than her heartbeat. The prisoner stood unmoving at the bars.

"I suppose," Mariah said, "that it won't do any good to ask why you are here."

His lips curled again in a half snarl. He didn't precisely growl, but it was far from a happy sound.

"I understand," she said, swallowing again. "I can leave, if you wish."

She almost hoped he would indicate just such a desire, but he shook his head in a perfectly comprehensible gesture. Ah, yes, he certainly understood her.

The ideas racing through her mind were nearly beyond bearing. Who had put him here?

There are too many similarities. He and Giles must be related. A lost brother. A cousin. A relative not once mentioned by anyone in the household.

Insane thoughts. It was her dangerously vivid imagination at work again.

And yet…

This prisoner had obviously not been meant to be found. And with Donnington gone, she couldn't ask for an explanation.

Dark secrets. It didn't surprise Mariah that Donbridge had its share.

This man is not just a secret. He's a human being who needs your help.

She twisted her gloved hands in her lap. "I won't leave," she said softly. "Do you think you can answer a few simple questions by moving your head?"

His black eyes narrowed. Indeed, why should he trust her? He was being treated like an animal, his conditions far worse than anything Mama had ever had to endure.

She examined the cage. It was furnished with a single ragged blanket, a basin nearly empty of water and a bowl that presumably had once contained food.

"Are you hungry?" she asked.

He pushed away from the bars and began to pace, back and forth like a leopard at the zoo. She had an even clearer glimpse of his fine, lithe body: his graceful stride, the ripple of muscle in his thighs and shoulders, the breadth of his chest, the narrow lines of his hips and waist.

Heat rushed into her face, and she lifted her eyes. He had stopped and was staring again. Reading her shameful thoughts. Thoughts she hadn't entertained since that night two months ago when she'd lain in her bed, waiting for Donnington to make her his bride in every way.

"Shall I bring you food?" she asked quickly. "A cut of beef? Or venison?"

He shook his head violently, shuddering as if she'd offered him dirt and grass. But the leanness of his belly under his ribs told her she dared not give up.

"Very well, then," she said. "Fresh bread? Butter and jam?"

His gaze leaped to hers.

"Yes," she said. "I'll bring you bread. And fruit? I remember seeing strawberries in the conservatory."

Hope. That was what she saw in him now, though he moved no closer to the bars. Who saw to his needs? She had no way of knowing and had every reason to assume the worst.

"You also require clothing," she said. "I'll bring you a shirt and trousers." His eloquent face was dubious. "They should…they ought to fit you very well."

Because he and Donnington were as close to twins as any two men Mariah had ever seen.

The Man in the Iron Mask had always been one of her favorite stories. The true king imprisoned, while the brother ruled in his stead…

"Your feet must be sore," she went on, her words tripping over themselves. "I can bring you shoes and stockings, and…undergarments, as well. Blankets, of course, and pillows. What else?" She pretended not to notice how ferociously focused he was on her person. "A comb. Shaving gear. Fresh water. Towels."

The prisoner listened, his head slightly cocked as if he didn't entirely take her meaning. Had he been so long without such simple comforts? Yet his face lacked even the shadow of a beard, his hair was not unclean, and his body, though not precisely fragrant, was not as dirty as one might expect.

Again she wondered who looked after him. Someone on the estate knew every detail of this man's existence, and she intended to find the jailer.

She resolved, in spite of her fears, to try a new and dangerous tack. "Do you…do you know Lord Donnington?"

His reaction was terrifying. He flung himself against the bars and banged at them with his fists. Mariah started up from the chair, prepared to run, then stopped.

This was more than mere madness, more than rage. This was pain, crouched in the shadows beneath his eyes, etched into the lines framing his mouth. He reached through the bars, fist clenched. Mariah held her ground. Gradually his hand relaxed, the fingers stretching toward her. Pleading. Begging her to overcome her natural fear.

Drawn by forces beyond her control, Mariah took a step toward him. Inch by inch she crossed the five feet between them. By the tiniest increments she lifted her hand and touched his.

His fingers closed around hers, tightly enough to hurt. His strength was such that he could have pulled her into the bars and strangled her in an instant. But he was shaking, perspiration standing out on his forehead beneath the pale shock of hair, his mouth opening and closing on low, guttural sounds she had no way of interpreting.

Desperation. Yearning. A final effort to make someone listen to the words he couldn't speak.

"It will be all right," she said. "I *will* help you."

His shaking began to subside, though he refused to let go of her hand. But now he was astonishingly gentle, running his thumb in a featherlight caress over her wrist. It was her turn to shiver, though she fought the overwhelming sensations that coursed through her body and pooled between her legs.

Oh, God.

"Please," she whispered. "Let me go."

He did, but only with obvious reluctance. She took a steadying step back, but not so far that he would become upset again.

Her feelings meant nothing. Not when he needed her so much—this stranger who had captured her mind and heart within a few vivid minutes.

"I…" She struggled to find words that wouldn't alarm him. "I must go now. I'll come back soon with the things you need. I promise."

He gazed at her as if he were trying to memorize everything about her. As if he didn't believe her. As if he expected never to see her again.

"I promise," she repeated, and retreated toward the door. His broad shoulders sagged in defeat, and she knew there was no more she could say to him now; he would not trust her until she returned.

Her stomach taut with foreboding, she picked up the chair, moved it back to its place in the antechamber and continued through the door. The prisoner made not a sound. She poked her head out the second door, saw no one, left the chamber and hastily locked the door.

She leaned against it for a moment, breathing fast, until she was certain of her composure. Then she assured herself that there was no observer in the vicinity, replaced the key under the stone and set out for the house.

He hates Donnington, she thought, sickened by the implications of the prisoner's reaction. *Why? And what if he knew that I am Lady Donnington?*

It didn't bear thinking of. And it didn't really matter. She would do exactly as she said. Help him, as she hadn't been able to help Mama.

Perhaps that would be enough to save *her.*

Do you know who you are?

He had understood the question, but he had not been able to answer it, just as he had been unable to tell the female what he wanted above all else.

Freedom. Memory. All the bright and beautiful things that had been stolen from him, though he had no recollection of what they had actually been.

She had not known him, though he had seen her before. She had been present on that day of pain and turmoil, when he had tried to escape his captors. The female…

Woman, he reminded himself, pronouncing the word inside his mind. The woman who had been with the *man,* his tormentor, in that time he couldn't remember.

She had been afraid then, as he had been afraid. She had fallen and grown quiet, so quiet that he had believed her dead. Then Donnington had taken her away, and *he* had been compelled to endure this numb emptiness of captivity.

Until today. Until she had come to him with her soft voice and a warm, half-familiar scent gathered in the heavy folds of her strange garments.

And asked him who he was.

He backed against the wall and slid down until he was crouching on the cold floor. He had greeted her with rage, for that was all he had known for so long. He had flung himself against the bars, ignoring the pain searing into his flesh, and sought to drive her away even as the silent voice within begged her to stay.

And she *had* stayed. She had told him her name.

Mariah. He rolled the name over his tongue, though it emerged as a moan. *Ma-ri-ah.* It was a good sound. One that he might have spoken with pleasure if his mouth would obey his commands.

I want to help you.

He grunted—a sound of amusement he had heard in some other life—and remembered the first thought that had come to him then. He had wanted her to open the cage door, but not merely to release him. He had wanted her to come inside, remove the heavy weight of fabric that bound her, open her arms to him and kneel beside him. He would place his head in her lap, and then…and then…

With a shudder, he flung back his head and plunged his fingers into his hair. There was still so little he grasped, so little he understood, yet he knew why she drew him. *Male and female.* It had been the same in that long-ago he had only begun to put together in his mind.

But never like this. Never like *her.*

Once more he tried to remember the events that had brought him to this cage. He pieced together terrible images of being violently reborn in this world, finding himself horribly changed, hearing a harsh and unlovely voice that made no sense. Men had taken him and carried him to this place where the taint of iron held him prisoner as surely as the bars themselves.

For the first while after he had been locked inside, he had staggered about on his two awkward legs, bumping into the high curved walls and fighting for balance. When at last he was able to walk, he had circled the room again and again, looking for a way out that did not exist.

They had left him alone for two risings of the sun, though he could see nothing but filtered light through the holes in the roof high above. Then another man, ugly and bent, had brought him food, water and a scrap of cloth to cover the most vulnerable part of his body. The man hadn't spoken to him, and after a few days he had realized that his keeper was as mute as he. When the man had returned, he had flung a slab of flesh, saturated with the smell of newly shed blood, into the cell.

Stomach churning with disgust, he hadn't touched it. It wasn't until after another sun's rise that the men had brought him things he could eat. Fruit. Bread. The same things the girl had promised him.

Girl. Mariah. She had seen only a man in him, not what he had been.

He had been mighty once. No one had dared…

Who am I?

There must be an answer. Mariah had promised to help him. He had believed her, until she had spoken the word he hated with all his heart.

Donnington.

He leaped up again, clenching and unclenching his fists, those useless appendages that could do nothing but pull at the bars until his palms were burned and raw.

And yet *she* had let him hold her hand.

He struggled to compose a picture of her eyes, far brighter than the sky lost somewhere above him. Captivating him. Holding him frozen with need.

Donnington. She spoke as if she knew him well; she had asked if *he* knew the man, and she was not afraid of him. *He* could not trust her, despite all her gentle speech.

No. He must learn to understand her—and himself. And until he could speak in her tongue, there could be no further communication.

He returned to his corner and began to memorize every word she had spoken.

MARIAH REACHED THE house in ten minutes, shook the worst of the wetness out of her skirts and strode into the entrance hall. As always, it was dark and grim, with its heavy wood paneling and mounted heads, daring the casual visitor to penetrate the manor's secrets. She walked at a fast pace for the stairs, hoping to avoid the dowager Lady Donnington.

She was out of luck. Just as if Vivian had anticipated her return, she swept out of the main drawing room and accosted Mariah at the foot of the staircase.

"Lady Donnington," she said, a false smile on her handsome face. Her gaze swept down to Mariah's hem. "I see that you have been out walking again. How very industrious of you."

Mariah faced her. "I must contrive to keep myself occupied somehow, Lady Donnington," she said, "considering my current state of solitude."

"Yes. Such a pity that my son felt the need to leave so suddenly after your wedding."

It was the same unpleasant veiled accusation the dowager had flung at her immediately after Donnington had left. *You were never really his wife,* Vivian's look said. *You drove him away.*

Mariah lifted her chin. "I assure you," she said, "he was not in the least displeased with me."

If her statement had been truly a lie, she might not have been able to pull it off. But it was at least half-true, for Donnington had shown no more disgust for her than he had affection. He'd simply ignored her, remained in his own room and left the next morning.

He'd said he loved her. Had it been the money, after all? Plenty of wealthy men could never be content with what they had, and she'd brought a large marriage settlement, in addition to her own separate inheritance.

But surely no healthy man would choose not to take advantage of his marriage bed. The other reasons why he might have left her alone were disturbing. And that was why, if the dowager did believe that her son hadn't consummated the marriage, she must feel compelled to blame that fact on Mariah.

"I'm certain that Giles will return to us very soon," Mariah said calmly.

"Let us hope you are correct." Vivian's stare scoured Mariah to the bone. "You had best go up and change, my dear. Donnington would never approve of your wild appearance."

And of course he would not. The quiet unassuming wife he'd desired must be proper at all times.

Mariah nodded brusquely and continued up the stairs. Halfway to the landing, she paused and turned. "By the way," she said, "Donnington doesn't have any brothers besides Sinjin, does he?"

"Why…why do you ask such a question?"

The outrage in the dowager's voice told Mariah that she had made a serious mistake. "I do apologize," she said. "It was only a dream I had last night."

"A dream?" The older woman followed Mariah up the stairs. "A dream about my son?"

"It was nothing. If you will excuse me…"

Mariah continued to the landing, Vivian's stare burning into her back, and went quickly to her room.

A hidden brother. How could she have been so stupid? It was all too bizarre to be credible. If she hadn't seen the prisoner with her own eyes…

You did see him. You touched him. He is real.

Preoccupied with such disturbing thoughts, Mariah opened the door to find one of the chambermaids—Nola, that was her name—crouched before the fireplace, cleaning the grate.

"Oh!" the maid cried, leaping to her feet. "Lady Donnington! I'm so sorry." She curtseyed, so nervous that she dropped her broom and nearly upset the contents of her scuttle. She bent to snatch the broom up again.

Mariah tossed her hat on the bed. "I'm not angry, Nola," she said.

The girl, her face smudged above the starched collar of her

uniform, paused to meet Mariah's gaze. "Thank you, your ladyship," she said, her country accent a little thicker as she relaxed. "I'll be gone in a trice."

"No need to hurry." Mariah sank into the chair by her dressing table and pulled the pins from her hair. She knew she ought to ring for her personal maid, Alice, but she had no desire to be fussed over now.

Not after what had happened an hour ago. Not after visiting a prisoner who had been treated so abominably, worse than any of the patients she had encountered in the asylum.

"Your ladyship?"

Mariah looked up. Nola was standing with her scuttle and supplies, watching Mariah anxiously. "Are you all right?"

It was a presumptuous question from a servant, at least by English lights. Mariah took no offense.

"I'm fine," she said. She took a better look at the girl, wondering why she hadn't really noticed her before. Nola must have been close to eighteen, with a round, rather plain face, vivid red hair tucked under her cap, light gray eyes, and a mouth that must smile frequently when she wasn't in the presence of her supposed betters. "How are *you,* Nola?"

The girl couldn't have been more surprised. "I…I am very well, your ladyship."

As well as anyone could be in this mausoleum of a house, Mariah thought. But Nola's reply gave her a sudden peculiar notion. If there was one thing she'd learned, both at home and at Donbridge, it was that the servants—from the steward to the lowliest scullery maid—always knew everything that went on in a household. If anyone at Donbridge had heard of a prisoner in the folly, *they* would have done so.

But she had to be very careful not to frighten Nola. Mariah had few enough allies, and Nola, so easily ignored by everyone else, might be just the ticket. "Sit down, Nola," she said.

The maid looked about wildly as if someone had threatened to cut her throat. "I—I should go, your ladyship."

"I'd like to have a talk, if you don't mind."

She realized how she sounded as soon as she spoke. Nola undoubtedly believed she was in for a scolding for being caught cleaning up, and that was the last thing Mariah wanted her to think.

"You're not in any trouble," Mariah said. "I really only want to talk. I'm alone here, you see."

Comprehension flashed across the girl's face. "You…you wish to talk to *me,* your ladyship?"

"Yes. Please, sit down."

Nola returned to the fireplace, set down her scuttle and brushed off her skirts before venturing onto the carpet again. She sat gingerly in the chair next to the hearth, her back rigid.

"Don't be concerned, Nola," Mariah said. "I'd like to ask you a few questions about the house, if you don't mind."

"I…of course, your ladyship."

Mariah folded her hands in her lap, hoping she looked sufficiently unthreatening. "How long have you been here, Nola?"

"Well…mmm…almost six months, your ladyship."

"You must observe a great deal of what goes on at Donbridge."

Nola blanched, and Mariah knew she'd moved too fast. "I realize you really don't know me well, Nola," she said. "If you don't feel comfortable confiding in me…"

"Oh, no, your ladyship! You've never been anything but kind to everyone." She paused, evidently amazed by her own frankness. "It must be very different in America."

"In many ways it is." Mariah leaned forward a little. "The former Lady Donnington hasn't been kind, has she?"

Nola glanced toward the door. "Why should she care about the likes of us?"

That was close to downright rebellion. Mariah might have

smiled if not for her more sober purpose. "I don't believe she cares much about anyone but her son."

The girl dropped her gaze. "That's not for me to say, your ladyship."

"Please don't call me that, Nola. My name is Mariah."

A stubborn expression replaced the unease on Nola's face. "It isn't right, your ladyship."

The subject certainly wasn't worth arguing over. "Very well. But this is very important, Nola. I believe you can help me with something that matters a great deal to me. Will you answer my questions honestly?"

The armchair creaked as Nola shifted her weight. "Yes, your ladyship."

"Do you know if Lord Donnington has a relative…a cousin, perhaps…who looks very much like him?"

Nola's eyes widened. "A cousin, your ladyship?"

"Anyone who might resemble him strongly, except for the color of his hair."

Mariah thought that Nola would have bolted from her chair and out the door if she'd thought she could get away with it. But the maid must have seen that Mariah was very serious indeed, for she gave up the battle.

"There are rumors," she whispered, her head still half-cocked toward the door. "Only rumors, your ladyship."

"What sort of rumors?"

"Of someone…someone being kept at Donbridge."

"Kept against their will?"

Nola shivered. "Yes, your ladyship."

This conversation was proving to be far more productive than Mariah could have hoped. "Do the rumors tell why?" she asked.

The maid shook her head anxiously.

"It's all right, Nola. Do you know who is supposed to be guarding this prisoner?"

She could almost feel the girl's trembling. "There's a strange man who lives in a cottage at the edge of the estate. They say he never speaks, and no one knows what he does. I heard—"

CHAPTER TWO

FOOTSTEPS SOUNDED IN the corridor outside, and Nola leaped from her seat.

"Begging your pardon, your ladyship," she gasped. "I must go!"

She was out of the room before Mariah could rise from her own chair. She listened for a moment, hearing the rapid patter of Nola's feet as she hurried toward the servants' stairs. There would be no more questioning her today, that was certain.

But she'd confirmed what Mariah had already surmised: the prisoner's captivity was not a complete secret. Was it possible that she'd been too hasty in assuming that Vivian didn't know about it?

Could she have kept such a secret from her own daughter-in-law for the ten weeks since Mariah had arrived at Donbridge? A secret her son must share…

Mariah shook her head. She was jumping to conclusions, which was a very dangerous habit. She had no evidence whatsoever, only the prisoner's reaction to Donnington's name. And confronting Vivian directly was unthinkable. Mariah could only hope that Nola wouldn't go running directly to the dowager, though the tone of dislike in the maid's voice when she'd spoken of her former mistress suggested she wouldn't. Nevertheless, their conversation might very well be the talk of the house by noon.

You've gone about this the wrong way, Mariah told herself.

In her eagerness to discover the truth, she'd trusted a girl she knew nothing about. She'd made wild assumptions based upon one meeting with a man she didn't know.

But that man still needed her. From now on, she had to be extremely cautious. If Nola held her tongue, no one else should guess what Mariah had discovered. She must, with utmost discretion, collect the things the prisoner required.

There was only one place in Donbridge where she might find them. It wouldn't be difficult to enter Donnington's rooms; they were directly next door to her own, with a small dressing room between them. And there was no time to waste.

Donnington hadn't locked his door. Mariah stepped into his room, briefly arrested by the faint smell of the man she'd married. He was prone to using a certain cologne, one she had liked when he was courting her.

She had never been in his suite before. It was his domain, like his study and the billiard room. The furniture was unmistakably masculine, and Donnington had managed to find space on the walls to mount a few more of the smaller animal heads.

Shaking off an uncomfortable blend of disgust and regret, Mariah went directly to his wardrobe. She opened one of the drawers, selected appropriate undergarments—which might have made her blush, had she not seen far worse at the asylum—chose two of the shirts he'd left behind, then moved quickly to the trousers. Stockings were next, along with a pair of walking shoes that had seen hard use. She filched the towels from his washstand, along with a spare shaving kit, a comb and a bar of soap.

She paused, quite in spite of herself, to glance in his mirror, wondering what Donnington had seen in her.

Black, slightly waving hair, now loose around her shoulders. An oval face with rather common blue eyes, straight brows, and a well-shaped nose and mouth. Not pretty, perhaps, but perfectly acceptable.

Was it really my fault that he left? Did he find out about Mama, despite all Papa's efforts to buy off anyone who might tattle?

Mariah turned away from the mirror and glanced once more about the room. A waistcoat? No, that was hardly necessary now. A jacket. The prisoner would need its warmth in that cold chamber, though it might be pleasant enough outside. She returned to the wardrobe and removed one of Donnington's hunting jackets, the one he preferred to wear on the estate. Searching for something in which to wrap the clothing and supplies, she found a rucksack tucked in a corner of the room, along with several empty crates and a pair of lens-less binoculars.

Stuffing the clothing into the bag, she returned to her own room. On impulse, she went straight to her small bookcase, where she kept the books she'd loved as a child. Most were volumes of fairy tales, which for months after Mama's death Mariah hadn't dared to open.

Now she had some use for them. If the prisoner was capable of regaining his speech—presuming he'd ever had it to begin with—reading to him would surely assist in the process.

I can't keep calling him the prisoner, she thought. But no appropriate name came to her.

She set down the bag, thumbed through a book of Perrault's fairy tales and found the story of *Cendrillon,* Cinderella. When Mariah was very young, Mrs. Marron had liked to collect stories from every country.

Cinderella in the German language was *Aschenbrödel.* Mariah vaguely remembered a variation on the tale where the main character had been a boy, not a girl.

Aschen. Ash. Ashton was a proper name, especially in England.

"Ash." She spoke the name aloud, nodded to herself and

placed three of the books in the bag. Then she hid the bag under her bed. She would go out again tonight, when the dowager was asleep.

Caution. Discretion…

A knock at the door broke into her thoughts. It was Barbara, the parlor maid, who bobbed a curtsey as Mariah let her in.

"The dowager Lady Donnington requests your presence in the morning room, your ladyship," she said, never meeting Mariah's eyes.

Mariah wondered if Vivian had already heard about her conversation with Nola. "What does she want, Barbara?" she asked warily.

Barbara was clearly dismayed by Mariah's directness. "Mr. Ware has come, your ladyship," she said.

"Sinjin!" Mariah instantly forgot her worry and smoothed her skirts. Not that *he* would care about her appearance; he had excellent taste in ladies' fashions and an extraordinary eye, but he was, after all, her brother-in-law. He and Mariah had been friends from their first meeting.

"Please inform the dowager that I'll be down directly," Mariah told the maid, who was off in a flash. Mariah glanced at the mirror over her washstand to make certain her pins were still in place, and then descended to the morning room.

St. John Ware rose to his feet as soon as she entered. He smiled at her…that sly, enigmatic smile that suggested he and she shared a secret no one else would ever know. Mariah nodded to the dowager and greeted Sinjin with an extended hand.

"Mr. Ware," she said. "How delightful to see you again."

He rolled his eyes at her unaccustomed formality and turned to Vivian. "The dowager was kind enough to let me in despite the early hour."

Vivian looked askance at him. "And why should I not welcome my own son at any hour?" she asked crisply.

"Your scapegrace son," he said. "Or ought that title now go to Donnington?"

The very room froze as Vivian understood his jest. She stiffened, her spine as rigid as one of Donnington's elephant guns.

"You will not speak so of your elder brother," she said.

Sinjin managed to seem chastened. "You're quite right, Mother," he said. "Please forgive me."

Forgiveness was not in Vivian's nature, but she nodded with the graciousness of a queen. "You may ring for tea."

He moved swiftly to the bellpull and summoned Parish, the butler. Barbara arrived with the tray a short while later. The dowager poured without acknowledging Mariah's right to do so.

She is still angry about the question I asked her, Mariah thought. *But why? Is it merely because it might have implied…*

"What brings you to Donbridge, Sinjin?" Vivian asked briskly.

Sinjin examined his fine china teacup. "Why shouldn't I pay my respects to my own mother?"

"You have never shown much respect for anything, let alone your mother," Vivian said.

"You quite wound me," Sinjin said, too lightly to be reproachful. "I have the utmost respect for you, my dear."

Vivian was incapable of being less than dignified, but she came very close to a snort. "What do you require, Sinjin? A loan for the repayment of your debts?"

Sinjin's expression grew pained. "I am not so mercenary as you think, Mother."

She sipped her tea delicately. "If you had gone into the army as your father intended, you would not be in such straits."

For all the relative brevity of their acquaintance, Mariah knew how much Sinjin despised this topic. "Lady Donnington," he said pointedly, "must find such a subject tedious, Mother."

Mariah knew it would have been politic to absent herself, but Sinjin's eyes begged her to stay, and she wasn't of a mind to hand the dowager an easy victory. "The army is a fine vocation," she said. "For those suited to it."

"Indeed," Sinjin said. "A vocation to which I could not have done proper justice."

A teacup rattled in its saucer. Vivian waited while Barbara mopped up the almost invisible spillage where the dowager had set down her cup with a little too much force. "You do proper justice to very little," she said in a brittle voice. "If your brother were here…"

"But he is not, is he?" Sinjin stood abruptly. "I shall not impose upon your sensibilities any longer."

Vivian looked almost surprised at the vehemence beneath his veneer of unruffled courtesy. "There is no need for you to go."

"But I cannot replace the earl as company for you and Lady Donnington," he said. He bowed with soldierly precision, first to his mother and then to Mariah. "If you will excuse me…"

His stride was brisk as he left the room. Mariah excused herself with equal haste, earning a glare from the dowager, and hurried after him.

"Sinjin!"

He turned, slightly flushed, and doffed the hat he'd already retrieved from Barbara. "Lady Donnington," he said. "I apologize for my hasty departure."

"Oh, pish," Mariah said. "Don't come all formal with me, Sinjin."

His anger evaporated into his usual good humor. "How you deal with her every day is beyond my capacity to understand."

"No it isn't. You've dealt with her all your life."

He offered his arm, and she took it. They left the house, and Mariah was distracted by thoughts of Ash, so near and yet so far away.

Ask Sinjin. He would be glad to help.

But what if he already knew about the prisoner?

She refused to believe it. Not Sinjin. He was a good man.

As Donnington is not?

"A penny for your thoughts," Sinjin said, peering at her face with his keen brown eyes. "You look positively pensive, my dear. Are you yearning for Donnington?"

"It's nothing," she said, refusing to rise to his bait.

"Ha! Mother won't leave it alone, will she? How can she blame *you?*" He laughed. "Then again, how can she not? It's in her nature. My brother can do no wrong."

It wasn't the first time the subject had come up between them, and ordinarily Mariah would have been glad for his sympathetic ear. But self-pity seemed very unimportant in light of this morning's encounter.

"I do find it a bit odd that she has remained so calm," he went on, oblivious. "I should have expected her to go a little mad, not knowing where her darling has gone."

Mariah flinched at the mention of madness. *It's only a word,* she thought. But it wasn't. Not today. Not ever.

"Mariah."

She looked into Sinjin's eyes. He wasn't laughing now. "How *has* it been with Mother?" he asked.

"I am perfectly fine, Sinjin."

He drew her hand from the crook of his arm and held it in his. "Has she made any sort of comment…any kind of intimation that you…that you might be…"

"Might be what?"

Seldom had she seen Sinjin look as uncomfortable as he did in that moment. "Seeing someone," he said.

"Seeing someone? I see Lady Westlake, Lady Hurst…"

"A man, Mariah. Seeing a man."

Slowly she began to take his meaning. "A man?" Her face grew hot. "Do you mean—"

But she really didn't have to ask. He was talking about an affair. Something she'd only read about in books and heard of in the ghosts of rumors about a society to which she didn't belong.

"Don't look so shocked, Merry," Sinjin said, using her nickname in the familiar way to which they both had become accustomed since her arrival at Donbridge. "You may not have much experience of the world, but I know you aren't that naïve. Mother's wanted an excuse to end your marriage to my brother ever since he brought you to England. She'd love to think the worst of you." He sighed. "She mentioned to me once—just in passing, you understand—that she thought it odd that you spend so much time walking alone in the early mornings. Ridiculous, I know. There is no one in the world less likely to be unfaithful than you."

But she scarcely heard his reassurances. All she could wonder was how long the dowager had harbored such suspicions. Since the very night Donnington had left? A week after? A month? Did she have someone specific in mind?

"I shouldn't have spoken up," Sinjin said, his voice tight with remorse. "I just thought that perhaps it would never occur to you that she might think such a thing. She isn't quite rational when it comes to Donnie."

Mariah removed her hand from Sinjin's. "I'm glad you did," she said. "I knew there was something more to her anger than blaming me for Donnington's sudden absence."

Sinjin puffed out his cheeks. "Well, then," he said. "You've handled the whole thing admirably." He caught her hand again and lifted it to his lips. "You know you may always count on me for anything."

She managed a smile. "And you may count on me. I shall send a check for whatever you need."

If he had been as mercenary as his mother supposed, he

wouldn't have looked so uneasy. "I'm not so badly off as all that. I shall recoup."

"If only you'd stop the gambling—"

"For God's sake, Merry. *One* Lady Donnington is quite enough."

"I apologize. Sinjin…?"

"Hmm?"

"Are you very busy at Marlborough House?"

"Not terribly. I come and go. Why?"

"If you can spare the time, I might ask for your assistance."

"With what?"

"I would prefer to explain when I have…certain additional information."

"How very mysterious." She could see he was about to make an unfortunate joke before he thought better of it. "Just as you wish, little sister."

They turned and walked back to the house. After Sinjin had gone, Mariah wrote a letter to her banker in London, authorizing a transfer of funds to the Honourable St. John Ware. At least it was her money to do with as she chose, now that Parliament had passed the act allowing wives to keep at least some of their own wealth.

Somehow she made it through the rest of the day, trying not to think about what Sinjin had told her of Vivian's suspicions. She wrote a cheerful letter to her father, sketched flowers in the garden and supervised the running of the household as much as the dowager permitted.

But she couldn't forget. The dowager wanted to end her marriage to Donnington. She wanted to believe that Mariah was capable of being unfaithful to her husband, a notion that offended Mariah deeply.

And yet you already knew you must hide your next visit to the folly, she thought. Even if her reasons had been entirely innocent, based upon her desire to keep anyone else from learning that she had discovered Donbridge's strange prisoner.

Now she had another reason for concealing her activities. *You are going to see a strange man. Alone.*

For compassion. For justice, since some wrong had clearly been done. To Mariah, Ash was simply a patient in need of healing, a human being worthy of assistance and respect. And there would be bars between them…at least until she could determine what had happened and what must be done.

He touched your hand.

She shut the memory away and moved through the afternoon like a wraith. Dinner was an unpleasant affair, with long stretches of weighted silence and the occasional tart comment from the dowager. The elder Lady Donnington stared pointedly and repeatedly at the empty seat at the head of the table. Mariah imagined that she could hear Vivian's thoughts.

I know why Donnington left you….

There was no lingering at the table when dinner was finished. Mariah excused herself to her own rooms. Night fell at last, though the sky remained suspended in twilight until past ten.

The dowager was slow about going to bed, but Mariah waited until the house was silent. Then she retrieved her rucksack and raided the linen closet for blankets. The kitchen was dark save for a faint glow in the huge hearth; she entered the dry larder and found half a loaf of bread, along with several peaches from the conservatory. She chose a small knife from a row hung on the wall. She found an empty bottle and filled it with water from the kitchen tap.

She wrapped the food in a kitchen towel and then in one of the blankets, slung it over one shoulder and looped the rucksack over the other. Satisfied that she had the supplies she needed, she lit a lantern and passed quickly through the entrance hall.

It wasn't a noise that made her stop, nor any sign of movement. But something caused her to look up at one of the heavy ceiling beams over the door, hung with a shield bearing the Donnington coat of arms.

Cave cornum meum: Beware my horn. The motto of the earls of Donnington was a silver unicorn rearing atop a blood-red field, ready to charge at any potential enemy.

There was no earthly reason to shiver. Mariah had seen the shield every time she left the house. But it troubled her now in a way she couldn't understand.

Beware my horn.

Taking herself in hand, she opened the door and set off across the park. As always, the night was silent; there were faint rustlings of small creatures in the grass and shrubbery, but no indications of human presence. London was far away, and the nearest village was hardly a hotbed of activity so late at night.

She reached the folly in record time. No sound came from inside, and though she knew the heavy walls of the interior chamber were thick, she faced a moment of panic. She dropped the bag and blankets on the portico, rushed to the stone at the foot of the stairs and felt under it frantically.

The key was still there. No one had moved it. Ash must be where she had left him.

Wasting no further time, she unlocked the outer door and set the bag on the chair, laying the blanket with the food on the floor beside it. She hesitated just outside the inner door.

He's ill, quite possibly mad. What will I do if I can't save him?

The fear paralyzed her for all of ten seconds. Then she raised the lantern, set the key in the lock and opened the door.

Ash was waiting for her, pressed against the bars, clutching them with the same ferocity. His black gaze met hers, speaking just as eloquently as before.

Help me.

As if of their own accord, her eyes took him in as they had

done that morning, cataloging every detail of his body. She had never seen her husband like this. She had glimpsed him once without his shirt, but that—and the brief touch of his lips and clasp of his hand—had been the extent of her experience with his body.

Would he look so magnificent, so powerful, so—

He is a patient. A patient, *Mariah.*

She turned away to collect the bag and blankets. "I've brought you some things you need," she said. "Clothing, blankets, food. It isn't nearly enough, but it should do for tonight."

Without looking up to observe his reaction, she removed the clothing, food and books, and immediately laid the bread and fruit on the kitchen towel. Only then did she pause to consider the narrowness of the gap between the bars.

There would be no trouble, of course, with the bread or fruit. They could be cut. She wasn't so certain about the bottle.

"You must be hungry," she said, simply to fill the quiet. She selected one of the peaches, cutting off several small slices. Sweet juice coated her fingers, and she wiped the excess on the towel.

She rose and turned toward the cell. Ash hadn't moved. Immediately she saw the second problem. In order to give him the food, she must venture within his reach.

You've done it before, she told herself. *He won't harm you.* But she remembered too keenly how she had felt when he'd run his thumb up and down the back of her hand.

"I am going to give you the fruit," she said slowly. "Do you understand?"

His dark gaze flickered to the slices of peach in her palm and back to her face. She moved closer. His eyes never wavered. She reached the bars and extended her hand just far enough that he could take the fruit.

He didn't. Mariah was both puzzled and frustrated.

Someone had fed him, though not generously. He wasn't mad enough to require constant care, like an infant. Perhaps the problem was that he still had no reason to trust her.

"See?" she said, and took a bite of one of the slices. Juice trickled down her chin, and she licked her lips. "Delicious."

His gaze moved from her eyes to her mouth. The floor gave the tiniest lurch under her feet.

"Here," she said, pushing a piece through the bars. "Try it."

He took the fruit as delicately as a butterfly alights on a flower petal. Long, strong fingers lifted it to his lips. With strange fascination, she watched him eat it with a kind of sensual deliberation, as if he were savoring every bite. When he finished, she saw what might have been real pleasure in his eyes.

"More?" she asked. She adjusted the knife to cut another slice, and the blade slipped. She felt a stab of pain as the sharp edge cut into her thumb. Blood welled on her skin.

Ash reached through the bars and grabbed her hand, pulling gently until her own fingers were inside the cell, and drew them into his mouth.

Sparklers exploded inside her head. She gasped. His tongue rolled over her skin as if seeking the wound. She closed her eyes, incapable of moving as he licked between her fingers and laved her thumb almost tenderly.

Her senses returned too late, and she snatched her hand away. Heat flowed through her arm, into her chest, and continued on to her stomach and thighs. Her most secret place ached as it never had before, not even when she had been most in love with Donnington.

But there was another unexpected change in her body. She examined her thumb. It no longer hurt. More remarkably, the cut was gone, leaving only a trace of pink healing flesh where it had been.

Impossible.

She set the peach on the towel, nearly dropping it in her haste. Her fingers trembled as she picked up a chunk of bread and placed it on one of the blankets. She didn't dare allow Ash to accost her again.

Her second approach was far more cautious. She laid the blanket on the ground, several inches from the bars. Then she backed away and watched.

Lithe as a panther, he crouched and took the bread. He lifted his head and continued to watch her as he ate, not wolfing the food as one might expect him to do, but eating with all the finesse of a courtier at a prince's table. Mariah put the rest down for him and withdrew again, half-ashamed that she should still be letting her fear rule her.

If it were only fear...

Ash made a sound in his throat. Mariah jumped, recovered, and saw that he had finished the bread. She remembered the water but could think of no way of giving it to him...unless she found a way to open the cell door.

It was unthinkable. She still knew nothing about him and was no closer to learning.

"Are you very thirsty?" she asked.

He lowered his chin, the veil of hair obscuring his eyes, and shook his head. She felt only a little relieved.

Remembering the blanket, she shook it out, refolded it and placed it at the foot of the bars again. Ash didn't touch it. That uncanny stare continued to follow her as she bent all her attention on selecting one of the books.

Will he understand? Or is this all just wasted effort?

No, not wasted if there was the slightest chance of discovering just how much he *could* understand.

She sat in the chair, the chosen book in her lap, and set the lantern a little distance from her feet. It cast eerie shadows about the room and provided the bare minimum of light she would need to read. Her hand still tingled from the feel of Ash's tongue on her flesh, and several times her fingers slipped from the pages.

At last she found her place. She cleared her throat.

"'East of the Sun and West of the Moon,'" she read aloud.

Ash cocked his head, dropped into a crouch against the wall nearest the bars and let his hands dangle over his knees. As she began to read about the girl whose destitute father had given her to a mystical white bear in exchange for wealth and comfort, she began to wonder why she had chosen this tale, in particular, of all those in the book, or why this book of the three she had brought.

And she wondered—as she related how the girl had been visited every night by the same handsome prince, only to be deserted each morning—why, instead of the great white bear, she saw another creature, pale and elusive as a ghost, a beast very much like a horse but a thousand times more beautiful, his eyes black as a moonless night, his broad forehead topped by a glittering spiraled horn.

Startled, Mariah lost her place and looked at Ash. He was listening intently, but otherwise neither his posture nor his appearance had altered.

The Donnington coat of arms. Why should it so vividly come to mind at this moment? No one could have looked less like such a magical creature than Ash. It was certainly beyond any possibility that he should guess what fancies tumbled through her mind, and he looked entirely unresponsive to the story she was reading.

He doesn't understand. How shall I ever hope to—

Suddenly he stood, moved to the bars and opened his mouth. His lips moved without producing any sound, but he pointed at the book and then gestured toward Mariah's face.

"What is it?" she asked, half rising.

He gave a sharp, impatient gesture, and something very

near anger crossed his features…not the savagery of their first meeting, but an arrogant, impatient emotion, as if he were no mere prisoner but a prince himself.

"You wish me to finish the story," she said.

He nodded and gestured again toward the book. With a sensation quite unlike the satisfaction she had expected to feel at his response, she bent to the pages once more.

She related how the girl lived in luxury but saw no other person by day and only the prince by night. The girl became very lonely. One night, she bent to kiss the prince as he slept but woke him by letting drops of tallow fall on his shirt. He told her that he had been cursed by his wicked stepmother to be a bear by day and a man only by night, but that now he would be forced to leave her and marry a hideous troll.

Glancing up again to gauge Ash's reaction, Mariah saw that his lips were forming a word she could almost make out: troll. It was if he recognized that one word out of all those she had spoken.

The possibility encouraged her. She continued the story until she'd reached the end, where the girl, who had undertaken a long and dangerous journey to reach her prince at the castle East of the Sun and West of the Moon, had helped him to outwit the trolls who held him captive.

"'The old troll woman flew into such a rage that she burst into a thousand pieces, taking the troll princess with her. The bear prince and his love freed all the trolls' captives, took the trolls' gold and silver, and flew far away from the castle that lay East of the Sun and West of the Moon.'"

She closed the book and let it rest in her lap, watching Ash out of the corner of her eye. Frowning, he walked away from the bars and began to pace the length of his cage with his long, graceful stride.

Suddenly he swung around, his nostrils flared and his eyes

unfathomable. He studied her so intently that her stomach began to feel peculiar all over again.

"Why a bear?" he asked.

CHAPTER THREE

ASTONISHED, SHE JUMPED up, nearly upsetting the chair, tripping on her skirts and stepping on the fruit that still lay on the towel. "You…you can speak!" she stammered.

He lifted his head and tossed his hair out of his eyes. "I speak," he said. His voice was a lilting baritone with a slight English accent, unmistakably upper-class. "I…" He hesitated, gathering his words. "I speak *now*."

Now. Which implied a *before*, a time…when? Before she had come? Before he had been confined to this tiny prison?

Why didn't you tell me? Why didn't you answer my simple questions?

But she didn't ask aloud. She had made progress. If he had deliberately deceived her, it must have been because he hadn't trusted her. All she'd done was read a fairy tale, and yet…

"Why a bear?" he repeated.

A whole army of questions marched through her mind, but the situation was far too chancy for her to ask them. The best thing she could do was play along.

"I don't know," she said. "It's simply part of the story, the way the writer wanted to tell it."

She could see the thoughts working behind his eyes. "But he became a…man."

Excitement began to build in her chest. "Yes. When his curse was broken by the love of the girl."

"Curse," he said. His frown became a scowl so intimidating that she was glad of the bars between them. A moment later nothing but bewilderment showed on his face. "I don't remember."

"Don't remember what?" she asked very quietly.

He gave her a long, appraising look. "You do not know?"

"I'm afraid…" She tossed aside the temptation to equivocate. "I didn't realize you were here until this morning."

If it were possible to swoon from nothing more than a stare, she might have forgotten that she'd never fainted in her life. She had the feeling that he could have snapped the bars in two if he'd put his mind to it.

"Who am I?" he asked.

As if *she* could answer. But surely he must have realized from her previous questions that she was as ignorant as he was.

"I don't know," she said, drawing the chair closer to the cage. "I wish I could tell you."

"Donnington," he said. Without hatred, only a calm indifference.

She braced herself. "What about Donnington?"

Ash gestured at the cage around him. "He…did this."

The validation of her worst supposition made her ill enough to wish that she could run from the room and empty her roiling stomach.

This isn't the Middle Ages. People don't imprison other people for no reason.

And Ash was deeply troubled, even dangerous. There was no telling what was real in his mind and what imaginary. Who could know that better than she?

But Nola had heard the rumors about a captive on the grounds. And he looks like Donnington's twin….

She sucked in her breath. "You believe that Donnington put you here," she said, matching Ash's emotionless tone. "Do you know why?"

His hair flew as he shook his head again, on the very edge of violence. One moment calm, the next raging. Sure signs of insanity.

There would be no logical answers from him. Only the bits and pieces she could glean from the most cautious exploration. She must put from her mind the enticing contours of his body, the intensity of his eyes, the hunger…

She bent abruptly to gather up the spoiled fruit and left just long enough to toss it into the shrubbery outside. Ash was clutching the bars when she returned, his face pressed against them.

"I will not leave you," she said, knowing her promise was only a partial truth. "I am your friend."

"Friend," he repeated.

"I care what happens to you. I want to help you."

Belatedly she remembered the bottle of water she'd brought and considered the basin Ash's keeper had left just inside the cage. She would have to take the risk of filling it with fresh water.

She crept toward the cage, knelt and poked the bottle's neck through the bars. Ash made no move toward her, and she managed to fill the basin halfway before it became too difficult to pour. She glanced at the towels that still hung over the back of the chair. Rising, she wetted one thoroughly, walked back to the cage and held the moist towel up for Ash's inspection.

"Wash," she said, demonstrating for him by bathing her hands and face.

He followed her every movement, his gaze finally settling, as always, on her eyes. "Wash," she repeated.

"Yes," he said. "Wash."

Her throat felt thick. "If I give this to you," she said, "you must not touch me."

He seemed to understand. When she extended the towel,

he simply took it. No flesh touched flesh. But as he withdrew his hand, she saw something that made the squirming minnows in her middle seem like ravenous sharks.

His hands were burned. Red and black marks crossed his fingers and palms, stripes matching the bars he had so often grasped. There were similar stripes on his face. Even as she stared in horror, they began to diminish.

"Good God," she whispered. Without hesitation, she seized his hand, wrapping it in the wet towel he still held. "How did you burn yourself?"

"Iron," he said in a low voice.

"Iron? You mean the bars?" She touched one gingerly. They were cold, not hot.

"I don't know how you did this," she said tightly, "but your hands will need to be bandaged. And your face…" She looked up from her work. The brands across his jaw, cheeks and forehead were gone. She peeled the towel away from his hand. The marks were disappearing before her eyes.

She dropped his hand. It brushed the bar, and an angry red welt formed across his knuckles.

Astonished, Mariah took his hand again. The welts were nasty and raw, but they lasted no longer than she could murmur a prayer.

She raised her head. "Ash," she said. "How is this possible?"

He seemed not to hear her. "Ash," he repeated.

Her face felt as fiery as his vanished wounds. "You…don't seem to remember your name."

His fingers tightened on hers. "Ash is my name?"

"I…" She felt utterly foolish, befuddled, incapable of harboring a single rational thought. "For a while. If…if you approve."

His head cocked in that way she found so oddly endearing. "Ash," he said distinctly. "I…approve."

Relief weakened her knees. "Very good," she said faintly. "Have you any other injuries?"

"No injuries."

She closed her eyes, grateful to be allowed a few moments to recover and focus again on the questions that must be answered.

"Ash," she said, pushing everything else from her mind, "who else has come here? Who has been bringing you food and water?"

His black eyes seemed to gather all the lantern's light. "The man," he said.

"What man?"

Ash hunched his back, slinking about the cage in a perfect imitation of the stranger she'd seen skulking near the folly.

"Who is he, Ash?"

"I do not know."

"When does he come?"

He frowned, lifted his hand and held up three of his fingers.

"Three days ago?"

The frown became a scowl, and he raised his fingers again.

"Every three days?"

His forehead relaxed. "Yes," he said.

He knows his numbers, Mariah thought. "When was the last time he came, Ash? Was it this morning? The first time I visited you?"

"Morning."

Thank God for that. Whoever this keeper was, he was unlikely to return for another two or three days.

"Did he ever speak to you?" she asked.

"No. Only you."

So no one had spoken to him. How long had he been wrapped in a shroud of silence?

Distressed and wishing to hide it, Mariah glanced stupidly at the damp towel in her hands. "I think you ought to wash now," she said.

"Dirty," he said, gesturing down at himself, compelling her

gaze to follow. She noted that his—she swallowed—his "member" was very much in evidence beneath his loincloth.

"Yes," she said thickly. "Quite dirty." She moved to wet the towel again. She managed to pass it to him without looking at him, and after a brief pause she heard him sweeping the cloth over his body, followed by the almost inaudible "plop" as his single garment fell to the floor.

She squeezed her eyes shut, wishing her mind to become a perfect blank. This feeling had nothing to do with the way he'd licked her fingers. A lunatic might make just such an inappropriate gesture, lacking the qualities of courtesy and judgment found in the sane.

But there had been purpose in it.

"Mariah."

The sound of her name nearly wrenched her out of her prickling skin. Involuntarily she turned. He was quite, quite clean, and he had neglected to retrieve his covering.

She shut her eyes again, edged to the chair, felt for the trousers—giving up entirely on the drawers—and used the tip of her boot to push them toward the cage. "Please," she gasped. "Put on these trousers."

"How?"

Good Lord. "Haven't you…ever worn trousers before?"

"No."

She opened her eyes for a fraction of a second and could barely stifle a gasp. He was quite…quite…prominent. And she was very, very hot.

He has not come to his present age in a perpetual state of nakedness. He has simply forgotten all his old life. How am I even to begin?

"Show me," he said.

Her eyes flew open again. "I beg your pardon?"

"Remove—" He pointed to her walking dress. "Remove that."

She nearly choked. "Ash!"

"Did I speak incorrectly?"

He spoke beautifully. Breathtakingly. For a man who hadn't been able to talk less than twenty-four hours ago, he'd become downright verbose.

"That is quite unnecessary," she said, knowing that outrage would do no good and possibly much harm. "One does not remove one's clothing in the presence of others."

"Never?"

The one exception flooded her mind with fantastical images that sprang unbidden from her imagination. "Not in society," she said as steadily as she could.

"This is wrong?"

His gesture and glance down at himself made his meaning exceedingly plain. In vain she made another attempt to shut her wanton thoughts away.

"It is not polite," she said. "You must dress." She held the trousers up against her body with shaking hands. "You put them on, so. Step into one leg, then the other. The buttons are here."

"Do they not make it difficult to run?"

Laughter burst out before she could think to forestall it. "Gentlemen seldom find occasion to run."

"Am I a gentleman?"

Very good, Mariah. A fine beginning. "You will not need to run," she said. "Can you put them on, Ash?"

"You wish it," he said, as serious as the monk he most decidedly was not.

"I wish it very much."

He held out his hand. Half turned away, she passed the trousers through the bars. The mad beating of her heart almost drowned out the sound of his movements. She counted to herself, waiting for him to gather up the garment, put it on, fasten the buttons over his…his burgeoning masculinity. If the buttons would close at all.

If the dowager could see what's in your mind, Mariah...

"I am finished."

Her skirts hardly rustled as she moved, stiff as an automaton, to face him.

Dressed he was not. But at least he wore the trousers, half-buttoned. She should have been grateful that they weren't on backward, though they were much more snug than she had bargained for. He was still quite...noticeable.

"A shirt," she said, before her imagination could run away with her again. Just as gingerly as before, she placed the shirt at the foot of the bars. He took it, frowned, turned it about, then snorted with something very like disgust.

"You put it over your arms," she said, pantomiming the action.

"Show me."

She was beginning to feel more than a little as if he were making sport of her. But had he a sense of humor? The mad might laugh, but seldom with any kind of understanding. If Ash were mocking her, it was a peculiarly subtle form of mockery. Thus far he had been far from subtle.

Despite the generous cut of the garment, made for a broad-shouldered, muscular man, Mariah had to struggle to pull the shirt over her snug sleeves and tight bodice. It belled out over her bustle, but she was able to fasten the buttons.

"There," she said. "You see?" She pirouetted to show him every angle. "Simple as pie."

"Pie?"

"Something very good to eat."

"Is it simple?"

It took a moment for her to grasp his meaning. "Well...my mother always found it—"

"Your mother?"

Mariah blinked and faced Ash squarely. "Let us return to the subject at hand." She unbuttoned the shirt and pulled it off, prepared to give it to him. Ash had fixed his gaze at the point where her gathered overskirt flared over the bustle.

"What is that?" he asked.

"I beg your pardon?"

"Is that where you keep your tail?"

Another shock raced from the soles of her shoes to the very tips of her hair. "My...my tail?"

"You do not have one?"

Oh. This was so much worse than she had feared, even when her doubts had been greatest. "People do not have tails, Ash," she said.

"No," Ash said, unaware of her inner turmoil. "Mine is gone, too."

Flight seemed the better part of valor until Mariah realized what she was seeing in Ash's black, sparkling eyes. He was teasing her. Teasing her, for heaven's sake.

Relief eased the pressure within her chest. "It is a very good thing, too," she said, "or you would look quite out of place in the world."

"The world." He looked over her shoulder at the door leading to the antechamber. "Outside."

"Yes." How long since he had seen anything but these whitewashed stone walls?

"We shall go outside," she said. "When you are ready."

"Now."

It was a command, not a request, not a plea. She better understood what she faced now; she must firmly remind him who held command, or he would never become manageable.

"Not yet," she said. "First you must learn to dress, converse..."

And *remember*. That most of all.

With a deep sigh that further revealed the complexity of his emotions, Ash took the shirt from her and shrugged into it, the handsomely formed muscles of his chest and shoulders rippling with the easy motion. He buttoned it without the slightest difficulty, letting the tail hang over his trousers. Mariah knew she must choose her battles, and asking him to tuck in his shirt was the very least of them.

She had not remembered to bring braces, but that was a complication she didn't need at the moment. Garters were also out of the question. But stockings, even if they would not stay in place, were a necessity. She presented them to Ash.

"These go over your feet," she said.

He looked at his feet, then at the stockings. "I don't like them."

Just like a child…in that particular way, at least. And it was much easier to view him so, she decided. "You will get used to them," she said. "You must have worn them in the past."

"Never."

At least he understood the concepts of past and present, which could not be said of many lunatics. "It is not in the least difficult." She sat in the chair and unlaced her boot. "I am taking off my shoe. This is my stocking."

Blushing would be ridiculous now, in light of all she had already witnessed. She lifted her skirts to her ankle and pointed. "Stocking," she said.

His unfortunate habit of staring at her would likely be very difficult to break, but in this case she could forgive it. She replaced her boot self-consciously and returned to stand before the cage. "Let me see you do it," she encouraged.

He took the stockings, sat down on the floor—doubtless dirtying his otherwise spotless trousers—and pulled the stockings over his long, very handsome feet.

And now you find feet attractive. How gauche of you. How very…

Ash stood—or rather leaped—to those very attractive feet, scowling. "I don't like them," he said in a lordly manner that would have brooked no argument had it come from Donnington. It would be so easy to forget that Ash was not the man he claimed had imprisoned him.

Stop it, she told herself. She rose and resolutely picked up the shoes. "Shoes are next."

The difficulty of getting the shoes through the bars was daunting, but Mariah was determined to accomplish it, with or without Ash's help. He, however, was equally determined to keep them out, and his strength was considerably greater.

The third time he pushed them back, she lost her temper.

"That is quite enough!" she snapped. "You will wear them, or I shall...I shall—"

"Go!" he said, his shout all but rattling the bars. "Leave me!"

A prince could not have spoken more decidedly. Or more arrogantly. Mariah spun for the door. She was almost out when the hiss of ripping cloth spun her around again.

Ash was removing his shirt—except "removing" was far too fine a word for the damage he was inflicting on the perfectly fine linen. In a moment, it would be in shreds on the floor and she would have lost the battle entirely.

"No!" she said, and returned to the cell. "No," she said more softly. "No shoes."

He stopped, his hands clenched on the ragged edges of his shirt. "No shoes?"

Not today, my friend. But soon. She picked up the shoes and tucked them under the chair. "You will wear the stockings."

His scowl didn't waver, but she fancied she saw a hint of yielding in his eyes. "Yes," he said.

Mariah blew out her breath. "We shall do without the jacket today," she said. "It is time to discuss what you remember of your previous life."

The endless night of his eyes threatened to swallow her. "Let me go," he said.

"Not today."

Deliberately he pressed his face to the bars. The welts appeared before her eyes. She gave a cry and rushed to push him back, her hands thrust through the bars to press the firm muscles of his shoulders.

"Are you mad?" she cried. "You…you…"

She found herself near tears and took control of her wayward emotions, withdrawing her hands before he could think to grab them.

"I shall not be blackmailed," she said, anger spilling out of her like poison. "I have seen what happens. You…"

Heal yourself. As he'd healed her thumb. Now it was happening again. The marks were disappearing, gone in the space of a dozen short breaths.

Ash was someone, some*thing,* even she could not define. Either she was beginning to lose her mind, or he was more than…

Not even a moan of protest could make its way past the constriction in her throat. She gathered up the lantern and fled…ignominiously, thoughtlessly, and as swiftly as her feet would carry her. She had stumbled halfway down the stairs before she remembered to return and lock the door.

Once it was done, she leaned against the heavy wood and sobbed for breath. She knew she ought to go back inside immediately, face her fears, prove to herself that the conclusion she had just reached was utter nonsense.

But she found she could not. As she walked away from the folly, the key still in her hand, she comforted herself with the knowledge that Ash had everything he needed for the time being and she would return before his keeper made another visit.

A little time. That was all she required to compose herself, to plan, to think rationally again. She must be prepared to find and question the keeper, and to continue her visits without arousing Vivian's suspicions. She must keep her wits about her at all times.

Especially when she faced his direct, merciless gaze, tempered only by that strange, contradictory innocence. That desperation combined with arrogance and subtle mockery. That mysterious past, that handsome face, that magnificent body…

She would never be free of him until she had all the answers.

ASH—FOR THAT was now his name—held on to the bars until the pain became more than even he could bear. He released them, flexing his fingers until his hands ceased burning, and sat in his usual place where the cool curved wall met the cage of iron.

She was gone. He had known she would leave him; she had another existence, one he could not touch. Yet she had given her word. And now he knew she would keep it. She could no more stay away than he could walk through the bars and out the door.

He dropped his head into his hands, weighted with sudden despair. He hadn't meant to frighten her. His feelings would not be still, driven this way and that like golden hinds during the hunt.

Hunt.

The word stung worse than his flesh where it had touched Cold Iron, but he still could not remember why.

A drift of warming air spiraled down from the small openings in the top of his cage, carrying with it the smell of flowers. Poor, pallid things they must be to produce such a faint and common scent, yet he would have given everything to touch them.

Everything but his freedom. Even if he should never see Mariah again. He would surrender the taste of her flesh, the softness of her skin. He would sacrifice the chance to hear her voice again, reading stories in which bears turned into men and were saved by the love of beautiful women. He would no longer wonder why his body tightened when she gazed upon him, or how she would appear without the ugly mass of cloth she wore.

Yet he could not win his freedom without her.

Freedom to what purpose? From whence had he come? What did he seek?

He held up his hands, turning them forward and back. They were still unfamiliar to him, though he knew much time had passed since he had been put behind these bars. He rose and stared down at his legs, at his feet in their "stockings." His limbs, too, had been wrong from the beginning, of that much he was certain. He could make them obey him, but that did not alter their strangeness. Nor could he explain the changes in sight, smell and hearing that rendered his senses so dull and distant. And when he had spoken to Mariah of a tail, he had not meant to make her smile. The question had come from memory, from a time when he had been other than he was now.

Beautiful. Perfect.

His gaze fell on the basin. He knelt before it and stared into the clean water. He touched his jaw, his cheek, the line of his nose.

Human.

He jerked back, the word ringing inside his head. He knew it well, though Mariah had never spoken it nor read it in her book. It described what she was, just as much as the word "woman." He touched his chest, feeling the organ beating beneath his ribs.

Am I not human?

He looked into the water again. The face was that of a man, like Mariah's and yet different. A face he almost recognized. But behind that face he saw another, pale as his hair, as different in form as iron was from silver: long, elegant, noble in shape and form. From the broad forehead sprang a horn, spiraled and sculpted as if from stainless ivory. A horn of incalculable value to those who would use it to command the obedience of others.

He touched his own forehead, naked and smooth. But the appendage was not entirely gone. It was only hidden, like the gleaming white hide and pearlescent hooves and the speed to outrun either human or Fane.

I am not human.

Rocking back on his heels, he felt the knowledge sweep through him in a rush like liquid fire. Not human, but rather that other he had seen in the water. A lord. A king.

A unicorn.

He tossed his head as the name slipped out of his grasp. He searched through the images that had come to him so suddenly, and another word arrested his thoughts.

Fane.

In his shattered memory he saw something that looked like a man, tall and wearing garments that sparkled as they caught the light. But its true self was to a human as Ash's former shape was to this foreign body he wore: seductive, certain of its power, outshining everything that stood in its presence.

Fane. His enemy. The one who had sent him into exile.

Shuddering with anger, Ash bared his teeth, and a growl rumbled deep in his chest. *They* had been together, the Fane and Donnington. They had conspired against him. They had made him nothing.

Nothing except to Mariah, who had given him a name and a purpose, though that purpose was only beginning to take shape in his mind. Escape, that first. Then find the ones who had done this, and…

No. There was more. More he must do.

A well of longing opened up inside him. A yearning to be again what he had been, to live his life among others of his own kind.

Why am I here? Why have I been punished?

There were no answers. His memory remained clouded; Mariah had no idea who he was now, far less what he had been in that other world. But punished he had been, driven from his home, given this mortal body in which to suffer pain and humiliation.

He upended the basin and watched the water darken the hard stone floor. Only a few moments ago he had been thinking of surrendering Mariah in exchange for his freedom. Now he began to see the course he must take. Mariah was not merely the path to escape.

Mariah was the key. The key to everything.

To give her up would be disaster.

Ash returned to his usual place and slid down against the wall. Mariah would come to him again. And when she did, he would begin to remember why she, more than anything else in the world, could save him.

CHAPTER FOUR

"WHY DID THE countess take Lord Donnington's clothing from his room?"

Nola shivered, afraid—as well she might be—to have been summoned into her former mistress's presence, but Vivian was in no mood to salve the girl's anxiety.

"Come, girl. I know you spoke to Lady Donnington privately. Why did she ask you to attend her?"

The maid gulped audibly. "My…my lady…the countess only wanted to ask about the coal and…she said she had taken a chill and would like a bit more to—"

"You are not a practiced deceiver, Nola, I can see that well enough."

"I beg your pardon, your ladyship." Nola straightened, and Vivian almost wondered if she were attempting some pathetic sort of defiance. "The countess only wanted to talk."

"To a chambermaid?"

"She was very kind to me, your ladyship. I didn't know the countess took any of his lordship's clothing."

This time Vivian's well-honed sense for duplicity told her that the maid was telling the truth, however much else she might wish to conceal. "Most peculiar," Vivian said, displeased. She folded her hands in her lap and leaned forward, fixing Nola with a gaze that had intimidated many a greater personage. "She said nothing about Lord Donnington?"

"She said she knew how much your ladyship missed his lordship."

Her words bordered on the impertinent, but once more Vivian detected a large element of truth in what the maid disclosed. Odd that Mariah should be concerned about her mother-in-law's feelings for her son.

"Did she say she missed him, as well?" Vivian asked shortly.

"Perhaps..." Nola brushed at her uniform and gazed at the figured carpet under her feet. "Begging your pardon, your ladyship, but if she took Lord Donnington's clothing, perhaps it was because she wanted something of him near her."

Nola's imagination was impressive for a girl of her age and occupation. Vivian allowed a little of the starch to go out of her spine, selected a biscuit from the silver tray on the table beside her and broke off the most minute piece she could. Her hands began to stiffen and ache with the old complaint.

"You are quite well-spoken for a maid, Nola," she said, doing her best to disregard the pain. "Where did Mrs. Baines find you?"

"In the village, your ladyship."

"Is your family there?"

"No, your ladyship. My mother is in Barway, and is not well. She must have medicines. I was employed as a seamstress's assistant."

Then her coming to Donbridge was a great improvement in her circumstances, for which she must be daily grateful, Vivian thought.

"I am sorry to hear of your mother's affliction," she said.

Nola curtseyed. "You are kind, your ladyship."

As kind as you are stupid, my dear, Vivian thought. "You have some education," she said.

"A little, your ladyship."

"Enough to make you worthy to converse with a countess."

Nola never lifted her gaze from the floor. "I never expected such an honor, your ladyship."

Vivian was rapidly growing weary of the interrogation. "Let me get directly to the point, Nola," she said. "I would like you to make the most of this new confidence."

The girl finally looked up, a flash of alarm on her round, seemingly guileless face. "I don't understand, your ladyship."

With the most delicate of motions, Vivian crumbled the bit of biscuit into a napkin without tasting it. "I should think a girl of your obvious intelligence would comprehend me very well. Are you capable of discretion?"

Nola hesitated, but not a moment longer than she should. "Yes, your ladyship."

"There are many things my daughter-in-law prefers to keep to herself, and I wish to get to know her better. You might be of great assistance to me in this enterprise."

"How, your ladyship?"

"By making yourself easily available whenever she wishes to talk. By proving yourself her most loyal confidante."

"But my duties, your—"

Vivian brushed the crumbs off her fingers. "You shall be excused from any duties which might interfere with your new appointment. There shall be no penalties…unless you choose to decline my suggestion."

Their gazes met. The girl was under no illusion as to what Vivian implied. "Am I to report anything she says to me, your ladyship?"

"I see we understand each other, Nola." Vivian permitted herself a beneficent smile. "You shall also discreetly follow her when she walks the grounds, especially in areas out of sight of the house. You must by no means allow her to see you."

"Does your ladyship fear she might injure herself?"

Such questioning from a maid was beyond anything Vivian

would ordinarily have allowed, but she had set her course and intended to follow it to the end.

"I do fear for her," she said with a sigh of mock concern. "One never knows what a young matron might do when she is so early separated from her husband."

Which was a topic even this bold chit didn't dare to address. "Yes, your ladyship," she murmured.

"You shall find me very appreciative of your services to me. Perhaps your mother will recover more quickly than you anticipated."

Nola flushed. Angry, Vivian guessed. But not prepared to let such unsuitable emotions rob her of her position and the hope Vivian had offered her.

"I am honored to serve your ladyship in any way," Nola said with a deep curtsey, which effectively concealed her true feelings.

"Excellent." Vivian glanced toward the drawing room door, aware that Barbara might return at any time to take the tray and refresh the tea. "Do you have any questions? Is anything I have said unclear to you?"

"No, your ladyship. Everything is very clear."

"Excellent." Vivian rose. "I shall expect you to present yourself to me, discreetly, in a few days' time. If the countess does not call for you soon, you are to find a way to attract her interest again. I know you åre clever enough to do it."

There was no answer, but Vivian required none. She swept past the girl and through the drawing room door, massaging her hands in a way that no one might see.

She *would* know what Mariah was scheming, one way or another. She had long been convinced, given Donnington's sudden departure following his wedding night, that his marriage to the girl had never been consummated. And though proof of the validity of Vivian's suspicions might be long in coming, she could certainly find other damning evidence against the hussy…evidence that, when combined with the almost certain fact of Mariah's virginal state, might prove the basis for dissolution of the ill-conceived union.

Donnington might already be longing for an escape from his ties to Mariah. If he were to be assured that such a dissolution was both possible and desirable…

As the Americans said in their usual vulgar fashion, there was more than one way to skin a cat. And if the cat's pelt might be acquired with so little trouble to herself, so much the better.

"WILL YOU HAVE ANOTHER piece of cake, Lady Donnington?"

Mariah smiled at Lady Westlake with her best attempt at sincerity. "It is a delicious cake, Lady Westlake. My compliments to your cook."

"Our chef is indeed an excellent practitioner of his craft," the viscountess corrected with apparent gentleness, a reminder that her household employed a real French chef instead of the simple cook who served Donbridge.

It was one of those not-so-subtle remarks meant to remind the young matron of her responsibility to make improvements at Donbridge in her husband's absence, responsibilities that had clearly remained unfulfilled in the wake of the dowager's refusal to relinquish control of the household.

Lady Westlake and her luncheon guests regarded Mariah with variations of secret glee, hostility and thoughtful speculation. Mrs. Jonathan Brandywyne took pleasure in any discomfiture Mariah might show, while Mrs. Joseph Roberts's expression was one of puzzled disapproval. Only Madeleine, Lady Hurst, appeared sympathetic to Mariah's unfortunate plight.

But Lady Westlake was obviously of the same mind as the dowager. Mariah must have driven Donnington away, or he would not have left so suddenly. She made little secret of her belief in the new Lady Donnington's faults, even as she served up cake and smiles.

Why do you suffer this? Mariah asked herself. But she knew why. She had committed herself to this life and this marriage for her parents' sake. Hiding away from those who had become her peers would do no good and would only confirm Vivian's low opinion of her.

As if I care for that. Nor had she, until she'd heard Sinjin's warning. And since she had found Ash, everything had changed. There was no telling what might happen when he left his cage, which eventually he must do.

Ash. Her thoughts wandered dangerously in his direction. She hadn't been able to see him today; household concerns, unexpectedly dropped in her lap by the dowager, had kept her occupied all morning. Then there had been this luncheon, which would not end until two at the earliest.

She might comfort herself with the knowledge that, since she still had the key, Ash was unlikely to be disturbed by his unknown keeper, but that didn't really ease her mind. Eventually she would have to put the key back, and she couldn't bear the thought of his being alone in that place. If only she could go to him now…

"Your cake, Lady Donnington."

She snapped back to the present and accepted the second piece from Lady Westlake. Mrs. Brandywyne smothered a titter. She, like many other Englishwomen, obviously thought Mariah's healthy appetite yet another sign of American ill-breeding.

"Tell me, Lady Donnington," Mrs. Brandywyne said sweetly, "how are you faring while Lord Donnington is away? How difficult it must be for a young wife."

"Difficult?" Lady Westlake said. "Some young ladies should be glad to see very little of their husbands after the first few days of marriage."

A silence fell, partly compounded of titillated shock and partly of agreement that could not be spoken. It was a generally accepted fact that English ladies bore their husbands' attentions from a sense of duty and the need to provide an heir as quickly as possible, but they were not supposed to enjoy the means of getting a child. Mrs. Brandywyne and Lady Westlake clearly hoped to provoke Mariah.

"I do regret his absence," Mariah said, meeting Lady Westlake's probing gaze.

"Of course you do," Mrs. Brandywyne opined. "Such a lovely young bride as you are, Lady Donnington."

"When he returns, we shall be all the happier to be together again."

"'Absence makes the heart grow fonder,' as they say," Lady Hurst put in.

"Let us indeed hope so," Mrs. Roberts said, her first words in a good half hour.

For a moment, that seemed to be the end of the skirmish, minor as it had been, but Lady Westlake was far from satisfied.

"How fares your father in America, Lady Donnington?" she asked, pretending to take another tiny bite of her own half-finished cake.

Mariah set down her plate. "Very well, thank you. He keeps himself busy."

"With business interests," Mrs. Brandywyne said. "How industrious you Americans are."

"Indeed," Mariah said. "Hard work agrees with us. Men like my father prefer to earn their own way to prosperity."

Mrs. Brandywyne nearly dropped her teacup. Lady Hurst smiled.

Lady Westlake smiled, as well, but far less pleasantly.

"We have our own of that kind here in England," she said. "They feel themselves quite equal to those whose heritage and titles extend back to the service of our greatest monarchs."

"But your workers are serving the current monarch now, by bringing prosperity to the nation," Mariah said, "and allowing the titled to continue to enjoy their more...stimulating pursuits."

This time there was an audible gasp, though Mariah wasn't sure from whom it emanated. Lady Westlake maintained her smile.

"Oh, their scheming for position only amuses us," she said in a bland tone. "Though our dear prince shows most admirable tolerance for individuals of lesser station."

"More's the pity," Mrs. Brandywyne said. She was not a part of the coveted Marlborough House Set, the prince's circle, though she very much wanted to be. Mariah had heard that Bertie preferred his women beautiful, witty and a little fast. Louise Brandywyne was on the wrong side of plain and completely lacking in conversation. Mariah could almost sympathize with her thwarted ambitions.

"How is that you have never applied to join our prince at Marlborough House?" Lady Westlake asked. "Even Americans are permitted there."

"It would be quite remiss of me to go gallivanting about while my husband is away," Mariah said. "I prefer a quiet life at Donbridge."

"Take care it does not become too quiet," Lady Westlake said with a touch a venom, "or you might be tempted to find some questionable diversion to dispel your loneliness."

Questionable diversion. Mariah worked to suppress her anger. After what Sinjin had told her, she could not mistake the meaning of Lady Westlake's remark. Now she knew that Vivian's unfounded and insulting suspicions were shared by someone else...one who was far more the dowager's friend than she was Mariah's.

Mariah rose abruptly. "Ah," she said, glancing pointedly at the clock on the elaborately carved marble mantelpiece. "I am behind today. Please forgive me, but I must take my leave."

Lady Westlake rose very slowly to take Mariah's hand. "I am sorry, Lady Donnington. I hope you will be able to join us at Newmarket."

"Thank you, but I believe I shall remain at Donbridge for the time being." She turned her attention to the other guests. "Mrs. Roberts, Mrs. Brandywyne." She reserved her warmest smile for Lady Hurst. "Please enjoy the remainder of your afternoon."

She left without further ado, sweeping past a startled parlor maid with a stride as long as her skirts would permit. Fury propelled her as the carriage drew up in the drive.

Vivian and Lady Westlake. It was not the first time that Mariah had been invited to one of Pamela's luncheons, but the woman had never made such insinuations before. The dowager had always encouraged Mariah to attend the neighbors' social events; had this particular invitation been a ploy to catch Mariah out?

It hardly mattered what the two of them intended. The appearance of a stainless reputation was every bit as important as the fact of it.

And her reputation could be in very real danger.

But will that stop you?

Never. Neither would Vivian's designs on her marriage, nor Lady Westlake's spite, nor her own increasingly disturbing feelings for Ash. She was in control of her own actions.

The catch was that she had no way of predicting what Ash might do next. For all his struggles with speech and memory, he could not be dismissed as a mere lunatic. He might be caught in a web of confusion, but he had not been humbled by the experience. He had spoken like a nobleman, like a lord accustomed to command.

"Am I a gentleman?" he had asked. At the time she

hadn't answered him, having no answer to give. But now his simple question sparked a new comprehension. He could not be anything *but* a gentleman. A gentleman who had, for some reason beyond her current understanding, been horribly wronged.

She climbed into the carriage, her heart beating with new purpose. Whatever the dangers to herself, she must help Ash recover his memory. She must teach him what he could not remember. And she must make certain that he was restored to whatever life he had been compelled to abandon—even if she must shock the dowager in the process.

But she could not do it alone. She must have an ally, one who would lend respectability to the endeavor once it was brought into the open.

And she knew who that ally must be.

More than a little worried, Mariah rode all the way back to Donbridge with her fists clenched in her skirts. She hurried up to her room to change into her riding habit and waited impatiently for a groom to fetch Germanicus, her favorite mount. She slipped away before Vivian could accost her and urged the gelding to a fast pace, eager to make the necessary call on Sinjin at his country home before he returned to London.

Presenting her card to the parlor maid who answered the door, she strode into Rothwell's entrance hall. She was immediately shown into Sinjin's study, a masculine sanctuary into which few gentlemen would ever admit a lady.

"Ah, Lady Donnington," Sinjin said, rising as he finished rubbing out the end of his undoubtedly expensive cigar into the ashtray on his desk. "I had not expected to be graced with your charming presence so soon."

Mariah removed her hat. "I hope it is not an inconvenience."

"An inconvenience?" He chuckled and waved her toward one of the hard, straight-backed chairs. "After your recent generosity, your coming could never be an inconvenience."

Mariah felt far too agitated to sit or bother with the niceties. "I hope you are prepared to listen to a very strange tale," she said.

Ware peered at her with interest. "Has this anything to do with your mysterious request for assistance?"

"Yes."

"Will you have tea?"

"I've only just had luncheon."

"With Lady Westlake?"

"How did you guess?"

"Something about the look on your face. And Lady Westlake holds you in particular fascination, you know."

"She seems to share the dowager's assumptions about my...my supposedly bad behavior."

"You do know why, don't you?"

Mariah was in no mood for further unpleasant revelations. "Sinjin..."

"She's been in love with Donnington for years."

"But Lady Westlake is married!"

"You're being naïve again, Merry. There are some who actually *do* ignore their marriage vows."

"You mean that she and my husband have been...they've—"

"Not as far as I am aware. But that doesn't keep Pamela from hoping."

Mariah played nervously with the hem of her riding jacket, striving to hide her agitation. "Do you know her well, Sinjin?"

He sighed. "Do take a seat."

She sat, and he did the same, drumming his fingers on the table beside his chair. "She's frequently at Marlborough House," he said. "One could scarcely miss her. And the Viscounts Westlake have been our neighbors since my grandfather's time. Pamela has recently become a great friend of my mother's." His face settled into a scowl. "I don't think Donnie has seen her since well before your marriage, but you'd do well to stay away from her, Merry."

"I may avoid *her*, but not your mother. She still hopes to discover grounds for her dislike of me. And if matters at Donbridge proceed without your assistance, I fear she may get her wish."

Sinjin started. "*What* matters?" he demanded. "Mariah, what have you done?"

"Nothing very bad, unless you consider discovering a hidden prisoner on the estate an evil on my part."

He laughed. "I beg your pardon?"

"I have found a man at Donbridge, imprisoned in a folly."

Sinjin leaned back in his chair and reached for the crushed cigar, which was quite beyond recovery.

"Get another, if you like," Mariah said. "I'm used to my father's cigars, you know."

Sinjin got up, paced around the room and swung to face her. "What nonsense, Mariah. I always suspected you had a vivid imagination, but this exceeds my wildest expectations."

She tried very hard not to flinch at his tone. Though her determination hadn't wavered, she had guessed that Sinjin would be bound to wonder about the state of her mind.

"It isn't nonsense," she said, very low. "Is anyone likely to hear us?"

"I usually banish the servants when I'm in my study," he said. "What has that to do with...with this fantastic story of yours?"

She took a deep breath. "This must be a secret between us, Sinjin."

"A secret." He waved his hand. "Very well, it shall be our secret." He laughed again, though the sound was strained. "Get on with it, then."

His rudeness was the least of her concerns. "When I was walking out by the mere yesterday morning," she said slowly, "I saw something at the folly—"

"You mean that Georgian monstrosity?" He chuckled to

himself, glanced at Mariah's straight face and sobered. "What did you see at the folly?"

"A man."

"A man?"

"A man caged up like an animal, behind bars. A man who has obviously been a prisoner for some time."

Sinjin frowned, wore another circle in the carpet, revisited his unhappy cigar, and finally took his seat again.

"A prisoner?" he echoed. "In the folly?"

"As I said."

It was too much for even an intelligent man to absorb all at once. Sinjin slumped in his chair, pinching his chin between his thumb and forefinger. "This isn't just a story, is it?"

"Do you think I'm a liar, Sinjin?"

"Good God, no." He raised his head. "Who in hell is he?"

Mariah released her breath. As miraculous as it seemed, he believed her. Or at least he was doing a very good job of pretending.

"I don't know," she said. "When I first found him, he couldn't speak. And though he has regained the power of conversation, he doesn't know his name."

"What do you mean?"

"Just that. It is as if he suffers from a form of amnesia. He was in a very poor state when I found him, with only stale water and no food."

"Good God," Sinjin repeated. He glared down at the crease in his trousers, his expression dark as storm clouds. "What *does* this fellow remember?"

"Very little," she said. "He has obviously suffered some sort of shock, but he is a gentleman, that much is clear."

"A gentleman?"

"Yes, though it might not appear so at first. His speech, his manner…"

"This is beyond anything."

"I know."

He remained deep in thought for several tense minutes. "How did you come to find this man, Mariah?"

"I saw a stranger lurking about the folly and found a key to an inner chamber. That is where I discovered the cage." She braced herself. "There is something else, Sinjin. This man… the prisoner looks almost exactly like Donnington."

"What?"

"Except for the color of his hair, he could be Donnington's twin."

Sinjin muttered something under his breath. "Are you quite certain all this wasn't a dream?"

The chair seemed to lurch under her. "I can see that it was a mistake to come here. I shall take my leave."

"Merry, I—" He stared into her eyes. "Good God. You're as white as a sheet. I'll ring for a glass of—"

"I'm all right." Mariah sat very straight and gazed at him earnestly. "What I have said is no exaggeration. I felt it was necessary to prepare you." She hesitated. *Should I tell you that he not only looks like Donnington, but blames your brother for his imprisonment?*

She had no choice. But that could wait until tonight…if Sinjin agreed to come.

"Did you or did you not mean it when you said I could count on you?" she asked.

"Of course I meant it," he said, though his usual aplomb had deserted him completely. "You haven't spoken of this to anyone else?"

"I did question one of the maids regarding rumors related to a captive somewhere on the grounds."

"Rumors? You'd already heard about this?"

"Not at all, but I thought if anyone would know…" She hesitated. "She confirmed that she'd heard stories of someone being held at Donbridge."

"For God's sake!" He shook his head. "I've never heard a word of this, and I can scarce credit—" He broke off. "A man who looks like Donnington. Did this maid say who is supposed to have committed this…this offense?"

"No."

"But you have a theory."

"I'll tell you what little I know tonight."

Sinjin didn't press her. He rose and walked to the sideboard, where he picked up a glass and set it down again. "The proof is in the pudding," he said grimly. "When shall I meet this…gentleman?"

Her heart resumed its normal rhythm. "Come to Donbridge," she said, "but secretly. I don't want to alert anyone who might have taken part in this." She hurried on before he could interrupt. "Meet me at eleven tonight, by the folly. I'll show you everything, and then we can decide what we ought to do."

"Why do I think you're about to get me into a situation I'm going to regret?"

"Will you do it?"

"Of course I will."

Once again he offered refreshments and tea, but she declined and hurried away. If she were very lucky, there would be time to speak to Ash and prepare him for the visit of another stranger.

But once she got back to Donbridge, the opportunity never arose. The dowager, uncharacteristically attentive in spite of her usual hostility, made it impossible for Mariah to slip away from the house until after dinner. It was gone ten when the dowager finally retired. Mariah waited for another half hour, made certain the house was quiet, and then put on her simplest dress, a shawl and half-boots. She was halfway down the stairs when Nola appeared out of the shadows.

"Nola!" Mariah hid the pillowcase of newly hoarded food

behind her back, though she knew she had little hope of keeping it concealed for long. Nola curtseyed, her face wreathed in concern.

"Begging your pardon, Countess," she said. "I didn't mean to startle you."

"You didn't. I was just going down to the kitchen. Why are you up and about so late?"

"I…I thought you might need help, your ladyship."

"Help, Nola? I can find my way to the kitchen by myself."

"I was just remembering what you told me, your ladyship," she said. "About the prisoner and all."

"I'm afraid my imagination ran away with me," Mariah said with a strained smile. "You needn't give it another thought."

The maid bent her head, peering at the level of Mariah's hip where the pillowcase protruded from behind her skirts. "You're going to see him, your ladyship?"

Mariah began to feel that the girl might prove to be every bit as difficult now as she had been helpful before. "What makes you think I'm going to see anyone, Nola?"

"Just a feeling, your ladyship."

A feeling. Mariah suppressed a shiver. "Is there something you haven't told me? Something about the subject we discussed yesterday?"

"No, ma'am."

"Then what I do is really none of your business," Mariah said, more harshly than she'd intended. She immediately regretted it.

"I know your intentions are good," she said, "but I'm really just trying to find out what's going on. It would be better if no one else were involved."

"But I saw Mr. Ware, your ladyship," Nola said. "Out in the park."

Nola's tone was anything but sly, yet Mariah was very

much on her guard. "And why were you creeping about outside, Nola?"

"I often go for walks at night, though Mrs. Baines doesn't approve." She performed another curtsey, which worked well to hide her expression. "I'm sorry, your ladyship."

"I should avoid annoying Mrs. Baines, if I were you. As for Mr. Ware, he is known to do just as he wishes. Our grounds are considerably larger than his and have excellent prospects by moonlight. There is a full moon tonight. Perhaps he had an urge to view it."

"Yes, ma'am. But…" Nola dropped her voice very low. "I could make sure *she* doesn't see you."

Mariah froze. Was that what the girl's interference was all about? Did she—did all the servants—know what the dowager suspected of her daughter-in-law?

"I am not concerned about the dowager," Mariah said sternly. "But I should not wish to disturb her. She has quite enough concerns as it is."

"Then you *are* going to see the man who looks like Lord Donnington."

Matters had proceeded to the point that denials would probably have little effect. *She* had begun this, and she could hardly blame the maid for behaving like the intelligent girl she was.

"Tell me, Nola," she said, "why should you want to help me?"

"Because Lord Donnington's going away wasn't your fault, not like some people say."

Good Lord. "You might find yourself in trouble if you gossip about such matters in the servants' quarters."

"But I don't, your ladyship," Nola said. "Never." She glanced over her shoulder into the entrance hall. "What can I do, ma'am?"

Countering Nola's stubborn resolve was no more likely than convincing her that her mistress had nothing to hide.

"Stay here," Mariah said. "If I find a way for you to help, I'll certainly let you know."

"I hope…I hope you will be very careful, your ladyship."

"I shall." Mariah held the girl's gaze. "No matter what else happens, you must keep our meetings absolutely secret."

Nola nodded solemnly. "I understand, your ladyship."

"Very good. You go up to bed now, Nola."

"Yes, ma'am."

Realizing full well that she was taking a very great risk, Mariah stood at the foot of the stairs until Nola had disappeared into the shadows. She could afford to delay no longer.

Outside, England's lingering twilight had finally given way to darkness. Mariah kept the lantern as dim as she could and went directly to the folly.

Sinjin was already there. He wore dark riding clothes and carried his own lantern, unlit. His horse, Shaitan, grazed contentedly on the long grass beside the lakeshore.

Sinjin turned into Mariah's light, hand raised to shield his eyes.

"Merry?"

"Sinjin! It isn't yet eleven!"

"Sorry, but I was rather eager to see what this is all about." He shifted slightly, and the lantern's light caught metal near his waist.

A gun.

"For God's sake, Sinjin!" she hissed. "There's no need for that."

"He might be a lunatic," Sinjin said, unfazed.

"I never said—"

"If there's a prisoner in the folly, there has to be good reason for it. A poacher, most likely. A temporary punishment—"

"A poacher who looks like Donnington?"

His eyes told her that he had not lost any part of his skepticism. "I am most eager to observe this resemblance."

"Observe it, but don't speak of it." She reminded herself that what she was about to say was absolutely necessary. "You suspected that I had a theory about who might have done this to him. But it isn't my theory, Sinjin. It's his."

"I thought you said he didn't remember anythi—"

"He blames Donnington," she said in a rush. "He believes that Donnington did this to him."

Sinjin was too stunned to laugh. "Do you know what you're saying?"

"I didn't say I accepted his claims," she said. "But you must be careful, Sinjin. Don't question him about it. I don't think he realizes how much he looks like…like the man he blames for what's happened to him."

"How is any of this possible?"

"I don't know."

Reflected light glazed the gun's barrel as Sinjin gripped it reflexively. "I'm sorry, Merry, but I—"

"Put that away. You won't need it." She stared into his eyes. "Wait here until I call you."

"Mariah…"

"Please, just do as I say!"

Sinjin subsided, though his expression was anything but sanguine. Mariah carried her pillowcase up the stairs, readying the key for the lock. She entered with every bit as much apprehension as she had the second time, half afraid of what she might find.

Everything was as she had left it. No one had been inside since she'd last come. Ash stood at the bars, his face turned so as to look beyond her, toward the square of darkness framed through the two doors.

"Who?" he demanded in a harsh voice. "Who is he?"

CHAPTER FIVE

ASH SMELLED THE man before he walked into the room, his hand near his hip and the glitter of iron at his waist. He was dark-haired and brown-eyed, lean and well formed, and he wore a shirt, trousers and the overgarment that Ash remembered was called a "jacket."

He smelled almost exactly the same as the enemy who had put Ash in this place.

Mariah blocked the stranger's path, but he clearly saw Ash. His eyes widened in astonishment.

"My God," he said. "My God." He stumbled into the wall, breathing heavily, and continued to stare.

Ash flung himself at the bars, and the stranger jerked away. Mariah approached the cage, hand raised, the slim, straight lines of her brows drawn over her eyes.

"Ash? Are you all right?"

He didn't know how to answer. "All right" meant feeling well, and he didn't feel well. Mariah had been away too long. He was furious at the presence of the second human, who intruded with his Cold Iron and his thick male scent that was so much like Donnington's. If there had been a way out of the cage, Ash would have charged him, knocked him down, impaled...

"Who is he?" he repeated.

"My name is Sinjin Ware," the man said hoarsely, pushing away from the wall. "Who in hell are *you?*"

"I call him Ash," Mariah said. "Please, Sinjin, stand back."

She turned to Ash again. "Mr. Ware has come to help us. There is no reason to be afraid of him."

Ash laughed, drawing a startled expression from both humans. "Ware," he snarled. "Donnington."

The man exchanged glances with Mariah. "My God," he repeated. "Did you tell him who I—"

"Do you still think he's a poacher, Sinjin?" Mariah said before he could finish.

"No. I had...no idea."

Ash banged at the bars with his fist. "He did this."

Sinjin drew his hand over the fringe of dark hair above his lip. "Believe me, Mariah. I had nothing to do with—"

"You are his," Ash said, no longer caring if his flesh touched iron. "His."

The human male looked ill. "What is he saying, Mariah?"

She took his arm. "We shall return soon, Ash," she said. She led the man she called Sinjin from the room and half closed the door. Ash realized at once that she did not want him to hear what they said to each other.

"We must be careful, Sinjin," she said in a low voice that Ash easily heard. "Ash is very—"

"What the hell is going on?" Sinjin demanded.

"I told you that Ash blames Donnington. He hates him. Somehow he's realized that you are related to him."

"How? Giles and I look nothing alike!"

"As I said at Rothwell, I am convinced that Ash has no idea how much he looks like Donnington. And I never mentioned you. I certainly never told him that you are Donnington's brother."

"Does he know Donnington's your husband?"

"No. And it is too soon to tell him."

"You're afraid of him. You *do* think he's mad."

She didn't answer. Ash pressed as close to the bars as he could without touching them.

"Think carefully," Mariah said at last. "Who in your family might resemble your brother?"

"You aren't suggesting—"

"Who, Sinjin?"

"No one!"

"No one that you know of."

"Don't you think I would be aware… Do you actually think this man is here because of my brother?"

"I don't know what to believe. Please stay here, Sinjin."

A moment later she returned to the inner chamber, fetched the bag she had brought with her and opened it, producing another loaf of bread, small red fruits, a white stone-like container and another shaped of clear crystal.

"Bread, strawberries, butter and jam," she said, smiling at Ash. She sat in the chair, spread a cloth across her heavy skirt and removed two pieces of the bread from its wrapping. She coated them with the yellow substance in the stone container and the thick, sweet-smelling fruit from the crystal.

Ash could see Ware peering through the crack in the door. Donnington's *brother,* though Ash didn't know what that word might mean. He only knew it was important. As was *husband,* though he refused to consider why it hurt so much to think of Mariah bearing a connection to his enemy.

And Mariah had said he looked like Donnington. Ash had not seen Donnington when he had gazed at his own face in the water, yet something in him knew it was true.

The thoughts flying through his head made his hunger go away, but he knew he must remain strong. He took the bread through the bars, and then Mariah left the room again.

"You speak to him as if he doesn't know what bread and jam are," Ware whispered. "And he's only half-dressed."

"He was left with almost nothing," she said. "Nothing to eat, nothing to wear."

"You brought him those clothes?"

"Of course. What else was I to do?"

"You said you saw another stranger by the folly. This man hasn't been completely neglected. Someone must come here to feed him, clean his…" He paused. "What did your maid say?"

"Nola said there was a strange man living in a cottage on the grounds, and no one knows what he does. Ash implied that someone comes to him every few days. Someone who doesn't want anyone else to know that Ash is here."

Sinjin made a harsh, angry sound. "This is a highly volatile situation, Mariah," he said. "Obviously this man has suffered, but as for his identity or Donnington's…involvement, we'll have to give this very careful thought. Acting too quickly can only—"

Mariah strode back into Ash's room, Ware on her heels. He caught at Mariah's arm. "Mariah, listen to me. We—"

The bars rattled as Ash banged against them. Fire coursed over his skin.

"Don't touch her," he commanded. "Don't touch her!"

Both humans started. "He *is* a lunatic," Ware said.

Mariah shook him off. "He's nothing of the kind." She moved as close to Ash as she could without touching the bars. "Don't, Ash. Please."

The fire licked at Ash's forehead. "Stay away from him."

"Sinjin won't hurt me, Ash. I promise you, he's our friend."

"Merry, this man is obviously disturbed," Ware said. "Don't promise him anything. Not until we know what he's done."

"Done?" She whirled to face him. "What could he have done to deserve this?"

"We need to keep our wits about us. You must see that."

"Yes. We must *all* keep our wits about us." She smiled at Ash, though her lips trembled. "Try to be patient, Ash. We both want to help, to find out why you're here so we can let you go."

"Merry…" Sinjin warned.

But she wasn't listening to him. "Have you remembered anything new, Ash?" she asked. "Anything you can tell us?"

To offer her the truth would be to admit too much. That he was not human. That there was some other world ruled by those who were not human. That he had possessed another life, another form far mightier than this one. No, he could not offer her the truth.

For she had not given *him* the truth.

"No," he said.

"We'll find a way, Ash."

"Which will require considerable finesse," Ware said. "And you will leave the investigation to me, Mariah."

"First we must find Ash's keeper."

"I'll look into it as soon as it's light enough to search," Ware said. "You go back to the house, Merry. Pretend that nothing has happened."

She flashed another glance at Ash and pushed Sinjin out of the room again. "Suppose Donnington does know about this?" she said. "Might Vivian not know, as well?"

"Mother? You're joking."

"Perhaps. But, as you said, we can make no judgments as yet. I'll learn what I can in the house. You find this keeper. And you must discover how Ash is related to your family."

"*If* he is—"

"No judgments, Sinjin."

"I'll do just as you say. But, Merry… Don't say anything to my mother. Not under any circumstances. She would be worse than shocked if she saw him."

"This can't be kept hidden for long."

"Go back to the house. I'll stay with him until dawn."

"That would not be wise."

"I'm not leaving you alone with him. He's shown a propensity for violence."

"Can you blame him?"

"Hasn't it occurred to you that you simply haven't been questioning him the right away?"

"What do you propose? Torture?"

"I'm beginning to wonder, given his startling resemblance to Donnington, if your desire to help isn't some sort of obsession."

"It ought to be every bit as much of an obsession with you, Sinjin! This man could be your direct relation."

There was a long moment of silence. "I was right, wasn't I? This isn't just natural concern on your part."

"Do you believe that compassion isn't sufficient reason to help someone?"

"I mean the way you look at him, speak to him—"

"We shouldn't leave Ash alone," she said. The door swung open again, and Mariah walked straight over to the bars.

"I'm sorry, Ash," she said. "Mr. Ware and I—"

"Release me."

She stared at him, her lips slightly parted. Ware walked up behind her, examining Ash through narrowed eyes.

"A gentleman, is he?" Ware said. "He does speak rather like a duke I once knew. Truly, Merry, you must realize that this man may not be sane, let alone capable of or willing to speak the truth. We—"

There was scarcely room between the bars for Ash's hand, let alone his arm, but he struck at once. His flesh screamed in pain as his fingers clutched the collar of Ware's jacket and jerked the man against the bars.

"Truth?" he snarled. "What do humans know of truth?"

The silence became frozen. Ware breathed sharply through his nose. Mariah, who had grabbed Ash's wrist, went very still.

"Humans?" she whispered.

Ash released the other man and pulled his arm back, holding it against his chest. "Men," he said. "Men like Donnington."

"Can you fail to doubt his sanity now?" Ware asked, straightening his clothing with sharp, angry motions.

"Considering your own behavior…" Mariah frowned into Ash's face, then glanced at his arm. Already the marks were fading. "Ash knows the meaning of truth. Would anyone not of sound mind understand such a concept?"

"Who knows what a lunatic might or might not understand?"

Mariah glared at him. "Do you know how to open this lock?"

"You aren't seriously thinking of letting him out?"

"Can you break it?"

"I won't. He's dangerous, Mariah. He's also strong, however badly he's been treated. I can defend myself, but you can't."

"He would never hurt me."

"How long have you known him? Two days?" Sinjin snorted. "No. I won't do it."

She turned back to Ash. "I'm sorry, Ash. You must wait a little while longer. A day, at most."

"I told you not to promise him anything," Ware said, his face darker than it had been before. "I've got to find that keeper first."

They looked at each in a way Ash could hardly bear. "Very well," Mariah said. "Ash, we shall both be leaving now. But it will only be for a little while."

He wanted to wail and beat his fists against the walls of his cage, to rage and roar and attack the bars again and again. But he merely withdrew into the shadows where their light boxes' feeble illumination couldn't reach. He watched as Mariah and Ware spoke quietly, and then, after touching Mariah's hand, the other man left the room.

A dozen heartbeats later Mariah was at the bars again. "Ash," she whispered, "I have an idea, but I must make sure the coast is clear first."

He remained where he was while she followed Ware, listening to her feet in their small tight shoes tap against the stone. When she returned, her face was flushed, and her movements were as quick and darting as those of a bird.

"I am going to get you out," she said. "Tonight, whatever Sinjin may say."

Ash knew then that he had won the battle. "How?" he asked.

"I shall find a way to break this lock."

"Why?"

She had never looked at him so directly or so clearly. "Because I see how it will be. I thought I needed Sinjin's help. I still do. But he won't soon agree to let you go, after what you…after how you behaved."

It was a reprimand. He did not like it. "What is he?"

"Sinjin? I meant to tell you—"

"Donnington's *brother,*" he said. "What does it mean?"

She searched his eyes, her face almost white. "You heard us, didn't you?"

"What does it mean?"

"Brothers are family. They have the same mother and father."

"*Mother* is the female who bore you?"

"My mother, yes. As *their* mother bore *them.*"

"What is *family?*"

The delicate skin over her throat trembled. "A mother and father and children—brothers and sisters—make a family."

The food in Ash's stomach would not remain still. "I am Ware's family? And Donnington's?"

"We…we don't know, Ash."

"I look like Donnington."

"You don't…you are different. It isn't as if—"

Ash laughed. "I am my enemy."

"No. No, Ash. There is so much we have yet to learn. You must give us time."

Time meant waiting. Time meant this room, this cage. He tried to think of something else.

"What is Ware to you?" he asked.

"He is a friend."

She had called herself Ash's "friend." But it wasn't the same. He knew it was not.

"He does not believe that Donnington did this to me."

"Whatever Donnington may have done, Sinjin knew nothing about it. You must remember that."

Ash looked from the tops of the bars to the point where they sank into the ground. "What is *husband*?"

"Ash—"

"Tell me."

"A…a husband is like a father. A husband…lives with his wife."

"Donnington is your husband and you are Donnington's wife."

As Ash had been before, so she was now: mute, voiceless.

Why had she not spoken the truth earlier, when she'd had the chance? She could not be afraid of Ash, or she would never have returned. But she *was* afraid.

"He kept you like this?" Ash said, his hatred doubling.

"Like…" Her hand swept to the base of her neck, where the heavy cloth covered her flesh. "No, Ash."

"You escaped," Ash said. "You found me."

"I…" Her face was beaded with tiny drops of moisture. "Ash, I am not living with him now, but he did not keep me in a cage."

"Then why were you his wife?"

"Because…because I didn't know what he'd done to you."

There was something hidden in her eyes and voice, but he could not make sense of it. Fury boiled under his skin. "Where is he?"

"Away. I don't know where. But he will return. That is why, when we leave this place, you must remain hidden."

"I will not hide."

"Only for a while. But you cannot stay in this cage for one more hour."

A promise, like the others she had made—and kept. Yet when she left, Ash could not forget that she had not told him about Donnington. Her husband. His enemy.

He paced along the front of the cage, striking the bars each time he reached the end and turned for another pass. The pain became a part of him, keeping his anger strong. His heartbeat slowed to match the steady rhythm.

And then they came.

Memories. Not like the others, fragmented and seen through the prism of a dream, but solid and bright and real.

He lay in the shadow of great gray stones cupped in a circle of trees, his mind a voiceless sphere spinning inside his head. Two others stood near him: one was Donnington—like Ash, save for the darkness of his hair.

The other was Fane. While the human was not unimpressive, the Fane would draw all eyes to him wherever he appeared. His body was lithe and slender, his features finely drawn, his hair a richer nut-brown than anything that could be conceived on earth. His eyes were silver shaded with green, his clothes woven of light and thread so fine it could hardly be seen. He gazed at Donnington with contempt, everything about him speaking of power and arrogance.

"I kept my part of the bargain," Donnington was saying. He gestured to the girl lying at his feet. "I brought her, as you asked. Where is my unicorn?"

The Fane slowly turned his head. Cold eyes surveyed Ash where he lay. "There," he said.

"This man?" Donnington started toward the Fane lord, who moved not a muscle, and then stopped to stare at Ash. "He looks exactly like *me!*"

Cairbre—for that was the Fane lord's name—smiled a little. "An odd effect of the transfer. You were the first human he saw when he passed through the Gate, so his body shaped itself in your image."

Donnington shuddered. "He wasn't supposed to be human!"

"He was cursed to assume human form in your world, but I expected this to be a temporary condition."

"You're saying it isn't?"

"Oberon is still powerful. He will not be so for long."

The human scowled. "Can it...can it understand us?"

"It has not yet learned human speech." The Fane lord stared at the human until Donnington dropped his gaze. "You have said that you kept your part of the bargain, but you have not fully succeeded, either. The girl is resisting my power. I cannot bring her through the Gate."

"Because you're nothing but a ghost."

"It has nothing to do with Oberon's restrictions on our appearance in your world," Cairbre said coldly.

"Then your weakness is no problem of mine," Donnington snapped. "She's barely conscious, and you can't get her through?"

The Fane's gaze fell on Mariah. "Some part of her hidden nature has thwarted me. I believe she will not enter Tir-na-Nog unless she is coaxed by one she trusts without reservation."

"What has that to do with me? Do you think she'll still trust me after what I've done?"

"If you fear that she will remember what has passed here, you need not. These memories will be concealed from her own mind."

"It doesn't matter." Donnington reached inside his pocket and drew out a silver object that sparkled with clear gemstones. "You gave me this talisman, and I found the girl for you. I brought her to England, and I haven't touched her. But I'll be damned if I'll woo her all over again just to get her through your bloody Gate. I'm willing to stick to the bargain, but not under these conditions."

"Very well." Cairbre said. He steepled his elegant fingers under his chin and glanced again at Ash. "I propose another solution. There is a very ancient bond between unicorns and virgin maidens. It was how men hunted the beasts before they fled to Tir-na-Nog. The unicorns were compelled to give themselves up to the maidens, but the enchantment had power over the females, as well." He forestalled Donnington's interruption with a lift of his hand. "If we permit the girl to meet with Arion, she will inevitably be drawn to him, and he to her. If he wins her trust, he himself can lead her through the Gate."

"That's utterly preposterous!" Donnington sputtered. "Allow *it* to meet the girl? Shall I throw a ball to introduce them?" He shook his head sharply. "Even if such a scheme would work, how do you propose to win the unicorn's cooperation in contributing to its own destruction?"

"By making him believe that I will convince Oberon to lift his curse if he cooperates."

"Then he mustn't learn anything about our scheme."

"It is dangerous to take me for a fool, mortal."

Donnington seemed not to hear him. He was staring at Arion, his expression filled with contempt.

"Are you sure it will be worth hunting?" he asked. "I expect to earn my trophy with a good chase and kill. It doesn't look as if it could walk, let alone learn to speak."

"Arion, unfortunately, did suffer a considerable shock, but in time—"

"You mean it has lost its senses?" Donnington worked his hands open and shut. "Is it insane?"

Cairbre floated a few feet off the ground. "He will be sane enough for you to hunt, mortal."

Donnington's skepticism gave way to contemplation. "You want them to meet," he said slowly. "I have an idea of how to bring that about." He met Cairbre's gaze. "Mariah's mother was considered mad because she saw visions of another world."

"Ah, yes. Fane blood coming to the fore."

"Mariah spent years looking after her mother. She has great sympathy for those who suffer the same affliction."

Something passed between Fane and human, but Arion's senses were fading, and he sank into a gray world, formless and still.

When he woke again, Donnington was gone and so was the girl. Cairbre stood above him, a giant shadow against the moon and stars.

"You heard all that passed," he said.

Arion tried to rise. There was something terribly wrong with his body, but he was only just beginning to feel it.

"Yes, you heard," Cairbre said, "though Donnington believes you did not understand." He smiled. "Do you remember, Arion? Do you remember what you have lost?"

Arion remembered. He remembered running in the perpetual sunlight of Tir-na-Nog, his mane and tail flying on the breeze that never grew too warm or too cold, his muscles rippling under his gleaming coat, his horn striking sparks that blinded the lesser beasts who bowed to him. Rabbit and hind, fox and red-eared hound, all crouched and cried their praise: Arion.

Only one other word had meaning for him: freedom. Freedom from the chains of mortality. Freedom to do as he pleased, whenever he pleased. As he ran, unfettered, his people followed, every one as flawless as the gems humans so coveted.

But he was mightiest of all. He was perfection, the most noble creature ever to walk the fields and groves of Tir-na-Nog, greater even than the Fane. He was king, and not even the lordlings dared to defy him.

Until Cairbre. Until a Fane had attempted to subvert Arion

and his people, who had ever disdained the doings of the humanlike creatures with whom they must share Tir-na-Nog.

You will help me defeat Oberon, Cairbre had said. *I shall rule, and give you all you desire.*

But Arion had desired nothing. He turned his back on the Fane and laughed in the way of his kind. Cairbre made many threats, full of boasts as such creatures always were when their will was thwarted. But Arion had only lifted his tail in contempt and led his people away. Cairbre had risen in a streak of smoke, wailing in rage as he disappeared. And Arion heard nothing more from him until the day he was brought before Oberon.

Though there was much Arion did not comprehend of Fane ways, he understood then that Cairbre had taken his revenge. It was Cairbre who whispered in the Fane king's ear, who made him believe that Arion, not Cairbre, intended to rebel. Cairbre who urged Lord Oberon to punish Arion for his supposed crime. Cairbre who watched, smiling, as Arion was cast from Tir-na-Nog and condemned to a human existence.

"Your condemnation served two purposes," Cairbre whispered in his ear. "I had my revenge for your defiance, and I could buy a human to aid me in the search for my bride." He laid his slender hand on Arion's head. "His price was one I was pleased to pay. I promised him that he might hunt the rarest game of all."

Arion bucked against the restraints that bound his limbs, but no part of his body would move as it should.

"You don't yet understand, do you?" Cairbre purred. "You have been cursed to take human shape and will never be restored as long as Oberon rules Tir-na-Nog. You will end your life on the spear of a mere human."

The hunt. The hunt which had not occurred in a thousand human years…the hunt from which the unicorn kind had fled, never to return to the world they graced with joy and light since the beginning.

On earth, Cold Iron ruled. On earth, under the right conditions, a unicorn might be killed.

"You are afraid," Cairbre said. "In all your life, you have never been afraid. Death was but an empty shadow. But now, my friend, it is real. If I but tell the mortal what Cold Iron may do to a creature of Tir-na-Nog…"

Arion's hornless head struck the ground, and his blood, red as the fireflower, dripped onto the ground. Arion reeled. Unicorns' blood was as clear as their crystalline horns, and it was never shed.

Except on earth.

Arion reared up, trying to strike at the nearest enemy. Cairbre laughed as Arion fell back to the ground.

"Humans have their great obsessions," Cairbre said. "Donnington's is hunting. He is willing to surrender this girl to me in exchange for you. When I have the female, with her mix of human and Fane blood, I will bring new hope to Tir-na-Nog and win the fealty of many."

Arion struggled to make the noises Fane and human created so effortlessly. He felt strange muscles move, but no sound came forth.

"You have but one chance, Arion-that-was," Cairbre said, his silver-green eyes dancing. "Donnington is stupid. He knows not the Fane. He believes that I am bound to keep my promises. But he is also clever, in his primitive way." He stared across the rolling field that stretched away from the stones and the trees. "She is a virgin. She will be drawn to you and you to her. You will make her trust you, and you will deliver her to me." He sighed. "Oh, I know that Oberon's curse prevents your return. But he will soon find himself weakened, and I shall open the Gate and allow you to pass."

In the distant realms of memory, Arion found a scene so far from his understanding that he knew no unicorn yet alive had ever experienced it. A unicorn knelt in the forest, humble and tamed, his head in the lap of a virgin girl. The hunters came, their common mounts winded and sweating, their faces triumphant as they saw their prey brought low at last.

"Yes," Cairbre said, seeing the tale of blood pass behind Arion's eyes. "But if you obey me, such things will never come to pass."

Arion tossed his head, and Cairbre smiled again. "You wonder how you are to meet and woo this girl in a world you do not understand," he said. "But that is the beauty of Donnington's scheme. The girl is afraid of inheriting her mother's supposed affliction, yet she is drawn to those the humans deem mad because of the emotion they call compassion." He bent to caress Arion's face with his fingertips. "It will not be difficult for you to appear as one of these mad humans, Arion. You have not yet learned to speak their tongue or ape their manners. All you need do is continue to wear the mask once you have come to comprehend them."

Freedom. A way back. A release from this ugly shape that imprisoned him in mortal flesh.

Life. Retribution.

"Yes," Cairbre mocked. "You must win more than the girl's compassion. You must win her love. But you must never touch her. Your human form may be tempted, but she must be pure when she comes to me. Win her, but do not let her claim your heart."

"Dahh…" Arion moaned. "Daahn…"

"Donnington was worse than foolish to take the girl in the mortal bond humans call marriage. But he has not violated her, and he will bring her to you. I shall not interfere. This is yours to accomplish alone, Arion. Prove your worthiness and you may yet survive. But *she* must not know. She must never know."

Ash snapped out of the past, his hands scored with a dozen stripes, skin hissing and crackling. In an instant, he had remembered all. He understood how he must have come to be imprisoned, though the details still escaped him. He grasped at last why he looked like Donnington, the first human he had ever seen, the mirror in which he had glimpsed his terribly changed body. He knew why he must remain close to Mariah, why he must court and claim her.

Death was the alternative. Death, all but unknown to his kind, and the complete end of his hopes of return to Tir-na-Nog and his own people.

As for *her*…

He sank to the floor. Her kind had hunted unicorns nearly to extinction. Females like her had lured his fellows to their destruction.

Though she could not know it, Mariah possessed power over him. He could easily fall under her sway, as his ancestors had.

Win her, but do not let her claim your heart.

Ash clenched his fists, though there was nothing to strike but the unyielding ground. He must remember that Mariah was part Fane, though that otherworldly blood had not permitted her to see Donnington's treachery. Donnington and Cairbre had locked Ash in this place with the intention that Mariah should find him and feel bound to him because of his supposed madness.

But something had not gone as they had planned. Too much time had passed before Mariah came to him, and when she did, it had not been necessary for him to feign madness. Long days behind the bars had driven him to it, and only Mariah had saved him.

Mariah, who feared madness herself. Who must never know what he knew now.

You must betray her.

Betray her to Cairbre, to a life in Tir-na-Nog, where she would be but a pawn in Cairbre's scheme to rule the Blessed Land.

Where she would be free of Donnington. Where she would live in luxury and beauty to the end of her days. Where she might come fully into her powers, free to defy Cairbre as she had unconsciously defied him earlier, when he had tried to take her through the Gate.

It would not be so terrible for her. She would be alive. Not even Cairbre could steal her spirit, her courage.

Ash sprang to his feet. Why had she married Donnington? What deceptions had he used to win her? Were they the same deceptions Ash must use now to save himself?

He felt the hunter's iron-headed spear already lodged within his body, twisting, stealing breath and life. The girl would *not* be harmed. When he won his freedom from exile and was back in Tir-na-Nog, he might even come to her aid against Cairbre.

And take my revenge.

He ran his hands through his short mane. He had no answers, only instincts. The instinct to return to his true self. The instinct to survive.

And it was not as if he *cared* for her. He must forget the softness Mariah had awakened in him. He must remember who he was.

Arion. But he would be Ash as long as he must, and become what Mariah wished him to be.

By the time she returned to his cage, a heavy bar of Cold Iron in her hand, he felt nothing at all.

CHAPTER SIX

"I BELIEVE SHE has a lover."

Vivian, the dowager Lady Donnington, poured another cup of tea for Lady Westlake, who took the fragile handle between her elegant fingertips.

"Of course," the younger woman said. "I had assumed that fact was already understood between us."

Understood, indeed. Nevertheless, Vivian chose subtlety over Lady Westlake's frankness. "She has only been married two months," she remarked.

"And has shown no signs of being with child."

Vivian found that her aching hands were remarkably steady as she offered Lady Westlake the plate of biscuits. "Although, if she were to become so now…"

There was no need to finish the sentence. Both women knew the unwritten rules of high society. It was far from unusual for married ladies to take lovers from among their own kind—discreetly, of course, with an eye to never being caught in a public place—and with the tacit permission, if not approval, of spouses who were engaged in similar clandestine affairs.

But this was only to be undertaken after a woman had given birth to "an heir and a spare," so that no illegitimate offspring could claim an inheritance not rightly his. For a new bride like Mariah to enjoy the intimate company of a man not her husband…

"She is a shallow child, to be sure," Lady Westlake said, "but to take such a risk…"

"Indeed. But since I believe she drove my son away before their marriage was…complete, I would not put anything past her."

Lady Westlake's expression took on a new and very keen interest. "I knew it," she said, half under her breath.

Vivian didn't know whether to be angry or pleased at having so perceptive an ally. "Did you?" she asked in a cool tone.

"I apologize if I have offended," Lady Westlake said hastily. "It was not my intention."

"Of course it wasn't, my dear." Vivian finished her tea and waited until Barbara had retrieved the tray and left the room. "How did you come to suspect?"

"I fancy that I have known Lord Donnington long enough to guess that he would not leave Donbridge immediately after his wedding without very good reason."

"He would not. And though he is a strong man, he would never dream of forcing himself on a lady, even his wife."

The two women absorbed this thought in silence. Lady Westlake was first to speak again.

"What do you propose to do about the situation?" she asked. "Until Donnington returns…"

"I shall take steps to see that he is provided with all necessary information to press for an annulment."

"You know you have my full support, Lady Donnington," Lady Westlake said.

"I am gratified to hear it." Vivian rose and swept around the room, walking past the window that let in a modicum of morning sunlight and stopping at last beneath the portrait of her late husband. "How William would have despised this state of affairs. But my son has always done just as he wished, even in his choice of wife."

Lady Westlake made a sound of agreement. "What shall be your first move, Lady Donnington?"

"To determine the name and nature of her lover." Vivian turned and resumed her chair. "For that I may ask your help. I already have an agent in place, but I am not sure how fully she can be trusted."

"May I enquire as to the nature of this 'agent'?"

"A maid in the household, one who has been taken into Mariah's confidence. I have encouraged her to continue to foster the relationship as much as she is able. Americans are remarkably informal with their servants."

"So I have heard. Odd that they should have servants at all, given their penchant for doing their own work."

But Vivian was in no mood to be drawn from the subject at hand. "You are in no sense obligated to help me, Lady Westlake, but if you are truly willing…"

"I am."

"Would it be possible for you to befriend my daughter-in-law more closely?"

"I doubt, even in her ignorance, that she would find me sincere. I have not always concealed my dislike. But I shall do whatever I can."

The two women smiled at each other in perfect understanding. Vivian knew that Lady Westlake had been pursuing Donnington for some time before his marriage and resented Mariah's very presence in Donnington's life. She was a matron with an ill and elderly husband and a son with whom she had little to do; according to gossip, she had already engaged in any number of affairs. But she was certain that she could snag Donnington with Mariah out of the way.

Vivian had given Lady Westlake to assume that she would not stand in the way of such an alliance, but in truth she would never permit it under any circumstances. Pamela appeared respectable on the surface but, beneath that pretty veneer, was a simple tart.

Nevertheless, Pamela must continue to believe that the field would be clear for her once Mariah was disposed of. The situation must be handled with the utmost delicacy, and all blame must fall entirely on the American heiress's shoulders.

Vivian stood up again. "If you will forgive me, Lady Westlake, I have household matters I must attend to. My daughter-in-law does not see fit to take on her proper duties, so I must perform them in her place."

A flash of waspish resentment crossed Lady Westlake's face and was quickly gone. She rose gracefully. "I look forward to our next discussion, Lady Donnington."

"As do I." They shook hands, each holding on a little longer and a little more firmly than was strictly polite. Vivian escorted Lady Westlake to the drawing room door and signaled Parish to send for her carriage. "Goodbye for now, Lady Westlake."

The women exchanged nods, and Lady Westlake walked out of the house. Vivian watched the footman hand her into her seat, where she settled gracefully in a flurry of overdecorated skirts and waved to her hostess before the carriage started away.

You shall serve my purpose, young woman, Vivian thought, *but you shall never get your hooks into Donnington. Our name shall not be further polluted. He shall marry a good, innocent English girl, fortune or not.*

And everything would be just as it had been before.

SINJIN MET MARIAH again the next night after sunset.

She had been compelled to spend most of the day with the dowager, who still seemed intent on finding as many things for Mariah to do as was humanly possible. Most of it was make-work, some of which Mariah suspected could easily have been left to a servant, but there was no way she could avoid it.

And no amount of work could clear her mind of her last

conversation with Ash. He had heard everything she'd said to Sinjin, everything she'd wanted to keep hidden from him until he was ready. Until she was ready.

Now there was no telling what might happen. She'd still attempted to free him from his cage, but the effort had failed. She had been unable to wield enough strength to crack the lock with the crowbar borrowed from the groundskeeper's shed and had naturally not been able to call on Sinjin for help.

But now he was here, pacing outside the folly with his gun still tucked into his trousers.

"Mariah," he said with obvious relief. "I thought you wouldn't be able to come."

"Vivian kept me occupied." She joined him, compelling him to stop his pacing. "Ash heard us, Sinjin."

He gave her a blank look. "Heard what?"

"Everything we said about how much he looks like Donnington and the possibility that you're related."

She couldn't see his eyes in the darkness, but she could imagine their expression. "For God's sake. How did he react?"

"With questions, many of which I was compelled to answer."

"And?"

"He seems to have taken it as well as can be expected."

Sinjin grunted. "I suppose I'd better be prepared for another attack."

"I made it clear that you had nothing to do with Donnington's actions."

"Which have still not been proven."

"I know." She raised her lantern and searched his face anxiously. "What were you able to learn?"

"Quite a bit more than I expected." He returned Mariah's gaze. "We should speak here, before going inside."

"You know I intend to release Ash tonight."

"And I approve."

His response was so unexpected that Mariah was left momentarily mute. "What changed your mind?" she asked.

He took her arm and led her to a bench overlooking the lakeshore a dozen yards from the folly. "Your guesses about him weren't far off."

"You found the keeper."

"Not exactly."

"Tell me!"

"From all I've been able to find out, your wild man must be the son of my mother's long-lost sister. He's my cousin, Merry."

Mariah stared into the dark water. "I knew there had to be a connection, but to hear it…"

"Yes." He sighed. "There's a great deal I still don't know, but this much appears to be true. Over thirty years ago, my mother's elder sister married an American and emigrated to the United States after a terrible falling-out with my maternal grandfather. She was disowned and never heard from again. Even my mother never spoke of her. It was eventually assumed she had died in America, and nothing was ever heard of any offspring from her union."

"How did you learn this?"

"From one of my father's old footmen. Apparently some sort of letter arrived at Donbridge soon after my father married my mother, but he chose to discard it rather than upset her."

"And you think the old earl knew your aunt had a child?"

"I do."

"What is Ash's real name?"

"The footman wasn't privy to that information. It will still be necessary for me to contact the authorities in America, or at the very least to employ an investigator to discover Ash's history."

Struggling to catch her breath, Mariah tried to envision a situation that could have brought Ash to Donbridge under such circumstances. Donnington had spent some time in America before his courtship of her; had he learned of Ash's existence then? Had he met his lost cousin? If so, what could have passed between them? How had Ash lost his memory?

Had Donnington truly imprisoned his own cousin?

"I know what you're thinking," Sinjin said. "Why is Ash here? What on earth could have possessed my brother to do this? I still can't believe it. How could he be so depraved?"

That was the very thing that Mariah still could not accept. Donnington had been a perfect gentleman during their courtship. Nothing untoward or disturbing had ever happened when they were together—quite the contrary. Surely she could not have known so little about him….

"What of his keeper?" she asked.

"I found a cottage on the border of the estate. Whoever lived in it must have fled."

"Because he realized I had discovered Ash?"

"Perhaps. Naturally I'll make subtle inquiries in the neighborhood."

"And in the meantime, the most important thing is for Ash to recover his memory."

Sinjin frowned at his clasped hands. "We must continue to keep his presence absolutely secret. And we must be prepared for my brother's return to Donbridge…"

"Yes."

They looked at each other in grim understanding. "Where can Ash be taken?" Mariah asked.

"The cottage, perhaps," Sinjin said. "If the servants weren't sure who lived there, it seems likely that no one ever goes near the place."

"It does seem reasonable." She leaned forward on the bench, staring into the still dark water. "How much should we tell Ash about what you've discovered?"

"He already knows that there is a connection between us.

And he's still potentially dangerous. I'd advise saying nothing more for the time being."

"I agree. We shall tell him nothing until we've learned more and have decided how best to handle…"

She realized that she'd been about to speak of Ash as if he were a child. She rose. "We can discuss this further at a later time. Now we must see Ash and tell him what we intend to do."

Together they went into the folly. Ash was waiting at the bars as he always did, his eyes flickering from Mariah to Sinjin and back again.

Mariah set down the two bags she'd brought with her. "I'm sorry to have taken so long," she said to Ash. "We're here to let you out at last." She took the crowbar from against the wall and handed it to Sinjin, who was staring bemusedly at Ash. He hesitated, weighing the heavy metal in his hand, and approached the cell.

Ash's lips peeled away from his teeth. "Ware," he said.

It seemed that her efforts to absolve Sinjin of any part in Ash's imprisonment had not been entirely successful. "I need his help to break the lock," she said. "Stand away from the bars, Ash."

He did so, but with great reluctance, as if he felt that giving way to Sinjin in any manner was a defeat. Sinjin studied the lock, then lifted the crowbar and swung. Iron clanged on iron. It required several blows to finally shatter the padlock.

Mariah darted in to pull the pieces apart, flinging them as far from the cage as possible, and then began to open the door.

"Wait!" Sinjin said. He pushed ahead of her and stood blocking the cell's exit.

"Ash," he said, almost gently. "You must be careful. We must all be careful. Do you understand?"

After a hard and silent stare, Ash nodded. Sinjin backed away. Ash stepped forward like a neglected horse finally released from its stall, head lowered and body tense.

"Ash," Mariah whispered. For the first time she was close to him without the impediment of bars between them, and the feeling was extraordinary, almost frightening. He projected something she had only glimpsed when he'd been confined: a nobility, a strength of mind and purpose so evident that even Sinjin seemed affected. His body, underfed though it might be, rippled with lean muscle, all the more obvious with proximity. His shoulders were so much broader than she had realized, his pectorals and ridged abdominals as finely developed as in the most perfect Greek statue.

But his face…his face was beautiful. Not in the way a woman is beautiful, for there was nothing delicate about it. But its lines were so handsomely formed that Mariah realized he didn't look exactly like Donnington at all. Feature by feature the two men seemed identical, but it was as if Donnington were a rough copy of an original sculpture, blunted and crude.

"This isn't going to be easy," Sinjin muttered.

Ash didn't seem to hear him. "Mariah," he said. He drew closer before she had time to prepare herself, his firm fingertips reaching to touch her cheek, sweeping down to her jawline.

"I say," Sinjin said. "That isn't at all the thing, old man."

Ash's head jerked up. Black eyes met brown in a battle of wills. "It is not how a *gentleman* would behave?" Ash said.

The sentence was so clear, so complete, so different from anything he had said before, that both Mariah and Sinjin were taken aback. If it hadn't been for the musical depth of his voice, that inexplicable "something extra" Mariah couldn't define, anyone standing outside the building would have sworn the earl himself stood within the folly.

"We'll be leaving soon," Mariah said, desperate to escape, if only by a few meager feet. "I've brought more food—"

Ash shook his head and gazed at the open folly door behind Sinjin.

"He must dress first," Sinjin said. He glanced at Mariah, who couldn't have agreed with him more thoroughly. She retrieved the new shirt, waistcoat, jacket, fresh stockings and shoes she had brought, and laid them over the chair.

"If you are to pass for a gentleman," Sinjin said stiffly, "you must begin by looking the part. One scarcely goes about wearing only trousers…and unpressed trousers, at that."

Ash looked fully capable of raising a clenched fist and introducing it to Sinjin's face, but he controlled himself. "Will we leave this place if I put those on?" he asked.

"Yes," Mariah said. "So long as you promise to stay with us."

"The shirt," Ash said.

No one could have mistaken it for anything but a command. Both pleased and annoyed, Mariah fetched the shirt. With easy grace, Ash put it on, leaving the top two buttons undone, then brushed past a startled Sinjin and picked up the stockings.

Mariah had already noted that he'd discarded the previous pair, which lay in a heap in the back of his cell; Ash's expression revealed his distaste, but he sat on the chair and pulled them over his feet.

Sinjin watched without speaking as Ash put on the shoes, tested them and finally stood up.

"They do not feel good," Ash said. "Why do gentlemen wear them?"

If Sinjin could have goggled, he would have done so then. "We aren't savages, Ash," he said.

Ash cocked his head. "What are savages?"

"The very opposite of gentlemen."

"Then the savages are the ones who put me here."

"'The ones'?" Mariah said, wedging herself between the two men. "You mean Donnington and the keeper?"

Ash stared directly into her eyes. "I don't know," he said.

She couldn't prevent the shiver that ran the full length of

her spine. One thing hadn't changed, and that was her response to him. If anything, it had only grown stronger.

Sinjin's words came back to her. *I'm beginning to wonder if your desire to help isn't some sort of obsession.*

"The jacket," she said hastily, lifting it from the back of the chair. Ash gave it the same cold, forbidding glare he'd bestowed on the shoes and then held out his arms. As she helped him put it on, Mariah's fingers brushed over his biceps, his shoulders, the top of his chest where the collar gaped. She closed her eyes and swallowed.

Remember what you're doing. He's still your charge, your responsibility. Nothing more and nothing less.

She stepped back as Ash straightened the jacket. He shrugged several times, adjusted the sleeves, frowned over the snugness of the arms.

"You must button your shirt," Sinjin said. "It isn't proper to display yourself in front of a lady."

"It is not polite," Ash said, emphasizing the second syllable.

"I see you have learned something," Sinjin said. "Have you a brush, Mariah?"

Discovering that her arms still had enough strength to function, Mariah produced the brush and shaving gear she'd brought on her second visit.

"A brush," she said, presenting it to Ash. "Do you know how to use it?"

He took it from her hand, examined it, set the bristles to his silver mane and pushed his forelock away from his temples. It did no good. The hair slid back across his forehead, impossible to hold in place.

"He'll require some macassar," Sinjin said.

"That doesn't seem necessary just yet," Mariah said, dreading the thought of weighing down Ash's beautiful hair with scented oil. She took the brush from Ash and examined his jaw. "No beard at all," she said.

"Peculiar," Sinjin said. He stroked his own modest moustache. "I doubt he'd submit to a shave, in any case."

Ash cast him a dismissive glance. "I have no need to remove hair from my face."

"Then I shall take the shaving kit back to the house," Mariah said. "Now you should eat."

Every movement elegance itself, Ash accepted the fruit and bread Mariah gave him.

"That's all he takes?" Sinjin asked. He addressed Ash. "You must have better than that if you're to put on weight, cousin. You—"

He broke off as he realized what he'd just said. Strangely, given his usual alertness, Ash didn't seem to notice the slip.

He doesn't know what a cousin *is,* Mariah thought. So many words he didn't understand. It was an enigma that he could speak so well and yet remain so ignorant.

If he grew up in America, why does he speak with an English accent? Did he learn it from his mother? Is she still alive?

Questions that hardly mattered in the face of so many others that were far more urgent. She waited while Ash finished his meal and handed him a napkin. She showed him what to do by dabbing at her own mouth with a second napkin, and he followed her example.

"Well," Sinjin said, "a very promising start." He nodded to Ash. "It would be best if you remained here for another day," he said, "so that we can prepare your new place for you."

Ash, who was perhaps only an inch taller than Sinjin, loomed over him. "I will go now," he said.

"For God's sake, man. This is Donnington's estate, and if he had something do with…with—" he couldn't bring himself to say it. "Until we know exactly who you are, we can't risk your parading about the grounds."

"He's right, Ash," Mariah said. "We have found a safe place where you can stay until these issues are resolved, and we can have it made ready tomorrow. I promise that you will have everything you need."

Ash stared into her eyes. "I will not have freedom."

CHAPTER SEVEN

FREEDOM.

Mariah looked away. Of course. Freedom was the one thing Ash wanted above all else. The freedom to know who he was. The freedom to go where he chose, when he chose.

And it was the one thing she could not give him.

"It will come," she said, and touched his arm.

It was a grave error. Even through his sleeve, she felt his heat, his vitality, that ineffable quality of power and assurance that made him seem so much more than merely human. And he responded to her touch, his gaze striking hers with all the force of a freight train hitting a flimsy wooden railing.

"Mariah?"

She started at Sinjin's voice and withdrew her hand. "I think we should take Ash away from here tonight," she said firmly.

Sinjin looked askance at Ash, deep lines etched between his brows. "I still think—"

"The longer he's in the folly, the greater the chance that someone will stumble across him."

"But if whoever put him here finds him gone…"

"We shall find the means to deal with that situation when it arises." She turned toward Ash without quite meeting his eyes. "Are you ready, Ash?"

Once again she felt herself being scrutinized, weighed, judged, as if by a monarch rather than a man who had so recently been a half-naked prisoner.

"Yes," he said.

"And you will stay where we take you, even when I must leave you?"

His mouth tightened, but he offered no objection. With Sinjin's help, Mariah gathered up all the bags, scraps of food and other necessities they'd brought to the folly, and carried them outside. She waited by the door for Ash to follow.

Step by hesitant step he walked through the inner door into the anteroom. His nostrils flared as if he had caught the scent of the flowers growing near the folly steps, heavy with perfume in the still night air. His face was lost in a kind of wonder, a gratitude that twisted her heart. So a convict must look when he was finally released from long incarceration, or a madman who had regained his sanity after years of black, hopeless suffering.

Against her better judgment, she reached again for Ash's hand. His palm was warm and dry. He closed his fingers over hers, and she felt in that instant that she, not the world beyond the folly walls, was his only desire.

"We shouldn't waste any time," Sinjin said. "I'll fetch Shaitan."

Deaf to Sinjin's words, Ash descended the folly steps, paused, and looked across the mere to the stand of ash and willow beyond. He seemed about to sprout wings and fly across the water, swooping, rising higher and higher until his shape blotted the stars from view.

Searching, Mariah thought. *He's searching for something he doesn't see.*

"Are you all right?" she asked.

He smiled. The expression was dazzling, entrancing, and she realized she had never seen him smile before. It was a gift Mariah thought she could never tire of, no matter how many times he might offer it to her.

"Merry."

Her nickname had never caused her such consternation as it did then, purred by the man standing so quietly beside her. The word had an intimate feel, rolling off his tongue with a slight trill that suggested some exotic clime.

"Why does Ware call you that?" he asked, his black eyes obsidian gems that stole all the moon's light for themselves alone.

"It's a…it's called a nickname," she stammered. "A shorter version of one's own name, used as a term of…a term of endearment."

"Endearment."

"It's a feeling. Like friendship. Like love."

"Love?"

She realized that she'd made a very foolish mistake. "I see Sinjin returning. We should—"

"Love is what the girl felt for the bear-man."

She was touched, despite herself, by his reference to the fairy tale she'd read to him that second night, the story of the girl and the bear who had become a prince.

In spite of her slip, she had been given the opportunity to end any misunderstandings before they could begin. "There are many kinds of love, Ash. Friendship is one. Another is that between a mother or father and a child, or brothers and sisters."

"Ware loves you."

"He is…like a brother, Ash. He feels affection for me."

That cock of the head, a sliding of silver hair over his dark brows. "Am I to be your brother?"

Her skin felt too tightly stretched across her face. "If that is what you wish."

She prayed that he was finished with his questions, but he was not done with her yet. "What does it mean?" he asked.

"What…does what mean?"

"Merry."

She seized the lifeline. "To be merry means to be happy. To enjoy life."

"Are you happy?"

"Of course I'm…" She met his gaze with every effort. "It isn't a question one generally asks another unless they are very close."

"But we *are* close."

Close indeed. Close enough that he could have pulled her into his arms without reaching out more than a few inches.

She nearly stumbled as she tried to put a safer degree of space between them. Ash lifted his hand but spared her his touch.

"You don't laugh," he said.

"Should I be laughing?" she asked stupidly.

"Does not one laugh when one is happy?"

Once she had laughed. She and Mama, so freely, so easily. They'd laughed—laughed too much, some said—and played together as if nothing could ever harm them.

Then the voices started, and Mama began to go away.

"Merry!"

Sinjin spoke, and the spell was broken as he led his horse to a halt beside them.

"You ride, Mariah," Sinjin said. "Ash and I can—"

Shaitan lifted his great black head and snorted, his ears pricked toward Ash. Like one walking in a dream, Ash approached the stallion with his hand outstretched.

"Take care," Sinjin said. "He's been known to bite strangers."

But Ash didn't stop. He cupped Shaitan's muzzle in his palm and leaned close, nearly brushing the stallion's face with his own.

"He only bites savages," he said.

"Oh?" Sinjin said. "Did he tell you so?"

"Why do you make him wear this?" Ash asked, fingering Shaitan's bridle.

Sinjin rolled his eyes at Mariah. "Hasn't he seen a horse before?"

Even if she'd had an answer, she wouldn't have had time to give it. Ash had begun to move in the direction of the mere, and Shaitan was following him like a loyal hound.

With a snort of disgust, Sinjin caught him, took the reins and helped Mariah to mount. Once she had set an easy pace, Ash walked ahead, his long gait carrying him with a kind of rhythmic fluidity superior to even Sinjin's natural grace. After briefly matching Ash's stride, Sinjin fell back to walk beside Shaitan.

"He seems to know what he wants well enough," he remarked to Mariah. "Are you sure you'll be able to control him?"

Thank God he hadn't noticed anything amiss with her during her conversation with Ash. "I have no wish to control him," she said.

"Someone must."

"If you try, Sinjin, he will rebel."

"Because he sees me as a rival."

"Don't be ridiculous. He has had a great deal to absorb in the past three days."

"So have you."

"If you still harbor the mistaken notion that I regard Ash as anything but a mistreated human being in need of assistance—"

"We shall see how much assistance he accepts."

The ominous tone of his voice warned Mariah that Sinjin was by no means satisfied. They both knew what might happen if Ash failed to cooperate. The shock to anyone who saw him would be considerable, and the consequences could break open a hornets' nest of trouble.

Mariah gave Shaitan a little tap with her heels and hurried to catch up with Ash. Following Sinjin's directions, she steered him around the mere, through the wood and over several low hills.

In spite of her extensive exploration of the grounds during her periods of enforced isolation, Mariah couldn't remember venturing into this more distant area, where a sizable wood of birch, willow, poplar and elm clumped around a meandering stream in a dense canopy. A few hundred yards on, beneath a pair of ash trees, stood the cottage.

The hovel—for hovel it was—might at one time have belonged to a groundskeeper charged with looking after the southern boundary of Donbridge, but there were obvious indications that it had been abandoned long before Ash's keeper had taken up residence. The badly overgrown pathway through the uncut grass suggested that no one had attempted to keep up the environs. The walls sagged, and the thatched roof threatened to collapse in on itself. Rusted scythes, rakes and shovels lay scattered about the yard, acting as forbidding barriers to a closer approach.

Yet there were signs of recent occupation. Sinjin, moving ahead, swung the door open, and Mariah caught a glimpse of furniture inside.

Ash went no farther. "*He* was here," he said.

No need to ask who "he" was. "He's not here now," she said. "And no one will find you in this place."

She dismounted, took his arm and led him closer to the cottage. It was like pulling a load of bricks. When at last she reached the door, she was breathing heavily and perspiring beneath her bodice.

"No one has been here since I left this morning," Sinjin said, poking his head out the door. "I should warn you that it is only slightly more pleasant than Ash's cell."

He wasn't exaggerating. The place stank of stale sweat, old cooking and unwashed cutlery. The single bed was unmade, the sheets stained, and what furniture graced the hovel was crooked or broken.

Well might Ash's keeper have fled; there was little

evidence that he'd been paid enough even for his own needs. Ash might have been left to starve to death, had she not found him. If she could have put her hands on the blackguard now…

"There isn't much to see," Sinjin said, prodding at the pile of ashes in the filthy fireplace. "Nothing of any use to us."

She nodded and looked back toward the door, where Ash hovered on the threshold.

"Come in, Ash," Mariah said, holding out her hand.

He didn't take it, but he entered the cottage. Something almost ugly crossed his face, a ferocity that suggested he would like nothing better than to smash everything in the room. No gentleman there, only the wild man. The savage.

"It's all right," Mariah murmured. "We won't let it stay this way. If need be, I'll carry new furniture here myself."

"That won't be necessary," Sinjin said, straightening from the hearth. "If you really trust her, ask your maid to clean the place. I'll see to the rest."

A great burden lifted from Mariah's shoulders. "Thank you, Sinjin. I shall owe you a great deal after this."

Ash moved so silently that Mariah was completely unprepared when he stepped between them. "I will not stay here," he said.

"Enough of this nonsense," Sinjin said, glaring at Ash. "Mariah is willing to risk a great deal for your sake. The least *you* can do is be grateful."

Bad blood boiled between the two men, but there was no room for Mariah to separate them. "Nothing will be gained by this," she snapped. "Ash, you agreed to do as I asked. Are you prepared to break that promise?"

Ash lowered his head and stared at her from beneath his level brows. "I will not break it."

It was a victory, though Mariah doubted that Sinjin would regard it as such. Neither of them had any choice but to take Ash at his word.

And what if he should simply disappear?

"Perhaps *I* should stay," she said slowly.

"I shan't permit it," Sinjin said. "It isn't proper."

"Just because he's no longer in a cage?"

"Do you desire to play into my mother's hands, Mariah? Your reputation is at stake. Do you want to provide fodder for her suspicions?"

"Reputation?" Ash repeated.

The prospect of explaining *that* delicate subject was daunting at best. "It's nearing dawn," Mariah said. "We've no more time. Sinjin, will you wait outside for a moment?"

He went, though not graciously. She circled the cottage, found a few relatively clean rags and stripped the soiled sheets from the bed.

"This will have to do for now," she said to herself, spreading the rags over the mattress. She cleared the small, crooked table and spread out what was left of the meal she'd brought.

"Try not to worry," she told Ash. "You won't be alone for long."

"I am not worried. If the man comes back, I will not let him leave again."

Something in his tone told Mariah that he meant more than simply detaining his keeper. She had no doubt in her mind that he was capable of taking revenge on anyone who had harmed him.

"You mustn't hurt him," she said. "There are other ways of dealing with those who commit such crimes."

His black eyes snapped. "I will not hurt him," he said, "if you stay."

Blackmail. How could he have become so adept at it so quickly?

"I cannot," she said, recognizing that Sinjin had been right. It wasn't merely her reputation, or even Vivian's ill will, that made her quail at the thought of sharing the cottage with

Ash. It was the weakness of her own body and emotions, the weakness that made her knees tremble in his presence and her memories unaccountably turn to her empty marriage bed.

"You have trusted me thus far," she said unsteadily. "Trust me now."

He took her hand, his fingers finding their way between hers. "Why can you not trust me?"

"I... Ash..."

"Go," he said roughly, releasing her hand. He began to turn away and stopped. "Bring books."

"Books?"

"Like the girl and the bear-man."

Of course. And why not? Mariah could think of no better way to stimulate his memory than by providing him with as many books as possible, as long as she could find the time to read to him.

"I shall bring as many as I'm able," she said. "Is there anything else you need?"

He considered, head cocked. "Yourself," he said.

The weakness returned, settling in her stomach and making her feel light-headed. She became aware of the diffuse light of dawn creeping through the cracked windowpanes.

"I will see you very soon," she said, edging toward the door. Ash didn't try to stop her. Sinjin gave her a searching look when she joined him, but he seemed to know she was in no mood for conversation.

She hurried back the house while Sinjin rode for Rothwell. She headed straight for the servants' entrance, shook out the hem of her skirts as best as she was able and carefully opened the door.

Dawn was breaking and the servants' area was already a hive of activity as Cook and her minions worked toward the completion of breakfast, Mrs. Baines and various maids discussed the day's chores around the house, and Fellows, the dowager's personal maid, arranged the drawing of a hot bath for her mistress.

That meant that Vivian was still in her rooms, Mariah realized as she swept past the curious faces she encountered in the corridor and continued to the servants' staircase. She bolted up the stairs and made her way to her own room, where she removed her boots and set them aside for cleaning.

Summoning Alice, who already resented her mistress's propensity for dispensing with her services, did not seem a very good idea. But since Mariah had deliberately chosen the simplest gowns she could find for her morning walks, she was able to negotiate the hooks by herself. When she had relieved herself of her heavier garments and put on her dressing gown, she sat on the bed and began to consider her next move.

She'd no sooner counted off the first step than someone tapped on the door. She knew it was Nola before the girl entered the room.

"Nola," she said, deeply self-conscious at the thought of her clandestine activities. "How are you this morning? Isn't it a lovely day?"

She knew she was babbling, but there was no help for it, and Nola seemed not to notice.

She curtseyed and said, "It is that, Lady Donnington. Is there anything I might get for you?"

Evidently the girl had been keeping close watch for Mariah's return, but her eagerness made it all that much easier for Mariah to enlist her in the work ahead.

"Do you still want to help me, Nola?" she asked.

"Oh, yes, ma'am."

"Come sit." Mariah indicated a chair and waited until the girl was perched on its edge and waiting alertly. "I have something important to tell you," she said, "and it must continue to remain a secret." She took a deep breath. "You guessed correctly when you met me leaving the house. I have seen the man who looks like Donnington."

"Cor," Nola whispered. "It's really true, then?"

"It is. And he is—has been—a prisoner, just as the rumors said." She leaned forward. "Have you heard anything else, anything at all, that you haven't told me?"

"Nothing, your ladyship. Hardly anyone speaks of it, and then only at night, when the wind blows and the trees scrape the attic windows."

Ghost stories. Tales to frighten impressionable young maids still in their between years, told while huddled under the covers in their cramped attic chambers.

"Very well," Mariah said. "We'll leave that for now. In the meantime, I must ask you to do something you might not find pleasant."

"Ma'am?"

"I shall need you to clean a cottage and make it habitable."

"A cottage?" Nola nearly jumped out of the chair. "The cottage where the mysterious man lives?"

"Yes." Mariah hesitated. "The man isn't there anymore, Nola. The prisoner is."

"Cor blimey!" The girl flushed. "I'm sorry, your ladyship."

Mariah waved her hand dismissively. "I've heard far worse, Nola. But I wouldn't advise speaking that way in front of the dowager."

"No, ma'am." Nola hunched down in a conspirator's posture. "Why would anyone want to lock up someone who looks like his lordship?"

"That's what we—Mr. Ware and I—intend to find out. But first we must help Ash as best we can."

"Is that his name?"

"He doesn't remember his real name, Nola. I gave that name to him."

"He has lost his memory?"

"Yes, though I believe it is only a temporary affliction."

"Do you want me to go to the cottage now, your ladyship?"

"Not now. Early tomorrow morning, before anyone is up." Mariah rose and went to the bookshelves. "We shall bring him more clothing and as many books as we can carry. The more he learns, the sooner he will recover."

"Yes, ma'am."

"You will have little chance for sleep if you do this for us, Nola."

"Oh, that doesn't matter, your ladyship!"

"Then I'll come for you early tomorrow morning, at three."

Excitement buzzed in every line of Nola's body as she left to resume her regular household duties. Mariah was scarcely less agitated. She must somehow make her way through another trying day, confined to this house, while Sinjin, who had so much more freedom than she did, set out to learn more of Ash's origins.

Perhaps he'll turn up something important tonight, Mariah thought. *Perhaps we will have all the answers.*

But that would be a miracle. Mariah didn't doubt for a moment that the next few days would consist of hard work with no miracles involved.

She went to the bookshelf and debated over what was best to take to Ash. Her collection seemed pathetic seen in the light of necessity. Yet Ash had responded well to the fairy tale she'd read. There couldn't be much harm in starting simply, with more children's stories.

At random, she picked out a book and read the title. *Mythical Beasts.* Her fingers seemed to move of their own accord, seeking the section under the letter *U.*

Unicorn. A creature of contradictions: capable of ferocity and yet also compassion, beautiful beyond measure, capable of using its magical horn to counteract poison and even, according to some legends, to heal.

Mariah closed her eyes, wondering why she thought of Ash when she studied the illustration that accompanied the text. Except for the horn, the words might have described *him*.

She closed the book with a snap and set it back on the shelf, turning to the novels—books she'd read in New York when she'd needed a brief respite from her time caring for Mama.

The Man in the Iron Mask. The Count of Monte Cristo. Ivanhoe. All romantic visions of the past, seemingly irrelevant to these modern times, each presenting an admittedly legendary example of how society functioned. And yet, at the very least, they would expand Ash's vocabulary and might serve to awaken new memories.

Both the man in the iron mask and the Count of Monte Cristo were prisoners who escaped their fates, she thought. Would that fact allow Ash to take some hope in his situation or only anger him further?

With an uncertain frown, Mariah stacked the novels on her bed table. Taking books from Donnington's library was out of the question, but he might keep a few volumes on geography, history and science in his room; she would see what she could find before dinnertime. By the time she was through with Ash, he would be well beyond the fictional world of novels and fairy tales.

Trying not to let her doubts overwhelm her, she dressed again and went down to breakfast.

CHAPTER EIGHT

PAMELA, LADY WESTLAKE, set her reticule on a side table and smiled at Mr. St. John Ware.

"How delightful to see you again, Mr. Ware," she said.

He smiled in return, though there was a certain lack of authenticity in the expression. Indeed, one might almost have believed that Ware had no desire to see her.

She, however, had a very strong desire to see him, though he must not under any circumstances guess just how strong.

"Please be seated, Lady Westlake," Ware said, indicating the most comfortable chair in his drawing room. The place was decidedly masculine; Ware was, after all, a confirmed bachelor whose numerous "lady friends" had no influence whatsoever on his life at Rothwell. Pamela had been certain to bring along a maid; though an established matron, she could not be too careful in the presence of one of England's most inveterate rakes.

"To what do I owe the pleasure of your visit, Lady Westlake?" Ware said, having rung for tea and taken his own seat opposite hers.

"I wished to inquire about your brother, Mr. Ware," she said, arranging her skirts in such a way that the ankles of her dainty boots were visible. "Have you heard from him?"

He sprawled a little in his chair—not at all proper in the presence of a lady, but indicative of his generally insolent manner. "I haven't, Lady Westlake," he drawled. "May I ask why the interest?"

His bluntness was no surprise to her, and she had come prepared. "I have been deeply concerned about your sister-in-law, Lady Donnington," she purred. "For such a young bride to be left alone is hardly conducive to marital happiness."

"A subject with which you are well acquainted."

They stared at each other. Ware knew very well that her marriage was scarcely a marriage at all, given that her husband was an invalid twice her age, uninterested in his wife and devoted to his grotesque collection of mounted insects.

"Yes," she said after a moment's pause. "Let us speak frankly, you and I. We know better than anyone what the poor child is missing…you with your—" a pause "—experience, I with my own. Donnington owes her more than he has given her. If anyone will have heard from him…"

"It would be the dowager Lady Donnington," Ware said, "not I."

"But surely, as brothers so close in age, you have always confided in one another," she said sweetly.

It was an entirely foolish thing to say, but Pamela hadn't meant it as a real question. Everyone knew that Donnington and his brother had been at odds since childhood and had very little to say to each other.

Ware seemed not in the least discomposed. "My brother confides in very few," he said. "Have you inquired of my mother?"

"Naturally. She has heard nothing."

Someone tapped on the door, and Ware's butler, an extremely thin man with a doleful face, entered with the tea. He bowed to Pamela, set the tray near her and retreated.

"Will you pour, Lady Westlake?" Ware asked.

"Of course." She did so with the elegance for which she had received so many compliments. Ware rose to accept his cup but set it down without drinking.

"Your concern for Lady Donnington does you great credit," he said, "but she appears to be coping with the situation very well. I think you need not trouble yourself on her account any further."

"Because she has your friendship?"

"Always."

"It is fortunate when a new bride can find such support among her relations."

"Indeed."

"I trust Donnington will not have cause to regret his absence."

The temperature in the room dropped several degrees. Ware stood abruptly.

"If you will forgive me, madam," he said, "I have an appointment with my man of business and am already running late."

His brusqueness should have been unthinkably rude, but Pamela welcomed it. She set down her cup, also barely touched, and rose, as well.

"Then I thank you for taking the time to see me," she said, offering her hand. "I am certain everything will all turn out well in the end."

He barely touched the tips of her fingers. "I am certain it will," he said, and herded, more than escorted, her to the door. "Hedley, will you kindly see Lady Westlake to her carriage?" Without waiting until she reached her conveyance, he retreated into the drawing room.

So, Pamela thought with no little sense of triumph, *Mariah has got a lover, but not one anyone of decency would ever suspect.*

Her own vague suspicions had been based on no more than the obvious affection between Mariah and her brother-in-law, but the outrageous notion had become a little more plausible when she'd followed Mariah on one of her oddly timed excursions across Donbridge's park and witnessed the two speaking intimately together by the mere.

The subject of their discussion had not been audible to her, but she had seen quite enough. Proof or not, she recognized an excellent opportunity to work mischief against the little American bitch.

She smiled as she accepted a footman's hand into the carriage. Dear Vivian would be beyond shocked. But she would have what she wanted: grounds for an annulment of the marriage once Mariah was caught and Donnington returned to testify that the union had never been consummated.

You have played with fire, my dear Sinjin, she thought, *but it is not only you who will suffer. And when it is all over, Donnington will finally turn to me.*

NOLA STOOD IN THE doorway of the cottage, bucket and mop in hand, and stared.

Well she might, Mariah thought. Though the candles were burning, there was no evidence that Ash had used the cot or eaten more than a mouthful of the food she'd left him.

Mariah set down her heavy bag of books near the doorway and strode into the tiny back room of the cottage. He wasn't there.

He's left. That was the only thought in her mind as she took up the lantern again and ran back outside. The dim light of false dawn was beginning to glaze the eastern horizon, and she knew she had little time to find him.

She paused at the end of the overgrown footpath to stare at the ground. His feet had been bare; that was obvious enough from the faint tracks he had left in the soft soil. She lost his trail when she reached the wood. Not so much as a broken twig marked his passage.

You should never have trusted him.

She walked deeper into the undergrowth with the lantern aloft, stumbling over shadows, batting aside branches and knocking away the brambles that clung to her clothing. She made numerous detours around areas too thickly clustered with vegetation for her full skirts to negotiate, and she began to wish for the trousers she had been permitted to wear during her parents' long-ago holidays to their former home in the West.

Only that experience kept her from falling into one of a hundred damp, hidden depressions or tripping over mossy fallen branches. She knew the wood couldn't be large compared to those in the United States, but her fears and the drag of her skirts made it seem interminable.

Without warning, she broke free of the trees and stepped out into a wet meadow thick with wildflowers. She lifted the lantern and focused on a flash of movement.

A naked man was running across the meadow, leaping over pools of open water and plunging amidst the reeds in graceful bounds, moving as no man should be able to move. There was no sense of the ridiculous about him, only sublime grace, the slide of sleek muscle, the very image of flight above the common ground.

Just like a unicorn. The mythical creature filled her eyes, pale coated, cloven hooves brushing the grass and sedge without ever touching the earth.

Mariah gasped as Ash landed so lightly that he made barely a splash in the green water. He turned, eyes reflecting the growing light like black glass.

Instinctively she began to back away. Ash started toward her. He paused only a few feet away, unclothed and very, very male. He seemed much more naked here than he had in his cell—here, where someone might see and assume…

"Ash," she managed to choke out. "You must go back to the cottage."

He tossed his head, sweeping the forelock of silver hair out of his eyes. She could smell the spicy, indescribable scent of him, so unlike Donnington in every way.

"I couldn't stay there," he said. "I had to get out."

His nearness was beginning to reawaken certain disturbing responses in her body. "Where have you been?"

"Here." He gestured at the trees around them.

Relief almost washed away the feelings she didn't dare examine too closely. "We must go back, Ash. You must dress at once."

"I prefer this."

She refused to consider the possibility that he might indeed be mad, no matter how much his eccentric behavior seemed to suggest it.

Who suffers most from delusion? she asked herself. *Ash, so unselfconscious and natural, or you, with your fantastic visions of mythical creatures?*

"You cannot go without clothing," she said. "Not even here."

His expression might best have been described as a scowl, but it was aimed not at her but in the general direction of the cottage. Gradually his features relaxed, and he gazed at her with that dark, direct stare.

"You are afraid," he said.

She laughed. "Of what?"

"Of me."

"Of course not. Why would you think such a thing?"

"If you are not afraid of me, what is it you fear?"

"I am *not* afraid," she said, "and you have no right to suggest…"

Her words trailed off as he closed the slight space between and took her face between his hands. She was surprised at how callused his palms felt. They were not the hands of an aristocrat; it was as if he'd worked all his life.

But she lost the thread of her thoughts as he moved closer still, his face inches from hers. His breath caressed her lips. She held herself as motionless as a rabbit between the paws of a fox, hoping against hope that he would stop. Praying that he wouldn't.

Her senses sprang to life as Ash gathered her close. The shadow of unacknowledged desire she had fought from their first meeting became a solid thing that cried out for acknowledgment and sang of frustrated hopes.

Mariah closed her eyes. She could hardly feel Ash through the armor of her heavy skirts and corset, but she knew he was as moved as she. Whatever he had been before, there were some instincts he had definitely not forgotten.

Instincts such as those that claimed her now. Sinjin had seen through her. *This isn't just natural concern on your part,* he'd said. *The way you look at him, speak to him...*

Almost as if *he* were her husband. But he wasn't. He never would be.

She set her palms against Ash's chest and pushed until he released her. She nearly tripped over her skirts as she fell backward. Her breath came harsh and fast as she broke out of the wood.

And there she stopped, her hands flexing into fists. The last thing she should do was run from Ash. He had to respect her or she would be useless as a teacher. And in order to respect her, he must know that she wouldn't tolerate further advances from him.

Even if she longed for them...

"Your ladyship?"

Nola stood just outside the cottage, staring at Mariah in puzzlement, and Mariah realized how she must look with her hair half undone and her clothing covered with twigs, last autumn's leaves and God knew what else.

"I've been walking in the woods," she said, far more calmly than she felt.

"Did you find Mr. Ash?" the girl asked.

"Yes," Mariah said. "He'll be along presently, if you'll just—"

"Cor blimey!"

Mariah didn't have to turn to know what had prompted Nola's outburst. "Look away, Nola," she said. "Mr. Ash has been swimming and forgot to take his bathing costume."

But Nola was less than cooperative. She stared and stared with nary a blush, her eyes wide and her mouth slightly ajar.

Mariah marched to the door, took Nola by the shoulders and turned her about. "Sit," she commanded, barely noticing how much the maid had already accomplished with the cottage. She found Ash's abandoned clothing lying on his cot, and gathered up the badly creased shirt and trousers.

She was halfway to the door when she heard a very unwelcome voice.

"Why, Mr. Ware. I am just on the way to visit the dowager. How very…unexpected to encounter you here."

Pamela Westlake. Mariah froze, the air congealing in her lungs.

"Lady Westlake," Sinjin said in a polite, measured tone. "How well you look at such an early hour of the morning."

Thank God Sinjin had arrived. To judge by the casual exchange, Ash must have hidden himself just in time. But what was Pamela doing at Donbridge before six in the morning?

"Thank you, Mr. Ware. You look very well also," Lady Westlake said. "Have you been out riding?"

"As you see." The sound of footsteps and the clop of hooves on packed earth reached Mariah's ears. "Shaitan was badly in need of a good run."

"Ah, yes. He seems most interested in my Queenie."

Mariah gripped the edge of the lopsided table.

"Your ladyship?" Nola said behind her.

"Hush," Mariah whispered. "Stay where you are."

"Mother is an early riser," Sinjin was saying, "but she doesn't generally receive visitors at sunrise."

"But she invited me for breakfast, and she does admire

those who appreciate her schedule." A rustle of riding skirts as Lady Westlake dismounted, undoubtedly with Sinjin's gallant assistance. "I thought I might take a turn about your lovely park for an hour before going to the house, just to make sure I arrive in time, you know. Perhaps you would care to join me?"

"If you dare to bank on Shaitan's good behavior."

"Oh, I've no doubt you can control him." The muted tread of her riding boots moved closer to the cottage. "What an interesting little cottage, Mr. Ware. Do you come here often?"

"I pass this way sometimes. It is a pleasant ride."

"Who lives here? One of Donnington's groundsmen?"

"It is currently unoccupied."

"Yet I could have sworn I heard voices earlier."

"One of the Donbridge maids is inside cleaning for a possible new tenant."

"Indeed?" The footsteps drew closer still. Mariah backed away from the door and signaled to Nola.

"Quickly!" Mariah said. "Go out to meet her and help Mr. Ware get her away from the cottage."

Without a moment's hesitation, Nola jumped up and rushed for the door. She barely made it outside in time. Mariah heard an "oomph" of surprise from Lady Westlake.

"Oh! I beg your pardon, madam," Nola said. "I thought I heard voices, so I—"

"Never mind," Pamela said sharply.

"I've a bit of cider inside, your ladyship, if you'd care to—"

"No, thank you." Lady Westlake was clearly annoyed. Her riding crop swished against her skirt. "Go back to your work."

"Yes, ma'am." Nola reappeared in the doorway, a little breathless. "I think she's leaving, Lady Donnington," she said.

"You did very well, Nola," Mariah said. Still, she listened intently, waiting to see if Pamela's curiosity had been satisfied. There was no more movement near the cottage.

"Shall we go on to the house, Lady Westlake?" Sinjin asked. "I am sure my mother will not object to your arriving a little earlier than expected."

"A change of heart, Mr. Ware?"

"A desire for breakfast, Lady Westlake."

"Then let us make haste, by all means." Hooves shuffled as she mounted again. "And perhaps you *should* keep that brute away from my Queenie."

"Are you all right, your ladyship?" Nola asked.

"Yes," Mariah replied, though in fact her heart was racing. A moment later she went to the open door. Sinjin and Lady Westlake were gone.

If Sinjin hadn't arrived just in time…

What if she'd seen Sinjin and me together at such an hour?

Mariah's thoughts whirled. Pamela had already made it clear that she believed Mariah capable of taking a lover in Donnington's absence. Was it only coincidence that Lady Westlake had been riding near the cottage? Or had she heard rumors that led her to believe that Mariah was meeting someone here?

Did she think that someone was Sinjin?

The idea was despicable. In England it was considered a crime if a man had an affair with his brother's wife. It was actual incest, unthinkable. Unthinkable to anyone but Lady Westlake.

Or was Mariah simply letting her imagination run wild?

Still, whatever fancies her imagination might harbor, Mariah knew that Lady Westlake clearly suspected something. And whatever that something was, it could only be a danger to Ash.

"Nola," she said, "I'm going out to find Mr. Ash."

"Yes, your ladyship. I'll finish up here."

With a nod, Mariah set off. Ash was just inside the wood and came out readily when she called.

"Who was that female?" he asked.

"Her name is Lady Westlake, and you must on no account allow her to see you."

"She is your enemy."

Once again Ash managed to startle her with his insight. "She is a neighbor, Ash. A neighbor with too great an interest in matters that do not concern her."

"You do not *like* her."

"No, I do not."

"She means you harm."

A truthful answer would certainly be of no help now. "She doesn't like me, either."

"Then she is my enemy, too."

Oh, Ash. "All I ask is that you stay out of her way."

He absorbed this with a long look in the direction Pamela and Sinjin had taken.

"She *likes* Ware," he said.

"I beg your pardon?"

"She wants to mate with him."

Fiery heat surged under Mariah's skin from her face to her bosom. "How…how did you get such an idea?" she stammered.

ASH KNEW BY THE LOOK on Mariah's face that she was upset at what he had said, just as she had been upset by what he had done at the edge of the meadow.

He had not been upset. He had embraced her because he knew it was what humans did to express affection and bind themselves to one other. As he must bind her to himself.

Yet such cold reasoning had led to something dangerous. All unknowing, unaware of her own power, she had begun to cast a spell that he found more and more difficult to resist. He had wanted to feel the shape of her, the heat of her body, the softness of her mouth as she looked up into his eyes. In all his years as a unicorn, he had never experienced such emotions before.

But he knew about mating. He was quickly learning the needs of this human body. He understood what Cairbre had meant when he warned Arion not to touch Mariah.

"She must be pure when she comes to me." So that Cairbre could be certain of the parentage of the Fane children he intended to sire on the woman whose human blood, mingled with that of the failing Fane race, could make his people strong again.

But Mariah *wanted* Ash to touch her, in spite of her protests. He had smelled it, sensed it, felt it. He imagined mating with her, and his loins grew heavy all over again.

What had seemed so simple when he had been locked in his cage had become far more difficult than he could have dreamed.

"You must dress," Mariah said, no longer waiting for his answer to her question. Her face was very red as she pointed toward the cottage.

He went ahead of her, feeling her stare on his back as if she were stroking his body with her fingertips. Hunger nearly blinded him. He snorted and kicked angrily at the earth with his heel. She walked past him, her expression so tight that Ash almost regretted what he had done to bring her pain.

But it was necessary. She must be won, kept near him, tied only to him until he could deliver her to Cairbre.

He entered the cottage without speaking to her again. The younger female he had glimpsed from the wood stared at him, her eyes very round. She clutched tightly at the wooden staff in her hand.

"Cor blimey," she whispered.

"Nola," Mariah said, "if you would please turn your back…"

While the girl called Nola did as she'd been told, Mariah thrust a bundle of clothes at Ash. Then she faced the wall while he put the garments on, even the stockings and shoes he so despised.

"Are you finished?" Mariah asked.

"Yes."

"Oh," Nola said in a soft voice. "He's that handsome."

Mariah half turned to face the girl. "Yes," she said very quickly. "Ash, this is Nola."

Puzzled, Ash stared at the human girl. There was nothing remarkable about her—none of Mariah's beauty nor stature, little that might demand his attention.

Yet she did. There was something about her he couldn't name. A sparkle in her eyes as she gazed at him, a wisdom that belied her common appearance.

It was as if she knew what he truly was.

Nola bobbed so that her skirts, so much simpler and darker than Merry's, billowed out around her feet. "Good morning, sir," she said.

Ash glanced at Mariah. "Is she your friend?"

"Nola is a servant at Donbridge," Mariah said.

"Servant?"

"Workers who…do things for the people who employ them."

"Then you are *my* servant."

She made a strange noise, as if something had stuck in her throat. "I am helping you without expectation of payment. Nola is…compensated for her work."

"Compensated." The word was not one he had heard before. "What does that mean?"

"She receives money for what she does."

Money was a word he *did* remember. "The round metal things," he said. "Coins."

"It's true, Mr. Ash," Nola said. "I work for Lady Donnington."

"I have no money to give you."

"Oh, sir, you needn't worry about that."

"Indeed not," Mariah said. She appeared eager to speak of something else and darted for the bag that lay near the door. "I've brought books for you, Ash. Many books which might help you to remember." She placed the bag on a chair and stacked the books on the small round table. "These are primarily fiction," she said, "like the story I read you before. We will begin by seeing if you remember anything about how to read and then test your ability to write."

Ash was far from certain what *write* meant. He had not even understood the word *read* until Mariah had demonstrated in his cell.

If she agreed to read to him again, she would be compelled to remain close to him. And he to her.

"Will you teach me if I cannot remember?" he asked.

"Of course. But I am confident you will. I believe in you."

He felt the warmth of her regard. She believed in him. In the one who must deceive her.

"Then I will try," he said.

She smiled, entirely unaware of his treacherous thoughts. "Nola," she said, "you ought to go back to the house. You may continue cleaning early tomorrow morning."

"Yes, your ladyship." The girl began to gather her things, objects Ash studied carefully as she tucked them into the vessel she carried by a metal handle. "It will be no trouble at all."

Mariah nodded, her gaze focused on something Ash couldn't see. "I have been thinking, Nola. It might be best if you become my personal maid."

Nola turned red, as humans so often seemed to do. "What about Alice, your ladyship?"

"I've had certain indications that she wishes to leave my employ. I shall speak to the dowager, of course. But I alone decide whom I can hire for my own service."

"Thank you, your ladyship."

"No need. Go on back to the house. If anyone questions you, refer them to me. I'll think of something to tell them."

"Yes, ma'am." Nola bobbed again, glanced sideways at Ash and left the cottage.

Mariah moved to the door to watch the girl walk away, then returned to the stack of books on the table. "I must go back to the house presently," she said. "But I informed the dowager last night that I would be out riding this morning, and I'm sure Sinjin will keep Lady Westlake occupied. There is time for a little reading."

Ash moved up behind her. "What is *dowager?*"

She hesitated. "The dowager is Sinjin's mother."

The anger moved inside Ash again. "Donnington's mother. Vivian. You don't want her to know about me."

"She might mistake you for Donnington, Ash. But Donnington has gone away, and—"

"Why did your husband go away?"

"I'll…I'll explain at another time. It isn't important now."

But Merry was not telling the truth. It *was* important. Donnington's mother was as much a threat to her as Lady Westlake.

As Ash was himself.

"What shall we read?" Mariah asked abruptly, gesturing toward the books. "Perhaps this one." She set one book aside from the others. "Please, sit down."

He took one of the chairs beside the table, and she took the one across from it.

"A rancher in Cochise County," she began. And soon he forgot about Ware and Lady Westlake and the dowager, though his thoughts were not for the book or the words she spoke, but were focused on the soft fragrance that drifted from Mariah's hair and the lingering scent of her desire. He lost the meaning behind the sound of her voice and heard only its beauty.

He rose and stood behind her chair as she bent over the table. For many heartbeats she wasn't even aware of his presence…until he leaned closer to inhale the smells that so enticed him.

Mariah jerked and turned her head, her face only a hand's

breadth from his. Her lips parted. She breathed in his breath, and he breathed in hers.

"I think we have done enough reading for today," she said, closing the book and pulling her chair away from the table. She moved too swiftly for the skirts that bound her legs, and she would have fallen had Ash not caught her.

"I'm—I'm all right," she said, breaking free of his hold. "I must go now. You have enough food to last until we meet tomorrow." She rushed for the door and turned. "Do nothing, Ash," she said. "Stay indoors, for God's sake. And keep the door closed. It will ruin all our plans if anyone sees you."

She was gone before he could answer. Instead he followed her to the door, watched her mount her riding beast and kick it into a run.

Ruin all our plans. She knew nothing of his plan. But, for a time at least, their purpose would be the same. And he would become what she wanted him to be.

CHAPTER NINE

"It is just as I feared," Sinjin said. "I'm convinced that Pamela suspects us. And I've no doubt that she's reported her suspicions to my mother."

Mariah shivered, knowing full well what his statement meant.

"What shall we do about it?" she asked as they rode together openly in the late morning sunlight.

"We must be more careful," he said. "And I must begin to show interest in another woman."

"Lady Westlake?"

"I can't think of a better. If I'm courting her, her little theory is apt to be ruined, don't you think?"

"How do you intend to engage her…affections?"

He gave her a long, probing look. "I have my ways," he said.

And how could he not? He was astonishingly handsome, well formed, charming when he wished to be. Even Lady Westlake, with her apparent devotion to the earl, might easily fall when the right kind of influence was applied. A little flattery and flirtation…

"You won't be able to help me with Ash if you're occupied with Pamela," Mariah said.

"Oh, I'll manage to steal some time away." He frowned at her. "Be very careful, Merry. In the asylum, you had others to come to your aid. You will be alone with Ash."

Mariah felt ill. "How did you know about the asylum?"

"Donnington mentioned it to me sometime or other. In any

event, I'll keep myself informed of our charge's progress. If he does well, then I will contribute what I can to molding whatever gentlemanly qualities he possesses."

"I'm convinced," Mariah said, finding her feet again, "that he'll continue to learn very quickly."

"And then? Have you thought about the future, Merry?"

"We must not move too fast," she said. "Have you learned more of his identity?"

He shook his head, clearly preoccupied. Mariah glanced toward the house. It was near noon now, time for luncheon, and Sinjin had decided to beard the lioness in her den by inviting himself to the meal.

He gave Shaitan a gentle kick and rode for the house. Mariah urged Germanicus into a trot, filled with doubt about Sinjin's tactics. Would the dowager confront them? It seemed unlikely, given the severity of their supposed "crime."

Luncheon was strained, as Mariah had expected. The dowager stared at both of them when she thought they didn't notice. It was evident that the dowager Lady Donnington was bursting with questions she dared not ask.

Mariah was deeply uncomfortable, but she was willing to endure the discomfort. She had only begun to realize that if the dowager continued to harbor her nasty suspicions, she would be unlikely to search for another lover and find Ash by accident.

The meal ended at last. Sinjin had obviously run out of small talk, at which he was generally adept, and looked pained at his mother's icy reception. Mariah excused herself to her room when Sinjin left to ride back to Rothwell.

She spent the entire day planning Ash's education and considering what to bring him next. Histories of England and America would be useful. Still, there were only so many books he could study at one time.

And what about the future? Sinjin's question had been a legitimate one. She hadn't allowed herself to think much beyond setting Ash free and confirming his identity. But what would happen when he was fit for society and they were certain that he was indeed who they believed him to be?

What if he should relapse into insanity even after they felt sure of him?

She remembered Ash's touch, his breath on her lips, on her neck, stirring her hair. She could feel again his unbridled masculinity, bold and unashamed. Was that insanity?

Feeling suddenly feverish, Mariah sat down before her dressing-table mirror and slowly unbound her hair. That was what Ash did to her…made her feel unbound. Free of convention, free of expectation, free to pursue her own forbidden desires.

She touched her lips, wondering what it would be like if he kissed her. *When* he kissed her…

She began to put her hair up again but dropped the pins and ended up with a rat's nest of dark curls. *I shall not surrender. Not to this…this lust. I shall be sensible, logical, sane….*

And faithful. For as long as it took.

"IT IS NOT NECESSARY TO tell me, Nola," Vivian said harshly. "I already know."

The little maid shrank in her chair at her mistress's tone. *And why not?* Vivian thought. She had utterly failed to bring forth any useful information. It had been Lady Westlake who had confirmed her suspicions.

And then Mariah had the gall to bring her lover into my home. My own son.

"It isn't Mr. Ware, your ladyship."

Vivian emerged from her ghastly musings and stared at the maid. "What did you say, girl?"

"I watched her ladyship, just as you instructed, ma'am," Nola said. "I saw her with someone. Someone who wasn't Lord Donnington's brother."

The revelation was too unexpected for Vivian to take in all at once. She had been so certain, even though she had prayed that her fears were groundless.

Nola might be lying. But what could she possibly have to gain by doing so?

"Who was this person?" Vivian demanded.

"I don't know, your ladyship. Only that he has white hair."

White hair? Would Mariah, so young herself, take an elderly man as a lover?

Vivian released her breath. If Mariah had been seeing a different man all along, she no longer need fear that Sinjin had cast aside his honor for that horrid girl.

"You must find out who he is, this man with white hair," she said. She opened the small purse that she had placed beside her on the tea table and poured a number of coins into her hand. "Take these, and hide them. You shall receive more if you succeed in learning this man's name."

"Yes, madam." Nola rose and accepted the coins Vivian offered, then left hurriedly when Vivian dismissed her.

Perhaps now, Vivian thought, it would be safe to approach Sinjin privately, even apologize if necessary. Lovers or not, he and Mariah were obviously close. She might even learn something new that she could use against the hussy.

If only Donnington were here…

She bowed her head into her knotted hands and began to weep.

A WEEK PASSED WITH no sign of Sinjin.

Mariah assumed that he was occupied with courting Lady Westlake and easing her suspicions as well as his mother's. Nola had come to Mariah shortly after that day at the cottage and informed her mistress that the dowager now absolved her of any improper relationship with Mr. Ware.

Feeling both more vulnerable and as if a great weight had

been lifted from her shoulders, Mariah devoted every night, from midnight 'til dawn, exclusively to Ash. Though he showed no sign of being able to read, he was a quick study. He rapidly expanded his vocabulary, and asked incessant questions about everything and anything that entered his mind.

When she finished the book about the rancher in Cochise County, he demanded further descriptions of the forbidding landscape, the cattle, the hard and capable men who fought man and beast for their livelihoods. He hung on every word when she shared a little of her early childhood in the same unsparing environment.

And always, always, he was close to her. Too close. He circled the table like a pacing tiger, pausing to sniff at her hair, pulling his chair beside hers so that their shoulders nearly touched. His clothing might disguise his body, but her memories of his nakedness would not let her be. She both longed for and dreaded Sinjin's return.

One early morning he came, scowling and impatient. He reported that he had been spending considerable time with Lady Westlake, but that he couldn't stand the woman.

"Your protégé had better make some progress soon," he said, casting Ash an almost hostile glance.

"What further progress have *you* made in learning about his origins?" Mariah asked, beginning to feel put out herself.

"I am still waiting for information to arrive from America. You can scarcely expect it to take less than several weeks, if not months."

"Then how can you expect Ash to regain his memory in a few days? He already knows a great deal more than he did a week ago. He—"

"I am here," Ash said, rising from his chair at the table. "Speak to *me*."

They both turned to stare at him. Mariah flushed. "I'm sorry, Ash."

"You should leave," Ash said, holding Sinjin's gaze.

"And you should put on different clothing," Sinjin said, sniffing audibly.

"That is my fault," Mariah said. "I can't go on taking clothes from Donnington's room, and I must be very cautious in ordering a new wardrobe unless I have packages sent to another address. Can you lend him some of yours?"

"I do not want anything from him," Ash said.

Sinjin ignored Ash's pronouncement and addressed Mariah. "Very well. If you can guarantee he'll look better than a monkey in them."

Mariah barely restrained herself from taking both men by the shoulders and giving them a good shake. "Sinjin," she said, "I believe I am making good progress with Ash's education. If you can provide a few additional things he needs, that will be most appreciated."

"And what of *your* education, Merry?"

"I beg your pardon?"

"You're alone with a single man of uncertain origins. What is he teaching *you?*"

She clenched her fists. "You have made such insinuations before. Do I take it that you have assumed your mother's position regarding my supposed lack of morality?"

His expression lost its harshness. "I'm sorry, Merry," he said. "Pamela's less than admirable behavior has apparently polluted my mind. I'm unfit for any decent woman's company."

"Yes," Ash growled. "Get out."

The air crackled with tension, but Sinjin chose not to engage in yet another battle. He turned to go.

Merry caught his arm.

"Then don't torment yourself with that woman," she said.

"I can't just drop her. It's gone too far, Merry."

"What do you mean, gone too far?"

He avoided her gaze. "I did tell you that she was one of those apt to ignore her marriage vows."

Mariah let go of him. "You mean…are you saying that you and she…"

"It would hardly be the first time. For either one of us."

Between one moment and the next, Sinjin became a stranger. His appearance hadn't changed. He was still her friend, her loyal companion.

But he was not the man she had known. Rumors were one thing; no one in his right mind would have taken the dowager's grotesque speculations seriously. But Sinjin had just admitted that he was engaged in an affair with a married woman.

"You would have found out sooner or later," Sinjin said. "I'm no monk, Mariah. You may think you're the teacher, but you've got a great deal to learn about the ways of the world."

Without another word he turned on his heel and left the cottage. Ash stood beside his chair, his fists working open and closed, open and closed.

"I don't want his help," he said.

Mariah returned to the table and fingered the pages of the book she had been reading. "You will need it eventually. Sinjin is far better suited than I to teach you a true gentleman's behavior."

"Does *he* know what *gentleman* means?"

He couldn't possibly have understood her exchange with Sinjin, she thought, but he had struck a little too close to the truth.

"We are none of us perfect," she said. "You must learn the proper manner of speaking, addressing others…basic courtesies, certain ways of doing things."

He swung into another of his lightning-quick changes of topic. "Ware said he was not a monk. What is that?"

"A—a monk is a man who doesn't consort…spend time with women."

Silver brows lifted. "He has mated with Westlake?"

There were definite disadvantages in his ability to learn quickly. "Whatever he has done, it has been for your good."

"Because we are family."

They had returned to the subject she had hoped to avoid a little while longer, but it was safer than the one he had been pursuing.

"We believe," she began, and found her own chair. "We believe that you are the son of the dowager's sister. You are Sinjin's cousin."

"Is that like a brother?"

"In many ways. The dowager's sister went to America long ago. That is why we believe you may have come from there."

"The place in the book."

"Yes."

His black eyes searched hers, and then he demanded that she read to him again. But the sun was coming up, and Mariah knew she had to get back to the house.

"More books," he told her, as she started for the door.

She was too agitated to laugh. "Yes, Ash. More books."

He gave her one of those rare and beautiful smiles that seemed to catch the rising sun and fill his eyes with radiance. It was difficult to leave him.

But when she thought of the meadow, and his nearness during their reading sessions, it was much easier to run away.

"DONNINGTON? IMPOSSIBLE."

Vivian's voice rang too loudly in the cool evening air of the garden. This interview, unlike the others, had been held outside, for Vivian no longer felt it safe to conduct them within the house.

Especially not now.

"Utter nonsense," she said more quietly, turning with a hiss of her skirts. "If you do not start providing me with truthful information, my girl, you will soon find yourself discharged without a reference."

Nola appeared chastened and humble, her gaze averted downward and her shoulders hunched. Vivian wasn't deceived. If this girl weren't a practiced liar, she was certainly possessed of a fantastic imagination.

Donnington, indeed. As if her son would return home and not come immediately to Donbridge.

"White hair," she said sharply. "You said this man had white hair."

"Yes, your ladyship," the maid whispered.

"Then it cannot be the earl. His hair is jet-black."

Which was not precisely true. It had been going a little gray of late, as was not unexpected in a man of one and thirty years. As earl, Donnington had been burdened with more than his share of worries.

But white? Some said a great shock could turn even the darkest hair pale. Could Donnington have endured such a shock during his mysterious absence?

Even giving the idea the slightest credence made Vivian furious with herself. "Your eyes deceived you," she told Nola. "I will give you one final chance. Provide me with something useful and you shall remain employed. Until that time, your salary is ended."

"Yes, ma'am."

"One last chance, Nola. No more ridiculous stories. Am I clear?"

The girl curtseyed so deeply that Vivian might have suspected irony in the genuflection. If Vivian had dared to confide in any of the other servants and ask for help, she would have discarded the girl in an instant. But she couldn't afford such a luxury.

She was about to dismiss Nola when she caught a glimpse of something in the girl's face that she didn't understand. It wasn't pity. If it had been, she would have discharged the girl on the spot.

No, it was a kind of patient understanding, as if Vivian were the young, foolish girl, and Nola the elder and wiser. It made Vivian feel very small, very uncertain.

"Get out!" she cried. Nola scurried away like a little mouse, and Vivian told herself that what she had seen had merely been an illusion.

FIVE DAWNS LATER, Ash followed Mariah to Donbridge.

She knew she was a fool not to have expected it. A man of Ash's vitality and will would not long be content to remain in any sort of captivity after spending weeks, perhaps even months, in a cage.

He was defiant when she asked him to return to the cottage. She wondered if she'd only imagined that his tone of voice was different, his manner of speech a little more refined than it had been a few days ago. But he remained stubborn, and she was compelled to escort him back to the cottage and remain with him another hour, reading *A History of England,* before he would agree to stay.

As a result, she returned to the house after dawn, and was forced to endure the dowager's icy demeanor and barely veiled hostility. When she deigned to speak at all, Vivian spitefully asked why her daughter-in-law no longer received invitations to teas and luncheons from her fellow matrons in the neighborhood.

Mariah knew the answer, of course. "Distracted" by Sinjin or not, Lady Westlake had undoubtedly encouraged talk that Mariah was not all she ought to be, even if Sinjin had been absolved of any wrongdoing. It was an excellent thing that Mariah had long since abandoned any pretensions of becoming a real part of high society, here or in America.

If you were a part of it, she told herself as she tried to recoup her lost sleep with a midday nap, *you would not be seeing Ash.*

And that thought was very nearly unbearable.

She slept fitfully until evening, went down to dinner—minus the dowager, who obviously had no desire to see her—and waited impatiently for nightfall. She followed her usual roundabout path to the cottage and lingered outside for a good twenty minutes before she approached it.

As always, Ash seemed pleased to see her, though his demeanor was sober after their quarrel, and he made few comments as she sat down to read more of *A History of England.* She noticed that the as-yet-untouched novels had been shifted about, and she briefly wondered if Ash had been attempting to put her lessons on the alphabet to use. She cherished the hope but kept it to herself.

The night fled quickly, as did the subsequent three. Every evening found Ash a little more fluent in his speech, a little more swift to pick up the words Mariah pointed out to him. Four nights after she'd completed *A History of England* and had begun on a survey of the states of the American West, she dared to enter Donnington's library to gather a new set of books. The moment she stepped into the room she felt a prickle of awareness lodge in her spine.

Someone was in the room with her, someone so quiet and still that she had not been able to detect his presence until now.

There was only one man in the world who possessed such a skill.

"Ash," she whispered.

CHAPTER TEN

HE ROSE FROM HIS CHAIR and bowed far more deeply than was the current custom, sweeping his arm low and to the side as if he held the wide-brimmed, plumed hat of a cavalier. The gesture was that of a gentleman born, and the man before her, book still in hand, stood as easily in a gentleman's clothing as if he had worn such things all his life.

The change was not so much in his bearing, which had always been proud. Nor was it in his steady expression. But there was a new confidence in his eyes, an almost daunting certainty, and it chilled Mariah almost as much as the dangerous fact of his presence in the house.

"Lady Donnington," he said in a supple, seductive voice. He set his book down on the table beside his chair and advanced, matching the rapid pace of Mariah's heartbeat.

"My God, Ash," she whispered. "You can't be here."

She was still in the midst of her warning when Ash reached for her ungloved hand, raised it to his lips and kissed it. Not the air above it, as was the common practice, but the soft skin just to the back of her knuckles.

"I came to see you," he said.

She trembled, as much from his kiss and the way he continued to hold her hand as from fear for him. "You will be discovered," she said, trying to escape from his firm but gentle grip.

His answer was to pull her toward the chairs beside the hearth, a leashed, irresistible power flowing from his body to hers. With the same utmost gentleness, he pressed her into a chair. He took the one opposite, farthest from the empty grate. Mariah stared, tongue-tied, as he picked up the book from the table and opened it.

"'It is a truth universally acknowledged,'" he read, "'that a single man in possession of a good fortune, must be in want of a wife.'"

Shock held Mariah mute for a long minute, and then heat rushed through her body.

"*Pride and Prejudice*," she whispered. "But I never read that to you. I—"

"I read it myself," he said, closing the volume. "A very interesting book, though I confess that the behavior of some of the characters is a trifle difficult for me to understand."

Mariah half rose, found that her legs wouldn't support her, and collapsed back into the chair. "You read it yourself?" she all but squeaked. "How? When did you…?"

"Learn to read?" he said, smiling in a way he never had before. "You taught me, Merry, or don't you remember?"

"I began to teach you only two weeks ago. It isn't—"

"Possible? But you yourself implied that my lack of literacy might only be a product of my amnesia, did you not?"

So she had said, but she hadn't been prepared for this…this new Ash who kissed her hand and spoke with all the eloquence of an Elizabethan courtier.

"I am quite certain that your assumptions about my past are correct," he said to her silence.

"You've…you've remembered?"

"Not as much as I would wish."

"Your surname?"

"No. But I have chosen one. Cornell."

Mariah was too anxious for his news to question his choice. "What else do you remember?"

He sobered and glanced down at his hands, resting on the

cover of the leather-bound book. "Not why I was imprisoned, nor why Donnington is my enemy."

"But you know where you came from? How you came to
England, why—"

"I know I am from America. The rest remains a mystery
as yet."

Mariah made an effort to slow her breathing. As incredible
as it seemed, Ash had become everything she had hoped for.

But this was neither the time nor the place for celebration.
"It's wonderful that you remember, Ash, but it's too soon to
reveal yourself to—"

"To the dowager?"

How could she make him understand? "She is an elderly
woman, Ash. She might suffer some harm if she saw you. You
see, she didn't know that her sister had borne a child in
America, let alone that he…so closely resembles her son."

"Do I not have the right to present myself to my family?"

"Of course you do. When the time is—"

"Did you not suspect that Vivian might know of what Donnington has done?"

One more revelation from that conversation with Sinjin he
had somehow managed to overhear. "Perhaps, Ash. But I do
not believe it any longer."

"I know what 'reputation' means, Mariah. Ware's mother
desires to ruin yours."

"She is upset that her son left Donbridge—"

"And you have never told me why."

She gripped the arms of her chair. "Donnington and I had
a misunderstanding shortly after we…began to live together."

"After you were married."

"Yes. The dowager believes I was to blame."

Ash's eyes flared, and she almost expected to see him toss
his head. "This is about Donnington, then," he said. "All
about Donnington."

"I am simply trying to explain why you can't meet the dowager yet," she said. "You must be calm, and she must be prepared." She rose. "We will discuss this further at the cottage. It will be difficult to leave without attracting the attention of the servants, so you must do as I say."

He got up and took her hand. Then he pulled her toward him again.

But this time he didn't stop.

His face was no longer that of a half-wild creature—acting more on instinct than with deliberate intent—but that of an experienced lover who knew the effect of every move he made. His lips brushed hers, as light as his footsteps on the Persian carpet. It was hardly a kiss at all, yet Mariah felt the jolt of it all the way down to her toes.

She should have run, just as she had run from him by the meadow. She should have jerked away and left him without a moment's hesitation. But she let him kiss her, returned the kiss…gently, as he had given it, her mind helpless, her body under his command.

Too late she recognized the change when his mouth hardened, becoming demanding, seeking far more than she had ever before been asked to give.

Not even from Donnington. Giles had kissed her, but never like this. He had wooed her respectfully, promising more with his ardent but gallant attentions, until she had agreed to marry him and escape a world no longer her own.

There was nothing respectful about Ash's kiss. His tongue was too busy with hers to let her speak, and she had no wish to do so.

This, she realized, was what she'd been wanting all along, ever since she'd begun to know him in the folly. He was handsome, strong, masterful. He was perfect.

Too perfect.

She reached out blindly, laying her hands against his chest

in a vain attempt to put distance between them. His heart drummed beneath her palm, but he only drew her closer, refusing to acknowledge either her silent plea or the rigidity of her body. He kissed her again, tracing his lips across the corner of her mouth, along her jaw and down to her throat. Her nether parts began to ache and grow wet.

No! She shoved at Ash, somehow managing to catch him off guard, then backed across the room until she stood under the ladder that provided access to the upper shelves.

"You must never," she said, breathing harshly, "*never,* do that again."

"You wanted me to kiss you," he said softly.

"I…did not. And even if I did, it would be wrong."

"Because of your reputation."

"Because I am married, and a person who is married does not kiss another man. Whatever my husband may have done—"

"*May* have done? Have you ceased to believe me?"

"Under English law, a man must be allowed to confront his accusers."

"Will you confront him, Mariah?"

She wanted to sink into the carpet. "I will not ignore anything that has happened," she said. "You will have justice, Ash. That I promise."

"And until then you are not to be touched, even though it is what you desire." His mouth formed an uneven smile. "I understand completely, my lady countess."

His sweeping bow mocked her, yet when he straightened, his eyes held no anger.

"You must leave the house without further delay," she said, averting her gaze. "I will make sure it's safe."

She moved quickly toward the door, but someone knocked before she reached it.

"The window," she whispered, planting herself against the door. "Go out the window."

Ash hesitated, almost as if he would prefer to be caught than flee. But in the end, he did as she asked. He raised the sash and climbed through without once glancing back at her. And then he was gone.

Closing her eyes, Mariah waited until she was in firm control of her own emotions before she opened the door. It wasn't Nola, as she had half expected, but Barbara, the parlor maid, who curtseyed and glanced curiously over Mariah's shoulder into the library.

"I beg your pardon, your ladyship," she said. "I thought I heard voices. Is there anything I might get for you?"

"Nothing, thank you, Barbara." Mariah smiled, left the library and closed the door behind her. "You're up and about late this evening."

"Her ladyship…that is, the dowager…said that Donbridge might be having guests soon, Countess."

Guests? Mariah had heard nothing about it—that was no surprise, given the strained relationship between her and Vivian—but she had no intention of letting the maid know how ignorant she was.

"Of course," she said. "You may return to your duties, Barbara. I believe I will go up to bed."

And so she did, knowing full well that she wouldn't get a wink of sleep until dawn. She lay tangled in the bedclothes, tossing and turning until perspiration dampened her nightdress.

What have I done?

But she knew all too well. She had encouraged too much intimacy with Ash from the very beginning, believing only the personal touch would allow him to recover. But he had recovered quickly—and too well. And she had responded. Oh, how ardently she had responded.

How could she face him again?

It wasn't until five o'clock in the morning that the fairies came.

She did not recognize them at first. They seemed like large

insects—fireflies, perhaps—glowing and darting and nimble as they fluttered about the room. Mariah got up to close the window, and one of them alighted on the sill.

Mariah sank to the carpet in shock. The tiny creature followed. It hovered before her face, its own miniature features as blank as a doll's. Its arms were as fragile as fine china, hardly wider than a pin. And its wings, iridescent in the filtered light, beat faster than a hummingbird's.

The fairies flew about her for a time, exploring every corner of her room, diving under her bedstead, examining themselves in her mirror. Never did they make a single sound. When Mariah reached for the sill, they flew for the window and streamed out into the morning air.

Mariah crawled back to her bed and pulled the sheets and coverlet up to her chin, unable to get warm in spite of the moderate temperature.

Fairies. Just as her mother had described. They had come to find her at last. Like the unicorn. And she could tell no one. Not even Ash. Least of all Ash.

She shivered under the covers until Nola came to find her.

SO THIS WAS WHAT it was like.

Ash strode away from the house, the hair on the back of his neck on end and his heart clenched around emotions that were still too raw for him to bear.

Human. That was what he was becoming. Human enough to model himself on the people in the books he had read, the men who won their ladies-fair with the most ardent wooing.

They had taught him, those books, more than Mariah had done in all the time since she had found him. They had taught him about gallantry, chivalry, honor…what it was to be a gentleman like Sinjin. He wore the right clothes, carried himself as a lord of nobility.

He'd thought it would be enough. But it was not. This body

was a cage and would continue to be until he made Mariah *care* for him.

He remembered the story about the man who had been wrongfully imprisoned but had gradually dug his way out of his cell, only to become a nobleman bent on finding justice. Ash had not failed to recognize the similarities to his own experiences. In the end, the count had won both his revenge and the woman he loved.

Love.

Not long ago, Mariah had tried to describe this paramount of all human emotions. She had said there were "many kinds of love," including friendship. But Ash had not understood her full meaning until he had read the books.

Now he comprehended love's terrible power. He recognized that a female must be won with deeds and words that proved a gentleman's love for her. As *he* must win Mariah.

He recalled a line from one of the books: *Rénée responded with a look of love, for the young man was truly elegant and handsome like this, with his blue eyes, his smooth complection and the dark side-whiskers framing his face…*

Ash stopped, running his hand over his face. He felt the first roughness of what humans named *whiskers*…a most terrible warning of what was happening to him. Soon he would find it necessary to cut the hair away like any true human male. Would he have won Mariah's admiration if he had blue eyes and dark hair?

Dark hair. Like Donnington.

But it was not Donnington for whom she held affection. Of that he was now certain. She had responded to Ash's caresses, the physical expressions of love. He had thought himself in control, but he could not forget how his own body had felt, how quickly his heart had beaten, how much he had desired her.

That was Mariah's power over him. But desire was not

enough for her. She required that the male she loved must be a gentleman of strength and honor, not a weakling who required her constant assistance as if he were a child.

Yet there must be a fine balance between strength and gentleness. He had been too rough, too hasty in his actions. He had learned that there were subtler means of winning a female's affections.

He could tell her that he loved her.

He began walking again, his legs stiff and graceless. Nevermore would he gallop as fast as the flight of a phoenix, or graze the emerald grasses and fragrant blossoms of Tir-na-Nog. In forty mortal years, fifty at most, he would die.

Unless he sacrificed Mariah to a lie. A lie despicable enough without a false declaration of an emotion he could not feel. Not even for her.

She had made a choice tonight. A choice to leave him. He could not allow that decision to stand. He must find a way to be with her at all times, in *her* world. He must sever her ties to Donnington before the human returned from wherever he had gone. And he could never forget that he must not let his thoughts stray beyond securing her trust and affection. There would be kisses, but nothing beyond.

He wrenched off his shoes, stockings and jacket, left them beneath the shrubbery and broke into a run. He ran until his shirt was wet against his skin and his breath rasped. The sun rode well above the horizon and he was at last beginning to slow his mad flight when he heard a horse's cry and a man's grunted curse.

Instinctively he turned toward the sounds and followed them to a stretch of field that bordered the Donbridge estate. A group of horsemen on glossy mounts was gathered about a ginger-haired man of perhaps forty years, the glittering metal on his mahogany horse's bridle catching the sunlight as the animal plunged and bucked. Each of the other men made attempts to reach the hapless rider, but none could approach the bay stallion for more than a few seconds.

"Your Royal Highness!" cried one of the men, his face half-covered with a heavy black beard and side whiskers. "Make no attempt to control him. One of us will assist you."

His "Highness"—who must be a kind of prince, according to Ash's reading—set his jaw and refused to heed the blackbeard's advice. His mount whirled round and round, trying to unseat his rider, as the man fought for control.

Ash hesitated. He did not know these humans; he had met none but the man who had imprisoned him, his keeper and the three—Mariah, Sinjin and Nola—who had assisted him.

But a prince was a man of power, the son of a king or queen such as the one who ruled England. He would be an ally of worth, and Ash might soon require such an ally.

Surely Mariah would be impressed by such a coup.

He ran toward the frantic scene, slowing only as he approached the horse. He made a low sound deep in his throat. There was a language for horses, just as there were languages for humans and unicorns. It was a simple dialect, no more similar to unicorn speech than the twittering of a bird to the golden cry of a phoenix, but Ash understood it.

He set his hand on the wet, quivering flank of the bay, and the horse grew calm—still shaking, but no longer prepared to continue the battle.

"Well," the rider said, looking down at Ash in surprise. "I must thank you for your assistance, sir, but it was a dangerous attempt. Starling is hardly to be trusted. I—" His eyes narrowed and then opened wide. "Donnington?"

Ash bowed. "I beg pardon," he said, "but I am not the Earl of Donnington."

The prince's escorts crowded their horses round Ash and their master, murmuring in shock and bemusement.

"What jest is this, sir?" the man with the black whiskers

demanded. He stared at Ash's bare feet and unbuttoned waist-coat. "If you are not Donnington…"

"Come, come, old man," the prince said, smiling broadly at Ash. "I didn't realize you were one to engage in such tomfoolery."

"My name is Ashton Cornell," Ash said. "Please forgive my unsuitable appearance. I was walking, and did not wish to ruin my shoes."

The prince burst into a full-throated laugh. "I fear you have come very close to ruining your trousers."

"Trousers are easily replaced, sir, but a good pair of shoes is quite a different matter."

"How right you are." The prince swung off his horse, regarded Ash with a twist of his lips and offered his hand. "Well met, Mr. Cornell."

He gave the name such an emphasis that Ash knew he still believed his rescuer was Donnington but had decided to honor the earl's masquerade. Ash took his plump, strong hand. "Good morning, Your Royal Highness."

"Let us dispense with such formalities, my friend. My name is Albert, but my friends call me Bertie."

Albert Edward, the Prince of Wales, second only to the queen. Ash knew he had acted correctly.

The prince peered into Ash's face. "What brings you to Donbridge, Mr. Cornell?"

"I am a guest here, sir."

"A guest! How convenient. We were bound for Donbridge ourselves."

"I know Lady Donnington will be greatly honored."

"Indeed. Has she remarked on your resemblance to the earl?"

"She has not yet seen me, sir."

"What? You are a guest, but your hostess hasn't met you?"

"I sent a letter of introduction before I arrived in England, but I have not yet set foot in the house."

"Ha! So you decided to walk there?"

"My horse was very tired, sir, and I was not."

"Such sympathy for the beasts! I've no doubt you are a prime rider."

"I would like to think that I am not unskilled in the matter of horses."

"You've proven that well enough. Come, let us walk." The prince matched his pace to Ash's, showing himself to be surprisingly agile in spite of his bulk. "What brings a man of such remarkable…likeness to Donbridge? Surely you must be closely related to the earl."

"We are cousins."

"Cousins! Then why have you and I never become acquainted?"

"I have just come from America, sir."

"From what part of America?"

"The West. Arizona, to be precise."

"But you have no accent."

"My mother, the dowager Lady Donnington's sister, always maintained the habits of her homeland."

"Then you have never been to England?"

"My mother and the dowager became somewhat estranged many years ago. I believe neither the earl nor his family knew of my existence until I sent my letter."

"Well, well," Bertie said. "The story becomes more and more interesting." He patted Ash's shoulder. "Does anyone at Donbridge know of your uncanny resemblance to the earl?"

"I did not know myself, sir, until you remarked upon it."

"Hmm. But you must know that the new Lady Donnington is American. Have you never met before?"

"We have not, at least to my knowledge."

"Were you aware that the earl has been absent from Donbridge for nearly three months?"

"I was not, sir."

"A pity. I should have liked to have seen his expression when he encountered his mirror image. Except for the hair, of course. And his eyes are a bit less..." Bertie looked thoughtful as he signaled to one of the men riding behind them. "Where is your mount now, Cornell?"

"I gave him his freedom, but he will find me again."

"Russell, be so kind as to share your mount with Mr. Cornell until we reach either his horse or his shoes."

The light-haired man the prince had spoken to dismounted and led his chestnut close to Ash. "Please take my horse, Mr. Cornell," he said courteously.

"I would not deprive you, sir," Ash said, and turned back to the prince. "I can match the best of your horses, even on foot."

"Ha! Any fit man can keep up with a horse at a walk."

"I refer to a run, sir."

"Is that a challenge, Cornell?"

"If you like."

The prince gave another of his hearty laughs. "Oh, what a day this shall be. What course do you propose?"

"From here to the oak that stands alone in the park nearest the house."

"Ha!" Bertie exclaimed again, then glanced around at his men. "We shall give you a sporting start, Cornell."

Ash smiled. "What are the stakes?"

"Stakes?" Bertie shook his head. "Given the odds..." He glanced at the dark-bearded man. "Ten pounds, Gothard?"

"Yes, sir," the other man said. "Ten pounds."

With an inclination of his head, Ash set off at an easy run. He retrieved his shoes and jacket well before the prince and his retinue came within his hearing. He had been standing beneath the oak for several minutes when the prince arrived.

"Good God!" Albert exclaimed as he pulled Starling to a halt. "How did you manage that, Cornell? Where have you hidden your horse?"

His men drew up behind him, every one of their mounts showing clear indications of having just completed a fast run. Ash finished lacing his shoes and stood.

"My horse is still at large, sir," he said.

"Are you telling me that you…" The prince stared at Ash's feet. "Impossible."

"Yet I believe I have won the race."

For the first time the prince seemed put out. He frowned. "I've no objection to a good race, but I won't abide deceit, Don—Cornell. Where is your mount?"

"I am no liar," Ash said, his own temper rising. "I rode no horse."

The prince's men murmured amongst themselves, obviously outraged on their master's behalf. The prince continued to scowl. He gestured to his followers, and three broke away. No one spoke until the men returned.

"I can find no sign of a horse in the area, sir," the first man said. "No hoofprints but our own." The others agreed, and all eyes turned to Ash once more.

"Well," Bertie grunted. "How very irregular." He stared intently into Ash's eyes. "Let no man say I do not pay my debts. Gothard?"

Blackbeard reached inside his coat, removed a leather wallet and withdrew several narrow sheets of printed paper. "Ten pounds, sir," he said.

Ash clearly sensed how little the prince liked being caught off guard. "There is no debt, sir," he said with a short bow.

"Nonsense. Gothard…"

Ash backed away. "Please forgive me, sir." He turned and began walking briskly away from the house, leaving a murmur of surprise behind him. Once he was out of sight, he waited to allow the prince and his retinue to reach Donbridge ahead of him, making his own appearance just as the prince dismounted and servants in matching livery appeared to lead the weary horses away.

"Never mind, Russell," the prince was saying. "The carriages will find us sooner or later…as I hope 'Cornell's' horse will find him." His men laughed. "He'll pay for his tricks with his abundant hospitality. I am quite peckish. Ah!" He noticed Ash. "I see that you have ruined your shoes after all."

"Well worth the honor of a race with you, sir."

"If you will not accept my debt, Cornell, I shall be compelled to send you twenty pairs of shoes to replace the ones you have lost."

"That will not be necessary, sir," Ash said. "I should be compelled to hold the shoes unused rather than sully gifts selected by the prince's own hand."

Slowly the prince began to smile. "What elegance of language, gentlemen," he remarked. "One would think our 'Mr. Cornell' was born in the age of chivalry."

"I fear I have much to learn in that respect, sir," Ash said. "Perhaps you would consent to instruct me."

"By God, perhaps I will!" The prince gave Ash a brief nod and strode toward the steps that led to the front door, his retinue behind him. Ash hung back, well aware that he was committing himself to an action that could not be undone.

An elderly man emerged from the house, followed by Mariah and a woman who resembled Donnington so closely that she was almost certainly his mother. The women bent before the prince, their stiff skirts creaking.

"Your Royal Highness," the dowager said. "We are honored by your visit."

"As I am honored by your hospitality." The prince was all smiles. "We intend to spend the night at Rothwell, but if you've a bit of refreshment to see us on our way…"

"Of course, sir," Mariah said, returning his smile. "I have very much looked forward to meeting you."

"And I to meeting Donnington's new bride." Ash bristled as the prince examined her from head to toe. "Lovely, my dear. As are all the American women I have met."

"You are too kind, sir," Mariah said.

"Not at all." He glanced over his shoulder. "In fact, there is another—" he cleared his throat "—American here, one who will be very happy to make your acquaintance. Come, Mr. Cornell."

As one, Mariah and the dowager looked toward Ash. He could not have said which appeared more appalled. The dowager's knees buckled before Mariah caught her.

"Donnington," the elderly woman whispered. "Donnington?" She started forward, Mariah still clinging to her arm, and her expression opened like a blossom. "Where have you been? When you left us so suddenly…" Confusion caught her tongue. "Your hair…what has happened? Donnington?"

The prince said nothing, though his round face was beginning to register concern. Mariah bent her head close to the dowager's ear, but the older woman pushed her away. Ash spent no time waiting for an introduction.

"My ladies," he said, bowing from the waist, "I am sorry to come upon you so unexpectedly. I fear my letter of introduction may have gone astray." He met the dowager's gaze. "Madam, my name is Ashton Cornell. I am your sister's son."

CHAPTER ELEVEN

IF MARIAH HADN'T taken Vivian's arm again, the older woman would have fallen.

Forgetting that the Prince of Wales stood on her doorstep, Mariah stared at Ash. The shock of seeing him in such a way was already passing, replaced by anger and fear.

Anger that Ash had taken such precipitous action without consulting her—and before royalty, no less. Fear that he would make an even more foolish misstep.

And what if this is no misstep at all? What if he truly has remembered everything?

Yet if that was true, he had not seen fit to tell her. She pushed away the pain that came with that realization.

"Cornell?" Vivian whispered, her arm trembling in Mariah's grip. "I have never... Vicki's son?"

Ash bowed again. "Yes, ma'am. I do apologize for this untoward intrusion."

Mariah saw no alternative but to make the best of the situation. "Lady Donnington," she said, addressing the dowager, "I am sure His Royal Highness would appreciate tea and cakes."

As if she were awakening from a dream, Vivian pasted on a smile. "Of course. Please forgive me, sir."

The prince waved his hand in dismissal. "I see that we have caused quite a bit of inconvenience for you, madam." His fair face reddened. "I must apologize. Mr. Cornell and I only met a short while ago."

"I would have delayed my coming had I known it would cause distress," Ash said.

That almost certainly wasn't true, Mariah thought, given his behavior the previous night. But he couldn't have known about the prince's penchant for practical jokes, or that he would deliberately delay introducing Ash just to see the looks on everyone's faces.

Clearly the prince now regretted his actions, but did Ash? Had he wanted to chasten her for her rejection last night? What did he want of her?

Hadn't he made that clear enough?

"Won't you come in, sir?" she asked the prince, refusing to look at Ash. She spoke to those members of his retinue she recognized and smiled at the others as they entered the house. Ash and the prince followed the dowager to the drawing room, where he and his entourage selected chairs but remained standing until Mariah and the dowager were seated.

Having heard of Bertie's habits, Mariah quickly assured him that he was welcome to smoke, but he continued to glance worriedly at the dowager. She barely spoke, save for the merest courtesies, ignoring Ash completely as she inquired about the prince's ride and wished him good fortune at Newmarket, where he and his retinue were bound. Mariah could hardly contain the questions she wanted to fling at Ash. But when Vivian left the room, ostensibly to oversee the tea preparations, the prince indicated that he wished to speak to Mariah alone and escorted her out of the drawing room.

"Lady Donnington," he said, "please allow me to apologize again for any part I may have played in disturbing you and the dowager Lady Donnington. It was not well done of me."

"Please, sir, think no more of it," Mariah assured him. "I doubt Mr. Cornell, having never met his family in England, would have written to warn us of his resemblance to Lord

Donnington in any case. We would have been surprised sooner or later."

"Indeed," the prince said, obviously relieved. He chuckled. "A pity Donnington himself wasn't here."

The prince was not entirely repentant, but Mariah couldn't be angry with him. It was Ash who was going to get a thorough tongue-lashing.

"Can you tell me anything else about Mr. Cornell?" she asked.

"He's deuced good with horses, I can tell you that."

Mariah glanced toward the coat of arms hung above the front door. *Beware my horn.* She shivered.

"You are cold, Lady Donnington. Shall I have a servant fetch your wrap?"

"No, sir. Thank you, but I am quite well." She heard a door open. "Ah, I believe I hear the tea and cakes. Should you wish anything else, please inform either myself or the dowager."

The prince all but rubbed his hands together in anticipation. "No, indeed," he said. "This will do very nicely."

With a smile, he offered his arm and escorted Mariah back to the drawing room, where his retinue were discussing such tepid subjects as the weather. After an hour of small talk, a carriage drew up in front of the house, bearing the Prince of Wales' coat of arms. With sincere thanks for the tea and cakes, which he had happily devoured, the prince made his farewells and expressed the hope that he might see the lovely Lady Donnington at Rothwell.

"And you, of course, Mr. Cornell," he said, speaking directly to Ash for the first time since their arrival. "I am certain that Mr. Ware will be delighted to meet his American cousin."

There was a bite to the prince's invitation, and Mariah wondered what Ash had done to provoke this strange combination of annoyance and friendliness from the prince.

It was one more question she had no chance to ask. A

flurry of grooms and footmen saw the Prince of Wales ensconced in his carriage, while his escort remounted and took up their places. Five minutes later, in a swirl of dust, they were gone.

The dowager retreated into the house. Mariah lingered with Ash.

"What have you done?" she whispered.

"Are you not pleased, Mariah, that I have the favor of the prince?"

"I asked you to wait before...before doing anything," she said with a feeling of desperation.

His gaze was as level and black as always. "The time for deception has ended," he said.

But you aren't ready. No matter how eloquent your voice or smooth your manners...

"I see that the dowager has been discomposed," Ash said, "but I shall do what I can to ease her mind."

"There would have been a better way, Ash."

"It is done."

She caught his arm and immediately let go, as if he had become a creature of fire and steel. "You have no conception—"

"She thought I was Donnington. So did the prince."

"Of course they did! I told you that the dowager would be upset." She gazed earnestly into his eyes. "She was deeply unhappy when my husband...when he left Donbridge. She had—has—no idea where he might have gone."

"Or when he will return."

"No. Please, don't tell her what happened to you. She is your aunt. Treat her as such."

He inclined his head. "I shall do as you ask."

Mariah closed her eyes in gratitude. "Thank you, Ash. Ashton." She opened her eyes again. "That can't be your real name."

"It will always be my name," he said. "You gave it to me."

The pit was opening up beneath her feet. "How did you meet the prince?" she asked too abruptly.

"Quite by accident. He could not manage his horse. I helped him."

"I could see he was not entirely pleased with you."

"He is proud, as princes are."

"And you offended his pride?"

"I outran his horse."

She tried to imagine such a scene, remembering all too vividly how Ash had leaped through the meadow as if his feet had wings.

Swift or not, he couldn't have outrun a horse. But Mariah didn't intend to pursue the truth of the matter. Ash had won the prince's interest, and that in itself was a daunting prospect.

She clenched her fists at her sides so that she would not risk touching him again. "If only we could begin again..."

Abruptly he caught both her hands in his. "You do not fear only for the dowager's discomfort. You fear for *me*."

How could she deny it? In less than a month he'd gone from mad prisoner to courtly gentleman. Only days ago she'd been angry on his behalf, so full of pity and outrage. Nothing had mattered more than justice, not even the consequences of turning against her husband.

Now Ash was free, confident, strong... stronger and more dangerous than ever before. He would be Donnington's match. His superior.

"Is it revenge you want, Ash?" she whispered. "Is that really why you're here?"

He lifted her right hand and kissed it, just as he had done in the library. "My memory is still uncertain. Trust me, Merry. I might have been mad before, but now I am perfectly sane."

"I know you are," she said. "But if you want me to trust you, you must trust me. We must trust each other."

He kissed her left hand. His warm breath bathing her skin brought back the memory of his kiss. Made her aware of how much she wanted him to kiss her again…

Stop it. "I still know this world better than you do," she said, "no matter how well-brought-up you were in America. Let me guide you."

Her hands felt empty when he released them. "I will speak to the dowager. As her nephew."

"Without accusations, Ash. And only after I have spoken with her first."

"And you will come with me to Rothwell. Today."

"We have no need to go there. Sinjin will soon have more information for us. He will come when he—"

"The prince has invited us. Should we deny him?"

"His invitation was simply a courtesy. What could you possibly have to learn there that you cannot better discover here?"

"Your dowager may not accept me."

"You must give her time. She has not seen her sister in well over thirty years." She heard the sound of footsteps in the entrance hall and knew their conversation was blessedly at an end. So did Ash.

He offered his arm. "Lady Donnington," he said formally.

She rested her hand on his forearm, hating him, hating Donnington…hating herself. Ash had taken his life out of her hands, and there was no telling what he might do.

At least he isn't mad. Even if I am.

She carefully measured her steps back to the drawing room and stopped outside the door. "I must speak to the dowager," she said. "Please remain here, Ash."

He swept her one of his cavalier's bows, went into the drawing room and found a seat. Mariah didn't go directly to the dowager, however. She went to her own room, sat at her secretary and wrote out a quick note to Sinjin. She summoned a footman to ride to Rothwell immediately and deliver it by hand.

Having completed that task, Mariah walked down the hall to the dowager's suite and knocked. After what seemed like an eternity, Vivian opened the door.

She could not have looked less like herself. Her usually well-coiffed hair was falling down about her ears, her face was streaked with tears, and her dress was rumpled, as if she had been lying curled up on her bed.

"Did you know he was coming?" she asked.

"I had no idea," Mariah answered honestly.

Vivian passed her hand over her face, but her eyes were sharp and angry. "But you *do* know him," she accused.

"No, Vivian. I do not."

And that was at least partly the truth. She hadn't known *this* Ash until last night.

The dowager regarded her through narrowed, glistening eyes, and Mariah could easily guess what she must be thinking. Vivian must believe that Ash was who he claimed to be—the physical evidence was simply too overwhelming to deny—but she clearly had no desire to welcome her sister's son into the family.

"Do you intend to come down and speak to him?" Mariah asked.

The dowager straightened and raised her hands to her disheveled hair. "By all means I shall speak to him," she said. "I shall hear what story he has to tell."

"Then let me call for your maid."

The dowager nodded, too shaken to protest Mariah's decisiveness. Mariah rang for Fellows, then went out into the corridor to find Parish hovering nervously at the head of the staircase.

"Everything is all right, Parish," she said. "Please see that

Mr. Cornell is provided with anything he wishes. The dowager and I shall be down presently."

With a nod of relief, Parish descended the stairs. Once Fellows appeared, Mariah sent her in to Vivian. Mariah lingered in the corridor, trying to prepare herself for the unpleasant episode to come.

It wasn't just her fear of the meeting between two stubborn antagonists. It was being in close proximity to Ash himself. Last night—early this morning—his actions had shown that his desires had gradually changed since he had wanted only to escape his cage and discover his identity. She was sure he understood that she had ample reason to reject his advances, but he was more than clever enough to use the forbidden attraction between them to manipulate her into doing as he wished. Whatever that might be.

You will come with me to Rothwell, he had said. What did he hope to accomplish there? Did he think he needed her to intervene between him and Sinjin, who would have no idea of the full extent of what had happened since he had last seen Ash? What could he want of her brother-in-law, when he had already gained the attention of the prince?

And that brought up yet another vital question. If Prince Albert had truly taken to Ash, he might very well invite his new acquaintance to Marlborough House. Did Ash understand enough about English society to join it? For undoubtedly that end would appeal to him, and his reasons weren't difficult to guess.

He did want revenge, of that Mariah was certain. Donnington had never been part of the Marlborough House Set, and his resentment of that fact had hardly made him reticent in claiming that he had no use for such society. If Ash intended to establish himself among the prince's followers in order to injure Donnington, he could have no better advocate than the heir to the throne of England.

She wondered why he had chosen not to extend his hatred of Donnington to Donnington's wife. Perhaps he had realized that by seducing *her,* he would spoil something that belonged to his enemy. Perhaps she was only another part of his revenge.

Horrified by her own bitter speculation, Mariah descended the stairs, her legs as heavy as stumps, then smoothed her skirts and entered the drawing room.

Ash looked up from his perusal of the bronze horse perched on the mantelpiece. "I missed you," he said.

Mariah stifled a laugh. She had been gone no more than half an hour, and he had *missed* her?

"I am here now," she said, taking a seat. "The dowager will join us directly." She swallowed as he came within touching distance. "Ash, you asked me to trust you. I must know—"

The dowager marched into the room, head high, her bearing ominously cool. Ash moved away from Mariah, unruffled and calm. Mariah could only pray that she appeared the same.

The dowager could not have failed to note their proximity, but she let no sign of her reaction penetrate the mask of her face. Ash bowed to her; she nodded in return.

"Please sit down, Mr. Cornell," she said.

He continued to stand after the dowager had seated herself. "Again, I must apologize, madam," he said. "Had I know you would have no warning of my appearance…"

"It is of no moment," the dowager said. "If my greeting was less than proper, I beg you will forgive me."

"Of course, ma'am. But the fault was all mine."

She smiled at him, a ferocious expression that belied her welcome. "Now we are here," she said. "And you are my sister's son."

"Yes, ma'am. It was my mother's dearest wish that our families be reconciled. When she left us…"

"Vicki is dead?" The dowager caught herself, and Mariah could have sworn she glimpsed tears in Vivian's eyes. "I am sorry, Mr. Cornell. Deeply sorry."

Ash bowed his head. "As are we all, ma'am."

Silence hung over the room. "I hope that you will tell me about my sister's years in America," Vivian said at last. "I…regret what came between us." She produced a handkerchief and dabbed discreetly at her eyes. "But it seems that I have not lost her completely."

He proceeded to tell her about how Wilfred Cornell had taken his wife to California, where he had become wealthy supplying gold miners not only with necessities but also with the comforts they so often lacked. He described his parents' happy marriage, their eventual move to Arizona, and how he had been educated at a large university in the East. He briefly mentioned his mother's long illness and her final wish that her only son travel to England to meet her sister's family.

The tale was so richly detailed that Mariah couldn't doubt that he had lived every moment of it.

"My mother often spoke of you, ma'am," Ash said to Vivian. "She had heard you had two sons, but never suspected…" He smiled wryly. "Perhaps it is best that the earl is away, so that you may put him on his guard."

"I daresay," the dowager murmured. "I expect to hear from my son at any moment."

"To meet my cousins will be a great privilege. I know that the prince was on his way to your younger son's estate."

"His Royal Highness is a frequent visitor there," Mariah said.

"Then you are indeed a fortunate family."

There was a pause in the conversation while Vivian unconsciously rubbed at her left hand with her right…a sign, Mariah knew, of the recurring pain in the joints from which she had suffered for some years.

"Are you in discomfort, ma'am?" Ash asked.

The dowager flinched as if she had been caught in some criminal act and hid her hands in the folds of her skirts. "I am very well, thank you," she said in a flat voice.

Ash leaned back, a faint frown on his face. After another uncomfortable few moments, they went on to speak more of Ash's encounter with Bertie and his amazing good fortune in so quickly winning the prince's friendship.

"The prince is so very affable," Vivian said. "He has many American ladies among his acquaintance…as well as those less commonly received in society."

"He must have very good taste in ladies, then," Ash said, smiling at Mariah in such a way that her chest constricted and that familiar intimate ache returned.

"In any event, Mr. Cornell," Mariah said hastily, "you shall receive all the hospitality Donbridge has to offer."

"Indeed," Vivian said. Mariah glanced at her and saw a fierce look of satisfaction on the dowager's face. It was more than simple acceptance of Ash's identity. She had already convinced herself that she had found a new candidate for Mariah's clandestine lover, in spite of Mariah's assurances that she had not known Cornell before his arrival.

Mariah had no idea whether Ash was capable of concealing their past relationship, or if he even intended to try. The longer he remained at Donbridge, the greater the danger of discovery.

But if he goes to Rothwell…

"I must inform the housekeeper that a room should be made ready for our guest," the dowager said, rising. She turned to face Ash. "Lady Donnington will provide you with anything you require until your room is ready."

She swept out before Mariah could respond, deliberately leaving her son's wife alone with her nephew.

"I must speak to the cook," Mariah said to Ash without looking in his direction. "I hope you will take advantage of the beauty of our grounds. Our grooms will assist you in choosing a mount from our stables."

"I will select one myself," Ash said, rising as she did. "I always take what belongs to me."

She stiffened. "If you will excuse me, Mr. Cornell," she said, and left to consult with Cook.

"There will be a third at luncheon," she told the thin birdlike woman who ruled the kitchen. Mrs. Gray's curiosity was manifest. By now, every servant would know of Ash's arrival and his first meeting with the dowager.

But where was Nola? Mariah realized that she hadn't seen the girl since two mornings ago. She would have been of great help today, being more than clever enough to counter any rumors that might arise regarding her mistress's possible relationship with Mr. Cornell.

Angry all over again, Mariah occupied herself with household concerns, letting Ash fend for himself until luncheon. She trusted him just enough to believe he wouldn't pester the dowager with unsupported accusations or mention his captivity. In fact, she had to admit that thus far he had done just as she had asked.

But that wouldn't last forever.

Mariah assured herself that Ash's room had been properly prepared and then summoned a footman to inform their guest that it was ready for occupation. She was grateful that she and Ash did not meet again before she sought her own chamber for a brief spot of privacy.

Nola was waiting outside her door.

"Nola!" Mariah said, unaccountably relieved. "Where have you been?"

The girl curtseyed. "I am that sorry, your ladyship, but I had an urgent message from my cousin in Barway. She said that my mother had taken a turn for the worse, and so Mrs. Baines gave me permission to visit her."

"I am sorry to hear that, Nola. Is she better now?"

"Oh, yes, ma'am. It was really nothing at all."

"Thank goodness." Mariah smiled. "I shall be requiring your services, Nola. Alice has come down ill, and I may shortly be making a visit to Rothwell."

"Mr. Ware's estate?"

"Yes. Please prepare what I will need for a stay of no more than three days. And pack your own things, as well."

"At once, your ladyship."

Nola tripped away, obviously pleased to be accompanying her mistress on her first visit to a neighboring estate. Wearily, Mariah went into her room and lay on the bed.

They had all made it through the first morning, but the challenges were far from over. The future that Sinjin had questioned her about had seemed distant, even implausible, as if she and Ash had existed in a timeless world all their own.

But now that future was here, and her world was quickly slipping out of her grasp.

CHAPTER TWELVE

SINJIN WAS STILL A LITTLE breathless when he took the letter from Hedley. He was aware that his tie was askew and his jacket creased, but far better to let any observers note his state of dishevelment than allow them to see Pamela in her present condition.

Not that the servants didn't know that their employer and the beautiful Lady Westlake were engaged in *une affaire d'amour.* There were moments when Sinjin almost forgot the initial hostility between himself and Pamela. But that was part of the charm of their relationship: neither one trusted the other.

So far he seemed to have succeeded in putting any thought of Mariah from Pamela's mind, and she was completely untroubled by her own infidelity to her ancient, ailing husband. Sinjin knew he was an excellent lover, considerate and tireless; his long string of former conquests was testament to that fact. The ladies enjoyed what he gave them, and he enjoyed them equally, with no expectation of loyalty. Already, so soon after his last bout with Pamela, he was eager to begin again.

But he'd had his warning. He read through the letter, crumpled it and pushed it into his pocket as he returned to the bedroom.

Lady Westlake looked up from the bed, her body sprawled lazily across the tumbled sheets.

"Well?" she purred. "What brought Hedley all the way to this lovely little cottage of yours?"

"You must go," he said, gathering up her clothes and tossing them on the bed.

She pouted. "But why? You said your servants are discreet, and no one else—"

"The prince is arriving several hours earlier than expected," he said brusquely. "Obviously you can't be seen here."

Pamela made a most unladylike noise and slid from the bed. "The prince ought to have more consideration," she said.

For a moment she busied herself with her undergarments while Sinjin watched from the mirror. She struck a pose, thrusting out her admirable breasts.

"No time for another bout?" she teased.

"No time." He finished knotting a fresh tie, grateful he had never learned to be dependent on his valet, and waited impatiently for Pamela to finish. She requested his help with the hooks and laces along the back of her bodice, and in ten more minutes she was presentable.

"I won't be able to escort you this time," he said, straightening his jacket. "It wasn't wise to meet in the middle of the day."

"How gallant of you to be worried about my reputation."

"You can take care of yourself, my dear. That is why we rub along so well together."

"In more ways than one."

Sinjin was growing hard again, but he ignored his body's demands and handed Pamela her fox pelerine. "I'll write when I can," he said.

She caught the lapels of his jacket and kissed him passionately. With the greatest effort, he held her away and steered her toward the cottage's rear door.

When she was gone, he sat on the rumpled bed and considered all the things that had so radically altered overnight. Mariah's letter had been brief but explicit; Ash had appeared and claimed to be the very person Sinjin and Mariah had suspected:

his American cousin, son to the dowager Lady Donnington's long-estranged sister. Moreover, the prince had apparently become acquainted with Ash and had invited him to Rothwell.

Sinjin was furious at Ash's rash move. Matters were moving much too rapidly to control. Merry hadn't given a reason for Ash's sudden rebellion or done more than guess at his subsequent intentions, but Sinjin could surmise well enough.

He laughed shortly. Now he need no longer play games with Pamela, not even of the sexual variety. He ought to be pleased.

He wasn't.

Damn her. That wasn't fair, of course. She was only being what she was, true to her own devious and often petulant nature. If she didn't get up to one mischief, she would find another soon enough.

And all that didn't change a bloody thing.

He sighed, got up and estimated how quickly he could ride back to the house. Considering the time it had taken for Mariah's message to be delivered, the prince might arrive at any moment.

Sinjin urged Shaitan to his fastest pace and reached the house just as the dust from the prince's carriage was rising up from the lane. Sinjin flung the reins to a groom, ran up the stairs and found his valet waiting for him. Together they managed to get him dressed in ten minutes, and he was greeting Bertie in the entrance hall within fifteen.

As usual, the prince's manner was amiably effusive, ready to be pleased. Sinjin had already arranged entertainment in the form of a gypsy fortune-teller and dancers, games of chance—some less than legal—and the exhibition of a trained elephant from a small country circus. That, he hoped, should keep Bertie amused until he and his party went on to Newmarket.

He had instructed Mrs. Blunt to refurbish Rothwell's best rooms and his French chef to prepare gourmet meals throughout the prince's stay, so there was little more to be done but provide Bertie with his best brandy and finest cigars. When they had been seated in the drawing room, the prince and his retinue laughingly recounted their meeting with the American called Mr. Cornell.

Having been warned by Mariah, Sinjin prepared himself for the event of Ash's arrival.

MARIAH ARRIVED AT ROTHWELL in the barouche an hour before dinner, Ash riding beside her on Donnington's favorite mare. It was a bit of poetic justice that the temperamental animal took to Ash immediately, nibbling affectionately at his fingers. And Ash was an excellent rider, as befitted someone who had grown up in the American West.

None of which eased Mariah's qualms. In the end, she'd had no choice but to accompany Ash to Rothwell. The alternative was to stay at Donbridge and watch him go off on his own, his intentions still very much in doubt, when she still might have a chance to guide him. Even Vivian's speculative smiles had failed to change her mind.

The prince seemed happy to see them. He was especially effusive toward Mariah, whom he complimented on her gown and general beauty.

Under other circumstances, she would have been nervous to find herself under the prince's eye, but her discomfort was of no importance now. Sinjin exchanged knowing glances with her as His Royal Highness and his retinue came down for dinner, Ash following quietly in their wake.

Just before they were to go into the dining room, Lady Westlake arrived in her own carriage. Sinjin was clearly surprised to see her, but he quickly hid his feelings.

Mariah was well aware that a very sly fox had just entered the henhouse. One look at Pamela's arch expression told Mariah that Lady Westlake was not in the least surprised to see Ash, and that she had somehow obtained a very clear idea of who and what he was. They were briefly introduced, and she responded with exactly the right combination of surprise and pleasure. While Mariah was granted the privilege of entering the dining room on Bertie's arm, Pamela accepted Sinjin's escort, clinging possessively.

Once they sat down at the table, it soon became obvious that Ash had forgotten a few of the essential skills Mariah had just begun to teach him. He began by using the wrong spoon for the soup, ignoring every course that contained meat, fish or fowl, accepting only the side dishes of greens and vegetables, and refusing the excellent wine Sinjin had brought up from his cellar.

"A vegetarian, are you?" the prince asked, observing Ash with a gimlet eye. "I was not aware that gentlemen dined so differently in America."

Ash met the prince's gaze. "I do not eat meat, sir."

Lord Russell laughed, and several of the other peers raised their brows in disbelief. Bertie leaned back in his chair and fingered his side-whiskers.

"How extraordinary," he said. "And I suppose they haven't the proper cutlery in the West, either?"

The question was not quite hostile, but the prince had always been a stickler for certain niceties. Mariah spoke up quickly.

"The West, as Your Royal Highness is aware, spans a very large area," she said. "I understand that Mr. Cornell was accustomed to few luxuries in the isolated region where he was brought up."

"Perhaps he was raised by Red Indians," Russell suggested with a smirk.

"Yet he speaks like an Englishman," Lord Gothard put in.

"We all have our little eccentricities," Mariah said mildly. Bertie laughed. "Truer words were never spoken." He smiled at her. "I can always bank on honesty from our American ladies."

"You do me too much honor, sir."

The prince waved her comment away. "You have a valuable friend in Lady Donnington, Mr. Cornell."

"I am quite sensible of that fact, sir."

"As you ought to be." The prince stretched and glanced around the table, favoring Lady Westlake with an appreciative nod. "An excellent meal, Ware, made all the more delicious by the presence of such lovely ladies."

Mariah had seen enough flirting in her day to recognize it in Bertie's tone. Pamela all but batted her eyelashes, simpering in a way Mariah found nauseating.

You needn't put up with her any longer, Sinjin, Mariah thought in disgust. *Let the cat find other prey.* But she knew very well that Sinjin was not the man she had at first assumed him to be. He was not troubled by Lady Westlake's infidelity. He might not be prepared to give her up her "favors." If the viscountess was less than honorable, then Sinjin, too, must be judged in a similar vein.

Unable to meet his gaze, she endured the rest of the meal in silence. When the dessert course was finished and general conversation ended, it was Lady Westlake who rose to escort Mariah from the room. Her proprietary air set Mariah's teeth on edge.

"What a marvelous surprise," Pamela said, sipping her after-dinner cordial. "I never would have guessed that there could be such a remarkable resemblance between two men."

"I take it the dowager informed you of Mr. Cornell's arrival, Lady Westlake?" Mariah said sweetly.

Pamela was unfazed by the insinuation that she and Vivian had been in such close communication. "It will soon be the talk of the countryside," she said, smiling just as sweetly. "And you say you never met him before this morning?"

"If I had, it would surely have been the talk of the countryside long before this."

"Ah. Yes." Lady Westlake continued to stare into Mariah's eyes. "You must miss your husband all the more with such an uncanny reminder so close at hand."

"Of course."

"What an interesting meeting *that* shall be."

It wasn't clear whether Pamela was referring to Ash and Donnington or Donnington and his wife, but she couldn't mean anything good by it either way.

Mariah herself had ceased to know whether she wished for Giles's swift return—making an end, for good or ill, to this untenable situation—or if she hoped he would never return at all.

Someone will suffer. If Donnington is guilty, he will be compelled to pay for what he has done to Ash. Even if he is innocent, he surely must know something of what went on at his estate.

"Why, my dear, you look positively ghostly," Lady Westlake said. "Here, drink this."

She thrust a glass of sherry into Mariah's hand. Mariah drank, and the liquor went directly from her lips into her legs, numbing her feet.

"There," Pamela said. "Much better." She drew her chair closer to Mariah's. "Something is troubling you, Lady Donnington. Has Mr. Cornell upset you? He was a bit…peculiar at dinner, and the prince seemed somewhat put out."

Mariah sat up straight and set the glass on the side table. "Mr. Cornell may have his eccentricities, but they are no worse than those of many an Englishman. He has been a perfect gentleman since his arrival."

"So I have heard." Pamela smiled as if she harbored a secret, then rose to fetch Mariah's glass and refill it. "My dear Lady Donnington, you and I have perhaps not been as close as I might have liked. I fear I have given you little reason to trust me, and I have been…improper in my attentions toward your husband. I have made other mistakes, as well." She sighed and shook her head. "I see that my frankness shocks you. But I prefer to be as American in my honesty as you are so very…English in other ways."

Mariah suspected another barb, but she was still reeling from the fact that Pamela had as good as admitted her designs on Giles.

"You continue to doubt," Lady Westlake said. "I quite understand, but I do hope to prove myself your friend. You see, I…" She blushed, an unnatural sign of modesty on such an experienced face, and glanced away. "I have found true love at last."

Mariah drank the second offered glass of wine before she could think. *True love.*

With Sinjin?

"You have guessed," Pamela said, her gaze still averted. "I confess I…was not prepared to face such a change of feeling when he and I first became better acquainted. But now…"

The chair squeaked as Mariah got up and walked across the room. "I might congratulate you, Lady Westlake, were it not for your husband."

Pamela's cheeks turned a darker shade of red, and she took several agitated steps. "My husband…" Her voice dropped very low. "I pity him, Lady Donnington. I truly do. But he is not interested in…" She drew a shuddering breath. "I was very young and naïve when we married. He was already ill and has declined much. He does not love me."

Nor, it would seem, does Donnington love me, Mariah thought. *Still, that does not permit us to betray our vows.*

"Your thoughts are so transparent," Pamela said with an edge of laughter in her voice. "You disapprove of me greatly, do you not? As you disapprove of Sinjin. You have lived a very sheltered life, my dear." She poured herself a glass and sipped at it casually. "Perhaps it might help you to know that

Westlake cannot give me children, even if he had any interest in attempting it. He cares nothing for what I do. I have no life with him. No—"

Mariah could have sworn that Pamela actually choked on a sob. Even her cheeks were wet. Unwanted pity knotted in Mariah's chest, but it could not overcome her disgust.

"What do you want of me, Lady Westlake?" she asked bluntly.

"Is it not obvious?" Pamela lifted her head. "I am as much in need of a friend and confidante as you, Lady Donnington. We can help each other."

"I do not take your meaning," Mariah said.

Lady Westlake dabbed surreptitiously at her eyes, and when she looked up there was no remaining trace of vulnerability in them. "Let us be entirely open with one another," she said. "You judge me, but I am not deceived by your veil of innocence, Mariah. I never have been. I have some influence in society, whatever you may think of me." She held out her hand. "Consider what I have said. Do not so hastily reject my friendship."

"You were never a friend to me, Lady Westlake." Mariah rose without taking the offered hand. "Good night."

PAMELA STRODE OUT OF the drawing room a moment after Mariah's exit, concealing her fury. She was glad she had done so when she nearly ran into Sinjin.

"Pamela," he said harshly, seizing her arm. "What are you playing at?"

"Sinjin!" she said, genuinely startled. "I don't know what you mean."

He released her arm with a scowl potent enough to slice through steel. "I heard what you said to Mariah. What did you mean by it?"

"Mean by what? Come, Sinjin, there is no need for—"

He steered her out of the corridor and into a smaller room, papered and furnished in yellows and pale greens. "You have no desire whatsoever to make up to Lady Donnington," he said, pushing her into a chair. "You dislike her. You envy her. Do you expect her to believe you are sincere now?"

Pamela saw that she must tread very carefully indeed. "But I am sincere, Sinjin. I understand why Lady Donnington has been so little at ease in recent days."

Only the slightest twitch of a brow betrayed Sinjin's concern. "You make no sense, Pamela."

"Is it not true that Lady Donnington had known Mr. Cornell for some time before he presented himself at Donbridge?"

Sinjin had himself under better control now and didn't rise to her bait. "Whatever gave you such an idea?" he demanded.

"Just a bee in my bonnet, if you like," she said lightly. "Obviously it is untrue."

"It is." He bent over her, trapping her with his hands braced on the arms of the chair. "You had best leave Lady Donnington alone."

"But she does need a friend, and I can be a very good friend."

He snorted and pushed away from the chair. "What about the other?"

"I beg your pardon?"

"The part about Donnington."

"I know…I do realize I have been wrong in…in attempting to—"

He walked to the mantelpiece. "Give it up, Pamela. Even you haven't the ability to make *that* sound sincere."

She got up and came to stand behind him. "You don't believe me. You truly don't believe me."

"That you've found 'true love' with me?" He snorted. "As if you were capable of such an emotion."

"You know what I said about my husband was true." She laid her hand on his arm. "I have nothing at home. I had nothing until I began to feel…what I feel for you."

"And all those other lovers?"

"They meant nothing to me." She pressed her cheek to his rigid back. "I do love you, Sinjin. More than I can say."

She fully expected him to reject her again. Instead, he turned and took her face between his hands.

"Pamela," he said, searching her eyes. "Tell me the truth. It won't change anything between us."

"Won't it?" She covered one of his hands with hers and brought his palm to her lips. "How shall I prove it to you, my darling? What will you accept?"

The muscles of his jaw flexed. "Leave Mariah alone. Leave Cornell alone. And when Donnington returns…"

"Your brother has no claim on my heart. It is already given."

He kissed her, savagely enough to bruise her lips. Then he walked out the door without a backward glance.

She found a chair and sat down heavily.

He does believe me. My God, he loves me.

For a moment she found the idea immensely amusing, though her amusement passed quickly. Sentiment had no place in what she intended to do, not for the dowager and not for herself. But she might make very good use of Sinjin's emotions.

Voices sounded in the corridor. Someone laughed. Pamela rose and went to join the prince in the drawing room.

ASH SPENT THE NEXT hour on the edge of the prince's group, listening to the men trade jokes and reminiscences, while the pale-haired Lady Westlake joined in their laughter and Mariah listened attentively.

His relative isolation left Ash plenty of time to think about what had passed in the dining room. He had seen the amused contempt on the faces of the men when he had failed to touch their filthy meat and when he had used the wrong tools. Such disdain would have been unimportant to him had Mariah not been there to witness it.

She had defended him. There was humiliation in knowing she had found such an act necessary. He should have spoken for himself, no matter if the prince thought the worse of him for it.

But would that not have embarrassed Mariah all the more? He had urged her to accept the prince's invitation and accompany him to Rothwell in hopes of getting her away from the dowager's influence and interference. But should she become weary of his errors and leave him…

Ash waited until the prince was fully occupied with Lady Westlake and edged toward Mariah.

"I would speak with you," he whispered close to her ear.

She smiled at something Lord Russell had said, her expression serene. "We have no privacy here," she said, matching his low tone. "And I cannot simply leave with you."

"Tell us the story of the tiger hunt in India, sir," Lady Westlake said loudly to the prince, her gray eyes flashing in Mariah's direction. "I should love to hear it again."

It was almost as if the woman had deliberately called attention to herself so that Mariah could escape the prince's notice. Ash well remembered Mariah's warning that he stay away from the woman, and he could think of no reason why Lady Westlake should assist them.

Yet he would not argue with the opportunity. He beckoned to Mariah, and after a moment of hesitation she drifted with him to the opposite end of the room.

"I hope you are enjoying your visit, Mr. Cornell," she said in a normal voice.

"I require your help," he said more quietly.

She gazed at him earnestly, her lovely eyes wide. "What is it, Ash?"

"You tried to make it seem as if what I did at the table was acceptable," he said, "but I know it was not."

"I understand that your memory is not yet complete," she said, lowering her voice. "And it is not as if you are conversant with English—"

"The use of cutlery is the least of my concerns," he said. "I did not want you to guess how much…" He glanced aside, allowing his expression to reveal the vulnerability he felt. "There are vast gaps in my memory, Mariah. They may cause you further difficulties."

"They have caused me no difficulties so far," she said. "The prince is not likely to remain annoyed for long."

The conversation on the prince's side of the room faltered, and several faces turned toward them.

Mariah laughed. "Mr. Cornell," she said loudly, "what an amusing story."

Her body was tense as she waited to see if the others would notice how close she and Ash had been standing. They seemed, however, to be more interested in the prince and quickly returned to their own conversation.

"We must be more careful," Mariah whispered. "We must show no partiality for each other."

"Do they not realize that we are friends, Mariah?"

"They believe we have only been acquainted since your arrival at Donbridge, but the dowager…" She sucked in her breath. "Let us return to more practical matters. How can I help you?"

"I would request further instruction in the proper way of dining and any other skills you believe I still require."

"How can I guess what skills you have forgotten?"

"It would be better to take no chances."

Her brow furrowed. "I can't teach you here. At Donbridge—"

"We would be under the scrutiny of the dowager, would we not?"

She didn't answer, but he saw the acknowledgment in her eyes. "You ride beautifully," she said, "and that is a skill the prince always admires. Sinjin had agreed to show you the proper mode of dress for each occasion, if it can be done discreetly. As for the rest…" She hesitated. "Do you remember how to dance?"

CHAPTER THIRTEEN

ASH REMEMBERED READING about dancing in his books, but he'd never seen a detailed description of how it was done. Waltzes, polkas, quadrilles…all words to describe movements he could only imagine.

"Will you teach me?" he asked.

"Not here," she said, glancing again at the prince's party. "Not now. But…" She seemed to reach a decision. "Tonight, after everyone has gone to bed, we shall meet on the terrace. We can practice there, if we are very quiet."

Her words were guarded, but her scent suggested that she was not nearly so reluctant as she pretended.

And he would be alone with her again.

The hours passed too slowly. The prince and his companions talked well into the night, seeking their beds only as midnight approached. Mariah bade everyone good-night and went upstairs, leaving Ash to linger by the banked drawing room fire. In the dark square of the hearth, he saw himself as a glowing ember, a spark of swift light leaving the mortal world behind.

Soon. Soon.

The very thought made his chest tighten, as if he had run for many miles.

He was waiting on the terrace when Mariah arrived. The scent of flowers and freshly cut grass was strong in the night air. The moon was bright enough to illuminate her figure; she had put on a simple dress with little of the foolish rear projection called a *bustle,* and her hair had been freed from its tight coiffure and left loosely pinned about her head. The one incongruity was the elbow-length gloves she wore. She approached Ash slowly, almost timidly.

"We must be very quiet," she said. "We shall have no music, but I will count out the beat."

Ash merely gazed at her. Every time he saw her again, no matter how brief her absence, he marveled at her beauty. Not the perfection of the Fane or of the unicorn kind, but something uniquely her own.

"Shall we begin?" she asked, as if she hadn't noticed his stare. "We shall start with a quadrille."

Her efforts to make him believe in the invisible humans dancing with them were not entirely successful. Ash was aware only of her, her grace as she circled and clasped empty air with small, strong hands. Only when she came back to him was he satisfied, and each time she had to wriggle free of his grip.

"You must not hold on so long," she scolded after the fourth figure. "It will give the lady in question the wrong impression of your regard."

"I do not mean to give a wrong impression," he said.

She stopped, faced him and looked him in the eye.

"Now," she said, "the waltz. The waltz is danced by a large group of couples. It is not only a matter of mastering the steps but of dancing amongst the other couples to create one lovely pattern." She took his hand. "This is how we begin," she said, "with my right hand holding your left."

"And not letting go."

"That is correct." She paused, her gazed fixed on his chin, and took his other hand. "You must put your right hand very lightly here," she said, setting it just above her waist. Ash felt a shudder run through her body. She placed her left hand on his opposite shoulder, barely touching, yet the fire coursed through him as if she had stroked his naked skin.

"The steps are very simple," she said. "First, imagine a triple beat. One-two-three, one-two-three. No pause between." She looked down at his feet. "Step forward with your left foot. Yes, excellent."

As he did as she asked, she stepped back with her right foot.

"Now step forward and to the right with your other foot," she said, and moved gracefully so that her motions were sublimely in harmony with his. But when he made the third movement, they became tangled together, her skirts wrapped around his legs.

"Oh," she murmured. "I think we had better start again. I shall lead this time."

She repositioned his hands, his right on her waist and his left in her right. "Now we shall try again," she said.

And then she began to move—not as he had, hesitantly following her instructions, but smoothly, inviting him to do the same. A sound came from her throat, a humming that resonated throughout his entire body. The melody was simple, and Ash clearly envisioned what Mariah meant him to do. Within moments they were sweeping about the terrace. The rush of rhythm reached deep into Ash's soul, and he saw himself running again…running with Mariah at his side.

But he, not she, must be in the lead. He stopped, eliciting a brief cry of protest from her, and adjusted their positions back to those with which they had begun. Suddenly Mariah smiled.

"Very well," she said. "Let's see how well you do now."

He did better than well. At first they waltzed in silence, Mariah looking away from him with each one-two-three. But then she began to hum again, and he felt her body loosen.

"What is this music?" he asked.

"It is by a man named Johann Strauss. The song is called 'Tales from the Vienna Wood.'"

"Is this wood far from here?"

"It lies in the world of the imagination."

"I would like to go there."

"Perhaps I will take you some day."

He thought of her imaginary wood as he carried her with him, and she was so light in his arms that he lifted her from her feet more than once.

"Oh," she said, breathless. "It has never been like this." Joy sparkled in her eyes, sheer joy in the dance, and he thought his own heart would burst. They had become so much as one that he might have waltzed her straight through the Gates of Tir-na-Nog. Waltz her there and keep her forever.

His own fancies carried him so far that he didn't notice that her song had ended until she came to a halt. She was breathing quickly, still smiling, her hair falling down over her shoulders.

"You were wonderful, Ash," she said, stepping out of his arms. "You must have danced the waltz many times before…in your other life."

"I don't remember," he murmured.

"You will."

He couldn't look away from her flushed, happy face. "Because of you," he said. "Only because of you."

"I am glad I could…if only we…" She trailed off. "We should go back to our rooms," she said, the brightness of her eyes clouding as the magic began to fade. "Tomorrow I will speak to Sinjin about your clothes, and then we shall see about the—"

He caught her hand before she could finish the sentence, pulled her toward him again. She didn't resist. Even when he lifted her arm and began to peel the glove away from her fingers, she made no protest. He worked the glove past her wrist, slipped it off and let it fall to the floor. Mariah closed her eyes and swayed as he took one of her fingers into his mouth. He licked and suckled it, then moved to the next, teasing the tip with his tongue.

"Ash," she said in a choked whisper. "This can't go on. You know it can't."

He was too busy to answer. He had tasted each finger, and now he turned her hand over and began to kiss her palm, running his tongue along each shallow crease. Mariah shuddered. "Ash, please… I beg you…"

Somewhere in the house a door closed. Mariah jumped back, her skirts swishing about her legs.

"Go," she whispered. "No one must know about this. It is our secret."

He nodded grimly. "Yes. Our secret."

She fled, and Ash bent to pick up the discarded glove, closing his eyes as he smelled her scent. Then he tucked the scrap of silk inside his waistcoat and walked slowly back inside.

IT WAS TRUE. They were actually in love.

Pamela pressed her back to the wall and remained where she was, though Cornell and Mariah had long since gone up the stairs to their rooms.

They might still be together, of course. But Pamela didn't believe Mariah was ready for that final step. She was still the tiresomely upright child Donnington had inexplicably chosen to marry.

They loved, but they were not yet lovers.

Pamela banged painfully against the French doors as she emerged from behind them, too angry to watch her step. Of course none of this had come as any surprise after what the dowager Lady Donnington had confided of her own new suspicions. But the idea that Mariah should betray Donnington with this American oaf infuriated her.

Oaf? She paused in her charge up the stairs, her hand on the banister. She had just seen Cornell dance with breathtaking grace, as if he had waltzed every day since he was a child.

His lean, muscular body had guided Mariah about the terrace as if they were both gliding on air.

No, not an oaf. A mystery. A man who made the most elementary mistakes at the dinner table, and yet could look into a woman's eyes and melt her principles as if they were no more substantial than ice on a summer's day.

"Madam?"

She started and turned. The girl she recognized as the chambermaid who had been cleaning the cottage at Donbridge—supposedly Vivian's "agent" in the observation of Lady Donnington—stood blocking Pamela's path up the staircase.

"Lady Westlake?" the girl said. "I am sorry to have disturbed you, but I—"

"What are you doing here?" Pamela asked, wondering how much the girl had seen and heard.

"Begging your pardon, ma'am, I arrived with Lady Donnington. Her own maid has come down ill, and I'm to take her place until she is well again."

"As Lady Donnington's personal maid?"

"Yes, ma'am."

Pamela laughed under her breath. Vivian must have had something to do with Alice's "coming down ill" and seeing that Nola accompanied her daughter-in-law to Rothwell. True enough, the maid had proved a disappointment until she had suggested, however improbably, that Mariah's lover appeared to resemble her husband in nearly every particular, but that had proved to be an apt observation.

Apparently the dowager must still have some use for the girl. And Mariah would continue to be unaware that a little red spider was observing her from its tiny, insignificant web.

"Your work has nearly been done for you," Pamela said disdainfully. "We know the name and nature of Mariah's lover. All you need do now is report on any changes in their relationship."

"I shall do my best, your ladyship."

There was an almost insolent edge in the girl's tone. "Thus far," Pamela said, "your best has not been good enough."

Nola curtseyed. "Yes, your ladyship. Please excuse me, your ladyship." She curtseyed again for good measure and turned in the direction of the servants' staircase.

"Oh, and, Nola," Pamela called softly. "Never forget who employs you."

"I shall not forget, ma'am." Nola bobbed her head and disappeared into the corridor. Disgruntled by the encounter, Pamela retired, her thoughts lingering on the image of Cornell slowly removing Mariah's glove from her arm. Pamela had been highly aroused by the sight and would have sought out Sinjin, if he had not been sulking in his room like a child robbed of a biscuit.

Damn him. Damn all men. Eventually she would see Ashton Cornell brought low for daring to mock Donnington with his pretensions and claims to kinship. She would find a way to expose Mariah for what she was. And she would have Sinjin completely under her thumb until she was through with him and his glorious body.

BY THE NEXT EVENING, matters were much improved. The prince seemed to have forgotten Ash's minor blunders at the dinner table, and Sinjin had generously lent Ash several suits and a fresh set of evening clothes, though he treated Ash with a distant air that suggested he didn't trust his American relative.

Mariah knew that Sinjin resented Ash's precipitous decision to reveal himself, but she had little time to talk to her brother-in-law; nor, were she to be honest, had she any particular desire to do so. She was still troubled by his relationship with Lady Westlake, especially since she was convinced that Pamela had been the real seducer and was using him for her own mysterious ends. The woman was a disgrace to her rank, and Mariah did her best not to think about what Pamela and Sinjin did when they were alone together.

In any case, Mariah couldn't spend much time worrying about Sinjin; her hands were full enough simply keeping an eye on Ash and offering "discreet" instruction where he required it.

He certainly needed none where riding was concerned. His Royal Highness, sated with the best breakfast Rothwell could provide, invited Sinjin's houseguests to join him and his retinue on a morning tour of the countryside. Ash rode so lightly and with so little effort that the prince himself commented on his ability more than once. They were in harmony again, and even Mariah could give herself up to the pleasure of enjoying the fragrant spring air from the back of her spirited mare. Occasionally she rode knee-to-knee with Ash, feeling at last that she might live up to her nickname, laughing at the foolish little things that for so long she had been unable to appreciate.

Mariah finished the ride in the best of spirits. She had almost allowed herself to forget what she believed to be Ash's true reason for desiring to become accepted in society; he still needed her. And she would continue to help him, as long as she was careful not to allow him to touch her body.

Or her heart.

Luncheon was a casual, pleasant affair, and the prince played cards for much of the afternoon, while Ash watched and learned. He did much better at dinner, looking stunningly handsome in his borrowed evening clothes, handling his cutlery with ease and propriety. He related stories of Indians on the American frontier, so smoothly told that Mariah almost suspected him of having pilfered them from a book.

Her desire to question him on the subject went unfulfilled. Sinjin had arranged an after-dinner amusement. He had employed several wandering gypsies to perform tricks, dance and tell the fortunes of his guests. The prince fell into the spirit of the thing, applauding enthusiastically after the

wild dances and observing the prettiest gypsy maiden with
an appreciative eye.

It was nearing midnight when the brilliantly clad fortune-
teller retreated into her tent at the edge of the garden behind
Rothwell. Torches lit the grounds, giving an air of ancient
ritual to the affair. The prince was first to avail himself of the
gypsy's talents; he emerged from the tent well pleased and
urged the others to follow his example. Sinjin was fourth to
enter; his face when he returned was unreadable, but Mariah
sensed that he had not liked what he'd heard, even if—as was
likely—he didn't believe such balderdash.

In contrast, Pamela seemed pleased with her consultation,
very much like a cat who had gotten into the cream.

Mariah did her best to make herself invisible, but in the end
the prince found her out and demanded she take her place at
the gypsy's table.

"Come, Lady Donnington," he said, laughing. "Surely you
are not so cowardly as to fear your fate."

"Of course I am not, sir," she said carefully. "I only wonder
how prescient such a woman can be."

"Oh, she is very good, you may take my word on it." And
with that, the prince made it impossible for her to refuse. She
lifted her chin, refusing to let the others sense her trepidation,
and marched toward the tent.

Ash intercepted her just as she reached the entrance.

"Do not go in," he said harshly in her ear. "She knows
nothing."

Mariah met his gaze. "But you haven't yet seen her."

"No morta—no one can predict the future."

"I believe you," she said, "but I have no choice."

He bared his strong, white teeth. "If she brings you unhap-
piness…"

"Why should she? As the prince said, there is nothing to
fear."

Giving him a brief smile, she entered the tent. It was dark, as was to be expected, lit only by a pair of guttering candles. The gypsy woman, in her bright layers of rags, looked up at Mariah with intense dark eyes.

"Be seated, my lady," she said in a deep, resonant voice.

Mariah sat, felt in her reticule for a few coins and laid them on the table between them.

"There is no need to continue," she said. "Let us simply wait, and then I will leave, with none the wiser."

"You cannot bribe the fates, my lady. They will not be denied."

"Perhaps I do not believe in your 'fates.'"

"Your belief is unnecessary." The woman produced a well-worn deck of cards and spread them out on the table in a specific pattern.

What she said as she read the cards was worse than anything Mariah could have imagined. When she left the tent, she found that her hands were trembling, and she could scarcely see the ground in front of her.

Ash was still waiting. He took her hand, his warm skin burning her icy palm.

"She lied," he hissed. "Do not fear what she told you."

She attempted another smile. "I don't, Ash," she said. "Stop worrying about me."

"Mr. Cornell!" the prince called from the terrace overlooking the garden. "You are the last."

Ash scowled so heavily that even Bertie must have seen the expression. "I will not," he said.

Mariah took his arm as if she were gently cajoling him. "If you wish to keep the prince's favor, you must. If you would only give up this quest for revenge—"

"I am doing these things only to make myself worthy of you."

"You *are* worthy, Ash. You have no need to—"

She broke off. Though no one on the terrace could hear their conversation, an expectant silence had fallen over the observers. Abruptly Ash spun and stepped into the tent.

When he came out again, he wore a stunned look, and his pupils were so dilated that his eyes had become bottomless abysses.

"What did she say?" Mariah whispered.

He walked past her without speaking. When he reached the terrace, he faced the prince and the other guests, sweeping his gaze across their expectant faces.

"She is a fraud," he said in a sharp, precise voice. "This female can no more predict the future than can any of you."

The prince half rose from his chair. "Now, Cornell—"

"You are all fools for believing her," Ash snapped.

Sinjin started up. "Calm yourself, Cornell. This has all been in fun. Whatever she may have said to you—"

"Lies. She accepts gold for telling you exactly what you wish to hear."

"You will not address His Royal Highness in such a tone," Lord Gothard protested, also rising. "You had best go inside. Your company is neither required nor wanted."

The prince grunted agreement, his face red and his whiskers twitching. Mariah reached the terrace as Ash charged into the house. She paused to curtsey to the prince in abashed apology, then mumbled an excuse and ran after Ash.

He was nowhere to be found. When she checked, she discovered that the mount he had brought from Donbridge was missing from the stable. With no other recourse, she waited out the rest of the night in her room, listening for his return. Nola hovered about until Mariah ordered the girl to seek her own bed.

Mariah was furious, knowing that she should have recognized the extent of Ash's agitation and done something to forestall his untoward reaction. If his intention had been to remain in the prince's favor, he had surely forfeited it now.

The next morning the prince informed Sinjin that he intended to leave for Newmarket early the following day.

A few hours later his plans went awry. He began to turn even more ruddy than usual, swayed when he walked, and soon took to his bed.

"The influenza," his personal physician opined when they sent for him. "It is fortunately a very mild form of the disease. There is nothing to be done but give His Royal Highness complete rest, fluids and simple foods until the disease has run its course."

Mariah soon understood why the prince was not an exemplary invalid; he was an active man, unused to confinement. He fretted and complained to the gentlemen of his escort, insisting he was better, only to fall back on his pillows weaker than before; called irritably for first one dish and then another, straining the kitchen's capacity; and found it impossible to maintain his generally amiable air.

He had been ill for two days when Ash returned to Rothwell at last, subdued and very quiet. As soon as he learned of Bertie's affliction, he asked for an audience with the prince. He was denied the privilege, but a few hours later Mariah heard, to her astonishment, laughter coming from the prince's chambers.

Sinjin came for her. "You won't believe it," he said, "but Ash got in to see Bertie. They seem to have become the best of friends."

"But how?" Mariah asked.

"Come see for yourself."

He led Mariah up the stairs to the prince's suite at the end of the corridor. The door was open, and a number of the prince's men stood just inside, chuckling or exclaiming as a familiar voice spoke from inside the room.

"Sinjin," Mariah said, "what has he done?"

"To hear Lord Russell tell it," Sinjin said, "your Mr. Cornell has cured Bertie."

CHAPTER FOURTEEN

C<small>URED</small> B<small>ERTIE</small>?

Mariah walked closer to the door and peered in over Sir Jeremy Ackland's shoulder. The prince was sitting in a chair by the bed, clearly whole and hearty, his skin a normal color and his gestures vigorous.

"Truly remarkable," he was saying to someone just out of Mariah's sight. "I had always understood that the Apache are the most bloodthirsty of all the American tribes."

"Not as bloodthirsty as one might suppose," Ash said. "What skills I possess, they taught me."

"And those savage skills work damned well, by Jove," Bertie said, then caught a glimpse of Mariah. "I beg your pardon, ma'am," he said with his usual courtesy.

"Not at all, sir," Mariah said. She glanced at Ash, holding pride of place in a chair opposite the prince's. "I am grateful that you are recovered."

"So am I, so am I." Bertie beamed at the room in general. "Ah, Sinjin. I trust that your chef is prepared to produce an excellent dinner tonight."

"I assure you that M. Mézières will be as pleased as I to celebrate your return from the grave," Sinjin quipped.

The prince belted out a laugh as he heaved himself up from his chair. "For now, I wish to go outside. Will you join us, Lady Donnington, and hear more of your cousin's entertaining stories of life on the American frontier?"

"With pleasure, sir," she said. But try as she might, she couldn't get close to Ash again. His popularity had taken such a turn for the better that every one of the prince's companions seemed determined to keep their new favorite occupied.

Only after everyone had finally gone to bed did she manage to corner Ash where he sat in Sinjin's library.

"How did you do it?" she asked. "How did you cure the prince?"

Ash had risen at her entrance. "Lady Donnington," he said, "I am sorry that I was not able to speak to you earlier. It was not of my design."

She moved closer, puzzled by this inexplicable new formality. "What is wrong?"

He hesitated, barely meeting her eyes. "Nothing is wrong."

"You have certainly achieved what you intended," she said. "You have the prince's unqualified approval, and this time I doubt that anything you can do will lessen it. How did you cure him? If you can simply explain…"

"I cannot," he said, meeting her gaze. "If I had an explanation, I would tell you."

"You learned this from the Apaches?" she asked incredulously.

"No," he said. "I never met an Apache. I never lived in the West at all."

"I beg your pardon?"

He continued to hold her eyes with his. "My entire 'past' was all derived from the books I read, and from what you told me of my probable origins," he said. "My past, my stories of the West…all—"

"Lies?" she whispered, too stunned to move.

"Necessary deception."

She sat down hard in the nearest chair. "Why?"

"I could not remain a prisoner any longer." His eyes were

dull with sorrow, and yet a fire burned beneath the veil of sadness. "Even before I met the prince, I knew I could only begin to find the truth if I made myself acceptable to you, the dowager and anyone else I might encounter."

Mariah could scarcely believe what she was hearing. "You were…always acceptable to me, Ash—"

"Was I?"

She hadn't forgotten her assumption that he was mad. But that was before she'd come to know him, respect him, love…

"Was any of it the truth?" she asked, clutching at her stomach. "Surely…some of it must be, or it would not have come so easily to you."

He didn't answer immediately but wandered about the room, randomly touching the spines of Sinjin's books. "The gypsy knew of my deception," he said. "She said that I could not keep it hidden for long, especially from you."

"And so you are now compelled to be honest with me?"

His fingertips stroked a volume of Greek philosophy as they had once caressed her skin. "I did not wish to burden you with the truth."

"And is that why you were so angry on the terrace?" she asked. "Because you wouldn't be able to keep up your pretense?" She twisted her hands together in her lap. "What else did she tell you?"

"That I could not continue without your aid."

"I see. And *that* infuriated you."

"You have already done enough."

"Evidently I have done too much."

Suddenly he was beside her, so close that he needn't have done more then extend his hand to touch her.

"You know I care for you, Merry," he said, "but I would not further disturb your life."

"You…you couldn't…" The memory of what the gypsy had told her was so vivid that for a moment she was unable to speak.

You love one who will betray you. Yet you will not see the trap until it is too late.

She had not been enraged at the woman's calm statement. She had been terrified, but had hidden her fear so successfully that no one but Ash had seen it.

The betrayal had already come true. Ash had lied to her. He had not trusted her, whatever his excuses.

You will not see the trap until it is too late. The trap of love, into which she had stumbled without recognizing how very near she was to falling.

Ash had said he "cared for" her. But to care was not to love. At least she could conceal her love, something she could not have managed if Ash returned her feelings. She was fortunate indeed.

She emerged from her painful reverie and looked up at him. He was standing in a glaring light that seemed to come from nowhere, far too bright for the gas lamps Sinjin had installed at Rothwell. His outline was blurred, wrong somehow, and his figure was white.

She had seen this before. Then she had thought it a trick of the light, a temporary affliction of the eye, a quirk of the imagination. For the shape was not that of a human but something larger, something that stood on more than two feet, and from its head…

Beware my horn.

Covering her eyes, she sank deeper into the chair. This was *not* madness, no matter what the gypsy had said. The fairies had not been real. They were but illusions brought on by her guilt over being with Ash.

You will have the choice between defeat and victory. Choice. That was the one word she could cling to, even as she glimpsed a vision just like the ones her mother had claimed to have seen a thousand times over.

Unicorns do not exist. I choose not to see it. I choose…

Immediately the radiance vanished and Ash stood in the ordinary dim light, staring at her with incomprehension.

"Mariah?"

She shuddered once and rose to her feet.

"What do you intend to do now?" she asked calmly.

He watched her in silence for a moment longer, then bowed his head, as if he were actually afraid of her disapproval. "The prince has invited me to Marlborough House after his return from the races," he said. "Will you come with me?"

Before, he had demanded that she go with him to Rothwell. Now he asked. Asked humbly, as if he had really meant it when he'd said that he feared "disturbing" her life.

As if he had not already done just that.

"I have not been invited," she said.

"But you have. I asked, and the prince was happy to extend the invitation."

He had thought of everything. "I will not help you seek revenge against my husband," she said.

"That is not what I want of you, Mariah."

What *could* he want, then, now that he'd stolen her heart? He had become so adept at prevarication that he could deceive her with no difficulty, and he continued to learn new tactics with frightful ease.

If he wanted…what she had shamelessly let him take, those stolen kisses and caresses, she could not let herself give them again. If she did, she would be no better than Lady Westlake. No better than a whore.

Then there was Marlborough House itself. She understood that it was the very center of high society, as modern as the queen's court was mired in the past. Mariah had no business moving in such a milieu. In spite of her father's strenuous efforts, she'd never joined New York's upper crust in their amusements. All her time had been spent nursing Mama at home and visiting her in the asylums where she had spent so many days of her final years. Even if the Four Hundred had opened their gates to the daughter of a self-made man, she wouldn't have belonged among them.

No. She ought to return to Donbridge and wait for Donnington. She ought never to have left. But her treacherous heart held her tied to Ash with bonds that could not be broken. Not until this drama played itself out to the very end— whatever that end might be.

Face your fears, Mariah. Choose your own victory.

She looked up into Ash's eyes. "Yes," she said. "I will go with you."

THE DOWAGER WAS not pleased when Mariah announced her intention to accept the prince's invitation to Marlborough House.

"You cannot go," Vivian said as they sat in Donbridge's quiet little morning room. "Donnington would forbid it."

"Surely the earl could not object to his wife being in favor with the Prince of Wales," Mariah answered, letting her cup of tea grow cold on the saucer beside her.

Vivian all but gritted her teeth. "And is *he* going, as well?" she asked.

"Mr. Cornell was also invited, but we will not be traveling together."

"As if that should make any difference! You will be together at Marlborough House, a place of scandal and immorality."

Mariah had had enough. "Along with many others," she said. "I no more approve of scandal and immorality than you do, Vivian. I shall be in no danger at Marlborough House… unlike your good friend Lady Westlake."

For once Vivian was at a loss for words. She had fully understood the reference to Lady Westlake, Mariah was certain. Their conspiracy had been found out.

Mariah rose. "I will come back the moment I hear that my husband has returned," she said, and left the room.

The dowager refused to speak to her daughter-in-law until the packing was complete. Mariah's maid, Alice, had suddenly, though not unexpectedly, left her position after having expressed dissatisfaction with Mariah's apparent indifference to her services. Mariah was happy to make Nola's new position permanent.

Only when she and Nola were climbing into the brougham did the dowager make an appearance.

"Kindly conduct yourself as the wife of the Earl of Donnington," she said icily.

There was no goodbye, not even of the most formal variety. With Nola sitting in the seat opposite Mariah and the trunks firmly stowed, the carriage set off.

The journey to London passed quickly. Mariah spent nearly every moment of it wondering how she could possibly fit in among the prince's Set, who had shown themselves to be both sophisticated and demanding.

And she was worried about Ash.

Yet when she arrived at Marlborough House, nearly every rational thought flew out of her head. The house was palatial in its scope, a vast brick edifice with scores of tall windows, its elegant interior filled with paintings by famous artists, including a vast Battle of Blenheim spread across the walls of the main saloon.

Mariah was efficiently taken in hand by experienced servants and assigned a lovely room in the north wing. She had no time to be afraid. She was soon granted an audience with the Princess of Wales—Princess Alix, as her intimates called her—who was as lovely and gracious as any princess ought to be. She and the prince had introduced an egalitarian element to the royal court by inviting into their home those generally excluded from more formal society: artists and musicians, the untitled nouveau riche, Americans and foreigners of all descriptions.

Only on the second day, while she was still becoming used to her grand surroundings, did Mariah catch a glimpse of Ash among the bevy of the prince's familiar friends. He seemed to have adapted immediately to his new surroundings. He had a natural elegance that drew all eyes to him, and everyone was intensely curious about his background and his resemblance to the absent Earl of Donnington.

His popularity had only been increased by the talk of how he had "cured" the prince at Rothwell. He was kept busy by members of the Set who were eager to experience his Red Indian "healing abilities" for themselves. He disposed of such minor maladies as warts and colds, and his reputation spread so rapidly that Mariah was lucky if she caught sight of him once a day, even in passing.

She quickly saw that she had been right in her instincts: any aid she might offer Ash now would be entirely superfluous. Instead *she* was the one in need of assistance, a country mouse shivering in the lair of a pride of elegant lions.

For the prince's court, while undoubtedly glamorous, was no fairy tale come to life. Bertie obviously found his older lady friends to be much more engaging than an inexperienced newlywed, and even the other American guests seemed to find Mariah's company uninteresting. She had nothing new to tell them, no store of witty tales to provoke their appreciative laughter. At times she was so overwhelmed that she found herself merely observing the vigorous, often unconventional, amusements Marlborough House had to offer: the frequent balls, nightly card games, riding every morning on Rotten Row, and various unusual entertainments to keep the easily bored prince diverted.

"You must not take it so to heart, my dear," said the very popular Lady Strickland, American wife of the Marquess of

Strickland, as she and Mariah stood near the wall of one of Marlborough House's many drawing rooms and listened to the sparkling conversation surrounding the Prince of Wales. "At least Bertie welcomes American upstarts like us, which is more than can be said of the queen."

Mariah only half heard her words. She was watching Ash, who had just finished relating some amusing bon mot that had his audience laughing and several of the more beautiful women watching him with a predatory eye.

"Your husband's cousin grows more popular by the hour," Lady Strickland remarked. She smiled teasingly. "Is that jealousy I see on your face, Lady Donnington?"

"Jealousy?" Mariah said lightly. "I am Lord Donnington's wife. And, as you pointed out, Mr. Cornell is my cousin by marriage."

"Ah." Lady Strickland chuckled. "Well, my dear," she said, taking Mariah's arm, "you must let me guide you in these complicated matters. You shall soon learn to find your way."

Her reassurance was far from comforting. Mariah knew that she was losing Ash; he moved among the highest ranks with a sense of easy superiority that no one seemed disposed to resent. He had almost begged her to come to Marlborough, but now she never saw him. It felt almost like a second betrayal.

Only if you are stupid enough not to realize that he has done you a tremendous service. You are safe now—unless you expect him to love you.

Such sensible thoughts made very little difference to her irrational feelings. When Sinjin arrived a week later, he greeted her with his usual courtesy, but it soon became very apparent that his mind was on something else: Lady Westlake, who arrived the day after.

Mariah quickly realized that they were pretending to be only slight acquaintances in public while carrying on their affair in the very precincts of Marlborough House. No one seemed to notice or object, and before another week had passed, she began to understand why.

Vivian had tried to warn her of Society's ways, but she didn't fully comprehend until, waking from a dream of Ash, she crept down to the extensive library in search of a book and overheard two maids gossiping about Lord Russell's affair with the Viscountess Stapledon.

Nola was waiting in the corridor when Mariah returned to her room.

"Nola," she said, "what are you doing here?"

Her agitation must have been apparent, for Nola suggested they go into Mariah's room. "I did not mean to disturb you, your ladyship," she said. "I was just returning from the kitchen."

The explanation was odd, given that Nola would not ordinarily pass through the guests' part of the house if she were coming from the kitchen, but Mariah let it pass. She was glad to have the company.

"Nola," she said, drawing the maid into a seat, "what do you know of Lady Stapledon and Lord Russell?"

The girl averted her gaze. "I have not met them, your ladyship."

"But what gossip have you heard? Do the servants say…?" She flushed. "Do they say that Lord Russell and the viscountess are often seen together when others aren't about?"

Hunching lower in her seat, Nola nodded. "Everyone knows, your ladyship," she said. "It happens all the time here, ladies and gentlemen meeting at night."

"Married ladies and gentlemen?"

Nola nodded again, her smattering of freckles darkening in embarrassment. Feeling a fool, Mariah let the girl go. She should have left it at that: servants' gossip that she ought to ignore. But she was certain now that Vivian must know about Sinjin and Pamela, for all her fine talk of scandal and immorality.

Are you not guilty of infidelity yourself? she thought.

In her mind, perhaps. But not like Sinjin and Pamela, or Lord Russell and Lady Stapledon. She could guess what they were doing when they were alone, though she tried to avoid imagining the details. She and Ash had never gone beyond a kiss. In fact, Ash had not even approached her in a week, let alone shown her any sign of affection.

She had been virtually accused of behavior that the dowager hoped would ruin her reputation, yet others carried out their illicit *amours* without apparent consequence. If she could be near Ash and not give in to her baser nature, why should others not exhibit the same control?

Angry and desperate to understand, she approached Lady Strickland the next morning.

"You seem shocked, my dear," the marchioness said with a sigh. "I was, as well, when I first arrived in England."

"But you are not shocked any longer?"

"I fear that constant perturbation would be very tiring at Marlborough House, Lady Donnington. Have you not realized that by now?"

"But this…this isn't just flirtation. Surely others here disapprove?"

"Not as many as you and I might wish." The other woman laid her hand on Mariah's arm. "Buck up, my dear. All we can do is remember that we are Americans, not members of the English peerage who regard their marriages as less than sacrosanct." She smiled with a conspiratorial bob of her head. "We Yankees must stick together."

Relieved that she'd found at least one person who shared her distaste for the immoral activities that went on at Marlborough House, Mariah reminded herself again why it was fortunate that she and Ash saw little of each other. But later that same day, while she was wandering about the grounds, Lady Westlake came to find her.

"Good afternoon, Lady Donnington," Pamela said, matching Mariah's stride. "I meant to speak to you as soon as I arrived at Marlborough House, but I have been kept very busy."

"No doubt," Mariah murmured, continuing on without slowing her pace.

"And how have you been, my dear? Are you enjoying your stay here?"

"I am finding it very interesting," she said, "though not perhaps as interesting as you do."

"I have been here before, of course," Pamela said. "You cannot be expected to understand all the working of the prince's court."

"There are some things about it I'd be happy not to understand."

"Indeed?" Pamela made a show of considering Mariah's declaration. "Ah, yes. I overheard your conversation with Lady Strickland."

"I would not have believed that eavesdropping was quite the thing, even in this place, Lady Westlake."

"You will soon learn that there are few secrets at Marlborough House, Lady Donnington."

Especially where you are concerned, Mariah thought. "Then you are aware that Lady Strickland shares my opinion about certain…activities here," she said.

"Your naïveté is occasionally charming," Pamela said, "but at most times rather tiresome."

"Because I find blatant misconduct objectionable?"

"Even our prince is very fond of the ladies."

Fond of the ladies. That had been obvious to Mariah from her first day at Marlborough House. But Pamela was clearly implying something very different from mere "fondness." To think that the man who might set the course for the entire nation could be unfaithful to his beautiful wife…

"It was the way I was raised, you see," Mariah said

coldly. "My father remained faithful to my mother until the day she died."

"How exemplary. Your mother must have been a captivating woman."

Mariah's throat became a narrow tunnel that would hardly permit words to escape. "She was strong and intelligent."

"Qualities so few men appreciate. I take it that your mother is no longer living?" Pamela smiled. "Let me advise you, my dear. Whatever you may have been taught, one of the most important rules you must learn is that it is neither wise nor polite to peer too closely into the private lives of others."

"I should pretend to approve of what I believe to be wrong?"

"You are a fine one to talk, my dear." Pamela's smile broadened. "Perhaps you envy those like Lady Stapledon. Perhaps you wish you had the courage to go to Mr. Cornell and enjoy with him what you've been longing to do since you first met."

"I wish nothing of the kind," Mariah said. "And I do not envy you, Lady Westlake. I certainly do not envy Sinjin."

There was no blush, no outward sign of offense, in Lady Westlake save for a slight pallor to her already fair skin. "And I, my girl, do not envy you."

"Donnington has yet to return. Matters may not turn out quite as you might wish."

Without offering a response, Lady Westlake walked away.

Shaken by the encounter, Mariah did her best over the next few days to ignore the behavior that had become so evident to her. That soon became impossible. She learned to recognize the men and women who were engaging in clandestine liaisons. She heard the faint tread of feet on the carpeted corridors after midnight, and observed the sly glances certain favorites of the prince gave each other in the midst of otherwise innocent diversions. All the participants were married; many, so she heard, had indulgent spouses engaged in affairs themselves.

But what really prevented her from forgetting what she observed was not Lady Westlake's ongoing affair with Sinjin, nor those of any of the offending guests. It was the treachery of her own thoughts…the thoughts she should never have allowed to enter her mind again. She felt the atmosphere that suffused Marlborough House every night in the bedroom corridors and imagined herself as one of the conspirators creeping to her lover's room. She tossed and turned as if in a fever, despising herself as much she did any of the others.

"Perhaps you envy those like Lady Stapledon," Pamela had said. "Perhaps you wish you had the courage to go to Mr. Cornell and enjoy with him what you've been longing to do since you first met."

She hated the all-too-familiar and unwelcome sensations stirring in her body, the wetness between her thighs whenever she envisioned being with Ash again.

You will have the choice between defeat and victory. Was *this* what the gypsy had meant? She was so close to defeat, to losing every standard she lived by.

The best thing she could do was to leave Marlborough House. With Ash so far away, the temptation would end. But, in doing so, she would be admitting that her own self-discipline was as weak as she secretly feared. She couldn't bear the thought. So she put off the decision to go, determining with greater resolution to rely on Lady Strickland and make the acquaintance of other respectable parties like her.

Then the fairies returned.

CHAPTER FIFTEEN

MARIAH HAD TRIED not to think of the fairies since she had seen them at Donbridge after Ash's kiss in the library. Once again she attempted to dismiss them as the creation of a mind disturbed by her indecent thoughts of him.

And once again logic did her no good.

The creatures followed her as she walked through the halls of Marlborough House, haunted her in her bedchamber when she tried to sleep, and tormented her during her strolls about the grounds and along the adjoining London streets. No one else seemed to see them, of course. Just as no one else had ever seen her mother's visions.

Nola noticed her perturbation. "Begging your pardon, ma'am, but you seem upset," she said one day as she was helping Mariah put on a morning dress.

Mariah had become accustomed to Nola's mother-hen concern for her and bore it stoically. "I am simply a little tired. Life at Marlborough House can be demanding."

"It can indeed," the maid said, stepping back from her work. The fairies chose that moment to reappear, and Mariah batted them away without thinking.

"What is it, your ladyship?" Nola asked.

"You don't see...something flying around us?"

"Insects, ma'am? No, I don't see them. Shall I call someone to check the room?"

"That isn't necessary, Nola." Mariah forced her hands to

remain still and went down to breakfast a few minutes later, struggling to blunt her panic.

She could not go to Ash for comfort. She understood that very clearly. Searching desperately for diversions, she overcame her distaste and began to join the other guests in their amusements.

The relief was wonderful. She began to enjoy the card games and morning rides, and even the prince took notice of her again. The fairies retreated in defeat, and she began to feel almost normal. Missing Ash became less of a burden on her heart. It was inevitable that she should find herself preparing to attend the next ball to be given by the prince and princess.

Nola was pleased. She had obviously found her mistress's reclusiveness disturbing, both because she wanted her part in making Lady Donnington beautiful—a task she obviously relished—and because she was genuinely concerned for Mariah's happiness.

The girl need not worry any longer, Mariah thought. Her own state of mind had vastly improved, and she intended that it should improve even further at the ball that night.

But if Ash were there…

It would be no different than the past three weeks, she told herself, when they had seen so little of each other. She would find it excellent practice to meet with him in a neutral environment and exchange the most basic pleasantries without the heat of emotion behind them.

"Your ladyship?" Nola asked. "What gown will you wear tonight?"

"The emerald velvet, I think," she said, as if such thoughts were all that occupied her, "with the lace *tablier.*"

It was one gown among several that Donnington had purchased for her before their marriage, but she'd never had a chance to wear it. Doing so now was a reminder to herself of her marriage vows and, at the same time, proof that she did not need her absent husband's permission to dress just as she chose.

"A lovely choice, your ladyship," Nola said with an air of satisfaction. "Shall I call for a light supper?"

Mariah knew that the ball would go on until well after midnight, and that only finger food would be served before a very late supper. She certainly didn't want to be distracted by hunger until then.

"That is a very good idea," she said. "But very light, mind. I can't be bulging out of my corset."

Nola laughed and left the room. Alone, Mariah stared into the mirror above her dressing table. Her face looked pale. She pinched her cheeks, but the color faded all too quickly. She considered the lip rouge she had bought but never dared use. Perhaps tonight was the night.

She experimented with her hair until Nola returned with scones, cream and cucumber sandwiches. Mariah picked at the food while Nola began arranging her coiffure. She had chosen a looser style than was strictly fashionable, but in a fit of defiance against convention, Mariah let her have her way. Black curls framed her face, and Nola wove tiny artificial flowers through her hair. There would be no feathers, bows or bands tonight.

Dreading, as always, this particular portion of the dressing regimen, Mariah stood very still and allowed Nola to tighten the laces of her corset over her cambric chemise.

The muslin petticoats came next. Nola straightened the flounces to perfection. The bustle followed, a padded monstrosity buttoned to the corset.

Then there were the skirts, piled one atop another, the pleated faille underskirt and velvet overskirts draped about the hips and bustle in elaborate layers. The matching bodice was lace-trimmed, with a deep neckline and tiny velvet flowers twined about the dropped shoulders.

Mariah gathered up her fan and put on her gloves, aware that she looked, in her own way, beautiful.

Not for the prince. Not for the ladies of Marlborough House. And certainly not for Ash. *For herself.* Because she was real, living in the real world.

The ballroom was always lovely, but tonight, on the occasion of the birthday of one of the prince's lady friends, the room was even more beautiful, dressed with festoons of flowers and a vast froth of lace like the foam on ocean waves. Everyone was in high spirits, from the intense young artist in his unconventional velvet frock coat to the handsomely dressed ladies clustered about the subject of the ball.

Mariah went at once to join them. Thanks to Lady Strickland, they welcomed her promptly enough, too much concerned with their own appearances to consider her a rival—as if she would compete for any of their admirers. Lady Westlake was standing beside a portly gentleman with a yellow beard and a smile that displayed far too many teeth. She appeared to be dreadfully bored as the gentleman tried to charm her, but when she noticed Mariah, she smiled.

"If you will excuse me, Sir Rudolph," she said to the gentleman in an offhand manner, and came to meet Mariah. "What a lovely dress!" she exclaimed. "It suits your eyes and hair so very well, Lady Donnington."

Mariah was aware that she was in a public place and could hardly cut Pamela as she so longed to do. Instead, she searched for a similarly insincere compliment. Pamela's dress was scarlet and black, a startling combination that set off her golden hair and made it blaze like a fire above her very low décolleté. No one else could have worn such a thing without attracting criticism. On Lady Westlake, it was a triumph.

And an unerring emblem of her character.

"You will be the envy of every woman in the room," Mariah said without the slightest emotion.

"What a charming thing to say," Pamela said, snapping open her fan. "I hope Sinjin will agree." Before Mariah could think of a suitable answer, Lady Westlake spoke again.

"My," she said, "but it is already so warm. In a moment I shall go stand beside the ice swan. Perhaps it will cool me."

"It is a lovely sculpture," Mariah said, determined to keep the conversation civil. "Do you know Lady Baddeley well?"

"I find her quite a bore." Lady Westlake stood a little taller and looked around the room. "Where is Mr. Cornell, I wonder?" she purred. "It would be a pity for him to miss such an event."

"He did not speak to me about it," Mariah said.

"Indeed. Why should he?" Lady Westlake took Mariah's arm. "Come, let us go fetch some punch. I'm sure it will be just the ticket."

Trapped by the demands of basic courtesy, Mariah went along.

Pamela poured them each a glass of punch.

"Whom shall you dance with?" she asked. "Lord Russell is particularly handsome tonight, as is Mr. Denham. Though you must take care with both of them."

"I was under the impression that Lord Russell's interests are otherwise engaged."

The older woman tapped Mariah's arm with her fan. "He *is* one of those dreadful sinners, is he not?" She lifted her head. "Ah, the music has started. And here comes Mr. Denham to claim your hand."

Knowing that Mr. Denham was not one of those rumored to be conducting an illicit affair, Mariah was glad to accept his offer. He was an excellent dancer, and as she, who had always adored the waltz, was able to match him in grace, they had a lovely turn about the room. Other couples flashed by, but Mariah simply gave herself up to the dance.

Until she began to remember another time and place, a silent terrace, a different hand at her waist…

Something drew her glance to the other side of the room. Ash was standing near the prince, watching her intently. Their gazes met, but Mariah caught herself before she could lose her place in the waltz, and at last the dance came to an end. Mr. Denham bowed and escorted her to the chairs along the wall. Mariah was too dazed to do more than offer the briefest curtsey.

"May I have the honor of the next dance?"

She looked up into Ash's face. As unlikely as it seemed, he was more handsome than ever before, with a calm and ease that could only come from perfect confidence.

She ought to have found an excuse to refuse. But she could not appear to be discourteous, and she knew she must face him—and her own weakness.

"I would be delighted," she said.

He smiled as he led her out to the floor. He moved like something inhuman, like the fairies, like the unicorn of her visions. His hand was firm on her waist, and as the dance began, she was no longer certain if the sound she heard was the rhythmic beat of the waltz or the drumming of her own heart.

I have missed you, she thought. *Oh, how I have missed you.* But she maintained her silence as they twirled around the room, trying not to look into Ash's eyes and failing utterly.

"You have been enjoying your stay here?" he asked at last, his voice outshining Strauss with its music.

"Very much," she said. "And you?"

"I have learned a great deal."

And without my help. She gave him a determined smile. "Have you made any progress in recovering your memory?"

"A little."

He didn't elaborate, and she didn't inquire further. She could scarcely think at all, enveloped in the warmth of his grip and that unique masculine scent. No one must ever know how swiftly her body reacted to the nearness of his.

He leaned closer as the waltz spun toward its finale. "Mariah," he said against her ear, "what has come between us?"

"You have moved well beyond what I can teach," she said. "This is your world now."

"But it is not yours."

"It need not be, Ash. Not if you've found your place."

"I have no place without you."

She flinched in his arms. "If that were true, this would not be the first time we have truly conversed in three weeks."

"I did not wish to stay away from you. I only—"

The final beats of the waltz broke abruptly into silence. Mariah tried to pull away, but Ash kept his grip on her hand.

"Do not dance with anyone else," he said softly.

"Is that a command, Your Royal Highness?"

He seemed to miss her irony. "There are no men in this room worthy of you."

"But there are plenty of women worthy of you. Enjoy them."

She worked her hand free and moved quickly toward the chairs. Oh, yes. Let Ash enjoy the ladies he had charmed so well. And she would enjoy this ball without giving him another thought.

But it was not to be. She danced a quadrille and a polka with two different and very presentable partners, but her mind refused to obey her will. Ash's gaze was on her every moment, even when he danced with the loveliest women of the prince's Set. Sinjin claimed her hand for the Schottische, but it was very clear that her brother-in-law was distracted by the presence of Lady Westlake, who flirted with one man and then another as if her lover didn't exist.

By the sixth dance, Mariah recognized the futility of remaining at the ball even a few minutes longer. She was halfway to the door when a man intercepted her. She tried to move past him, but somehow he was in front of her again, smiling with such sympathy that she was compelled to give him a second glance. And then a third.

He was attractive, like many men in the room. But unlike most, he was clean-shaven like Sinjin and Ash. And his face…

Ash was undeniably handsome, but there was a strength of masculinity about him that removed any hint of the feminine in his face or manner. This man was simply gorgeous, like a romantic poet, with his long, fair hair, his strangely colorful garments, and eyes more silver than green. He moved as gracefully as Ash, something she would have thought impossible.

"Do you find it too warm, ma'am?" he asked in a lilting voice. "Perhaps I might fetch you a drink, or escort you out to the terrace?"

His forwardness deserved a brisk refusal, but she could not look away. "I do not find it too warm," she said. "I merely sought a few moments of privacy."

He laughed, the sound as silvery as his eyes. "Privacy? At one of Bertie's balls?" He searched her eyes. "I am sorry, Lady Donnington. We have not been properly introduced. I am Julius Caber."

Mariah had never heard the name, yet there was something familiar about him. Something she couldn't put her finger on, no matter how much she tried.

"Mr. Caber," she said with an inclination of her head. "I am Lady Donnington, as you are obviously aware."

"How could a man not know of one of the most beautiful women at Marlborough House?" he asked, reaching for her hand. He kissed it, and she could feel the warmth of his breath through her glove. "If you can spare the time, will you do me the honor of a dance?"

"Mr. Caber…"

"Bertie can confirm my credentials, if you wish," he said.

"That is not necessary. It's just that—"

"Please don't deny me, Lady Donnington. It is only one dance."

She permitted Mr. Caber to lead her onto the dance floor, where the other couples were gathering as a new waltz began.

If she had found Ash to be a superb dancer, he was a mere apprentice compared to Caber. They seemed to fly across the floor. At last she had been shaken free of her melancholy. At last she could forget the invisible ties that held her to the man across the room.

Only as the music drew to a close did she noticed that everyone in the room was staring at them.

Caber didn't seem to notice the stares at all, nor the whispers that buzzed from couple to couple. Someone tittered. Bertie stood with a lady on his arm, watching Mariah like the others. Even his pleasant face wore a mask of bewilderment.

"Mr. Caber," she whispered, "what is wrong? Why are they…?"

He didn't answer. He had vanished, no more solid than London fog, and she could find no sign of him anywhere in the room.

"Dear Lady Donnington." Lady Westlake was suddenly at her side, her voice all consolation. "You are ill. I shall accompany you up to your room."

"I am not ill!" Mariah said. "What is the matter? What have I done?"

"Nothing, my dear. You only require a little rest."

"Tell me what is going on!"

Pamela sighed, took Mariah's arm and began leading her toward the double doors that led to the hall outside. "Do you really not know?" she asked. "You were dancing alone. Quite alone."

Mariah was certain she hadn't heard the other woman correctly. "I beg your pardon?"

"You behaved as if you had a partner, but there was no one there. You laughed and held out your arms and danced in a most elegant fashion, but—"

"What do you mean, I was alone? Mr. Caber invited me to dance."

"Mr. Caber? I am not familiar with the name." Lady Westlake steered Mariah out into the hall. "Clearly you are overtired. A good night's sleep will surely cure what ails you."

"No," Mariah said, batting Pamela away. "You're lying."

"Even if I were," Lady Westlake said, "I'm quite certain that Lady Strickland would tell you the truth. Shall I fetch her? Shall I collect the opinions of the entire ballroom?"

Mariah made her way to the nearest chair. Lady Westlake might lie to her, but she wouldn't mention Lady Strickland if she believed the other woman would contradict her account.

There had been no partner, no Mr. Caber. He had existed only in her imagination, just like the fairies—and she had displayed herself, her madness, in front of society's best and brightest.

I am not mad! There is some explanation. Some other reason.

She rose, clinging to her dignity, and met Pamela's gaze. "I will excuse myself to the prince," she said.

"That is hardly necessary, my dear. I will make my apologies for you."

Mariah could guess what such apologies would consist of. Ignoring the other woman's offer, she turned and walked into the ballroom. The buzz of gossip had begun to fade, but her reappearance quieted all the voices at once.

She approached Lady Strickland. "Lady Strickland," she said, "I am sorry to have caused such a commotion."

The marchioness gave her a frigid smile. "My dear, your high spirits might better have been spent in engaging conversation than in mocking everyone in this room."

Mariah was stunned. "It was not mockery, Lady Strickland. It was…it was only—"

But the older woman was already turning away, and the cut was as deliberate as anything Mariah had ever experienced. She looked around the ballroom. They could not *all* believe that her behavior was some sort of playacting or mockery. But the curious, disapproving and even sympathetic eyes refused to meet hers for more than a moment, and even the prince pretended not to notice her.

Isn't their disapproval better than their belief that I am mad?

She backed away from Lady Strickland and her circle of friends, lifting her chin high as she walked toward the door. Familiar warmth rushed over her as Ash took possession of her arm.

"May I escort you, Lady Donnington?" he asked.

"It is not necessary," she said.

"You should not be alone."

"But I wish to be alone." Nevertheless, she allowed him to support her until they were in the empty corridor and then faced him squarely. "You saw what occurred."

"Yes. You surprised them." He touched her cheek with the back of his hand. "I was not surprised."

"Why not? Because *you* think I am…I am—"

He leaned into her, his lips against her hair. "Mariah," he murmured. "What is it? What is wrong?"

She almost laughed. "Why should you think there is anything wrong? I merely danced all about the ballroom in the arms of an invisible gentleman."

"He was not invisible to you."

She could not think of any response, especially an honest one, that would do anything but lend credence to her private fears. "I must leave," she said. "It is time that I returned to Donbridge."

"No. I will speak to them. I will tell them—"

"No!" A flush of heat started in Mariah's toes and worked up to her face. "I am very well. I…" Her hands began to tremble, and then the tremors spread throughout her body until she could no longer stand.

A dark veil fell behind her eyes. The last thing she remembered was Ash catching her in his arms.

SHE WOKE QUITE ALONE in her own chamber. Nola had evidently retired to her own small room in the female servants' quarters, but Mariah knew she had been there; her shawl lay across a chair pulled close to the bed, and an empty teacup, evidently forgotten, stood on the small side table. Mariah couldn't possibly have undressed herself and put on her nightclothes without assistance.

How long had it been? Mariah sat up, swallowing the unpleasant taste in her mouth, and found that her dizziness wasn't completely gone.

Neither were the fairies. They floated around her head like dust motes that had escaped the maid's mop and broom. They fled the wave of her hand and then returned, their tiny voices piping.

She forced herself to get up, nearly fell, and righted herself again. The night table and chair provided some support until she could reach the washstand, where she splashed her face and rubbed it with a towel until her skin was pink. There were deep circles under her eyes. She looked ten years older than her age.

Just as mother had before she died.

Mariah blinked the tears from her eyes. Her best hope was to return to Donbridge and seclusion. If the worst happened, she could hide it there better than anywhere else.

She half stumbled back to the bed and put on her dressing gown, pulling the sash tight. She had just finished when she heard a tap at the door.

It must be Nola. She didn't really want to see anyone, but she couldn't ignore the young woman who had so obviously tried to help.

She opened the door. There was no one there. The corridor seemed empty until she saw a ghostly form moving away. She bit her lip.

"Nola?"

The figure paused and looked back. In the light of the candle Mariah held, she could clearly make out the face of Lady Strickland. Another door opened, and Mr. Denham stepped out into the hall in a state of undress.

For a few seconds they stared at Mariah. Then Lady Strickland hastily walked away, and Mr. Denham closed his door.

Nauseated, Mariah closed her own door and leaned against it. Lady Strickland, who had expressed such disapproval of the goings-on at Marlborough House. Lady Strickland, who had said that "we" Americans should stick together, only to turn her back on Mariah in her time of greatest need.

The hypocrisy didn't astonish Mariah as much as numb her to all feeling entirely. She sat down on the bed, digging her fingers into the counterpane.

They would all turn their backs on an odd and naïve little fool, she thought. *Everyone but Ash.*

There was another tap on the door, barely audible. Mariah determined to ignore it, but the visitor didn't leave. Instead, the door opened soundlessly, and Ash stepped into the room.

CHAPTER SIXTEEN

MARIAH SPRANG TO her feet.

"Ash," she whispered. "What are you doing here?"

He closed the door and approached the bed. He was still fully dressed, but his warmth was like a blessing, his face filled with quiet concern.

"I could not leave you alone," he said.

"You cannot be here," she said. "Not alone with me, in the middle of the night."

"It is nearly morning." He went straight to the chair beside the bed. "How are you feeling?"

She twisted to face him, clutching her dressing gown closer across her chest. "Very well," she lied. "Ash…"

"You are *not* very well," he said, leaning forward to look into her eyes. "What do you fear, Mariah?"

She might have said she feared the rejection of the prince's court, but that would have been a lie. There was only one person in the world to whom she could confess her greatest fear: the man who had known what it was like to suffer from madness.

Still she hesitated, knowing that she would be taking an irrevocable step. She would be revealing to him her innermost heart, opening the door to a new, even deeper kind of intimacy, one scarcely less shameful than what she had witnessed between Lady Strickland and Mr. Denham in the corridor.

"Tell me," he said, the dark pools of his eyes drawing her

in with promises of complete and selfless understanding. He reached across the bed to brush her cheek with his fingertips. "Tell me, Merry."

His touch nearly undid her. She closed her eyes and threw away the last of her scruples.

"Ash," she whispered. "I fear I am going insane."

He dropped his hand, his gaze tilted away from hers. "Insane," he said softly. "How?"

No condemnation, only gentle inquiry. Relief rose like a tide into Mariah's throat and brought tears to her eyes.

"I have been…seeing things," she said.

His gaze swept back to hers. "The man in the ballroom."

"Yes." Now that the worst was out, there was nothing else to stop her. "But there is more. Have you ever heard of creatures called fairies?"

It must have been her imagination that he stiffened, that his pupils seemed to constrict as if all the darkness of his eyes had gathered in one pinprick-sized spot.

"Yes," he said, a little hoarsely. "Small creatures, often with wings."

"Yes." She swallowed. "They are only imaginary, of course. But I have begun…begun to—"

"You are seeing these fairies."

"I am. I have been seeing them since before we came to Marlborough House."

He cocked his head, his expression intent. "When, Mariah?"

"I…I don't remember."

But she did. And she couldn't tell him. Not now.

She reached across the space between them to grip his hand. "I'm seeing things that aren't really there."

"And this frightens you."

"Of course it frightens me!" She heard the shrillness of her own voice and took herself in hand. "Should I not be frightened of…of losing my—"

"Mariah." He turned his hand in hers to clasp her fingers. "I am here."

She felt her heartbeat begin to slow. "I have not begun this properly," she said steadily. "There is something else I must tell you. My mother…she was not an ordinary person. In fact, she was quite extraordinary in many ways. But she paid the price for her uncommon nature."

"You mother saw the same creatures."

She started. "How did you know? I never…"

"Go on, Mariah."

"She…she began having visions before we moved to New York from Denver, but they were very minor at first. It wasn't until we were living in the city that they became worse. She claimed to hear voices and catch glimpses from another world." The very thought of her mother's suffering made the tears overflow. "I tried to take care of her, but after a while…my father had to send her to a place where she could be treated by special doctors."

"An asylum," he said grimly.

She briefly wondered how he knew, and realized that she didn't care. "After a while," she said, "Mama couldn't see this world at all. She didn't want to. Oh, she was lucid sometimes, but at the end…"

Ash rose abruptly and walked across the room. "Can you describe her visions?"

"She said she saw a beautiful place, where no one ever dies. There were beautiful people in garments no seamstress could have envisioned, and all kinds of fantastic animals. She especially loved—" She twisted her fingers into the bed-clothes. "She especially loved the unicorns."

She almost thought she saw him flinch. "This madness began when she first saw the Fa—the fairies?"

"Yes. Just as it is now happening to me." She stared at him

without seeing more than a vague dark shape. "Am I becoming like her, Ash? Am I going mad?"

His breath exploded. "No! No, Merry. You are not going mad."

"How do you know?"

He swept toward her like an invincible force and knelt at her feet. "You are not mad," he said, gripping her arms. "Such things have been seen by men before."

"By...by you?"

"By others. The ancients, men of intelligence and wisdom. Others no more mad than you or I."

She searched his eyes, seeking the presence of some comforting deception. But he never looked away.

"Are you saying that such creatures exist?" she asked.

"Yes."

"But how can you know if you've never seen them?"

"I cannot tell you. But I believe there are many things that exist beyond this world."

She collapsed against him, resting her forehead on his chest. "If only I could believe."

"You must." He spoke into her hair. "Since you are sane, there is no alternative."

She burbled a laugh into his waistcoat. "But my mother... if what she saw was real—"

"You could not have known." He put his arms around her. "Do not be afraid, Merry. Trust me."

He had asked that of her before. To trust him. *Believe* him. But she couldn't. There had been too many days in the asylum, too many days when she had known Mother was too ill to be reached even by the deepest love.

She raised her head and disentangled herself from Ash's arms. "Thank you," she said. "Thank you for trying to help." She met his gaze. "Oh, Ash."

How stupid it was that they'd avoided each other. Ash had

never attempted to force himself upon her. He knew she intended to remain loyal to Donnington, at least until his guilt was proven. But she had let herself fall victim to her fear of temptation, her wounded pride when she realized that Ash no longer needed her to survive and thrive in the world.

Now, when they looked into one another's eyes, it was as if all those things that had seemed so dreadfully important no longer mattered.

She never knew quite how it began, but suddenly Ash put his hands on her shoulders and carefully eased her down onto the bed. She lay very still as he shed his jacket and tossed it across the chair. She was just a little afraid until he set his mouth to hers.

It was only their second kiss, and yet their lips fit together so perfectly that they might have done it a thousand times. He was gentle at first, exploring her mouth with his, his tongue probing tenderly at the hollows and dips.

Mariah arched her back, her nipples already aching, pushing their sensitive peaks into the thin lawn of her nightdress. Wetness flooded between her thighs as he slipped his tongue inside her mouth and curled it around hers. She imagined then that this was what it would feel like to have Ash inside her, this thrusting and teasing, these soft moans and cries emerging from her throat.

And imagination was all she'd had until now…the imagination that had made it so difficult for her to bear the thought of what other lovers did in the privacy of their chambers. They would lie together, just so. They would kiss, just so. They would—

The moist warmth on her nipple brought such a shock of pleasure that she forgot every thought that had been floating through her brain. Ash had his mouth *there*…kissing her through the fabric of the nightdress, molding the silk to her nipple, sucking the peak between his lips. The pleasure was so intense that she almost cried aloud.

She did not, but the pleasure-pain of Ash's caresses was excruciating.

"Do I please you?" he asked, drawing away.

Please her? She bit hard on her lower lip, knowing that if she dared speak now, she would beg him to continue instead of demanding that he leave her before they had gone too far.

He took her silence for approval and bent to her other nipple. This time he licked as well as suckled, moistening the fabric so that she might as well not have been wearing anything at all. He made her aware of her breasts as she had never been aware before…of their plump roundness, their fullness as he touched them with his fingertips, of the joy that could be derived from anatomy she had once believed suited only to nursing babies.

Ash was no infant. But he suckled her eagerly, hungrily, pushing her breasts from beneath so that her nipples thrust up into his mouth.

"Ash," she moaned. "Stop."

He didn't. He kissed his way up the slope of her breast to lick the crevice between them, moved higher to the base of her neck and kissed the hollow of her throat, the soft skin just below her jaw. And all the while his hands were busy lifting her gown higher—above her knees, her thighs, her hips.

How many times has he done this before? How many women has he taken to bed, caressed, loved…?

She jerked as she felt her body exposed to the cool air and Ash's stroking hands. Her gown was bunched above her breasts now, and Ash had returned to his original work. Only this time there was no fabric between her nipple and his mouth. His tongue made tight little circles, stroked the darker brown around the tip until it had contracted into a tight band of pleasure.

It would have been enough. It would have been enough for

her if he'd never done anything else but kiss her and lick her nipples as he did now, making the moisture trickle from between her legs.

But it was not enough for *him*. His hands moved from cupping her breasts to stroking the skin over her ribs, drifting down to her stomach, venturing lower still.

She bucked, struggling to pull the hem of her nightdress below her breasts. But she stood no chance against Ash, much less against her own desires. Almost against her will, she lifted her hips, aware only that something was missing, that something had to ease the terrible ache in her woman's parts, fill the great empty space between her legs.

"Merry," Ash whispered. His fingers slid into the bush of hair above the wetness, teasing and rubbing. Merry knew there was more to come. Yet nothing could have prepared her for the moment when his fingers moved still lower and dipped into the crevice beneath.

She tried to squeeze her legs together, but they only fell wider apart. Begging, inviting. He began to rub the cleft, lightly at first. She dared to open her eyes. He had lifted his fingers to his lips. They glistened with her body's rapture, and he licked them, closing his eyes in pleasure.

Mariah understood then what she wanted. The thought was so daring that she could not articulate it even in the privacy of her own mind.

She wanted him to kiss her there.

Her tongue refused to break its silence for such a terrible request. But Ash heard her nonetheless. His fingers slid lower and deeper inside the hidden cleft, finding a place where all sensation gathered. He began to do something to that place, rubbing it and tugging on it until her breath came in harsh pants and the sheets were damp beneath her bottom.

"Ash," she gasped.

He raised his head and met her eyes. His were black gems

that swallowed up Mariah's reality, leaving her nothing but all-consuming hunger.

And then, just as she felt herself begin to rise up and up into something very like heaven, he stopped. She reached down to snatch at his hand, to make him continue. But he set her hand aside and bent very low, only the crown of his silver head visible between her thighs.

He kissed her. There. Light exploded behind Mariah's eyes. His tongue took the place of his fingers, nimble, hot, wet. It darted into her cleft, found the little button of pleasure and flicked rapidly over it. Mariah felt a warm gush of liquid spill out of her, felt him lick it up.

Once again he took her very close to the edge of the that mysterious paradise that waited just beyond. Once again he drew her back. Then, as she cried out quickly, desperately, he pushed his tongue inside her.

There was the place. *There* was the ultimate ache, the emptiness that had to be filled. And he filled it, thrusting inside, withdrawing in a rhythm as natural and necessary as breathing itself. With each push she lifted her hips higher, higher, knowing there was still something missing. Knowing that what she wanted was not his tongue but the ultimate manifestation of his masculinity.

Breath sawing in his throat, Ash rose up above her, then knelt between her thighs, and she saw that his trousers were unbuttoned.

She had never seen an erect male member before. Her mother had briefly mentioned it as a giver of pleasure, but what Mariah saw now was a delicious shock. It was a magnificent thing, meant to fit inside her like a key into a lock.

Unthinking, she reached for him. Her fingers touched skin that was remarkably smooth, even silky. Ash groaned and flung back his head. She pushed herself up on the pillows and slid her hand lower, then up again. The expression on Ash's face was one she'd never seen before, as he thrust forward into her hand.

A little shift in position, a little lifting of her hips, and that powerful organ would be inside her. The emptiness would be filled. She would know the mystery of what those other women knew, those women who crept through the corridors to risk everything in pursuit of *this*.

The other women. The adulterers. The ones she had determined to despise…

She snapped her legs together and scooted back into the pillows. Ash lunged away as if he had been burned. They stared at each other, flushed, barely breathing, horrified.

Mariah averted her gaze and fumbled with the sheets, trying to cover her lower body. Ash retreated into the corner of the room, his hands working at the buttons of his trousers.

Bitter memories darkened Mariah's vision. "I shall be in no danger at Marlborough House." How utterly foolish she had been to make such a promise to her mother-in-law. How hypocritical she had been to judge others for *their* behavior. She should have known from the moment she left Donbridge that the end result would be this: falling into Ash's arms without a thought for her "reputation."

She had nearly surrendered what remained her only valuable possession: her honor. Surrendered her virginity— and not to the man to whom it rightfully belonged, but to the one she loved, the one who might get her with child in the course of a single night.

She knew she was, in a very real way, betraying Ash, just as she knew she had no other choice.

You will have the choice between defeat and victory. But where was the victory in this?

Mariah struggled into her dressing gown and sat on the bed with her knees drawn up to her chest, unfulfilled, shivering as if all warmth had seeped out of the room. Ash's harsh breathing was the only sound. He didn't approach her but stayed where he was, frozen, his eyes abyss-black.

"Please, Ash," she whispered. "Please go."

He left as silently as he had come, without a single word between them. Sick and shaking, Mariah fell into bed, wrapped in the scents of Ash's body and her own desire. The aching inside her was worse than ever, and she knew it would never go away.

An hour before dawn, after a sleepless night, she saw the fairies again…and the unicorn, silver and white, who looked at her through Ash's black eyes.

ASH LEFT THE HOUSE, his shirt loose and open, his feet bare in the wet grass. He walked blindly, leaving the grounds of Marlborough House behind and plunging onto the streets of Westminster. Few were abroad to see him: a handful of servants, sleepy coachmen, and a pair of inebriated gentlemen, perhaps returning from a late party, who gaped at him in drunken amazement. He ignored them all and walked until he began to glimpse carts on their way to market and knew he would soon lose the privacy he so desperately craved.

Tonight had been a disaster. During the past three weeks he had deliberately avoided Mariah; he had known that her stubborn sense of honor would not permit her to remain too close to him. He had hoped to provoke her jealousy of the other ladies who sought his company, compelling her to desire a return to their former intimacy. He had watched her fail to make a real place at Marlborough House, expected her to come to him so that they might grow closer still.

But he had been more stupid than even the dullest human. If he had simply maintained their friendship from the moment they had arrived, tonight would not have happened.

For tonight he had almost destroyed himself, destroyed his only hope of returning to his world. And all because he had wanted Mariah with such a deep and overwhelming passion that he had been unable to control himself.

Until *she* had pushed him away. She, with her virgin's power over the unicorn within him.

He looked around to make sure he was unobserved, then leaped the wall surrounding the Marlborough House park. He paused just inside, then turned sharply to follow the park's border. He still ached with wanting her; his cock was hard, his breathing rapid, and his vision so blurred that he could scarcely see the ground directly in front of him.

Rage. It ate at him, and he could not escape it. He raged at the fates that were tearing him in two. He raged at himself for allowing Mariah to believe, in spite of his reassurances, that the things she'd seen might not be real. And he raged because he knew the true identity of the "man" with whom Mariah had danced.

Cairbre, who had remained invisible to all but Mariah herself. Cairbre, who had demanded such an impossible price for Arion's former life.

In spite of his assurance that he would not directly interfere in Ash's attempts to win Mariah, the Fane lord had obviously chosen to become involved. Perhaps he had grown impatient with Ash's painstaking work, though time often passed far more slowly in Tir-na-Nog than in the mortal world. Or perhaps…

The sprites.

Of course. Cairbre's sprites, which Mariah called fairies. Cairbre's spies, who could very well have been watching Ash and Mariah from the very beginning. Watching, and reporting Ash's progress to the Fane lord. But they had not been able to hide themselves from Mariah's Fane blood.

Ash broke off the low-hanging branch of a tree with a violent snap. He remembered Donnington telling Cairbre that Mariah's mother had been considered mad in the mortal world. Mariah herself had confirmed the story and revealed how much she feared the same fate.

Now Cairbre's actions in the ballroom—and even earlier, when Mariah had seen the sprites before she'd come to Marlborough House—had made her doubt her sanity. Cairbre must have known the trouble he would cause by appearing to her.

How could driving Mariah to such a state serve Cairbre's purpose? It was true that Mariah had turned to Ash in her time of extremity, but if Cairbre's intention had been to use her fear to bring them together, he had made a serious error. The Fane had relied on Ash's desperation to keep both himself and the human girl under control, but he had not calculated on the strength of human desire.

Human desire, powerful enough to steal Arion's true self forever.

With a toss of his head, Ash began to run. There was little enough space, but he made use of it, his two human legs pumping, his heart slamming against his ribs. If he hadn't smelled and heard her first, he would have collided with the woman who stepped out from behind a mass of shrubbery, her wool-and-fur manteau moving slightly in the early morning breeze.

"Mr. Cornell," she said.

He came to a halt. "Lady Westlake."

She smiled at him, a lovely expression that dared anyone to doubt her extraordinary beauty. Even he felt it, and the tightness inside his trousers grew more uncomfortable.

"I have been watching you," she said. "I believe you could best even the swiftest competitor in a footrace anywhere in the country."

Ash caught his breath and stared at her, surprised that she could meet his eyes without lowering her own. "I was not running for your entertainment," he said.

"No, indeed. But I wonder why you found it necessary to run at all."

His mind told him to walk away, but his legs would not obey his thoughts. "I enjoy it," he said.

"Ah." She continued to smile, and her gaze moved slowly from his face to his feet and back again. "I believe you are not enjoying yourself at the moment."

Ash clenched his fists. "What do you want from me?"

"It is not so much what *I* want from *you* but what *you* want from *me*."

She could not have made her meaning more clear. Her manteau blew open, and Ash saw that she wore nothing but a thin chemise underneath. He could easily make out her taut nipples and the pale triangle of down between her thighs.

"Do you not admire what you see?" she asked.

Deliberately he looked away. "Cover yourself and leave me."

"Are you the prince himself, to give me orders?"

His nostrils flared, taking in her ripe scent. She was aroused, as aroused as Mariah had been, but *she* had no doubts about her desires.

"I know what you want," she said, moving closer. "I can give it to you."

He swallowed thickly. "Why?"

"Why do I want you to share my bed, or why do I come to you now?"

"I don't understand."

"You most certainly do understand, my friend. I know where you have been, and how the liaison ended."

He grabbed her arm. "How do you know?"

"It could not be more obvious." She fingered the fur of her collar. "Never fear. No one else shares our secret…yet."

He wanted to shake her as much as he wanted to push her to the ground and take her then and there. "I know what you are," he said. "You are Mariah's enemy."

She laughed, a sound almost as bright as that of a Fane lady of the highest rank. "I am hardly a threat to the little girl to whom you are so devoted. She is an *honorable* woman. She will never know the pleasures of love. She will wait for Donnington with her purity intact, but he cannot love her. She will live out her days in sorrow and loneliness."

Her words stung like the scrape of Cold Iron against Ash's skin. "Donnington is *my* enemy. I will not let him hurt her."

"Your enemy?" Her eyes widened. "How can that be, when you have never met him?"

"He left Mariah…he—"

"Thought so little of her that he abandoned her on her wedding night?"

That he had not known. But of course humans regarded their weddings as the prelude to consummation, and Donnington, being a human male, could not risk the temptation of taking her himself.

Pamela stepped closer and rubbed her fingers over her nipples. "Tell me," she said, "when did you fall in love with her?"

He shivered. "I am not in love with her."

"But you desire her, and she will not have you. You can have me, at no cost to yourself, and cause Mariah no pain. She will never know."

"I forbid you to speak of her again."

She continued to smile, unmoved. "You cannot forbid me, Ash, just as you cannot forbid yourself what you see before you." She opened her manteau and ran her fingers from her breasts to her thighs. She moaned as she rubbed herself.

"I want you inside me," she whispered. "I have from the first moment I saw you." She leaned down, and her breasts swayed. "How many women have you had since you arrived in England?" She reached out to touch his groin with damp fingertips. "None, I think. And a man as virile as you cannot be expected to abstain long."

Ash's head had begun to throb in time to the blood pulsing in his cock. "Remove your hand."

She did not. She only squeezed…lightly but firmly…and he closed his eyes.

"Now," she said hoarsely. "Let it be here and now, where no one can see. I will give you what no woman has ever given you before."

His sight dimmed. He grabbed her by the shoulders, pushed her in among the shrubbery and bore her to the ground. She sighed, flung her manteau open wide and spread her legs. He undid the buttons of his trousers and crouched over her, panting, teeth bared.

Then he saw the image of Mariah, her lips parted, her breath coming sharp as he caressed her. He saw her innocence, her beauty, all the things that had made it nearly impossible for him to leave her.

He jerked away, awkwardly buttoning his trousers as he did so. He was gone before Lady Westlake had recovered enough to pull her manteau over her half-naked body.

PAMELA WAILED. She made not a sound, but inwardly she was crying out her anger.

By God, he had left her. The bastard had left her lying here alone on the wet grass. No man had ever refused her before. And now her plans were ruined.

Pamela wanted much more than just to see Mariah openly humiliated, her marriage destroyed, her reputation cast into the gutter. She wanted to see Mariah's love for Cornell crushed, once and for all.

But she had failed. She had failed.

Pamela got up, brushed the grass from her all but ruined manteau and buttoned it to cover her own humiliation. Sinjin would never guess, of course. He was blinded by his feelings for her. But she might still use him to destroy Lady Donnington—and Mr. Ashton Cornell.

Her usual confidence restored, Pamela was walking briskly toward one of the house's several rear doors when the stranger appeared.

He didn't come from the house, nor from anywhere on the grounds. He was simply not there one moment and standing before her the next, a gentleman in perfectly fitted evening clothes, a vision with silver-green eyes and hair far more resplendent than anything that might have been called "brown."

Nonplussed and wary, she tugged her manteau as close as she could and smiled. "How do you do," she said. "I do not believe we have been introduced."

"We have not," he said, a sort of curtness in his voice that didn't please her. "You are Lady Westlake."

"And who are you?"

"Someone who believes that you and I can be useful to one another."

She took a moment to study him more closely. If he had been a guest at Marlborough House, she would have noticed him...as would every other woman in residence.

"I am afraid I must go into the house," she said. "Perhaps we might talk later, Mr.—"

He caught her arm as she turned, and though his fingers were slender, she might as well have been fighting the grip of a bulldog.

"You must not go just yet, Lady Westlake," he said in a voice that matched his eyes and breathtakingly glamorous features. "I have a proposition to make to you."

She had never heard any man speak so bluntly. She almost wished she were capable of blushing.

"Kindly release me, sir," she said in a freezing voice. "I am not interested in any proposition you could possibly make to me."

He laughed. "You are indeed attractive—for what you are, Lady Westlake," he said, "but I have no interest in your body."

All at once she felt steady on her feet again. He was one of *those*. She should have known at first glance.

"Then we have even less to discuss," she said, trying to free her arm.

"You're wrong, my lady, as you shall discover." He waved a beringed hand, and suddenly she couldn't move. Not so much as a finger.

"You see," the stranger said, "I can force you to do whatever I will. But I require your intelligence and cunning, such as it is."

He waved his hand again, and Lady Westlake sucked in a breath, nearly fainting as she fought a wave of dizziness. She put her hand to her throat.

"What did you…do to me?"

"A very simple matter for one of my kind."

"Your kind? What is your kind?"

"That is of little moment. It is enough to say that I know what you desire above all else, and that you may achieve your goals by assisting me in achieving mine."

"I don't understand."

"You witnessed the events in the ballroom tonight."

"Yes, of course. I—"

"I was the one dancing with Lady Donnington."

CHAPTER SEVENTEEN

THE LAUGH DIED on Pamela's tongue. "You?"

He gave a shallow bow. "Lord Caber, at your service."

The very name Mariah had given to her invisible dancing partner. A man who didn't exist.

"No one saw you," she protested. "How could you—"

The stranger smiled, dazzling enough to make Pamela weak in the knees. "I simply chose to make myself invisible." He lifted one languorous hand and was gone. Pamela blinked, and he was there again.

"You see," he said, "I am not really here. I have permitted my spirit to travel to your world. It was my desire tonight that no one else should see me."

Pamela wished that she dared to simply sit on the path and catch her breath. "What are you?" she whispered.

"As I said," he said sharply, "that is unimportant." He made a graceful warding gesture, as if to toss her questions aside. "My spirit can somewhat effect the events of this world, but it has its limitations. Do you desire the man you know as Ashton Cornell?"

She knew a sudden blinding fear that he had seen her with Ash a few moments ago. "Why should you care?"

He directed such a frown at Pamela that she felt faint again. "Must I tell you again that such things are not for you to know?"

"No. I care nothing for Cornell."

"If you lie to me…"

"I am not lying. I…was with him, but he refused me. And I meant it only to his harm."

"Then you hate him."

"I—" A flash of insight interrupted her answer. "*You* hate him."

"It is enough that he is your enemy, and that you despise Lady Donnington. This is true, is it not?"

"Yes."

"Then you shall be my agent. Together, we shall eliminate Lady Donnington as your rival and compel her to serve me."

"Serve you?"

"Yes."

She knew then that this was no game. There was something more here that she couldn't see, something even further beyond her ken than the powers of invisibility or holding a woman paralyzed and silent.

But she didn't care.

"I know Lady Donnington's greatest weakness," Lord Caber said, apparently satisfied with her reaction. "She fears madness above all else, because she believed her own mother to be mad. My purpose tonight was to strengthen that fear."

A great deal began to make sense to her. "You intended others to believe the same?"

He smiled. "I was not mistaken in you, mortal." His smile vanished. "I have but one purpose here—to drive away all of Lady Donnington's friends and allies. I have already laid the groundwork. You will take the next step by compelling the people of this house to turn their backs on her. She is to be isolated in every way, so that there is only one to whom she can go for comfort."

"Who?"

"Cornell."

"She has already gone to him. She refused his advances."

"And that is exactly what I wish. The one thing that must not happen is that she and Cornell should lie together."

"If they are to be driven into one another's company…"

"You must discourage her from breaking her vows to her husband."

"How?"

"I have no interest in your methods. These things must be done quickly. In recompense…" He opened his hand, and diamonds glittered in his palm. Pamela almost reached for them.

"No," she said. "It is not enough."

"I warn you…"

"I want Donnington."

He laughed. "Is that all?" The diamonds disappeared. "If you please me, Lady Westlake, you shall have what you desire."

But how can I trust you? Pamela asked herself, not daring to speak aloud. *How can you guarantee my prize?*

Caber saw through her. "I am not one to break my word," he said. "Even to mortals. You may have your Donnington when he returns."

When he returns. She sighed and closed her eyes. All would be well. All would be very well.

"We are agreed?" Caber asked.

There was no shaking of hands, no further explanation. Caber simply vanished as he had come, leaving Pamela to marvel at what she had just experienced.

Drive Mariah to Ash, but keep them from consummating their passion. Pamela's thoughts hummed with satisfaction. What she had in mind would surely achieve her goal, and on two levels: advancing her own revenge, and carrying out Caber's plan.

Mariah was torn between her antiquated notions of fidelity and her repressed desires. But she and Cornell would never complete the act they had begun. Pamela would do it for them, creating such disgrace for Mariah that she wouldn't dare attempt another liaison. And when Pamela was finished, even the most liberal of the Marlborough House Set would be compelled to turn their backs on the couple who had exposed their own decadent sins.

VIVIAN NOTED THE address on the letter and immediately took it into her private salon. It was the first real news she'd received from Lady Westlake since the younger woman had followed Mariah and Cornell to Marlborough House, and as Vivian read eagerly, she began to believe that there was hope at last.

Mariah was mad. Or so some were saying. The information was quite extraordinary and entirely unexpected; there seemed little basis for the accusation given the girl's odd but harmless behavior in the ballroom, hardly more peculiar than the eccentricities of many an English peer. Yet certain members of the easily bored Marlborough House Set seemed to delight in vindictive gossip, especially when the victim was a pretty American who had not yet earned the right to be called one of their own.

The talk would die, of course, if Mariah didn't repeat the deed or commit another like it. But Pamela had already indicated that she would do her best to keep the rumors alive, if only Vivian would play her part.

Vivian looked up from the letter, blind to the sunlight streaming across the polished surface of her writing desk. Her part was to locate and provide the evidence and basis for Mariah's apparent "defect," anything that might lend credence to the speculation about the girl.

She had already written to certain contacts in America, hoping to learn more about Mr. Ashton Cornell. As yet she had received no reply. But in this case, she would be inquiring about a specific family well established in New York. Even though she might receive little cooperation from Mr.

Marron himself, there would surely be other relations or acquaintances available to answer her questions—especially for a generous remuneration.

Vivian scanned the letter once again, flexing her fingers gingerly as she turned the sheet over. It was odd that Donnington had never indicated that he knew of Mrs. Marron's mental condition, but if things were as Pamela had claimed, Vivian could see nothing but advantage to herself in exposing Mariah's dubious background. Especially since the girl was terrified of going mad like her mother.

Leverage. Vivian had sought it, and now it was in her hands. Rather than have her family's history of madness confirmed, Mariah might agree to an annulment by admitting that she had never intended to consummate her marriage to the earl.

If not, she could always be compelled to admit that she had been too mentally incompetent to consent to the marriage. There would be ways to make certain that the world believed that to be the unfortunate truth of the matter.

Vivian carefully folded the letter, placed it in her desk and locked the drawer. This was all speculation. Time alone would tell how much benefit she could glean from this new information. All she need do was continue to be patient, and Mariah—poor, sad girl—would take a tumble from which she would never recover.

And if Vivian could take "Mr. Cornell" down with her, so much the better.

"I KNOW YOU WERE with him."

Sinjin had never felt the slightest desire to strike a woman, but Pamela's expression in the face of his accusation made him feel tempted. No shame, no denial—only a calm, self-satisfied air, as if they had been discussing her growing popularity with the prince and his Set. She didn't even ask him how he'd come to know of the liaison.

"Deny it," he said hoarsely, ready to take her shoulders and give her a good hard shake. "Deny that you went to find Ash in the garden, and that he had you right there."

She sighed. "I do not deny that I went to find him," she said. "With excellent reason. But I cannot tell you the rest as long as you are so irrational."

"Irrational?" He lowered his voice, remembering that his room was not nearly as private a venue as he would wish. "Irrational to find that you have been unfaithful to me—and with Cornell?"

"You assume that I was unfaithful. How very gallant of you," she said sarcastically.

He was only momentarily silenced. "Explain yourself," he said grimly, "or I shall toss you out of my bed in such a way that everyone in this house will know."

"How dare you?" She approached him with her hand half raised, as if she had nurtured the same thoughts as he. "How dare you think you can possess me, when you have long been known for your many assignations?"

"That is different. I—"

"It is no different." She retreated again and stood watching him, her chest rising and falling rapidly. "My purpose was for the greater good…and *I* did not seduce *him*."

Her words were so implausible that they stopped Sinjin cold. "What are you trying to say?" he demanded.

"I was merely attempting to expose Cornell for what he is—a fraud and a swindler. He was angry, and he attempted to take advantage of me."

He seized her arm. "Did he hurt you, Pamela?"

"He did not, but—"

"Did he force himself on you?"

Her expression became almost severe. "Is that prospect so

unbelievable? Have you never suspected that he is both more and less than he seems? You have accepted him as kin, an American cousin worthy of your family name. But have you ever considered that his purpose in coming to England might be less than honorable?"

Sinjin was by no means prepared to lay aside his suspicion of Pamela's story. He knew that she was completely unaware of Ash's imprisonment.

"In what way is Cornell less than honorable?" he asked.

"Aside from his behavior toward me? He may be a relation to your family—his appearance would seem to confirm such an assumption. But what if he were after the Donnington fortune?"

In spite of himself, Sinjin laughed. "Your supposition is ridiculous. He has no claim on the fortune. If Donnington were to—" He looked away. "I am the next in line. Even if Cornell assumed that he was entitled to some part of our inheritance—"

"He is American. Perhaps he is unaware of our laws. Or perhaps he simply wished to get into the dowager's good graces— and yours—in hopes of persuading you to part with some small portion of the family's money."

The idea was preposterous. "And you thought that by simply demanding the truth from him that you would get him to confess to this…improbable scheme?"

"I am not unattractive. Men have confessed their sins to me before."

"But you admit that your plan did not succeed."

"No. He is too obsessed with that little tart, Mariah."

"*You* call her a tart? *You?*"

She worked her arm free. "Since I believe her to be in league with Cornell, 'tart' seems rather mild."

"Mariah 'in league' with Cornell? Have you gone mad?"

"I know they were…acquainted long before Cornell introduced himself to the dowager. That is obvious to anyone with eyes to see. Why, then, should she have kept his presence a secret?"

"She didn't. She…" He stopped, aware that he was on the verge of telling Pamela everything about Mariah's discovery of Ash. "I know that there was no conspiracy of the sort you suggest."

"How do you know?"

"I am not in a position to share confidences."

"Confidences you do not question?"

"I know Lady Donnington."

"Do you know that she and Cornell believe that they love each other?"

Sinjin swallowed his immediate denial. Hadn't he seen the signs, even from the very beginning? Hadn't he warned Mariah not to allow her sympathy to get the better of her? And things had changed immeasurably since Ash had recovered his memories, or at least the memories he professed to recall.

Why shouldn't Mariah turn to the man who had become such an intimate companion when her husband had all but abandoned her?

Even if that were so, Mariah could not have been involved in any sort of swindle. What reason could she possibly have for coveting her husband's money when she possessed her own independent fortune?

And yet, what if Ash's behavior—his claims of having been imprisoned by Donnington, everything he had done— had been a highly ingenious act? What if he had deceived Mariah, and Sinjin, as well?

No. There was no truth to any of it. But inwardly, Sinjin found that a tiny sliver of doubt had entered his brain.

He shook his head. "You are deceived, Pamela," he said.

"Am I?" She shrugged. "Believe what you wish, then."

"I will. And *you* will have nothing more to do with Cornell."

"You ought to be grateful that I care so much for your well-being"

With a snort of disgust, Sinjin walked away. But he was far from sanguine. If she'd been telling the truth, if Cornell had abused her in any way…

He gritted his teeth and swung about to confront Pamela once more. But she had gone, leaving him with the frustrated need to mark her as his in a way she would never forget.

By God. He would have begged her, here and now, had she not left. That was how low he had sunk. And he had no desire to rise to the surface again.

THE RUMORS OF MARIAH'S eccentricity were still flying the evening after the ball. Though Ash waited, she didn't come to him, and he knew why. She didn't dare risk repeating what had happened between them. She was ashamed. And while she bravely refused to confirm the gossip by returning to Donbridge, she made little attempt to refute the talk about her "performance" in the ballroom.

The gossip heightened when someone put it about that Lady Donnington came from a line prone to madness, and that her family had been known in American as the "Mad Marrons" for generations.

No one knew how egregious these tales were better than Ash. He was certain that knowledge of Mariah's mother could not be so widespread in England without help.

Ash waited for nightfall, chose a fast horse from the stables and rode hard to the very edge of London, where the city gave way to a scattering of mansions and country houses. He stood on the crest of a hill and sent his thoughts out into the night. There was no response. Again he tried, and again. Thunder rumbled in the sky, and finally a flash of lightning illuminated a single figure, limned in a silver glow.

"Cairbre," Ash said. "What have you done?"

The figure moved forward. "Well may you ask me that, Arion, considering the foolish errors you have committed."

"I committed no error," Ash said. "I have done as you asked."

"Have you?" Cairbre's teeth glinted in the eldritch light. "You went too far, Arion. You nearly destroyed the girl's worth to me."

"But I did not."

Lightning flashed again. "Consider this your last warning, Arion," Cairbre said. "You have delayed too long, and—"

"Is your position in Tir-na-Nog so tenuous, great Fane lord?"

Cairbre's eyes glinted with anger. "Do you think to defy me?" he asked. "Think again, beast. If you do not do as we agreed—"

Ash didn't let him finish his threat. "Who at Marlborough House is serving you, Cairbre? Who is working against Mariah?"

Cairbre shook his head, his expression one that in a human might have been called pity. "You care for her, don't you? Poor deluded fool. That the magnificent Arion should come to this…" He glanced up at the sky, his clothing untouched by the rain that had begun to fall. "The girl is already in a state of fear and confusion. I can drive her truly mad with but the slightest effort. In such a weakened condition, she will not be able to thwart my will as she did before."

Ash began to tremble. "She'll do you no good in Tir-na-Nog if she's mad."

"I would prefer that she maintain her sanity for the sake of my people's approbation, but her virgin body is all I truly require."

Without thinking, Ash lowered his head and charged. Cairbre vanished and reappeared several feet to the left. He laughed.

"You have made yourself ridiculous over this human," he said. He snapped his fingers, and the lightning struck at Ash's feet. "Consider my words. If you obey, you are restored and the girl will be well—or at least alive. Otherwise, you both lose everything."

With another snap of his fingers he vanished, leaving Ash soaked to the skin.

For uncounted minutes he stood in the rain. "You care for her, don't you?" How many times had Ash implied as much to Mariah, only half meaning his words, thinking only of himself?

But he was not the man he had been when the memory of his mission had returned to him in the folly. Self-deception was no longer possible. There was only one way to put Mariah out of her misery, and that was to tell her the truth. The truth of who and what he was.

And of what he had wanted from her, even though she might hate him forever. Even though it would destroy every hope he had of regaining his true self.

Driving the horse as hard as he dared, Ash returned to Marlborough House. Mariah was nowhere to be found. After an hour of inquiry, he learned from a servant that Lady Donnington and her maid had left the house and apparently gone to a hotel, though the servant did not speculate as to why the lady had done so. Ash considered searching her out, but it was far more practical to wait. Wait until she had returned, restored by her time away.

Or so he told himself.

He did what he could in her absence, moving among the guests as he defended Mariah with a sharp word here and a quiet rebuke there. Those he had cured with his healing powers were grateful enough to listen; some even began to dismiss Mariah's peculiar behavior as mere "youthful high spirits" and ignore any less charitable interpretation.

Three days after Mariah had gone, a fresh rumor made its way through the house. Lady Strickland had received a letter from her husband in Derbyshire, though the contents of the letter did not remain confidential for long. Someone at Marlborough House had broken the unwritten rule of discretion and informed the marquess that his wife was engaged in a torrid affair with Mr. Denham.

Lord Strickland's letter had condemned his wife in the strongest terms, demanding that she return to his estate at once to tender an explanation. Lady Strickland's humiliation could not have been more complete. Then another question arose among the Set. Who had written to the marquess? Who had dared to break the unspoken agreement that bound the unfaithful residents of Marlborough House, and their prince, together in their enjoyment of extramarital pleasure?

Mariah Donnington.

At first it was only a whisper. No one had any proof, no concrete reason to believe in her guilt. But she was still fresh in the guests' thoughts, and it was only a short step from rumors of madness to murmured accusations of deliberate malice against a woman who had chosen to cut her fellow American. Even the most tolerant of the Set's members began to think her guilty when Lady Strickland's friends related how Mariah had expressed her distaste for the practices of the English peerage. Further talk confirmed that she had observed Lady Strickland and Mr. Denham in the guest wing late at night, giving her both motive and ammunition.

Ash himself had no doubt that this was the work of Cairbre or his unidentified human ally. And though the likely identity of Cairbre's servant was not difficult to guess, as yet Ash had no proof that anyone but Mariah had seen the Fane lord. Still, he did what he could to quash this new trouble.

"I have not had time to get to know her well," he said to a coterie of the prince's favorites as they gathered in the billiard room, "but she is not malicious. Even if she were inclined to revenge, she would hardly act in such a way as to draw suspicion to herself."

The gentlemen present glanced at each other, clearly caught off guard by Ash's disconcerting frankness. Several of them flushed in embarrassment, and one man began to leave the room. Lord Emory stopped his cohort with a gesture, glowering from under his thick gray brows.

"There are no ladies present," he said, "so I shall be equally direct. You speak of these matters very casually, but would you still defend Lady Donnington if she were not your relative by marriage?"

"She is my cousin, but I would defend any person wrongly accused," he said, staring into the man's eyes. "But perhaps that is an American habit."

"We have long known that Americans make much of propriety while they freely break their own rules."

"Much like the English." Ash smiled, his gaze sweeping the room. "Every one of you has chosen a wife who will be accepting of your infidelities, while you permit your females to lie with other men. You are scarcely in a position to speak of hypocrisy."

The others muttered and shifted about, unable to find a ready answer. Lord Emory subsided with a scowl, and Ash knew he had accepted at least a temporary defeat.

But one small victory was not enough. In spite of Ash's popularity, it was no longer a simple matter to swing the humans to his point of view. Some began to avoid his company. Even when Sinjin, too, took up a defense of Mariah, he kept well away from Ash. When their gazes met, Sinjin's burned with hostility.

He knew. Somehow he had learned—perhaps from Pamela herself—what his paramour had done that early morning in the park, and he placed the blame on Ash.

Finally he caught Sinjin at a time and place where the

human could not easily escape. "Good afternoon," he said. "You have a desire to say something to me?"

Sinjin narrowed his eyes. "I must say, Cornell, your nerve is almost admirable."

"Because I would prefer to speak more frankly about your lover than you dare to?"

The human paled. "You bastard. You'll either admit that you took advantage of her or I'll make you regret it."

Had Sinjin not given some assistance to Mariah when Ash had been at his most vulnerable, he would, at that moment, gladly have knocked the human off his feet.

"It was she who offered herself to me," Ash said.

"Liar."

Ash cocked his head. "It amazes me how irrational men can become when they are in thrall to a female."

"Do you deny having approached her?"

"Would it serve any purpose if I did? You are aware of her nature, yet you would defend her to your last breath."

"I'm aware," Sinjin said, breathing harshly, "that you are concealing something, Cornell. I don't know what it is, but I intend to find out."

"You might better ask yourself what Lady Westlake is concealing." Ash turned to go. Sinjin caught him by the arm and spun him around.

"Whoever you are," he said, "I know you have designs on Mariah. If you so much as harm a hair on her head…"

"I would be the last one to harm her," Ash said softly, shaking off Ware's grip. "And if your paramour should attempt to work her malice on Lady Donnington again, I will not be merciful."

"She and Mariah…" But Ware found nothing more to say. He turned on his heel and strode from the room. Ash stood where he was, his ears still ringing with Sinjin's accusations.

"I know you have designs on Mariah. If you so much as harm a hair on her head…"

Ash had said he would never harm Mariah. The time had come to prove it.

CHAPTER EIGHTEEN

MARIAH SAT ON THE edge of her mattress at the hotel. The unsigned letter lay open on the bed table.

Come back immediately, it said. *Mr. Cornell needs your help.*

She picked up the letter and studied it, as if it might give up its secrets. Who had written it, and why should Ash require her help?

She had known she was a coward when she left Marlborough House. She had meant to stay. She had intended to face Ash again and explain, make him understand that what had happened between them could not be repeated.

But she hadn't been able to do it. Even when she chose to retreat to a London hotel instead of Donbridge, leaving herself the option of returning to Marlborough House at a moment's notice, she had remained a coward. Thinking about Ash, about what they had done, left her weak and shivering with desire. If she were to go near him again, she might not be able to resist. She feared she would be paying for those few moments of pleasure for the rest of her life.

And as for the rumors…

Perhaps she was not mad after all. Ash had told her as much, and she had nearly believed him. He had absolved her of blame for her mother's suffering with a gentle firmness that had given her hope for the first time in many years.

Ash…

A few days, she'd told herself. *A few days and the memories of his touch will pass.*

But they did not. Nola's company was no help, and guilt mingled with hunger in Mariah's bewildered mind. Ash had branded himself upon her body. Each restless night brought him to her bed, if only in her imagination. The fairies left her alone, yet she would have welcomed them rather than face the dreams of her lust whenever she dared to close her eyes.

He will come to me, her unreasonable heart insisted. *He will find me.*

But he did not. And she began to understand that he had accepted her rejection and was honorable enough not to test it. He had been true to her, and now she must be true to him. Loving him had been a mistake…her mistake. She had forgotten herself because of it, betrayed her husband, herself— even Ash—in a way she had never intended.

Now, as she looked again at the anonymous letter, she realized that she could put off her return no longer. She alone could make the next move to restore their friendship to what it had been before, then hold to that friendship and keep it safe, something precious she would never let escape her again.

I will never leave you, Ash. Even if we never touch each other again, I will never—

A hand covered her mouth. She struggled, thrashing among the bedclothes, until she recognized the familiar and beloved presence.

"Hush," Ash whispered, removing his hand. "You are safe, Mariah."

She sat up, her heart beating so fast that she couldn't catch her breath.

"Ash," she whispered. "Are you all right?"

"Should I not be?"

"Someone sent a letter that said you were in trouble."

"Someone?" He frowned. "That someone was mistaken."

"But why would anyone—"

"That doesn't matter now, Mariah," he said, sitting on the chair near the bed. "There are things I must tell you. Important things that you must understand."

"But I *do* understand," she said, recovering her self-control. "I understand my weaknesses. They will never again take me unaware." She reached toward him, then pulled her hands back before she could touch him. "I treasure our friendship, Ash, but I put it in jeopardy. I blame only myself." Her eyes began to sting. "I ask your forgiveness."

He averted his face. "You are wrong," he said. "It was not your doing. It was mine."

"Oh, Ash. You mean more to me than I could ever say. If you were to leave me…" She tried to steady her voice. "I know you have found your place, my dear friend. You are accepted by society, and in time your memory will return. We may be parted by circumstance, but you will always be with me, as I will be with you."

He lifted his head. "You do not know what you are saying, Mariah." His eyes were obsidian-black, fathomless, unreadable. "I was never a friend to you."

"Please, Ash. Whatever guilt you may feel is entirely unnecessary." She leaned toward him, willing him to listen with an open heart. "From the beginning, even before I realized how much you would change, I knew there would be a bond between us. It may not be the sort of relationship society would sanction, but it is ours. It will not die even when Donnington returns, no matter what he has done. Not as long as we don't let it."

The intensity of his gaze was such that she almost wondered if he intended to renew his overtures. But surely he would not. He must realize that what she said was the truth, because only the truth must be spoken between them from now on.

"Ash," she said, laying her hand over his. "We have what most people seldom do. Trust in each other. Please trust me now, as you once asked the same of me."

"But I deceived you, Mariah. From the moment we met in the folly."

Immediately she tried to imagine what he meant, a hundred wild possibilities racing through her mind. *It is something small. Something unimportant,* she told herself.

"I lied to you," he said. "I *was* mad at the beginning—that much is true—but I was never what I pretended to be."

He slid his hand out from beneath hers. "I said that you were not insane. That was also truth. But the reason I know…" He drew a deep breath. "I have seen what you call fairies, Mariah. A hundred times. A thousand. And I have seen them in the place your mother envisioned."

The mention of her mother froze Mariah's insides. "I don't understand."

"Of course not. You could not possibly guess. I lived in that place, Mariah. It has always been real, just as your mother believed."

Mariah clutched at the bedclothes. "You're mocking me," she said.

"No. That I would never do." His gaze dropped to the carpet under his feet. "The place your mother saw is named Tir-na-Nog. It is the land of the Fane lords, who rule the sprites and hobs and lesser creatures in their domain."

"Tir…na-Nog?" she repeated slowly, feeling as though she were dreaming. "I have heard that name before. But it doesn't…it *can't* exist."

"It does. I will show you."

Nothing in the world could have prepared her for what happened next. He was in the chair one instant and then beside her on the bed, his movement so swift that she never even saw it. He gripped her shoulders.

"Look, Mariah," he said.

She lifted her hands as if she could ward him away, but it did no good. Suddenly, as if in a gaudy picture book, another world unfolded. She saw the trees first—elegant, too perfect, with leaves of silver and gold and emerald-green. At the bases of their trunks were carpets of flowers stretching to the tawny hills in the distance, a riot of color and shape Mariah could never have envisioned. Animals played in the fields: badgers, foxes, deer with crystal horns, exotic creatures that must have come from distant lands.

Then there were the buildings. Scattered across the fantastic landscape, they seemed to have been constructed from some substance that gleamed and sparkled in the sun like diamonds, each one a fantasy of spires, domes and traceries of delicate carving that would have made the greatest artist envious.

Like the pictures in a zoetrope, the images quickly shifted again. This time Mariah saw people. Oh, not ordinary people, but gods and goddesses, graceful beyond any human conception, in bejewelled clothing spun from clouds and dreams. They moved alone or in small groups, speaking in voices Mariah couldn't hear, gesturing with languid hands as they passed through gardens so elaborate and symmetrical that no human skill could have shaped them. Colored lights sprang from their fingertips; they waved casually, and great platters of fruits and breads and sweet confections spread before them as if by magic.

The last thing Ash showed her was more amazing and yet more real than anything that had gone before. A magnificent beast stood in a meadow of delicate fronds, a beast as much like a horse as a lion is like a kitten. Its glossy coat bore no resemblance to the word "white," so pure it was. Its mane and tail were made up of platinum strands that lifted and fluttered in a gentle breeze. Its ivory hooves were cloven, and in the center of its noble forehead a spiraled horn caught the sunlight and reflected it like a prism.

And its eyes… The creature stared at Mariah as if it could see her, and its eyes were black. So black that no light could plumb their depths. The same eyes she saw before her, gazing at her from Ash's face.

ASH STOOD IN THE meadow, reveling in the glory of his true shape. The blood flowed through his veins like honey as vibrant birds circled overhead, scattering many-hued feathers over his back like a royal cloak. Even the very air sang of his purity.

He saw Mariah from a great distance, as if through an imperfect glass. She seemed unreal to him, a character in one of the many books he had devoured during his time at Donbridge: a mortal woman with dark hair and blue eyes, waiting for him on the other side. She reached out to him, and her lips formed a single word.

Ash.

But that was not, had never been, his name. He lifted one leg and pawed the ground, crushing fragrant blossoms under his hoof. He remembered how he had lived in that other world, the things he had seen and done, the human language he had spoken. Memory called to him just as the girl did…soft, yearning, refusing to withdraw from his innermost sight.

Stay, whispered the soft wind. *Stay,* cried the trees and the gentle sun and the lesser beasts gamboling at his feet.

He turned his head toward the Fane structures that glittered beyond the trees. They were empty. No king, no queen, no courtiers currying favor—not even the half-Fane children who were supposed to be the saviors of the once-immortal race.

This was *his* world now, his entire, and his people were

racing out of the trees to meet him. They were beautiful in a way no creature in human skin could be, liquid silver and gold and bronze sliding over powerful muscle.

"Our king," they said in the language of their kind. "Our king."

He turned to meet them, head high, nostrils flared. The first to arrive knelt before him, touching her horn to the ground. One by one the others bowed, dark eyes joyful.

But then one, silver-coated, lifted his muzzle. The others rose with him in a silent wave.

"Who are you?" the first one asked.

"You are not our king," another said.

"Tainted. Impure. Impostor."

"Human."

Tir-na-Nog shuddered around him, blurring in his vision. His subjects, eyes wild, galloped away. The birds ceased their song. All the colors ran together in a flood that stopped his nostrils and carried him toward the flawed glass and the girl behind it.

The glass shattered. He sat again in the small room, his hands frozen on the girl's shoulders.

"Ash!" she cried.

"My name," he gasped, "is Arion."

Her eyes were dark, a narrow blue ring setting off the dilated pupils. Her body trembled. She opened her mouth but didn't speak.

"I am Arion," he said, knowing he must make her believe.

She closed her eyes. "One of us is mad," she said in a still, small voice. "Or perhaps we both are."

His fingers were numb on her body. "Mariah," he said, shaping the name with a clumsy tongue. "Not...mad."

She rolled away from him, curling her body like a hedgehog. "I don't know how you did what you did, how you made me see those dreams. But you are not a unicorn, Ash. You are simply a man."

A man. He got up, his two legs almost refusing to support him, and went to the mirror above the washstand. He ran his hands over his flat human face.

Tainted. Impure. Impostor.

Nothing had changed since he had first woken in the cage. He could feel himself sliding backward, losing everything he had gained. His eyes still saw Tir-na-Nog, glorious and untouchable. They would always see it.

"I am Arion," he whispered.

Mariah came up behind him, the reflection of her face beside his own. "It is time we went back."

Back to the cage. He banged his head into the glass.

"No." She pulled him away and forced him to sit. "We will return to Marlborough House. You will…be better again, Ash, when you are around the people you have come to know."

He tried to look at her, but her face would not come clear. "They…they blame you," he said.

"For what I did in the ballroom? I know that, Ash. You helped me."

The horn weighed heavy on his forehead. "More," he said. "Do not go back, Mariah."

"I'm not afraid of what they think of me."

"They will hurt you."

"Only if I let them."

She reached for his hand, curling her fingers around his. He remembered holding that hand through the bars of his cage, healing the small wound in her thumb without any thought at all.

"We will return together," she said. "I will fetch Nola."

She left the room, and Ash was alone. The room was dark, the only illumination coming from the sliver of that other world that still lingered in his vision. He heard movement outside the door, and voices, very low.

"Is something wrong, your ladyship?"

"Ash has come," Mariah said. "But…something is not right."

"With Mr. Cornell?"

"I don't know. I don't know at all."

The door opened, and Nola entered, followed by Mariah. The maid, red hair undone for sleep, averted her gaze and quickly began packing Mariah's things. Mariah took a dress behind a tall screen and remained there until Nola joined her. She emerged in a gown of pale blue, several shades lighter than the color of her eyes.

"Ash," she said, touching the back of his chair. "How did you get to the hotel?"

He knew the answer, but the word refused to come. "Horses," he said. "Box."

"A carriage." She turned away and spoke quietly to Nola.

"But if you travel together at this hour…" Nola said.

"I know. But I can't leave him alone. And I will have you as chaperone."

Nola's lips turned down, but she made no argument and quickly left. The thing on the mantel—the clock—ticked for a long time. Mariah said nothing, gone far away inside herself.

Finally Nola returned.

"The carriage is ready, your ladyship."

Mariah nodded. "Ash?"

He rose, staggered, felt for the support of the chair. Mariah reached for him, but he shook his head and made for the door.

No one stirred in the corridor, though there were smells of food coming from another part of the building, burning flesh that made Ash's nostrils close in disgust. Men stood with the horses in front of the carriage. The sun was at least an hour from rising, and the lights on the carriage cast their brightness in Ash's face. The horses bobbed their heads at him, sensing what he was. The men helped Mariah inside the box, and Nola climbed up after her.

He followed, though the walls of the box closed in like great stones meant to crush him. Mariah sat across from him, watching him, her face calm but her eyes almost frantic.

The carriage rattled over cobblestones, past wagons laden with greens and ragged men with their hands stuffed into their threadbare jackets. The horses drew up before the palace, and the man holding the reins jumped down from his high seat.

Something came to Ash before Mariah could leave the carriage. He jumped out ahead of her and offered his hand. She took it, paused to meet his gaze, and then climbed out.

"Thank you, Ash," she murmured. "Please, give me your arm."

He did. It was easier now that he was remembering again. They walked together toward the house, leaving Nola behind to speak to the men. They entered the building and passed into the wide vestibule. Only a pair of liveried footmen were present to greet them.

Mariah slipped her arm from the crook of his and continued on to the north wing. Ash waited, recalling a room where he had slept alone. He traced his way there, closed the door and went to the window.

I do not belong here, he thought. And yet he belonged nowhere else. He was in a place humans called *limbo,* neither fully human nor fully unicorn. Perhaps he would never truly be either one again.

PAMELA HAD FOUND it astonishingly simple to win Mr. Denham's agreement.

Even before she had given her reasons for her unconventional request, his reaction had been more than satisfactory. But when she explained that the entire purpose was to further humiliate Lady Donnington and take revenge on the woman who had exposed both him and his mistress, he simply could not turn her down.

They arranged the assignation for the day of Mariah's return. Pamela would send an anonymous message to Mariah's hotel, urging her to come back to Marlborough House as quickly as possible. Pamela would keep a careful watch out for Mariah, and the scheme would be put into motion immediately upon her arrival.

The place they chose was a corridor frequented by servants going to and from the kitchen. Someone was sure to pass by and see them. If that alone didn't precipitate the kind of gossip Pamela expected, she would give the rumors a little push. In the meantime, she would take thorough pleasure in the deed that would drive Lady Donnington to disgrace at last.

Mr. Denham met her a little before dawn, his face revealing his eagerness to take advantage of Pamela's offer. So much for his fidelity to his mistress, she thought as she straightened her dark wig and drew him close.

There was little delay after that. They waited until the distant voices of the kitchen servants echoed in the corridor, and then Denham pushed her against the wall. He lifted her skirts and petticoats, his hands feeling her naked skin beneath.

"My God," he whispered as his fingers came away wet. He unbuttoned his trousers as Pamela lifted one leg to grant him access.

There was no love-play, no murmured words of affection. Denham grabbed her bottom, pushed her against the wall and entered her with an almost savage thrust. She cried out and gripped his shoulders as he pushed and withdrew, each time harder than the last.

"Ash," she moaned.

He slowed, as if he found her use of the other man's name disconcerting. But he had known this was all part of the game and quickly recovered himself. "Mariah," he whispered, moving inside her more slowly. "I've waited so long."

The voices drew nearer. Denham increased his pace again,

thrusting with such force that her back scraped against the wall. She called out Ash's name again, and he repeated Mariah's.

The voices stopped. Over Denham's shoulder, she could see the dim shapes of two young women. They had come to a halt in the corridor and were staring, their mouths little O's of astonishment.

It was fortunate that they had arrived when they did, Pamela thought. Denham was very close to coming, and so was she.

"Ash," she groaned.

"Mariah." He pumped into her almost violently and gave a great shudder as he spilled his seed. Pamela gasped and flung her head back as she reached her own completion.

By then the servants had fled.

"My God," he said as he withdrew. "Pamela…"

She pushed him away and smoothed her skirts. "I hope that Lady Strickland appreciates what she has in you, Lord Denham," she said with a wry smile.

"Pamela, I must see you again."

"You mean you must have me again." She let her fingers drift across his flushed face. "Perhaps…when this is over."

He tried to kiss her, and she was very much aware that he was growing hard again. She slipped out of his embrace.

"Go to your lover," she suggested. "I am certain she will appreciate your vigor all the more tonight."

"You know…you know I can't see her now."

"Then find a willing maid. We are finished."

Before he could protest, she had walked away, her body and her schemes well satisfied. If everyone in Marlborough House didn't soon know what had happened by tonight, it would be a miracle indeed.

ASH WAITED BY THE window for a long time, listening to the humans move through the corridors and thump up and down the stairs. He hardly heard the soft knock on his door.

"Sir?" Nola opened the door and peeked in, her hair disheveled and her round face drawn. "I'm afraid there is trouble, Mr. Cornell."

Her words formed slowly into something that made sense. "Trouble?"

"For Lady Donnington." She entered the room and closed the door. "They are saying that...that you and her ladyship were seen together early this morning in the servants' area."

"Seen...together?"

Her cheeks turned scarlet. "Seen committing an indiscretion, sir."

Indiscretion. Something of which others disapproved. Of which Mariah disapproved.

"But I have been *here*," he said.

"It does not matter, sir. The rumors have already begun."

Ash remembered that servants had seen them enter the house just before sunrise. "Why would anyone say this?"

Nola's face wrinkled. "I don't know, sir."

He stirred from the window, beginning to remember how certain humans had spoken of Mariah after they had blamed her for sending the message to Lady Strickland's husband. Now they had more reason to hate her. Anger began to simmer in his blood.

"I will go to her."

"Please be careful, sir. If you are seen together now..."

"I shall be." There was simply no question of leaving her to face the humans alone. He would make them realize that he and Mariah had done nothing wrong—even though he had wished it with all his heart.

He bared his teeth and walked out into the corridor.

NEVER COULD MARIAH have been prepared for what occurred after her return to Marlborough House.

At first she assumed that the icy stares were only a lingering consequence of the ballroom incident, that the prince's guests had not let the matter fade, even in her absence.

But those ladies and gentlemen she met in the hall after she emerged from her room did not simply give her odd looks or acknowledge her with a certain coolness as she passed. They avoided her as if she were a leper, and she heard whispering behind her when she went in to luncheon.

On her way back to her room she was intercepted by a most apologetic butler, who regretfully informed her that her chambers had been assigned to another guest. She was directed to a small, cold room, one without so much as a dressing closet or a fireplace to ward off the chill.

She sat on the bed, her mind a weary blank. After what had occurred at the hotel, she wondered that she still had the ability to care what the Marlborough House Set thought of her.

It was so real. The sky, the trees, the…

The unicorn. The one called *Arion*. The creature Ash had claimed to be.

One of us is mad.

No not one, but both. Ash with his delusions—his seeming return to what he had been when she had first found him. And herself…

Herself for believing he had somehow made her enter another world. The same beautiful, perfect world her mother had seen so many times. Somehow she and Ash had shared a vision, and Mariah could find no explanation for that. She knew only that she had imagined it all.

She spread her hands and stared at them, at each slender finger so well formed for its tasks. If she were indeed on the final path to going insane, it wouldn't matter what anyone thought of her—not here, not at Donbridge, not anywhere. She would retreat into a world of her own creation and choose, as her mother had done, never to leave it again.

For several hours she lay on the narrow lumpy bed and tried to sleep. No one came to her door. Sometime after noon, she went to the mirror at the tiny dressing table and unpinned her hair. Nola had gone about her own business, but Mariah felt she was far better off alone. Slowly and deliberately she put up her hair again, caring little whether or not the style was fashionable or flattering to her face. Working patiently through the difficulties of dressing herself, she changed into the most conservative afternoon gown she owned.

There was nothing more to be done but to go downstairs and face her judges.

"Mariah."

She looked up into the eyes of her brother-in-law, who had entered the room without knocking. His expression was so grim that she braced herself to hear some terrible news.

"Are you all right?" Sinjin asked, taking a seat beside the dressing table

Giving him the real answer was out of the question. "Is there a reason why I shouldn't be?" she asked calmly.

"You don't know?"

"I have been away, as you must be aware," she said.

He shook his head. "Oh, Mariah."

"Tell me."

In terse sentences he explained how she had been blamed for a letter exposing Lady Strickland as an adulteress. Those rumors alone would be enough to damn Mariah in the opinion of many in the Set.

But there was worse to come. "You were seen with Ash in the servants' corridor near the kitchen just before dawn," he said.

"*Seen* with him?"

"I know of no polite way to phrase it. Nearly everyone at Marlborough House now regards you as the worst sort of hypocrite."

She began to understand, though her anger and shame still hid behind a protective veil of despair. The upstart American girl, only a few months married, had resented the behavior of her betters, so she had taken petty revenge for the cuts she had endured after the ballroom incident. Then she had committed the very same act for which she had exposed Lady Strickland to the condemnation of her husband and the more conventional society outside the Set.

"We returned together to Marlborough House an hour before dawn," she acknowledged, beginning to shiver, "but we parted soon after. Ash and I were never near the kitchen. Whoever reported this must have seen someone else." She held his gaze. "Do you believe these stories, Sinjin?"

He looked away. "It doesn't matter what I believe. Those who might never have suspected anything untoward between you and Ash have now been dissecting every moment that you have been observed in one another's company. And the fact that you are only recently married and have borne your husband no heirs…" He cleared his throat. "It would be best if you left Marlborough House."

Anger pierced the veil of distress. "Leave without defending myself—or Ash? No. I did that before, and it made everything worse. I will not do so again."

"Your detractors will not be persuaded otherwise now," he said.

She rose and walked across the tiny expanse of unobstructed floor, pacing from the narrow bed to the washstand and back again. "I won't run away."

"You must."

Ash stood in the doorway, his expression twice as forbidding as Sinjin's.

Sinjin got up. "Get out of here, Cornell."

Ash ignored him. "I know what has happened," he said to Mariah. "I will make these humans see that they are wrong."

Mariah shivered. *Humans?* "You can't help, Ash. The others blame it on me, not you. You might win back their favor, but I—"

"Their favor is of no interest to me." He stared at Sinjin. "Take her back. Protect her."

"That's exactly what I intend to do." Sinjin strode across the room until he stood toe-to-toe with Ash. "There is something you should know about this man, Mariah. He attempted…he made advances on Lady Westlake."

His full meaning didn't penetrate Mariah's consciousness all at once. She put the words "advances" and "Lady Westlake" together as if they were pieces of a difficult puzzle that she had just begun to solve.

"Pamela?" she said stupidly. "Ash?"

"She told me," Sinjin said, his mouth curled in disgust.

"And you believed her?"

"Cornell did not deny it."

She stared at Ash, her body going numb with shock. "Ash?"

He wouldn't look at her. "Yes," he said, "it is true."

The numbness spread to Mariah's legs. She sat down carefully.

"Why?" she asked.

"Does it matter?" Sinjin said.

But she thought she knew why. She'd denied Ash her body. She had behaved like the worst sort of hussy by allowing him to reach a point of arousal that must have far exceeded her own. And Pamela was a born seductress. How could Mariah blame anyone but herself for what Ash had done?

"There is clearly no reason for you to stay now," Sinjin said, turning toward her again. "You can have nothing to gain except further suffering."

Perhaps that was exactly what she deserved. She and Ash *had* been lovers in every way that mattered. She *had* been a hypocrite in disapproving of Lady Strickland and those like her. She ought to pay for her hypocrisy…and her foolish belief that Ash couldn't want anyone but her.

But the strength to face her accusers seemed to have drained out of her. She'd been no less than honest when she'd said that Ash could win back the favor of the guests where she could not. He was a man, and the standards of behavior were different for men and women. The scandal would eventually blow over. For him.

But not if she remained to keep the flames burning.

"Mariah," Sinjin said, sitting beside her and taking her hands. "If you still have any doubts…" He cleared his throat again. "The prince asked me to attend him this morning. He also thinks it best that you return to Donbridge with as little fuss as possible."

Of course. Even the Prince of Wales, for all his tolerance, could not appear to approve open scandal in his own residence.

"I see," she said. "I see very clearly. I will return to home immediately."

He squeezed her hands. "I will take you myself."

She was very careful not to look in Ash's direction. "I never belonged here, Sinjin."

"I should have discouraged you from coming."

"But I had to come, you see. Ash—" She stopped and looked toward the door. Ash was gone.

Sinjin released her hands. "You really do love him, don't you?"

With all my heart. For the rest of my life.

"Our association has been nothing but disaster since he met the dowager," she said. "It is best that we part. I will be packed and ready to leave by this evening."

There was no more to be said. Sinjin left her alone. Nola reappeared just in time to help her pack her things. Sinjin's

carriage was awaiting her at the appointed time. Hostile onlookers watched as her trunks were being loaded, each one
containing a ragged piece of her soul.

Sinjin led her toward the brougham's door and offered his
hand, but the rattle of an arriving carriage made her pause.

"My God," Sinjin said.

She followed his gaze. At first she thought that the man
descending from the carriage was Ash, but even before she
realized that was impossible, she saw the sweep of black hair
and the fresh scar across his cheek.

Donnington.

CHAPTER NINETEEN

SINJIN WAS MOVING BEFORE Mariah could catch her breath.

"Donnington!" he said, offering his hand to his elder brother. "For God's sake, man, where have you been?"

The earl offered no embrace, and his manner was stiff. He had not yet noticed Mariah. As the men exchanged a few brief words, Mariah was keenly aware that the men and women awaiting her departure had noticed Donnington's arrival. If he hadn't yet heard of the scandal surrounding his new wife, he soon would.

Mariah braced herself and walked toward Donnington's carriage. He saw her immediately.

"Mariah!" he said, striding toward her. She expected him to seize her arm, but instead he stopped and glared at her from his dark, penetrating eyes.

"I went to Donbridge," he said, "and my mother informed me that you were here. What mad whim drove you to come to Marlborough House by yourself?" He continued speaking before she could answer. "By God, Mariah, I ought to—"

"It was my doing, Donnington," Sinjin said, stepping between them. "I felt she was too much alone at Donbridge and a change would do her good."

"*You* felt?" Donnington gave a sharp laugh. "As I seem to recall, Mariah is *my* wife."

"Whom you left without explanation." Recognizing that several guests were drawing closer, Sinjin lowered his voice.

"What did you expect her to do? Wither at Donbridge for months on end?"

"I expected her to behave as a countess should," Donnington said, obviously struggling with his fury. He signaled to his footmen. "See that Lady Donnington's luggage is transferred to my carriage. We shall be leaving immediately."

"I was already leaving for Donbridge," Mariah said as calmly as she could.

"Were you?" His gaze swept around the growing audience as if he sought one face in particular and couldn't find it.

Ash, Mariah thought. *He's looking for Ash.* How much had the dowager told him? Did he know that his "cousin" had left Donbridge at the same time as Mariah?

She prayed that Ash would stay away, but God was in no mood to answer her prayers.

"Donnington!"

The voice was more growl than speech. The people observing the little drama made way for the tall, well-formed man with white hair, black eyes and Donnington's features.

Donnington raised his head. For an almost incalculable second his face went slack. Then it hardened again, and he stared as if he were as astonished as the guests watching the two nearly identical men come face-to-face.

"You dare to return?" Ash said, his words and voice once again what Mariah had come to expect of him since their meeting in Donnington's library.

"Who is this man?" Donnington asked the crowd with a gesture of perplexity.

"His name is Ashton Cornell," Sinjin said coldly. "He is our American cousin."

"Our cousin?"

"Why are you so surprised, Donnington? Have you not seen him before?"

"No. How should I have done?" The earl stared at Ash as

if reassessing his first judgment. "Ashton Cornell," he said. He made no move to offer his hand. "Perhaps I ought to welcome you to England."

"You bastard," Ash said quietly. "You are a coward and a traitor. You betrayed your wife and imprisoned me, and I will have satisfaction."

Murmurs of surprise rose from the observers, many of whom shook their heads in disbelief. Someone laughed.

"Imprisoned you?" Donnington said in a subtly mocking tone. "What is this man talking about, Sinjin? Is he mad?"

Sinjin gritted his teeth, the muscles in his jaw flexing. "I think we had better discuss this privately."

"No, no. Let the poor man have his say." Donnington briefly met Mariah's eyes. "Do you know this Mr. Cornell, my dear?"

"Come away," Mariah begged him. "Let us return to Donbridge."

But Ash was having none of it. He advanced on Donnington.

"You are a villain," he said. "You believed that you had everything arranged to your satisfaction, but it did not turn out as you wished."

"He *is* mad," Donnington said. "Someone call for a doctor."

"No!" Mariah clutched at his arm. "He is only confused. Once we are gone—"

"Have you some interest in this fellow, Mariah?" Donnington asked without looking at her. "Is that why you defend him?"

"He is your cousin. We have become acquainted since his arrival in England."

"'Acquainted'?"

"I understand that he has been through a great deal," she said. "You are just arrived home. This argument can be resolved at a later time."

"It will be resolved here," Ash said. He removed one of the gloves he was wearing and threw it at Donnington's feet. "I challenge you, Earl of Donbridge."

Murmurs rose to cries of disbelief. "What have we here?" Donnington asked. "Have we returned to the days of chivalry? How very quaint." He played to his audience. "Will someone fetch me a pistol? Or perhaps it ought to be swords at dawn?"

He laughed, and others joined in his laughter, though there was a thread of unease running through the mingled voices. Donnington gestured to the footmen, who began to transfer Mariah's boxes to his carriage.

For a moment it seemed as if Ash might back down, recognizing the futility of his challenge. But then he closed the distance between himself and Donnington in a few strides and struck the earl in the face with the full weight of his fist.

Donnington fell, hard. He scrambled to his feet immediately, blood flowing from one of his nostrils.

"By God," he swore under his breath, rubbing at his face. "You'll pay for that." In a louder voice, he said, "Someone restrain this man!"

Mariah flung herself between them, gazing into Ash's eyes, begging him to *think*.

But he was well beyond rational thought. He set her aside and lunged at Donnington, seizing the shoulders of the earl's jacket. "You will pay," he snarled. "You will never hunt me. And you will not keep *her*."

A pair of men from among the onlookers grabbed Ash's arms. He nearly knocked them down, but a third man joined them, and together they held Ash tightly. Mariah had no doubt that he could fight them all off, but he subsided, sudden weariness and confusion in his face. He never so much as glanced in her direction.

"This man is clearly ill," Donnington said, dabbing at his nose with a handkerchief. "I will not press charges if he is seen to properly."

Everyone fell silent. Another man in the crowd turned and walked briskly toward the door to the house, doubtless to call for a doctor as the earl had demanded.

Mariah could barely control her trembling. She hated Donnington then, with the same vehemence she'd felt when she'd first heard Ash's accusations. Time, and Ash's encouraging progress, had tempered her feelings and given her hope that Ash's returning memory might somehow absolve Donnington of his crime.

Now she was all but certain of his guilt. But if she defended Ash, any hope of getting the truth from Donnington would be lost.

She pretended to stagger, as if the events of the past few minutes had overwhelmed her.

"Please, Donnington," she whispered. "I would like to go home."

He stared at her through narrowed eyes and finally helped her into his carriage. The men holding Ash simply waited, as if debating what to do with their prisoner.

They will let him go. They will see that he isn't really mad. He'll make them see.

If he could overcome his rage at Donnington…if he could be again the man who had moved so easily through Marlborough House, before the visions…

She would have given ten years of her life to let Ash know that she was with him, if only in spirit. But he didn't look up, and her attention was caught by another coming to greet Donnington with a pretty moue of sympathy.

Lady Westlake. Sinjin went stiff, only his head moving as he watched Pamela offer her hand to the earl.

Mariah couldn't hear what they said to one another. The conversation seemed light enough, as it must be in the presence of others, but she could almost feel the heat between them—at least from Lady Westlake's side.

Sinjin must have felt the same. But he stood by the carriage door until the conversation ended and Donnington was watching Pamela return to the house. The earl cast a dark glance in Mariah's direction and strode after Lady Westlake. The men holding Ash followed him.

The velvet seat squeaked as Sinjin climbed in and sat opposite Mariah.

"You did the right thing by not interfering," he said in a grim voice.

"Did I?"

"You need my brother's trust, at least for the time being. We all want the truth."

Sometimes the truth was almost too hard to bear. "Why didn't you go after them?"

"Donnington never listens to me. I could make matters worse."

Or perhaps Sinjin was a coward, unwilling to face his brother's anger.

She schooled herself to remain calm. "You did not try to speak to Lady Westlake," she said.

He closed his eyes. "She was otherwise engaged."

"What did she tell you when she accused Ash of…approaching her?" Mariah asked.

He opened his eyes again. "Don't torment yourself."

"My feelings for Ash haven't changed," she said.

"What *could* change them, Mariah?"

His question made her heart drop into her stomach. "What did she say?"

"She implied that you and Ash have been conspiring to claim some part of the earl's fortune."

Mariah nearly wept but laughed instead, covering her mouth to stifle her laughter. "Conspiring since when? Am I supposed to have imprisoned Ash, only to pretend to find him and help him to cheat my husband?"

"She doesn't know anything about the time before Ash came to Donbridge."

"She is still a liar."

"I am aware of that possibility."

"Then why did you accuse Ash—"

"I wanted you away from here, away from Ash. He can only bring you trouble. His bizarre behavior—"

"I don't care about what happens to me as long as Ash is safe."

"But you must." He hesitated, his expression as weary as Ash's had been. "Could Pamela have been correct in that one matter? Could Ash have arranged in some way to feign imprisonment and win your sympathy, all in order to insinuate himself into—"

Mariah realized that her laughter was teetering on the edge of hysteria. "Surely you don't believe that?"

He dragged his hand across his face. "No. My brother must in some way be responsible. But getting him to admit it—"

"I shall find a way." She leaned back in her seat, unable to keep from thinking about what Ash must be enduring. If she heard that he had been confined again, she would tell them the whole story. Let them think her mad.

"Your ladyship?" Nola said from the carriage doorway.

The maid's voice was like a balm. "Nola," Mariah said, leaning toward the carriage door, "we shall be leaving presently. Is everything stowed?"

"It is, your ladyship." Her brow creased in concern. "Are you well, ma'am?"

"Quite well."

"I am glad, your ladyship. But Mr. Cornell—"

"If you have no other tasks, Nola, you may ride with us."

"But won't it be…won't it be a little crowded, ma'am?"

As in answer to her question, Donnington arrived. He pushed Nola aside, his shoulders framed in the doorway.

"Sinjin," he said, without looking at his brother, "you and the girl will ride in your carriage. Mariah will ride with me."

Mariah said nothing as Sinjin climbed out of Donnington's carriage and, followed by Nola, entered his own. Once the doors were closed and the carriages were moving, Donnington began his assault.

"Do you think I don't know what you've been doing?" he asked in a deceptively quiet voice.

"I have been staying at Marlborough House, under Mr. Ware's protection," she said, matching his tone.

"Sinjin's protection! Does his idea of 'protection' include letting you drag the Donnington name in the mud and have affairs with other men?"

"What Lady Westlake told you is a lie," she said. "Mr. Cornell and I were not together near the kitchen, nor did I send the letter condemning Lady Strickland." She clenched her skirts in her fists. "If you wish to know the origin of those rumors, you might want to question Lady Westlake further."

Donnington raised his hand, and she prepared herself for a blow. But he lowered it again, contempt on his face. "I never thought *you* would leave Donbridge for the pleasures of Marlborough House," he said. "Our agreement—"

"Did not include your leaving immediately after our marriage. I am hardly your wife, Donnington. You chose to abandon Donbridge for *your* own pleasures."

"You are my wife." He seized her arm with the speed of a striking snake. "You are to be obedient, loyal, and appropriate in your behavior at all times."

"And you are to have no standards of behavior at all?"

His fingers tightened on her wrist. "Did you lie with Cornell?"

"No."

His gaze remained fixed on hers. "You were seen with him many times."

"No more than I was seen with other men." She searched his eyes. "Why did you leave? You were so different in New York. I actually believed…" She looked out the carriage window. "How can you have changed so much?"

"I haven't changed. It is you—"

"Why did you imprison your own cousin?"

His skin blanched. "Imprison him? I had never seen the man before today, when he attacked me."

"Then why did I find him locked up in the folly by the mere, half-starved and irregularly fed by a keeper no one at Donbridge knew about?"

Donnington opened his mouth and closed it again with a snap. "My dear," he said very carefully, "I fear for your sanity."

"I have another witness," she said. "Your own brother."

Surely he ought to have anticipated that someone would have found Ash eventually, but he seemed completely unprepared. "The man you call Cornell," he said, the words half-strangled in his throat, "tried to kill me."

"I beg your pardon?"

"He appeared shortly before our wedding. It was clear that he was a relation, but his behavior was beyond eccentric. He claimed he was the son of my mother's sister, and that he had come to England to receive his portion of the Ware fortune."

"You mean that he did not know that he was entitled to nothing except what you might choose to give him?"

"What would you expect? An American, believing himself entitled to anything he can steal by any means."

The insult was surely calculated, but Mariah would not be distracted. "So he arrived in England, without revealing himself to anyone else, and approached you with outrageous demands. And you found that sufficient reason to cage him like an animal."

"I told you, he tried to kill me. When I refused to grant his demands, he obtained a gun and twice tried to shoot me when I was riding across the estate."

"And instead of summoning the police, you took the law into your own hands."

"He proved himself entirely mad, capable of anything. I would not under any circumstances see you put at risk. But I hoped he might regain his sanity before I summoned the authorities."

Donnington must have known that what he said was not only improbable but outrageous, beyond the behavior of any civilized person. And yet he spoke without apology, without regret.

Mariah was having none of it. "You went away without telling me, without telling anyone. You left Ash to rot. Why?"

"I had my reasons."

"And I am supposed to be satisfied with such an explanation?"

"Some day you will understand."

"I want to understand *now*. You must have known that he would be found eventually. He was a little mad, but how could any man not be, wrongfully imprisoned in a cell scarcely big enough for a dog?" She held her husband's stare. "Sinjin and I did what we could to help him. He was finally able to tell us the truth about what you did."

"What truth? The truth of a madman?"

"The truth of an evil perpetrated upon an innocent man."

If Donnington could have stood up, he would have done so. As it was, he simply became more menacing.

"You were taken in, Mariah. You accepted his lies." He laughed. "You came to care for him, didn't you? To believe that *I* was the villain?"

"I didn't know what to believe for a long time," she said. "I tried to withhold judgment. But now I see that you have no defense."

"You are a child and a fool, Mariah."

"I was, yes."

"I can still destroy your precious Mr. Cornell. He attacked me in a public place. All I need do is testify that he was already mad when he first came to me, and he will be put away forever."

"And all I need do is join my testimony to Sinjin's."

He leaned back again. "Are you so naïve as to think that they would ever accept your story over mine? They already think you are mad."

"Sinjin is well regarded by the prince and the Marlborough House Set. What reason would he have to speak falsely, especially about his own brother?"

"To gain the earldom. To take revenge for what he perceives as injustices in the past."

The words were accompanied by a sneer, but suddenly Mariah was certain that Donnington was genuinely shaken. "Did you intend to kill Ash and hide his body?" she demanded. "Whatever your real reasons for what you did, they are certainly not what you claim."

He breathed harshly through clenched teeth. "You are quite a clever little girl, Mariah. But you have stepped into waters much too deep for your dainty feet." His eyes glinted. "My mother has urged me to seek an annulment to our marriage. She has a number of witnesses willing to testify that they heard you arguing with me on our wedding night, refusing to let me approach you and swearing I would never have you. Refusing to honor your vows is grounds for dissolution of the marriage."

"*I* refused?"

"Then there is the matter of your apparent infidelity. I believe we can find other witnesses happy to testify there, as well."

"Your mother and her witnesses are liars. And why should I contest an annulment? My reputation has already been ruined. I have no more desire to be married to you than you do to me."

"Ah." He smiled almost sweetly. "But there you are wrong, my dear. I *do* intend to remain married to you. I had my doubts before the ceremony, but as an honorable man I went through with it, even though I had come to believe I was making a mistake. I changed my mind while I was away. And now…" His smile broadened. "I would never let you go, Mariah. I know you think you love Cornell, but you will never have him."

"You would stay married to a woman you clearly despise simply to take revenge on another?"

"But I don't despise you, Mariah. I admire your—what do you Americans say?—your 'spunk.' When enough time has passed, you will turn to me."

A knot of realization began to twist in Mariah's stomach. "How do you suppose you will ever manage that, Donnington?"

"By striking a bargain with you, my dear. If you cooperate, I shall not pursue my contention that Cornell twice attempted to kill me. I will simply testify that he was bent on causing trouble in our family and that I warned him to return to America…which clearly he did not do." He narrowed his eyes to slits. "You have wealth of your own, Mariah, but I have far more. It isn't difficult to buy men of a venal nature, which is a majority of the human race. If you do not agree to my proposition, I can see to it that 'Mr. Cornell' is put away for a very long time."

"Why?" she whispered. "Why did you marry me?"

"I want you, Mariah. That is all that matters."

But it wasn't. She sensed that there was much more behind Donnington's strange behavior than she could yet determine. Why had he married her if he'd had doubts about her? As he'd reminded her, he didn't need her money. How could going away for several months, never communicating with her or any member of his family, have convinced him that he wanted her?

But Donnington could not be reasoned with. He had committed a crime and would get away with it. The alternative was to see his wealth and power focused on destroying Ash.

They rode on in silence, stopping for the night at an inn in Hertfordshire, where—much to Mariah's profound relief—they were given separate rooms.

The next day they reached Donbridge, where the dowager was overflowing with joy at her beloved boy's return.

For all her efforts, Donnington paid his mother scant attention. In turn, she barely acknowledged Mariah, her demeanor as cold as an Antarctic iceberg.

Dinner was a horrid affair. Mariah imagined Ash being held by "doctors" bought and paid for by Donnington, prepared to do anything necessary to keep their "deranged" patient quiet. After she and the dowager left the table, Mariah made an excuse and returned almost immediately to the dining room.

"I will do as you say," she said. "I will be your wife in every way. But you must release Ash and allow him to leave the country."

Donnington sipped his port. "I am happy to see that you have come to your senses, my dear," he said. "We will enjoy our marriage bed tonight."

"No." She lifted her head. "Not until I see Ash board a ship bound for America."

He set his glass down, hard. "I could force you."

"Then our bargain will be null and void. I shall never be yours."

He rose, nearly knocking his chair backward. "Mariah," he said, his voice suddenly hoarse. "I have never humbled myself to a woman before. I do so now."

"You?"

"Yes. I was wrong to leave you. I did love you, Mariah. I just didn't realize how much until I went away." He touched the scar on his cheek. "When I left, I went to hunt in Germany and

Hungary. I almost died. I was ill for many weeks. A man near death begins to see many things to which he was blind before."

Mariah closed her eyes. He appeared sincere, even vulnerable in a way she had never observed in all their time together. Yet she could not believe him. He might have reasons for wanting her now, but they had nothing to do with love.

"Once I thought I loved you, Giles," she said. "But how can I love you now, knowing what you did to Ash?"

"I do not demand your love." He raised his hands in a gesture almost like a plea. "Cornell is not what he appears to be. I ask only for time, time to show you."

"How can I trust you?"

"Give me a chance, Mariah. I forgive you for any past indiscretions. It will be as if they never happened. And I will let Cornell go."

"You will allow me to see Ash off on the ship?"

"Yes. And he will have all the money he requires to make his way when he returns to America."

"Then—when he is gone—I will be yours in every way."

Donnington circled the table and held out his hand. "Shall we shake hands on it, Mariah?"

She stared at his outstretched fingers. Then she slowly put her hand in his.

CHAPTER TWENTY

"SHE IS QUITE MAD, you know," Vivian said.

At first she wasn't certain that her son was listening. Then, abruptly, he turned toward her, morning sunlight streaming through the window onto his broad shoulders, his expression as closed as one of the books in his library.

"Why do you say that, Mother?" he asked. "Has she done something to provoke such an accusation?"

She quickly softened her tone. "She refused to fulfill her wifely duties," she said. "She drove you away."

"She did not refuse. I had doubts about our marriage, and—"

"As well you might! I have heard about her shocking behavior at Marlborough House. Surely there can be no better reason—"

His stare was savage. "Mother," he said, "it would be best if you stay out of such matters. The dower house is quite comfortable. Perhaps you would be happier there."

Even his threat of exile, frightening as it was, couldn't silence her. "You doubt that she is mad? Perhaps she is not—at the moment. But her mother was quite insane. She ended her life in an asylum."

"I know."

"You know?"

"Did you think I didn't look into her background before I courted her?"

"Then why…why did you marry her?" She reached out to touch his arm. "I am your mother, Donnie. I want only what is best for you. Once you are no longer able to annul your marriage, you will be compelled to provide for her for the rest of her life. If she does go mad…" She shuddered. "And your children, Donnington. Think of your children and what she may pass on to them."

"May," he said. He stepped back, so that her hand slipped from his arm. "I am prepared to take that risk."

"But why? You can't possibly love her, or you would never have—"

He turned on his heel and left her standing in the drawing room as if she were a child begging for sweets before dinner.

For the rest of the day, Vivian wandered the house in a daze. Mariah remained in her room. Donnington saw to his business. No one spoke to her except the servants, and then as little as possible. They knew her own son had treated her like a parlor maid, dismissing her concerns as if they were so much meaningless babble.

He wanted the girl. It made no sense, and neither did his vague accounting of why he had failed to write while he was on his supposed "hunting trip" in Germany and the Balkans. It seemed she merited no real explanation.

When night fell, she found herself in the entrance hall, unable to consider even the idea of sleep. Behind the closed door of the library she heard voices, one of them Donnington's.

The other was also male, but of a much lighter timbre. Not Sinjin, nor any of the servants. She could not make out the words, and she knew she should turn away and leave her son his privacy.

But she did not.

Instead, she moved closer to the door, close enough so that she could set her ear against the wood.

"…our agreement," the lighter voice was saying. "It was

your task to leave them alone together so that Arion could win her cooperation and bring her to the Gate."

"Cornell has failed," Donnington snapped. "Or did you not know that he has already taken her virginity?"

"But he has not. I know."

"It doesn't matter now. His desire for Mariah is moot. He is in custody for attempting to attack me, and he will remain so unless I authorize his release."

"What becomes of him is of no moment to me. In coming to care for the girl, to *love* her—" the unknown man gave the word a snarl of contempt "—he has become little more than human himself. But that can still change to your benefit." A silence. "You have one final chance, Donnington. I have almost consolidated my power in Tir-na-Nog, but even after I have won, Mariah will be a prize. When I am ready to come for her—"

"I am no longer interested in our agreement. I have changed my mind."

"Has your absence addled your wits, human? How is it that you can have 'changed your mind' when you have not seen the girl in months?"

"She is my wife. *Mine.*"

Vivian closed her eyes. The rest of what they had said made no sense, but this did. Now she would have her answers.

"You would not understand, Fane lordling," Donnington said. "Your kind have no feelings. I came to care for the girl even before we were wed, but I honored our bargain until I came to my senses."

"Your senses?"

There was another silence, pregnant with hostility. "I've no proof that you would ever have kept your part of the bargain. If you do not overthrow Oberon, your powers remain limited in this world. And without the ability to change Cornell back to his true form, you would renege even if

Mariah were delivered to you. But if you did gain that power, you could force Mariah through the Gate yourself. Why, then, should you keep our agreement?"

"You dare to doubt my word?"

"You want her, Cairbre, at any price. I choose not to let you have her. You used me, believing in your arrogance that you could manipulate me as you would have manipulated Arion. You were wrong."

"Do you think the girl trusts you now? She found Arion in his prison, just as we intended. But her feelings for him have grown too strong. Does she not believe his accusations that you are responsible for his suffering?"

"I told her that he tried to kill me."

"Lies which you cannot back with proof."

"They will suffice. Return to your country and seek your own bride."

"Be warned, mortal. When I come fully into my power and Oberon can no longer enforce his will, I will be free to enter this world in my physical form. I will be free to destroy you."

"There must be some way to destroy *you*, Cairbre. And I'll find it."

"You will suffer for your insolence, human. Make no mistake. Even now, I can do you harm."

Vivian started as a loud crash rattled the walls. Without thinking, she opened the door and stumbled into the room.

Donnington was just getting up from the floor, a fallen bookshelf directly behind him. The man to whom he had been speaking stood well out of reach.

Except he was not standing. He was floating in a nimbus of light that might have belonged to an angel.

Vivian covered her mouth with her hand. Neither man so much as glanced in her direction.

She backed out of the room and closed the door, as quiet as a whisper.

"Think carefully before you attempt that again," Donnington said, his voice shaken but unafraid. "Cornell shall meet his end soon enough, and you shall never interfere in my life again."

"This is not the last time you will hear from me, mortal."

Then there was no more talk, no sound from the room. After a few minutes, Vivian heard the noise of something heavy being scraped across the carpet, and she turned and fled up the stairs to her room.

She had *seen* the…man, or whatever he was, called Cairbre. She had heard the words he spoke to Donnington. He had threatened her son. And they had both referred to Cornell as if he were part of some sort of agreement between them. An agreement that somehow would have seen Mariah delivered to Cairbre, with Donnington's assistance.

It made no sense. Only two things were clear: Cairbre wished harm to Donnington—harm Vivian was certain he had the ability to inflict—and Donnington intended to kill Cornell.

Vivian laughed under her breath. She wondered if *she* were the one going mad.

But no. She saw her path clearly, perhaps for the first time in months. She liked Mariah no better than she had from the beginning. The girl was at the center of some contest of wills between Donnington and a seemingly human creature who could float above the earth. She was also very likely an adulteress. But neither like nor dislike had anything to do with Vivian's next decision.

Shivering, she peeked into the corridor. There was a chance that Donnington had already gone to claim his husbandly rights, but she was prepared to take that chance.

She pushed Mariah's door open without knocking. The girl was standing by her window; even when she heard the door, she didn't move.

"Donnington," Mariah said softly. "I thought we had an agreement."

"Mariah."

The girl turned, her face an almost frightening blank. "What do you want, Vivian?"

There was not an ounce of respect or courtesy in Mariah's tone, but Vivian found she couldn't blame her. "I must speak with you."

Mariah glanced toward the door that opened to the small room connecting her chamber with Donnington's. "What can you possibly have to say to me?"

"Is Donnington in his room?"

"I heard him come up."

"Then we cannot speak here."

"You wish to keep secrets from your own son?"

"Please. Come downstairs to the kitchen."

Mariah searched Vivian's eyes. "If you still expect Donnington to seek an annulment…"

"I know he will not. But there are questions only you can answer."

With another glance toward Donnington's room, Mariah followed Vivian out the door, down the servants' staircase, through narrow corridors and into the deserted kitchen area. Mariah stopped just inside the door.

Vivian was too unsure of her legs to remain standing. "Forgive me," she said, seeking a chair, "but I have heard disturbing things that I must discuss with you."

A spark of interest—or perhaps concern—lit Mariah's eyes. "What have you heard?"

"How did you first meet Mr. Cornell?"

A look of distress wiped the calm indifference from Mariah's face. "What does that matter now?"

"You did not first meet him when he came to Donbridge, did you?"

"Why should *you* care about the truth?"

Vivian clasped her hands, hoping that Mariah would not detect their weakness. "I know I have not treated you well. I believed you responsible for my son's disappearance. I am no longer so certain."

"Why?"

"Please. Answer my question."

Mariah leaned heavily against a worktable. "I found him imprisoned in the folly by the mere."

Sharp lights whirled about in Vivian's head. "Imprisoned… how?"

"He was in a small cage, barely clothed and fed. He could hardly speak."

"And he…he told you that my son—"

"Yes. He said that Donnington imprisoned him, though he has never told me the reason why."

"But Mr. Cornell claimed to be my sister's child!"

"He had lost part of his memory. Given his resemblance to Donnington, it was the best explanation we could find."

Vivian found a mote of courage. "Donnington said that Cornell tried to kill him."

"So he claims."

"You don't believe him."

"No."

"Then why are you staying with my son?"

"Because he threatened to hurt Ash if I didn't."

"How can I accept any of this?"

"You don't have to." Mariah started for the door.

"No. Wait!" Vivian tried to stand but sank back into her chair. "You love him, don't you?"

"I will never love Donnington."

"Cornell. You love Cornell."

"Yes."

"You would do anything to protect him."

"Yes."

"I…" Vivian closed her eyes against the swaying of the room. "I do not know if you were unfaithful to my son. But I know that Donnington intends to harm your lover."

"We struck a bargain. He will leave Ash alone as long as I stay with him willingly, as his wife in every way."

Vivian's eyes filled with tears. "I do not think that will stop him."

In an instant Mariah became one of the Grecian Furies, her slender body shaking with anger. "How do you know?"

"I heard him…speaking with another man. A man called Cairbre."

"I don't know the name." Mariah advanced, hands clenched into fists. "Tell me what else Donnington said."

How could she, when she still only understood a fraction of the conversation? "They spoke of 'this world,' as if there were another one."

Mariah stopped, looking as though she had just found herself on the edge of a precipice. "Another world?"

"They called it…Tir-something. And this Cairbre said he wanted to take you from my son."

"Did you see this stranger?" At Vivian's nod, Mariah asked, "What did he look like?"

"He was like an angel…or a devil. Beautiful, wearing rich clothing of a type I have never seen before. And he was…" She drew in a breath. "Floating above the ground."

She watched Mariah's eyes, waiting for a disbelieving laugh or an accusation of madness.

But Mariah only felt for a chair and sat down near Vivian.

"Just as Ash showed me," she murmured. "But why should Cairbre want me?"

"I don't know. I only know that your Ash is in danger, and so is my son." Vivian paused, struggling to fill lungs that seemed to have shrunk to the size of walnuts. "Whatever he may have done, I have come to believe that my son truly loves you. But you could never make him happy. And I will not permit him to commit an act that he will regret for the rest of his life."

Mariah met her eyes. "I'll go to Donnington," she said, rising abruptly. "I'll make him tell me—"

"No. You must leave, Mariah."

"And let him hurt Ash? Never."

"I will tell him that I know what he plans. I can stop him."

"That's not good enough." Mariah charged for the door and strode through it before Vivian could find her feet. Panting, Vivian followed her up the stairs. At the last minute Mariah entered her own room, and Vivian went after her.

"You were right," Mariah said. "I can't let him know." Her gaze turned inward. "Vivian, you must help me get Ash away. You and Sinjin. You must act immediately, while I distract Donnington by whatever means necessary."

"Yes. Of course. But—"

The fury was back in Mariah's eyes. "Swear to me that you'll keep silent and help Ash."

"Yes. I swear it."

A rush of cool air swept into the room. As Mariah spun to face the window, a dark figure pushed his way through the casement and dropped to the floor.

"Ash!"

Vivian pressed her hands to her mouth. Cornell gave her the barest glance before snatching Mariah into his arms.

"You are safe," he said, cradling her head between his hands.

"Yes." She returned his frantic kisses. "How did you get away?"

"That is of no importance."

"Are they after you?"

He kissed her again. "They will not find me. I am here to take you away."

."No." She pulled back and curled her hands around his shoulders. "*You* must leave. Donnington intends to kill you. Go to America, where you will be safe."

"Not without you." Once again he looked over her shoulder, pinning Vivian with his stare. "Where is Donnington?"

Vivian was afraid, as afraid as she had ever been her life. "In the next room," she said. "And if you do not leave immediately, he will hear us."

"I already have."

Donnington walked through the door of the dressing room, fully dressed and bearing a rifle. He pointed the weapon casually at Ash's chest.

"I thought I was finally done with you," he said. "But I see you are like the proverbial bad penny." He smiled. "There is only one way to dispose of a housebreaker who threatens one's wife."

ASH MET DONNINGTON'S cool gaze and saw in this human his greatest enemy, the man who had believed Lady Westlake's lies, who had taken Mariah away, who had nearly succeeded in confining him to yet another cage.

But he saw his enemy through eyes that were no longer entirely human. He was no longer weak, no longer a victim to be used for the purposes of others. The men who had tried to hold him had ample cause to regret their actions. And just as he had defeated his captors, he knew that he could defeat Donnington, as well.

Donnington would die, as he deserved.

Just as Ash readied himself for attack, Mariah walked directly in front of the muzzle of the rifle.

"You may kill *me* if you choose, Donnington," she said, "but you will not lay a finger on Ash."

Donnington grinned. "I don't intend to *touch* him, my dear." He jerked his head toward the dowager. "Mother, take my wife downstairs. I should not wish either of you to witness what is about to happen."

The old woman remained still. Ash's vision went red.

"Stay where you are, animal," Donnington snarled, "or my dear wife may meet with an unfortunate accident."

"I will kill you."

"I fear you will never have the chance."

"No!" the dowager gasped. "Donnington, don't be a fool!"

Donnington continued to stare at Ash. "Don't you see?" he said. "I have been a fool. Not anymore."

"You cannot commit murder!"

"It is self-defense, Mother. I caught this madman attempting to assault my wife. Naturally I had no choice but to defend her."

Mariah pushed the rifle barrel toward the floor. "Are you so certain that your mother will defend you, Donnington?"

Donnington blinked. It was the moment Ash had been waiting for. He charged, but the human was astonishingly fast. Donnington pulled a smaller weapon from his trousers and fired. Mariah screamed. Ash stumbled as the bullet grazed his shoulder and pierced the wall above Mariah's bed.

"No!" The dowager rushed toward Donnington as he prepared to fire again. "You will destroy yourself!"

He pushed her aside with a sweep of his hand. She fell against a chair and slid to the carpet.

Ash roared. Mariah crashed into him, sending them both tumbling. Ash threw himself over her, bracing himself for the killing shot.

"I'm afraid I cannot permit this, your lordship."

Mariah tensed, and Ash felt her amazement. The voice belonged to the servant girl, Nola. But the sound of it was different—low, calm, confident, not the voice of a servant at all.

Donnington's astonishment was almost palpable. "Get out of here!"

"I cannot do that, Lord Donnington," Nola said. "I had

hoped it would not be necessary for me to interfere again, but I fear you have gone too far."

"Nola?" Mariah whispered.

Her bewilderment and Donnington's disbelief were as nothing to Ash's. He had seen this girl a hundred times before. She looked the same: plain, unremarkable, hardly worthy of notice. Yet now he saw her as she really was, and he cursed his own blindness.

"Please put down the guns, Lord Donnington," she said.

He laughed. "Who do you think you are? Get out!"

She raised one work-roughened hand. The earl stopped in mid-motion, the pistol clenched in his fist. He dropped the rifle from slack fingers.

"That's better," Nola said. "Lady Donnington?"

Ash helped Mariah to her feet. "Nola?" she said. "What… what have you done?"

"What I should have done long ago." Nola glanced from the dowager, who was staring with her mouth half-open, to Ash. "I cannot maintain this spell for long. My abilities are no longer as great as…" She shook her head. "I have called the earl's brother." She looked again at the dowager. "If you do not wish your son to commit an act he will regret, you will aid Mr. Ware in restraining his lordship until the next moon's rise."

"You never truly worked for me, did you?" the dowager asked.

"I did what was necessary. Will you help?"

The dowager nodded slowly. "Who are you?"

"My name doesn't matter. Your son has broken his agreement with Lady Donnington. He has forfeited his right to her loyalty." She lifted her head, haloed by light only Ash could see, and gestured toward him.

"Mariah, do you trust this man?"

She met the younger woman's gaze. "With all my heart."

"Will you go with him, wherever he leads you?"

"I will."

"Then leave us for a moment."

"But I…"

"Go."

Mariah left the room, compelled by the power of Nola's words. Nola waited until the door had closed and stared at Arion. Her eyes were full of sad wisdom, neither Fane nor completely human. Those eyes said what her lips would not.

Be worthy of her.

He lowered his head. "I will keep her safe."

"Do you understand what you will be sacrificing, Arion?"

"Yes."

"Then be warned. Cairbre will not surrender his purpose, neither here nor in Tir-na-Nog. Take Mariah to London. It will be more difficult for Cairbre to find her there." She hesitated. "You must travel by train. You will be surrounded by Cold Iron, there and in the city. Can you bear it?"

Ash met her gaze. "Yes."

She inclined her head briefly. "You have until the next moon's rise." Her gaze lighted on the dowager. "Have you funds?"

"Yes, and Mariah has her own fortune. Most of it is in the bank, but I know she has kept some of it on hand for her personal use."

"Then she must take all she can."

Donnington tried to speak, but his mouth was as frozen as his body. His cold eyes promised vengeance.

Ash moved toward him. "You will not harm these other mortals," he said. "Or I shall return and find you."

Nola silenced him with a gesture. "He will harm no one if you leave England and never return. Go and fetch Mariah."

A moment later Mariah followed Ash back into the room, worry in her eyes. Nola repeated her instructions, leaving out all mention of Cairbre.

"Do you understand?" she asked.

"Yes." Mariah frowned at Nola in confusion. "I don't know who or what you are," she said, "but I trust you. Have I time to pack and change before we go?"

"If you are quick about it."

Mariah turned without a word and began to remove clothing from her wardrobe. She selected a plain brown riding habit and entered her dressing room to change.

Nola glanced toward Donnington.

"You will return to your room," she said, "and wait quietly."

Stiff as a wooden doll, Donnington backed toward the door, pushed it open with the weight of his body and passed through. Ash turned the key and locked Donnington out as Mariah emerged from the dressing room and finished gathering her things. Within minutes she had placed a small collection of garments and several books in a neat stack on the bed.

"I assume we shall be riding to the station," she said.

"That would be wise," Nola said.

Mariah added another book to the stack and removed a satchel from under her bed. "What of the servants?"

"They are asleep and will not awaken until morning."

Mariah circled the bed and offered her hand. "We have much to thank you for."

"It is not yet finished." But Nola took Mariah's hand, short calloused fingers around fine slender ones, and pressed something hard and smooth into Mariah's palm. "My powers are no longer reliable, but if you are in desperate straits, simply hold this talisman and call my name. I will do what I can."

Ash saw the object in Mariah's hand: a tiny piece of carved bone, the markings on it too tiny even for him to read. Mariah wrapped the bone in a handkerchief and began to pack the bag, each movement steady and precise.

Ash stared at her…at her grace, her composure, her faith in the face of so much that must be beyond her ken.

Be worthy of her.

CHAPTER TWENTY-ONE

ASH CLOSED HIS EYES, suddenly afraid. When he opened them again, both Nola and the dowager were gone, and Mariah stood waiting with the bag in her hand. He took it from her, and they descended to the entrance hall.

No one stirred. The night was lit by a nearly full moon as they hurried to the stables. Even the horses were quiet, making no sound as Ash spoke softly in their ears. Once the animals were saddled and bridled, he and Mariah rode at a gallop away from Donbridge.

Moonlight flowed over on his shoulders like the rays of the sun. He felt the horse's muscles bunch and release between his thighs, the animal's energy flowing through his body like the near-magical invention humans called electricity. He became one with his mount, the barriers falling one by one until it was *his* hooves beating the earth, *his* ears pricked for the slightest sound, *his* tail a banner flying on the wind.

No human thought told him where to go. One moment he and Mariah were headed toward the train station, and the next the horses were standing before the scattering of stones and small, circular wood that marked the Gate.

"Ash?"

He woke from the dream. His sweat-flecked horse stamped the ground as if to remind him that he was human again.

But he was not.

"Ash, where are we?"

Her voice was strained…perhaps from fear, or the exhilaration of the escape. But he thought it was something else. He saw the pupils of her eyes shrink in spite of the darkness, her gaze fix on the cluster of stones.

"I know this place," she whispered. "I have seen it before."

Ash clenched his fists in the coarse strands of his horse's mane. Was she beginning to remember that day when Donnington had dragged her before the Gate, intending to give her to Cairbre? Arguing over the part he himself must play in her capture?

She dismounted and took a few dazed steps toward the Gate, almost as if she were inexorably drawn to it. *Cairbre could not make her enter,* Ash thought. *But what if she did so herself?*

The very thing he had sworn she must never do. The *human* half of him. The half that now came up with a dozen excuses for why he should take her through.

I cannot lie to her anymore. She can never know me until she has seen what I have been. If she sees, she will know she is not mad, that her mother was not mad.

All rational justifications. All sensible, perhaps even necessary. Had he been less Arion and more Ash in that moment, he would have rejected them outright.

But reason had nothing to do with it. Instinct belonged to Arion, and instinct would not be denied. Arion had led him here. Arion hated Cairbre. Arion believed he could overcome his enemy if only he could return to Tir-na-Nog.

And if he were victorious…

Then wouldn't Mariah be safe? Would not all of Tir-na-Nog be free of Cairbre's schemes?

He tossed his head. Arion, the king of unicorns, had a chance against the usurper. Ash did not. Yet Ash could use words as Arion never could. Words to convince Mariah what must be done.

"Ash? Why are we here?"

He turned to her, breathing quickly with excitement. "Do you remember what I showed you in the hotel?"

Her body grew still. "Please, Ash. I know you think—"

"I do not *think*. I *know*."

She leaned against her horse's firm shoulder. "We must go on to the station. We haven't much time."

"No." He felt desperation begin to take hold of him. "Donnington may be defeated, but Cairbre will not stop."

She started. "Who *is* Cairbre?"

She *must* have remembered at least part of what had happened at the Gate months ago, but he knew he must turn her away from such memories as long as he could.

"It would be better to ask who *you* are, Mariah," he said. "You are part Fane, and the Fane rule Tir-na-Nog."

He saw her puzzlement quickly turn to comprehension. She *did* remember the visions he had shown her, however much she had rebuffed them.

"Fane?" she echoed.

"What humankind have called the Fair Folk. But they are so much more. And you share their blood."

Her eyes showed nothing but bafflement. He hurried on. "Somewhere in your ancestry," he said, "a Fane mated with a human and left the offspring in your world. The mating might have taken place many generations in the past, but your Fane blood gave your mother the power to see Tir-na-Nog."

"My mother? She was—"

"Perhaps she was a little mad because no one else could see what she did. But what she envisioned truly existed. It *does* exist. Just as I showed you."

She took her horse's reins and brushed her skirts aside as if preparing to mount again. "I will not listen to this, Ash. You are ill. We can find help—"

"You must listen!" He seized her shoulders and spun her

around. "You saw the sprites. You saw Cairbre when he danced with you in the ballroom, invisible to every other human present."

"Lord Caber?" she whispered. "He was real?"

"Yes. You have been drawn into the contentions of the Fane. You will no more be able to reject your heritage than your mother could. But there is more in you than the power to see." He gave her a little shake. "Within you may lie the ability to open the Gate to Tir-na-Nog."

MARIAH LISTENED AS he had demanded, too bewildered to protest again.

The Gate. This pile of ancient stones, fallen down, moss-covered and crumbling with age. This place that she had just begun to remember.

A passage to another world.

Ash had brought her here, not to the train station as they had agreed. He had deceived her, and now he offered an explanation. He claimed he could prove once and for all that her mother had not been insane…and that she herself would not fall into insanity.

She shook her head sharply. What Ash said could not possibly be true. But what if it was? What if that other world did exist and she need never fear madness again?

They spoke of "this world," as if there were some other one. Vivian's words, describing the overheard conversation between Donnington and Cairbre. A man—a creature—who wanted to take Mariah from her husband.

"Who is Cairbre?" she repeated.

Ash dropped his hands from her shoulders and stared at the Gate. Perspiration moistened his forehead. "Cairbre is a lord of the Fane," he said. "A high and powerful lord who believes he should rule Tir-na-Nog." He met Mariah's gaze. "He plans to steal the throne from the Fane's rightful ruler."

Mariah's brain felt like a block of lead inside her skull. "What has this…this Fane lord to do with me?"

"He wants you as his mate. He believes that by presenting you to the Fane as his bride, he will gain the support of other lords and more swiftly succeed in his purpose."

Marian concentrated on each breath she took, counting them one by one. "Why should these lords care about me?" she asked. "Do they have no women of their own?"

"They have females in plenty. But those of pure Fane blood are rarely able to bear offspring." He lowered his voice, as if the words he spoke were too dangerous for anyone else to hear. "They are a dying race, Mariah. Their only hope lies in stealing human females to bear their children."

"But you said I was not fully human."

"You are human enough to be of great value to the Fane, but Fane enough to be worthy of Cairbre."

A laugh burst from her, choking the words in her throat. "He wants me because I can give him children?"

"And because winning you will give him status to defeat Oberon."

Oberon. Shakespeare's King of the Fairies. Had the great playwright known he'd written of more than myth?

"You said that Cairbre is powerful," she said. "He can make himself invisible—"

"That is the least of his abilities."

"If he wants me so much," she said, "why did he appear as Lord Caber and then disappear again? Why didn't he take me then?"

"Oberon has declared that no Fane can enter this world save as a spirit…a spirit that can work some limited magic on earth but not physically interfere beyond a few simple tricks." He seemed to gather his thoughts. "Cairbre was bent on finding a woman of mixed blood who would serve his purposes, but he required human assistance. That is why he recruited Donnington."

Mariah's knees began to buckle. Ash caught her and eased her to the ground.

"Donnington?"

"He has been working for Cairbre since before you met him."

"I—I don't understand."

"Humans with Fane blood have become rare in England. Cairbre must have given Donnington a talisman to help him recognize any female who would fulfill Cairbre's conditions. Donnington traveled across the ocean in hopes of finding just such a candidate. He discovered you and brought you to England under the guise of marriage, intending to deliver you to Cairbre."

Lies and more lies. "But why?" she asked. "How did Donnington come to be working for a man from another world?"

"Perhaps Cairbre chose the earl because the Gate is so near his estate. Any Fane has much to offer a mortal—gold, jewels, wealth beyond imagining."

Greed. Even for a man already wealthy, the temptation of more was great. After all he had done, avarice was the least of Donnington's sins.

And yet something must have gone wrong. Donnington had *not* "delivered" Mariah to Cairbre. He had left Donbridge without explanation. And when he'd returned, he had claimed to want Mariah for himself.

"Donnington broke their agreement," she said.

Ash crouched before her. "I do not know why he changed his mind. But Cairbre has other allies." He hesitated. "Mariah, he would rather see you driven mad than go to any other man. When he knew that you and I...that we had been together—"

"What have you to do with Cairbre?" she demanded. "How do you know all these things? Who *are* you?"

"I tried to show you, Mariah."

"That you come from Tir-na-Nog. That you're…a unicorn."

"You could not accept what I told you, but I tried to protect you from Cairbre as best I could. I believe that he employed Lady Westlake to act as his agent and work mischief against you. Against us."

"The rumors," she said. "Lady Strickland. The stories that you and I—"

"I do not know what Cairbre promised her. She already hated you, Mariah. She had her own reasons for making you suffer."

But Mariah was already pursuing another impossible idea. "You have not told me what you have to do with all this…why you tried to protect me, why we almost…" She shivered. "Why did Donnington imprison you?"

"I was Cairbre's enemy in Tir-na-Nog. He wished to use me in his scheme to rule. I refused. He did not have sufficient power to do me harm in Oberon's domain, and yet he could not allow me to remain in Tir-na-Nog while I knew his secret. He had me exiled to earth as a human and instructed Donnington to hold me captive."

Mariah hugged herself tightly. "How could he hope to hold you indefinitely without someone finding you?"

"I do not know, Mariah. The keeper told me nothing."

"But if you were Cairbre's enemy and *he* couldn't harm you, why didn't he simply tell Donnington to kill you?"

"It is not easy to injure one of my kind."

"Then you were never really human at all."

"But I am, Mariah." He touched her face. "I am human enough."

Mariah knew he wasn't telling her the full truth. There were many secrets here, layers upon layers of secrets she might never uncover.

"What else haven't you told me, Ash?" she asked. "How much have you withheld from the beginning? Was it all an act?"

He leaned forward and took her into his arms. "At first, when they brought me here, I was driven mad by my imprisonment and the physical changes I could not understand. Then, as I began to remember, I wished only to destroy my enemies." He rubbed his cheek against her hair. "But as I came to know you, Mariah—as you began to save me—it was no longer simply a matter of revenge."

"You still wanted to hurt Donnington. You would have tried to kill him at Donbridge."

"But I chose *you*, Mariah."

She melted into his chest as if all her bones had lost their ability to support her. He *had* chosen her. Her.

She rubbed at her eyes. "I believe you, Ash," she said, hardly louder than a breath. "I believe everything you've told me."

His sigh rushed through her hair. "Mariah…"

"I have only two last questions."

"Tell me."

"Who is Nola?"

"I do not know. She is not Fane, but she has great power."

"My maid," Mariah said with a little laugh. "What was her purpose, pretending to be a servant? Do you think she was watching over us?"

He buried his face in her shoulder. "Perhaps," he said. "We owe her much."

She pulled away to look into his eyes. "And why are we here, Ash? Why did you say that I could open the Gate?"

"I must go through, Mariah."

A renewed sense of dread stopped her heart. "Why?"

"Because we will never be safe so long as Cairbre is allowed to meddle in human affairs."

"You couldn't defeat him before, Ash. He drove you away from Tir-na-Nog. There must be somewhere we can go to get away from him. Surely he couldn't find us in America!"

"The Fane are not confined to England. They have become

weaker over the centuries, but where there are Gates, they can pass through to this world and subvert other humans to their will." He lifted her chin. "Cairbre is not alone in his desire to find a mate who will bear him offspring. Other women may be taken. I can do nothing to save them if I remain here."

"And if Cairbre finds a way to kill you?" She took his face between her hands. "I love you. I won't let you go."

He kissed her, and she gave herself up to the kiss with the sheer rapture of total joy, knowing that she belonged to him and he belonged to her. No one could tear them apart again— not society, not Donnington, not the most powerful Fane lord himself.

Any last scraps of loyalty she had felt toward Donnington were gone.

She was free to take Ash at last. And to let him take her.

They lay down together, wordless, on the grass under the trees. She was fully clothed, but in moments Ash was naked, and something about the disparity excited Mariah in a way she had only just begun to understand. This time she would be the one to begin; she would examine and absorb every aspect of his beauty, from the crest of his silver hair to the elegant strength of his feet.

She kissed the corner of his mouth and let her hand drift down to his chest. She had never found a better word to describe him than *magnificent,* but now even that description seemed inadequate. She traced her fingers over the hard curve of his pectoral muscles, fascinated by their shape, so very unlike her own. Ash sighed as she rubbed her fingertips over his nipples. They intrigued her, and she spent some time simply touching them. Then she pressed her lips to his left nipple and flicked it with the tip of her tongue.

The sound that emerged from Ash's throat was one she had never heard from a man before. He speared his hands into her hair, setting it loose from its pins. Basking in his pleasure, she licked his other nipple. He grasped at her arms, and she knew he wanted to return the favor, but she would not have it. Not yet.

Far more than merely curious, she rested her cheek on his chest and looked down the length of his body. The organ she had first glimpsed in the folly and touched in her room at Marlborough House was fully erect, a large, firm shaft that stood proudly against his stomach. Any sense of shame was gone; she longed to touch it, stroke its smoothness and hear Ash's low cry.

But she denied herself—and him. She pressed her face into the hollow beneath his ribs, taking in the scent of him, feeling the texture of the pale hair that ran from just below his clavicle to this curve of bone and muscle. She stroked his arms, his shoulders, the flat stomach ridged like a washboard.

Again he tried to stop her. Again she forbade him. She massaged him with her palm, circling lower as she gazed into his eyes. His pupils were dilated, black on black. She traced the V that ran from his hips to his groin. His chest was rising and falling rapidly, his excitement flowing into her so that she could no longer tell his from her own.

Without looking down, she slid her fingertips lower and lower, until she found the silky head of his shaft. Fascinated, she explored it with her hand. Ash closed his eyes, his back arching. She knew without asking that this gave him the most pleasure of all, her hand on him, touching this place forbidden to any but a lover. It was more than merely hard; its circumference was so large that she wasn't sure at first that her hand would fit around it.

Soon it will be inside me. But she didn't dare think that far ahead. She cupped her fingers over it and slid them down, then up again, listening to the music of Ash's harsh breathing

Once she had thought herself no better than a whore. Now

she knew it must be true, but she didn't care. She kissed his stomach. He flinched, and she extended her tongue and touched the tip of his shaft. He drew a great shuddering breath.

"Mariah," he groaned.

It might have been a plea. A plea for mercy. A plea for her to continue. She chose the latter course. Her tongue worked lower, tasting him, curling around him until her lips were sliding over the fullness of him, catching the silky cap between her teeth.

He moved, pushing himself into her mouth. She suckled him as he had suckled her nipples, as he had kissed and licked the hot, hungry cleft between her thighs.

That part of her was beginning to ache more than ever before. One of a woman's deepest instincts was claiming her now, the instinct to mate, to take a man inside her body.

She felt his cool strong fingers grip her shoulders, pulling her back. She rolled to Ash's side, her mouth filled with the taste of him. The top button of her riding jacket popped free before she realized what Ash was doing.

His lips pressed into the hollow of her neck, exposed by the opening at the top of her jacket. The second button followed, along with another kiss. Then he freed the upper buttons of her shirtwaist, baring her skin.

She wore no corset. There had been no time to put one on before they'd fled Donbridge, and only the tight jacket of her habit held her breasts in place. When he unbuttoned the jacket to the bottom, they lay exposed save for her shirtwaist and the chemise beneath it.

Her breath came faster as he continued to undo the buttons of the shirtwaist. She pushed it aside and waited eagerly for him to do what he had done before.

He did not disappoint her. But he didn't begin by suckling her nipples through her chemise. He simply tore it open, as if he couldn't wait to feel his tongue against her naked flesh. And he did not begin gently. He drew her breast into his mouth, as much as he could hold, and rolled his tongue over and around, mouthing, devouring. First one breast and then the other, until her drawers were nearly soaked with her woman's juices.

Instinctively she snatched at her skirts, pulling them above her ankles and her knees. She undid the ties of her drawers, letting the center fall open. She felt for the swollen, hot flesh and rubbed herself where Ash had kissed her before, heat rushing up into her stomach with each stroke of her finger.

Within moments Ash's fingers replaced hers. He continued to suckle her breasts while he made magic with his hands, exploring the valley between her lower lips, sliding until one wide finger found her throbbing center and thrust inside.

She cried aloud. She had known such penetration was supposed to hurt, but she felt only the wild abandon of incredulous pleasure. He moved his finger in and out of her, then added a second finger. She spread her legs wide, her core still too empty, too incomplete.

Who removed her skirt and petticoat she could never remember. All at once she was wearing only her torn chemise and open drawers, and Ash was over her, braced on his powerful forearms, the head of his shaft lying along the inside of her thigh.

"Mariah?"

The question was both tender and rough, demanding and pleading. She grasped his shoulders. The torment was unbearable.

"Yes," she gasped. "Yes."

He settled his hips between her thighs, and his shaft slid inward and upward, barely touching her, growing slick as her wetness covered it. The tip grazed her cleft. She arched up, opening herself, begging him to fill her at last.

He thrust. It was a sharp, quick plunge, and she felt the snap of something breaking, the mildest discomfort before the waves of pleasure began. He withdrew almost all the way, teasing her cleft with the head of his shaft, and then entered again.

Nothing came from Mariah's lips but moans as he settled into a rhythm, thrusting and withdrawing, his thickness stretching her wide, making his mark deep inside her body. Deep, but not deep enough. She raised her legs and clasped her ankles about his chest, and he cradled her bottom with one hand as he drove into her again.

She knew instinctively when it was nearly finished. A strange thrumming began in her belly, a feeling as if a dam were about to burst. Ash moved more rapidly, his eyes closed, his head tilted back. Just as the thrumming filled her entire body, he stopped. She tried to hold him inside, but he left her, and the opening he had filled wept with grief.

But he was not so cruel. He clasped his hands around her waist and lifted her, carrying her with him as he rolled onto his back. He eased her down onto his hips, and she slid over him, crying out again in relief and ecstasy. She spread her hands on his chest and moved as he had moved, impaling herself while he grasped her hips and shuddered in time to her motions.

This time there was no stopping the wave. The dam gave way, and she drowned in it, the small muscles inside her contracting in release as Ash thrust into her over and over again.

She collapsed into his arms, laughing and weeping. He wrapped himself around her, stroked her hair, murmured words of praise and adoration. Then there was quiet, a silent melody of life that had finally opened up to her.

"I must go through the Gate."

She didn't hear him. His words were so much empty noise, meaningless in this blissful new existence.

"Mariah." He cupped her face, lifted it, stared into her eyes. "It is time."

Stunned realization shot white inside her head. All the lazy warmth fled her body, and she felt as if he had reached inside her chest and torn out her heart.

Nothing had changed. It was over. He was leaving her.

"Please understand," he murmured. "Mariah…"

She tried to pull away, but he wouldn't let her go.

She had told him that *she* wouldn't let him go. She had told him that she loved him. She had given herself to him after so many days of longing, of waiting, of doubt. And yet the first words he had spoken afterwards were about the Gate, about leaving, and she hated him for it.

"Mariah," he said, kissing her forehead, her brows, her eyelids. "I would never leave you for any other reason than stopping Cairbre. But I must go—and I cannot manage the Gate myself."

A blossom of bitterness opened up beneath her ribs. "You mean I am still of some further use to you?"

He glanced aside, something like pain in the set of his mouth. "I have tried to explain."

"Explain? Is that what you call…what you call—"

"No, Mariah." He stroked her back. "Tell me, would you love a coward?"

Oh, yes. She would stay with him no matter what he was. But she saw now that, no matter how little she really understood his reasons, Ash would not abandon his determination to defeat Cairbre, if only for her sake.

She could not hate him. She could only love him all the more.

"How can I help?" she asked in a small voice.

He looked away again, and she knew he was suffering, too. "Think carefully, Mariah. Did your mother ever disappear?"

"I…beg your pardon?"

"Did she ever go where you could not find her?"

Mariah wriggled free and sat up, suddenly self-conscious and aware of her near-nudity. "She spent most of her life at home or…or in asylums."

"Then you and your father were not always with her."

A peculiar memory entered her mind, as incongruous as anything that had happened since they had left Donbridge.

"There was a time," she said, "when my parents and I traveled into the mountains of Colorado. It was a wilderness with few roads, but my mother seemed more…sane there than anywhere else. We stayed in a lodge with a few other guests. One morning…" The memories were becoming clearer now, as sharp as broken glass. "One morning we couldn't find her. We were terrified that she had wandered away and become lost. A search party was sent out. That night they found her…" She turned her head to stare at the fallen stones. "She was sitting under a tree next to a cairn of heavy rocks. She said she had walked through the cairn into another world."

"A Gate," Ash murmured.

"She said she had been in that other place for only a few minutes."

"A few minutes in the Blessed Land may pass as hours in this world," Ash said. "She was partly Fane. She found a way from your country into Tir-na-Nog."

"And now you think I can open the Gate, too."

"It is possible that if we try together, we may succeed."

The moon was sinking low in the sky. In a few hours it would be dawn. Sinjin and the dowager couldn't hold Donnington forever. He was an expert hunter, and once he was free, he would track them down. If she waited for Ash outside the Gate…

"I'm going with you," she said.

"No. If Cairbre discovers that we have entered Tir-na-Nog, he will be able to take you anytime after you have stepped through the Gate."

"I am not afraid of him."

"You do not know him. Once the Gate is opened, you must go on to the station. Find a place to stay in London. I will follow when I can."

"*If* you can." She got up, pulled on her petticoat and picked up her skirt. She reached into the pocket and fingered the cloth-wrapped talisman. "That isn't good enough for me."

A look of bitter self-contempt crossed his face. "I swore to protect you."

"Even you can't protect me from everything." *Least of all my own fears.*

"Listen to me—"

"Both Cairbre and Donnington have tried to use me. This is my battle as much as it is yours. Either I go with you or I won't help you open the Gate."

She watched him struggle with the choices she had given him. A moment of blazing intimacy passed between them, as overwhelming as their loving, as those first few times in the folly when she had not even begun to guess how much he would mean to her.

"You must do exactly as I tell you," he said. "We will have only the element of surprise on our side. I will confront Cairbre as soon as I see him. You will remain out of sight. If he comes for you, you are to return to the Gate and your own world."

"I agree," she said. "What about the horses?"

"We will take them through with us. No harm will come to them in Tir-na-Nog."

She turned away, fastened her skirt, then pulled on her shirtwaist and jacket. She still felt horribly exposed.

"What shall I do now?" she asked.

Gently Ash turned her to face the stones. "Your mother knew," he said. "You will know, as well, if you open your heart."

She thought of Mama, of her flashes of humor and deep

compassion, so often mingled with bewilderment and that terrible distance Mariah had never been able to cross. She imagined that crossing now, between herself and her mother, between Mrs. Marron and that other world she had once seen so clearly.

Ash's warm hand took hers. Their flesh became one. Light shimmered over the stones, and their shapes seemed to waver, to become as insubstantial as clouds.

There was no literal opening, no enormous gate creaking inward to let them pass, but Mariah knew when they had succeeded. Her body felt light, as if she might simply fly into Tir-na-Nog.

"It is done," Ash said. "You are well?"

"Yes."

"Release your mount the moment you enter Tir-na-Nog. Find a place to hide."

"I understand."

She waited while Ash unsaddled the horses and removed their packs, then took the reins of her mare and followed Ash and his gelding toward the stones. She flinched as they drew level with the Gate, but nothing blocked their path. The stones had become ghosts, like the ground and the trees around them. She closed her eyes. Her feet touched grass as soft as down.

Light. Wondrous light. The smell of the most delicate perfume. A feeling of such contentment that she stood where she was, unafraid, while the new world opened up around her.

"The horses," Ash said. His voice was strange, thin, as if it were fading away. She released her mare's reins, and the animal burst away in a run, the gelding by her side.

Mariah quickly lost sight of them, but she felt no concern for their well-being. She was transfixed. The sky arced above, a perfect azure lit by a perfect sun, neither too bright nor too dim. The clouds were no more than wisps of lace tumbled about by a fragrant breeze. Each tree was an ideal of its kind, embraced by vines that might have belonged in a tropical paradise. Red and white deer with crystal horns grazed undisturbed on the luxuriant grass. And the flowers were just as she had witnessed in Ash's vision…thousands upon thousands of every variety she had ever seen and many more besides.

No, Ash had not deceived her in this. Neither one of them was mad. Her mother had been right all along. Sane, misunderstood, abandoned for being more than human.

And she felt a part of her she had never recognized—the Fane within herself—begin to blossom just like the flowers at her feet. Now at last she knew what she was. Surely there was no suffering in this world, no fear, nothing such as Ash had described.

The sprites appeared out of nowhere as they had done before, tiny winged creatures buzzing around her, uttering tiny cries like the stings of minute wasps.

"Cairbre," Ash whispered. "Go back, Mariah."

Going back was impossible. He must know that. But as she opened her mouth to explain, a man appeared before her. A man who resembled Lord Caber, but only in his barest outlines, as if someone had created the mortal lord from an imperfect sketch of a god.

This was the original—this gorgeous creature with eyes of silver-green and hair only a blind man would have dared to call brown. His brilliant garments were seamless and so finely woven that not a single thread could be detected.

The dream of beauty slipped from Mariah's grasp. Cairbre. He was no longer merely a name nor a version of the man she had met in the ballroom at Marlborough House. She had seen him long before.

"Arion," Cairbre said pleasantly. "And Mariah. How delightful." He twitched a finger, and the tiny fairies darted to form a moving halo around his head. "I confess I had not expected you to manage the Gate, Arion, let alone surrender her to me. But it seems that your true nature has overcome your human scruples."

More than once during the past weeks Mariah had felt as if she were walking on a narrow bridge suspended over nothingness. Now she stood on that bridge again, and it was Cairbre's words that threatened to send her sailing over the edge.

"Yes," Cairbre said to her, ignoring Ash. "You and I met before that night at Marlborough House, but the human part of your mind could not accept what you had witnessed. We shall remedy that presently."

Ash roared. He charged at Cairbre, teeth bared and eyes wild. Cairbre's raised hand stopped him as if he had flung himself against a brick wall.

"Now, now, Arion," Cairbre said. "You kept your part of the bargain, and I shall keep mine." He made another gesture, fingers dancing in midair.

Ash was gone. Another creature stood in his place, the creature Mariah had seen in her dreams, in Ash's vision…the magnificent beast whose rearing shape graced the escutcheon of the earls of Donnington.

"You seem surprised, my dear," Cairbre said. "But of course you never did meet Arion in his true form." He reached toward the unicorn with his graceful hand. The animal snapped fruitlessly with strong white teeth and trembled with rage.

"You cannot harm me now, Arion," Cairbre said. "Once your horn could have done me grave injury, as it might have mortally wounded my enemies had you chosen to cooperate. But I have become too powerful for you."

The unicorn made a terrible sound, so full of despair that Mariah nearly sank to her knees in sympathy.

"Ash," she whispered.

"Did he tell you?" Cairbre said with patently false sympathy. "Did he make you believe that he had a chance against me?"

"He told me what he was," she said. "I had faith in him. I still do."

"And do you have faith in what you see around you?"

"Yes." She met his gaze steadily. "I know what you want. You won't get it."

"If Arion cannot touch me, you certainly cannot defy my will."

"I shall certainly try."

"So much spirit." His eyes glinted with pleasure. "Tell me, did Arion claim that he loved you? It is said that we Fane cannot feel human emotion. Why should *he* know any better, beast that he is?"

Ash squealed and bent his head, the razor tip of his spiraled horn nearly touching Cairbre's chest.

"I wonder what he would say if he could speak?" Cairbre said. "Does enough mortal remain in him that he would beg your forgiveness? Or is taking his revenge all that fills his mind?" He sighed. "I see that you still don't understand. It is time for you to remember."

CHAPTER TWENTY-TWO

MARIAH SWAYED. She was no longer in Tir-na-Nog but another place, a familiar place beside the stones in her own world. And others were with her: Donnington, his voice a roar in her ears; Cairbre, lips curled in anger...and Ash, bound, sprawled on the earth, his black eyes both bewildered and stark with the same rage she'd just seen in the beast he had become.

She heard them speaking, Donnington and Cairbre, weaving their web as she lay at her husband's feet. She heard them discuss their scheme for her, just as Ash had described: how Donnington had located a virgin girl of Fane blood to become Cairbre's bride; how she had struggled against Cairbre's attempts to carry her through the Gate.

"But there is one thing you could not have heard," Cairbre said aloud, cutting into the memories. "I gave Arion one chance to return to Tir-na-Nog. Since I could not compel you to enter the Gate, he was to win your affection and loyalty, so that you would willingly follow him wherever he led you. Once he had brought you to the Gate, I would open the passage, and he would take you through it."

And then, she realized, Ash would at last resume the life he wanted so desperately, as king of the unicorns, all but immortal, beautiful, free.

Now she was here in Tir-na-Nog, all according to plan. Ash had brought her, and he was himself again.

You love one who will betray you. You will not see the trap until it is too late.

Lies, nearly everything he had told her. Except…*Cairbre wanted a virgin. Ash made love to you. He begged you to stay on earth. Why?*

Perhaps some part of him had really cared for her. But it hadn't been enough.

She pressed her face into her hands. She would rather have been insane than face this terrible truth. And yet…

Part of the memory was missing. She couldn't grasp it. Cairbre wouldn't let her.

"I pity you, Mariah," the Fane said. "I would have spared you this pain. But the sorrow will fade, here in this world where you belong."

Through strangely dry eyes, Mariah saw Arion drop to his knees before Cairbre, a supplicant begging mercy.

"Oh, no," Cairbre said. "You have no worth to me now. You are humbled at last, great Arion." He returned his attention to Mariah. "You shall have everything you desire in my world, my dear. Every luxury, every indulgence, to bring you perfect happiness. You shall be my queen."

The only possible response was a grim sort of laughter. "You have done nothing but bring suffering for everyone you've touched," she said. "In my world, I'd simply call you an evil man. But you are much worse than that, because you truly believe you are a god."

Cairbre's face twisted into an ugly mask. "I *am* a god, human. In every way your little mind can comprehend." He snapped his fingers. Arion grunted in shock as chains appeared around his fore and hind legs, jerking him to the ground. He lay there, sides heaving, like a sheep awaiting slaughter.

And then he gave up. His bright intelligent eyes dulled with a film of despair; his neck was stretched across the grass, throat exposed as if for the knife. The glitter of his horn vanished, replaced by the rusty tones of a tarnished blade.

"You see what is left of your lover," Cairbre said, setting his foot on Arion's withers. "Except he never was your lover, was he, my dear? The gift of your virginity has been saved for me."

He was wrong. Even his superior senses, his vaunted powers, couldn't discern the truth. But Mariah knew she had to play along.

"That's a gift you'll never have," she said. "Unless you give me something in return."

"And what is that, little mortal?"

"Arion's freedom."

"You would have me set Arion free, in spite of his deception?"

"It was *your* bargain with him. If you swear, by whatever you call holy, that you'll let him return unmolested to his old life and never seek to do harm to him again, I'll give myself to you. I'll bear you all the children you wish."

"Is this what humans call *forgiveness?*" he asked. "How extraordinary."

"Do you agree?"

"I could still force you."

"Someone else said that to me. But I am still part Fane. It might not be quite so easy as you suppose."

A beautiful smile spread across Cairbre's face. "What is it that you fear most, Mariah?" He answered his own question before she could speak. "It is obvious, of course. Donnington informed me about your mother, your close acquaintance with what humans call insanity."

"My mother was not insane."

"But your fear of losing your mind might have been a useful tool had not Arion upset my plans." He sighed. "Do you now know why I danced with you in the mortal palace? Why you were subject to the petty spite of your fellow humans?" The smile left his face. "I had intended that your fears and your isolation from your fellow mortals should bring you closer to Arion. But you grew too close." He cast Arion a contemptuous glance. "Arion came to his senses too late. You, however, may never again come to yours."

Mariah took a step back. "You're speaking in riddles," she said.

"I despair of your intelligence, Mariah. Do you not realize that I have the power to condemn you to real madness?"

She tried to stop her shaking and failed. "I will make a very poor queen if you choose that course," she said. "But I've already agreed to stay with you if you set Arion free."

He hesitated, weighing her worth to him. "I am pleased, Mariah," he said. "Your spirit is admirable, in its way."

"Then you accept."

"Yes. Oddly enough, I believe you will keep your word."

He snapped his fingers again, and the chains binding Arion dissolved. "You are free to go, beast," he said. "See if the others of your kind will accept you as leader now." He prodded at Arion with the toe of his bejewelled boot. "Let me never see you again."

Arion lay where he was, unmoving, barely breathing. Ash had been restored to his true form, but he'd lost everything else: his pride, his hopes of defeating Cairbre, his honor.

She approached him slowly and crouched beside him. The urge to touch that once-satiny coat was powerful. She kept her hands folded over her knees.

"I forgive you," she said. "Get up, Ash. Go away, where Cairbre can never find you."

If she hadn't been certain that Arion was incapable of such emotions, Mariah might have suspected that she saw a tear in the huge black eye. He tucked his forelegs under his chest and heaved himself to his feet. His powerful legs trembled. His head hung low, and he looked neither at her nor Cairbre.

"You are forgiven," Cairbre said, mockery in his voice. "Go."

Muzzle nearly brushing the grass, Arion walked away, his cloven hooves making no sound. Mariah's heart closed. From now on, she would allow herself to feel nothing. She would go about her life here as if it were a dream—and pray she never caught another glimpse of Arion as long as she lived.

She met Cairbre's gaze. "I am ready," she said.

He paused as if hearing some distant sound too faint for Mariah to hear. "We must return to the city," he said. He took Mariah's arm. "Quickly…"

A white blur filled her vision. Cairbre fell with a startled expression as Arion shouldered him aside and stopped before Mariah.

Up, his eyes said. Cairbre was climbing to his feet, his shrieking sprites like a hive of angry bees darting around him.

In one desperate leap Mariah flung herself onto Arion's back. She clung to his mane as he plunged toward the invisible Gate, then jumped into the mist.

They flew. The passage seemed to take an eternity, but to Mariah it was an eternity of glory. Riding Arion was like riding Pegasus, like soaring high above the clouds where no earthly fear could touch them.

Then his forehooves struck solid ground. Mariah nearly took a tumble but righted herself just as Arion came to a stop on the other side of the Gate.

Where Nola was waiting. Or a person who might have been Nola. She was not tall, nor was she particularly beautiful, but she was striking in a way few women could hope to be. Her red hair tumbled about her shoulders. She no longer wore a maid's clothing but a simple green gown without corset or bustle, simply belted by a sash around her small waist.

"You must not remain here," she said, as if she had anticipated everything that would happen from the moment they left Donbridge. "While you were in Tir-na-Nog, Donnington was able to escape. And while you were passing back through the Gate, Cairbre warned him that you were returning to earth."

A few minutes in the Blessed Land may pass as hours in this world, Ash had told her. It was already well into the morning here on earth. Cairbre had called upon his former ally…but why? He must have realized that he could no longer trust Donnington, who had claimed to want Mariah for himself.

"How do you know all this?" Mariah demanded, instinctively reaching for Ash and feeling Arion's smooth coat under her fingertips.

"I still have a few tricks left," Nola said with a wry smile. "Did you think that Cairbre would simply let you go? He and Donnington may be adversaries, but the earl is certainly no threat to Cairbre. As long as Cairbre has some use for the human…" She turned to Arion. She didn't speak, but he heard whatever she intended to say. He scraped his hoof violently through the dirt, leaving a deep furrow, and made a low sound more like a growl than anything an earthly horse could have managed.

"Yes," Nola said. She addressed Mariah again. "Arion has taken a great risk by returning you to earth. Nothing, no pleading from you, will win him mercy now, and you also are in great peril. If you go immediately, you may still escape Donnington. He may no longer want you as his wife, but he has ample reason for taking you before you can get away. Go directly to the station and board the first train bound for London."

"And what of Ash? Why hasn't he become human again?"

"Cairbre must have bespelled Arion to keep his original shape while he is on earth."

"For what purpose?"

"What happens now is Arion's to face alone."

"Whatever he may have done, I won't—"

"Mariah!"

Sinjin's horse pulled up in a veil of dust. He dismounted, glanced at the beast standing beside Mariah, and froze.

"*She* told me about him," he said hoarsely, indicating Nola, "but I couldn't believe it."

Mariah stepped in front of Arion. "Why are you here, Sinjin?"

He glanced at Nola. "Mother and I tried to hold Donnington, but he had help in escaping us." His face tightened in rage, quickly suppressed. "He's got his guns and dogs with him. Mariah, you have to leave."

Mariah was sick to death of being told what she must do. "What of Ash?" she repeated. "Where is he to go? If Donnington and his dogs find him…" Suddenly she understood. "Cairbre always intended to betray Arion, didn't he? He never planned to let Arion return to his own life." Her voice began to shake. "Donnington isn't just after me. He intends to kill Ash."

"It was part of the bargain with Donnington," Nola said. "Cairbre promised the earl that once his goals were achieved, Donnington would be permitted to hunt the rarest game of all."

"How can he hope to kill a creature from Tir-na-Nog?" Mariah demanded, bolstering her courage. "Aren't they supposed to be immortal?"

"Yes, but—"

"Ash outran the prince's horses, even as a man. How could Donnington possibly catch him?"

"There is but one foolproof way to catch a unicorn…with a virgin. Cairbre demanded that you be brought to him in a state of purity so that he could be certain that any offspring you bore him would be his own. He also told Donnington that only a virgin would be capable of weakening Arion enough so that he could be taken in a hunt."

But I'm not a virgin anymore, Mariah thought. *Ash made sure of that.*

"So," she said calmly, "I was to betray Ash as he betrayed me."

"You are a danger to him if you remain," Nola said.

Arion shook his head wildly from side to side, flecks of

foam flying from his lips. He turned his horn on Mariah and came within an inch of touching her chest with the razor tip.

"You can't frighten me, Ash," she said. "None of you can. I'll go back to Cairbre. There must be a way—"

"There is too much bad blood between Cairbre and Arion," Nola said. "And you have broken *your* agreement with him."

"This woman," Sinjin said, glancing at Nola, "told me that Cairbre has the means to drive you mad. Not just to appear so to the world, but truly insane."

"That's a risk I'm prepared to take." Mariah edged her way toward the Gate. "Protect him. Don't let Donnington—"

The baying of hounds interrupted her pleas. She turned to Arion.

"Run, Ash," she begged him. "Run."

He reared, his hooves scraping the air inches from her face. A moment later a naked man stood in his place, his breath sawing in his throat. He swayed, and Mariah moved to catch him.

He shook her off and stared first at Nola and then Sinjin, his face expressionless. "Leave us," he said.

His voice was that of a king expecting instant obedience. Sinjin lingered, scowling, but after a few moments he joined Nola and led his horse away from the Gate.

Ash stared after them until they had gone far enough that they could no longer hear his words.

"They told you to go," he said. "And so do I."

ASH KNEW EXACTLY HOW he must sound. His voice was flat, emotionless, conceding nothing to their former relationship—the relationship that had been a falsehood from the very beginning.

But any cruelty he might inflict on Mariah was a small price to pay for her survival. *He* was already lost. He had no notion of how he had been able to change his form again;

likely he would never have the chance to learn. All he could do was use the chance to save her.

"There is no reason for you to interfere," he said, not waiting for Mariah's response. "It is as Cairbre told you. I used you to regain what had been stolen from me."

She heard him well enough, but she only stared...stared into his eyes as if she sensed his lie, as if he would return to the man he had pretended to be and embrace her with protestations of love.

But he had never claimed to love her. And he never would.

"It was all a deception," he said in the wake of her silence. "The arrangement that you would find me in the folly, the feigned madness, the winning of your trust."

She kept her gaze locked on his, though her eyes had filled with very human tears. "You're lying, Ash," she said.

"I do not lie. I—"

"When you first tried to explain," she said, "you told me that the madness was real, that it came from your change and the imprisonment. That part was true, wasn't it?"

"I—"

"Donnington was to lock you away for me to discover— so that I would sympathize with you, wish to help you. But it didn't turn out quite as you had planned. Whatever he intended, I didn't find you until he had been gone nearly two months. You couldn't bear the captivity."

"You are wrong."

"I have seen madness all my life. That was no deception. And whatever he promised you, Cairbre never planned to let you return to Tir-na-Nog. He intended for Donnington to kill you."

Ash bared his teeth. "Cairbre is a fool," he said. "Donnington shall never catch me. Why do you think I took your virginity? So that Cairbre could not use it against me."

All emotion drained from Mariah's face. "Even if you evade Donnington, Cairbre will remain your deadly enemy."

"Not forever. I am still a king."

"A king without a kingdom."

"You will never comprehend what I am. *You* are human. Mortal. Did you believe I could ever come to care for you?"

She stared at the earth he had torn with his hooves. "If delivering me to Cairbre was all you ever intended," she said calmly, "why didn't you try to bring me to the Gate sooner? I was already in your thrall long ago."

"I had to be sure of you. I—"

"Why did you try to make me stay behind? Why did you protect me?"

"I did not protect you."

"You defied Cairbre and brought me home."

He began to feel himself losing any advantage he might have won. "I do recognize that you have done me some service, for which I felt an obligation. There are now no more debts between us."

He heard the pounding of her heart, smelled her distress. After a long while she lifted her eyes to his.

"Where will you go?" she asked him.

"I will buy time by allowing Donnington to chase me. Then I will go back to Tir-na-Nog."

"To fight Cairbre?"

"Cairbre made one miscalculation. In changing me again, he restored enough of my power that I can open the Gate without assistance. I will have my revenge."

"On Donnington, too?"

"I will stop him."

"You mean you'll kill him."

He arched his neck as if to display the horn so proudly borne by his other self. "I can heal. I can also kill."

She clasped her hands in supplication. "Don't take his life, Arion. He, too, is ill with his own kind of madness."

"You care for him still."

"No. Not for a very long time."

"Then do not presume to interfere."

She was silent for a long while. "Thank you, Arion," she said. "You have made things very clear. You have shown me that there has never been anything between us. I certainly have no desire to rob you of your heart's desire."

"Then go."

She tilted her head, hearing the sharper cry of the hounds. "Run, Arion. Find your revenge."

He forced his thick human legs to carry him away from her and found Nola, who waited alone under a willow tree.

"You have done well, Arion," she said wearily. "She believes you."

Arion concealed his self-contempt. "If you care for Mariah, help her. Don't let her travel alone. Do what you can to keep her hidden from Cairbre. I will see that Donnington no longer interferes."

"I cannot keep her safe forever," Nola said, her face as drawn as an old woman's. "I tried, you see. After I became Mariah's maid, I went to Tir-na-Nog and attempted to reason with Oberon on your behalf. But Cairbre had already gained too much influence. I was cast out again, and now I am too weak. My magic is failing."

He stared across the parkland that stretched away from the Gate. "You say you have lost your magic, but I have regained mine. I can return to Tir-na-Nog. When I have dealt with Donnington, I will find those who will fight Cairbre."

He turned away, but Nola caught his arm. "You say you have power now," she said. "Do you know why, Arion?"

Arion could not bear the question. "Farewell, Nola."

"My name," she said, "is Nuala. And, Ash…Donnington is a greater threat than you realize. He carries iron bullets."

Arion strode away without answering, paused before the Gate and changed again. The scent of the approaching hunters was acrid in his nostrils. He glanced at Mariah, tossed his head and began to run.

All the glory, all the joy he had once taken in this simplest of actions was gone. He was tormented by thoughts of Mariah, of what would happen to her if he failed.

He must defeat Donnington. And then, if he survived, he must find a way, against all odds, to bring Cairbre down.

But even if he succeeded, he would never see Mariah again.

SINJIN WATCHED THE creature flee, so lost in anger that he had little room left in his heart for astonishment.

A unicorn. Nola—Nuala—had not deceived him with her seemingly mad talk of other worlds and legendary creatures. This was what Ash had always been—not a lunatic, not a long-lost cousin, not a man of rank who deserved a place at the prince's side.

He was not even human. And now he was running from the man who intended to hunt him to the death—the Earl of Donnington, who would have remained safely confined if it hadn't been for Lady Westlake. Pamela, who had come to Donbridge with heartfelt reassurances that she cared nothing for Giles. Who had finally admitted that she'd lied about Ash's advances and had begged Sinjin's forgiveness. Who had sworn that she would never give herself to another man again.

And then she'd set Donnington free.

Sinjin had not struck her; he had never yet hit a woman. He hadn't even cursed her. He'd simply tried to stop Donnington. And turned his back on Pamela one too many times.

Nola—this new Nola, who called herself Nuala—had revived him from unconsciousness. The simple maid who had earlier rushed to tell him of trouble at Donbridge had revealed herself to be something else entirely.

Sinjin stared at the ginger-haired woman who stood gazing

the way Ash had gone. What in heaven's name was she? She'd turned from chambermaid to goddess in an instant.

No. Not a goddess. *A witch.* That was what she'd claimed to be. A witch who had compelled his attention and explained, in words that made a terrible kind of sense, the truth behind Giles's erratic and inexplicable behavior.

Tir-na-Nog. The world of the Fair Folk, who called themselves Fane. A place shaped by magic and inhabited by unicorns who could change into men. Ash was one of these creatures, and as a man he had fallen in love with Mariah, who, abandoned and sold by Giles to a Fane lord, had come to love *him.*

"I am here to help both Arion, whom you know as Ash, and Mariah," she'd said, when he had asked why he should trust her. She'd claimed she had been watching everything that had been happening between them since Mariah had found Ash in the folly…watching and trying to give aid whenever she could. "Mariah and Ash are destined to be together," she'd said.

And that, she obviously thought, was sufficient reason to make Sinjin obey her hasty commands. She'd never told him *why* she had felt compelled to bring two strangers together— what she had done to ensure it, why she'd posed as a maid, or what benefit she received from such an apparently selfless act. And above all, she had never explained why she, having gone so far to insinuate herself into the lives of the Wares, had chosen to reveal herself only now, when matters had become so desperate.

Sinjin didn't trust her. He couldn't, not when she had revealed so little of herself or her motives. But he'd done as she'd asked. He hadn't tried to stop Donnington again. He'd ridden directly to the Gate. And now he was waiting…waiting to be told what to do, as if he were a child.

Helplessness was not an emotion he'd often felt in his life. Pamela had unmanned him, and now Nuala was doing the same. As for Ash, he'd done nothing but hurt Mariah, betraying her just as surely as Pamela had betrayed *him*.

And he could do nothing. Nothing.

Nuala appeared beside him, her arms wrapped around her chest as if she were chilled. "You may still help Mariah," she said, as if she had heard his thoughts. "She should not be alone when she travels to London, but I cannot go with her."

Sinjin stared at her, despising her for using him just as Pamela had done.

"Why?" he demanded. "I thought *you* were her mystical guardian."

"There is more I may yet do here."

"Aren't you losing your magic?"

"I…" She avoided his gaze.

"You're going to stop my brother."

"I will try."

"Isn't my brother in danger himself? That creature has powers, too, doesn't he? He could kill Donnington."

"I doubt that is possible," Nola said softly. "A unicorn's horn has the power to heal, and no doubt it may kill, but no unicorn has ever used it for that purpose." She grasped Sinjin's arm with a strength that startled him. "Donnington has iron bullets, and iron has the power to destroy any inhabitant of Tir-na-Nog. Would you see your brother become a murderer?"

"What will you do? Wave your hands and make Donnington fall off his horse?"

Her expression turned suddenly hard. "If necessary."

Sinjin clenched his fists. He wondered if he ought to defend his brother against this woman with her unknown powers. But Giles had done much wrong. He had to be stopped, and Mariah had to be protected. She was the one most in need of it.

He stepped back, putting more distance between himself

and Nuala. "I don't know who you are," he said, "and you refuse to tell me. I wouldn't trust you to look after Mariah in any case." He glanced away from her sad and weary face. "I'll take care of her. I don't need the help of a witch."

She closed her eyes. "I wish things could have been different."

"So do I." Without a word, he took his horse's reins and strode toward the Gate.

"Mariah!"

There was no answer. He glanced among the trees surrounding the ancient pile of stones.

"Mariah! Damn it—"

"She's gone," Nola said, her voice tight with distress. "She's gone through the Gate."

"And you couldn't stop her?"

"I didn't see. I am sorry."

"Sorry?" Sinjin strode to the fallen arch and pushed against the stones in a cold fury. "For God's sake, why? Why did she go?"

"To keep her bargain with Cairbre. She doesn't believe that Arion can defeat the Fane. She'll try to beg for Arion's life."

"She'd risk so much after what he did to her?"

"Love is not a rational emotion, Mr. Ware. As you well know."

He flinched, feeling the knife twist inside his chest. "Do you have another command for me, madam?"

"I must do whatever I can to help Mariah, however little that may be. *You* must ride after Donnington." She laid a fine-boned hand on his shoulder. "If you care for Mariah, you will not let Arion die. Do your best to stop the earl until…"

"Until what?"

"I do not know. We can but try to do good when we can."

Sinjin met her gray-eyed gaze. She appeared so harmless, yet she scared him in a way he didn't understand. And he despised his weakness.

He shook her off. "I ought to thank you," he said, "but I've no more gratitude to spare."

He clambered into the saddle and set off without a backward glance.

CHAPTER TWENTY-THREE

TIR-NA-NOG WAS EXACTLY as Mariah had left it. The only difference was that Cairbre was no longer waiting.

That fact left her in a desperate quandary. She was in a strange land she knew nothing about save through visions and a single previous visit; she had no idea how to find Cairbre in this vast and exotic world, and every moment she lingered brought Ash closer to death.

She still didn't know how much of what he'd said had been lies, but she didn't believe for a moment that Cairbre would let Ash escape unless he was certain that Donnington could kill him, with or without the help of a virgin. She must convince Cairbre to call off his mortal hound. Convince him that she could still become what he wanted her to be…even if he chose to drive her mad.

There was no more time for thinking, let alone regret. She looked in each direction, seeking some sign of where to go. To the east the meadows stretched endlessly to the horizon; to the west rose a range of mountains, violet in the distance. To the north, beyond the meadow, lay the barrier of a forest, and beyond that…

She set off across the meadow, silver trees swaying above her. The lush emerald grass rustled with the movements of small animals: a stoat popped up its pointed muzzle to watch her pass, a fox emerged from some hiding place, and a badger scuffled along in her wake. The herd of crystal-horned deer lifted their heads as if to judge her friend or foe.

She couldn't have said why she headed toward the forest. Her feet seemed to move by themselves; only after she had gone half the distance did she realize that she was being guided, chivvied along by the creatures she had glimpsed: stoat and fox, grumpy badger and shy hedgehog, the herd of deer who paced at her side, creatures she could not quite see but which seemed to belong in a place few mortals could ever have imagined. Birds of brilliant plumage swooped and banked overhead, twittering as if in encouragement.

Perhaps they meant her ill. More likely they were all under Cairbre's command and were simply leading her to him. But they didn't frighten her. She lowered one hand, and the fox nuzzled her like a friendly dog; she lifted the other, and birds alighted on her fingertips.

The forest filled her vision. The animals grew quiet; even the birds had stopped singing. Trees with bark of woven gold and leaves like colored glass closed in over her head, tinkling in the faintest of breezes. One by one the animals fell behind: first the hedgehogs and mice, then the deer, then the badger and stoat, until only the fox remained. It pushed its damp nose into the palm of her hand.

Go forward. She went, expecting Cairbre to appear at any moment. The trees blocked the sunlight, yet the reflections from their leaves lit her path like a thousand candles.

"Cairbre!" she called.

The fox shook out its russet fur and yipped as if to urge her to silence. She entered a small clearing and stopped. Something was coming. She could feel the tiny hairs on her arms rising, her skin tingling with anticipation.

White shapes drifted like ghosts among the golden trunks. Dark eyes caught the light and cast it back like black diamonds.

Unicorns.

Mariah didn't dare move. They crept out of the trees' dense shelter with fearful steps, heads bobbing, nostrils flared. One by one they approached her, stretching their necks and then snapping them back as if they expected her to strike out.

If Mariah hadn't seen Ash in his true form, she might have sunk to her knees in obeisance to their beauty. But these creatures were faint shadows compared to their king, frightened prey prepared to flee at the slightest threat.

"I won't hurt you," she said, and spread her hands. "See? I have no weapons. I mean you no harm."

The boldest of the unicorns, her coat a dull bronze, extended her head and nickered.

"She asks who are you."

Mariah turned sharply. The fox sat on its haunches behind her, as serious as a judge waiting to pronounce sentence.

"Nola?" Mariah whispered.

The fox flattened its ears and glanced toward the female unicorn, who tossed her head.

"I've told Adara that you have come from Arion," the fox said.

The unicorns drew closer, forming a loose semicircle around her. Perhaps two dozen beasts crowded into the clearing, rubbing shoulders and shifting from foot to foot in nervous anticipation.

Arion, a voice whispered in her mind. *Arion.*

"They want to know what has become of him," the fox said.

Mariah rubbed her face. "How can I explain?" she asked. "I don't even understand what has happened here. Why did you lead me to this place?"

The fox gave a very human sigh. "They do not speak your language, nor you theirs. But you are still of Fane blood. If you are willing to open your mind…"

"I must find Cairbre."

"You will. But you must also have allies."

"For what purpose? Arion's only hope—"

"Lies in what happens here and now."

The unicorns moved so near that Mariah could have touched them without stretching her arms. *Arion. Arion.*

"See what they have seen," the fox said. "Until you have shared their fear, you cannot convince them."

"Convince them of what? I have no time—"

The words became garbled on her tongue. Shapes drifted through her mind, gaining form and substance as she followed their passage. A herd of unicorns, perhaps two dozen of them—not dull now, but shining brightly enough to rival Tir-na-Nog's glorious sun—so stunningly alluring that every other creature, no matter how magnificent in its own right, bowed down before them.

And leading them was Arion. He was indeed a king—a king with no need of a crown or any other human badge of royalty. It lived in him, in his grace, in his eyes, in the horn he bore so majestically.

The scene changed. Cairbre stood before Arion in the depths of a forest, gesturing with bold, forceful strokes of his hands. The unicorns ranged behind Arion shook their heads, and stamped in distress and anger. Arion, his neck arched proudly, showed his strong white teeth to the Fane lord, and Mariah realized that he was laughing. He swung his hindquarters toward Cairbre and trotted away, his subjects behind him.

Cairbre, his face dark with fury, vanished into thin air. There was another confused blur of images, and suddenly Arion was alone in a sort of courtyard, enclosed by intricately engraved stone walls set with rows of velvet-draped seats. Three score Fane, lords and ladies both, sat overlooking the central arena where Arion waited, his neck weighted with chains that held him captive.

At the head of the courtyard rose a throne carved as if from a single enormous ruby. A dark-haired Fane sat on the throne, an obsidian scepter in his hand, his robes like midnight scattered with living stars. Lord Oberon. It could be no other. Beside him stood Cairbre. He bent to whisper in Lord Oberon's ear. Oberon raised the scepter, and all at once Arion and Cairbre stood by the very Gate through which Mariah had passed.

A handful of Fane, cold as graven images and no more merciful, formed a circle around the Gate. Cairbre, his face turned away from them, grasped the chain around Arion's neck and spoke in the long, ivory ear.

Mist gathered, lightning flashing within it like fireflies caught in a bottle. Cairbre and Arion plunged into the mist.

Mariah blinked. She was in the forest again, the unicorns watching her with flattened ears, the fox slightly behind her.

"Do you understand what you have seen?" the fox asked.

"No," Mariah whispered. "Arion defied Cairbre in some way…"

"Cairbre demanded that the unicorns use their horns to injure Oberon's supporters," the fox said, "and then refuse to heal them unless the king's men surrendered to Cairbre. But Arion denied Cairbre, who caused him to be punished and cast out of Tir-na-Nog. If you surrender yourself to Cairbre now, you will gain nothing. Arion will not be permitted to survive unless Cairbre is stopped."

"Stopped?" She looked into the crowd of silent unicorns. "How? What do they want of me?"

"They are afraid," the fox said. "Their king was punished for daring to defy Cairbre. They fear that he will do the same to them."

And yet they still had power. Mariah felt it clearly; theirs was a match for any but the most potent Fane magic—power that resided in their horns, magic that could wound the Fane, who were very nearly invincible. It was that inborn ability, the fox explained, that Cairbre had hoped to use in his coup against Oberon, who would never anticipate the interference of creatures who had always held themselves aloof from Fane life and politics.

But Cairbre had failed to convince Arion to aid him. Too late, blinded by his own arrogance, Arion had discovered that Cairbre had won the ear of the very man he hoped to unseat from the throne of Tir-na-Nog. With his lies, Cairbre had convinced Oberon that the unicorns had planned their own coup against the ruler of Tir-na-Nog, and he had urged his king to cast Arion out of the Blessed Land.

But it hadn't been done merely for revenge. It had been carefully arranged to support Cairbre's bargain with Donnington.

"Cairbre gained the power he sought," the fox said, "but he is not secure in his rule. Rebellion is already brewing."

"The other Fane are fighting Cairbre?" Mariah asked.

"Yes. But even the Fane who hate him cannot overcome his allies without help."

Mariah finally understood. "The unicorns…*they* could hurt him."

"But they have been too long away from your world and have forgotten what it is to fight for their lives."

Could the same be true of Ash? Would he allow his own life to be taken rather than defend himself?

Mariah tried to put such paralyzing thoughts out of her mind. "If they won't fight," she said, "why hasn't Cairbre come after them?"

"Because he knows they present no threat without their leader to guide them."

"What can *I* do?"

As if in answer, the bronze female, Adara, stepped closer. She bent her head in a kind of obeisance, then delicately lipped Mariah's hand.

"They know, you see," the fox said. "They smell Arion on your skin, they feel him in your heart. They will trust you as they would no other."

"You think that I—"

"You must, if you wish to save Arion."

"Can they…can we truly make a difference?"

"Once Cairbre hoped to use the element of surprise to overthrow Oberon. Now that advantage is in your hands." She hesitated. "You still have a choice, Mariah. You may choose to return to earth, where you may very well escape Cairbre in the end. And honesty compels me to tell you that if you stay and fail, Cairbre will surely follow through with his threat to destroy your mind."

Shaking, Mariah looked at each of the unicorns in turn. They were watching her, waiting for a sign. Waiting for the signal to take their own kind of revenge.

It is up to you now.

Mariah lifted her chin. "Will you come with me?" she asked them. "Will you fight Cairbre to save Arion?"

The unicorns shifted and stamped their feet in a kind of rhythm, like tribesmen pounding their spears upon the ground. They tossed their heads, displaying their horns, and it seemed to Mariah that their coats began to gleam as if lit from within.

Adara pushed at Mariah's chest with her muzzle, then knelt, a sign for Mariah to mount. There was no sidesaddle to accommodate Mariah's riding habit, and she looked around for some sharp object to tear her skirts, so she could ride astride.

The unicorn dipped her horn, and fabric ripped like paper. Mariah climbed onto Adara's back. Muscle rippled underneath her, and the creature's magic flowed into her arms and legs. She was no longer Mariah Marron or Lady Donnington. She had become a queen.

Turning about, Mariah's mount bobbed her head at the other unicorns. The fox leaped up onto a silver unicorn's back, balancing easily with her front paws planted on the beast's withers. The others fell into place behind Adara and trotted single file along the path by which Mariah had entered the forest. As soon as they were clear of the border of golden-barked trees, they began to run.

Had Mariah not already experienced the glory of riding on Arion's back, she might have come very near to swooning with sheer joy. Instead, she bent over Adara's neck and breathed deeply, gathering her courage for the fight to come.

In a little while the city rose up out of a mist, its diamond towers reaching toward the sun. The thought of deadly conflict going on behind its elegantly inscribed, richly colored walls seemed inconceivable.

But something was happening. Even as the unicorns raced closer to the city, Mariah saw streams of colored light burst skyward from somewhere within its walls: red and green, gold and blue.

"The battle has been joined," the fox said, as its mount drew level with Adara.

"How do we get in?" Mariah asked.

"There is a Gate to the south, hardly used by the Fane. It will almost certainly not be guarded now that Cairbre has been challenged from within. You must maintain the element of surprise for as long as possible. Ride directly for the center of the city, and do not pause until you have encountered Cairbre and his allies." She leaped from her mount's back. "You will not need me, Mariah. Your heart will guide you."

"I have no power."

"You possess more than you know. Farewell."

"Nola…"

But the fox was gone. Mariah wrapped her fists in Adara's mane.

"Are you ready?" she asked the unicorn.

With a fresh burst of speed, the beast lowered her head and flew toward the city's southernmost wall. In minutes hey were plunging through an open ivy-shaded gate and nto a broad lane lined with russet trees. Painted columns rose to support delicate roofs, the rooms beneath open to the scented air.

But Mariah had no interest in Fane architecture, no matter how beautiful. She heard the distant sounds of conflict: the clash of weapons, shouts of challenge, cries of anger.

For a moment the unicorns faltered. Adara slowed to a trot and then a halt. The others stopped behind her.

"This is not the time to give up," Mariah said urgently. "Win your freedom! Fight!"

Adara bobbed her head, sweat darkening the hair on her sleek neck. Mariah rested her forehead against the unicorn's mane.

Listen to me. I am one of you.

Adara cocked her ears back as if Mariah had spoken aloud. But Mariah knew the time for words was over. She opened her heart as the fox had urged, felt herself sink into the body beneath her, into the mind so different from her own. She found the fear, shared it, fought to overcome it.

Muscles flexed. Mariah gasped as Adara began to run again. Courtyards and gardens and shaded porticos passed in a blur. Colored light spread across the sky like ink in water.

And suddenly they were there, in the thick of battle: Fane against Fane, lord against lord, armed with slender swords and bright magic. In the space of the time it took to draw a few rapid breaths, Mariah recognized the enemy.

Cairbre, urging his cohorts on with cries in a foreign tongue. Cairbre, spears of light shooting from his fingertips to strike down the rebels. Those who fought against him were severely outnumbered; they were about to fall back in defeat.

Adara needed no further encouragement. She lowered her horn and rushed toward Cairbre's men. Fane looked up in astonishment, but too late. The unicorns fanned out and attacked, their horns piercing rainbow armor as if it were the cheapest tin. Mariah clung to Adara's back, longing for magic she didn't possess.

The assault was so swift that she never felt it. An invisible hand struck her, sent her flying from the unicorn's back. She landed on something hard, and her skull cracked against the ground.

Cairbre's face was the last thing she saw before darkness claimed her.

SINJIN RODE AS FAST as his mount would carry him. The baying of the hounds had gone silent; he had no idea which way they had turned, and his only hope of picking up the trail was to return to Donbridge and follow his brother's track from that point.

Twenty minutes of hard riding brought him to Donbridge's park; he continued on to the stables, finding the ground outside well churned by the hooves of Donnington's stallion and the paws of a dozen hounds. The prints of both horse and dogs were easy to follow away from the estate; they led in the direction of the Gate.

An anxious groom emerged from the stables and tugged at the brim of his cap. "Mr. Ware," he said, eying Sinjin's sweating mount. "Can I be of service?"

Sinjin passed his reins to the groom. "Take care of her, but first saddle Shaitan as quickly as you can."

With a bob of his head, the groom led the weary mare into the stables. A few minutes later he emerged with Shaitan, who rolled his eye at Sinjin and danced with excitement. Sinjin mounted, turned Shaitan in the direction Donnington had taken and urged the stallion into a run.

The tracks led across the park, north in the direction of the Gate, then broke off to the east toward the fen country. If Arion had run before the hunters, his hoof prints were completely obscured by those that followed. But Sinjin had no doubt that the hunt was on in earnest.

He bent low over Shaitan's strong neck. Late morning sunlight beat on Sinjin's shoulders, warm as blood. He had no idea whom it was he was riding to save.

Someone was going to die. Sinjin felt it as a chill along the back of his neck, a heavy weight in his heart. Mariah had gone to face an implacable enemy. Donnington cared for nothing but revenge against the creature that had bested him. And Arion...

Mariah loved him. Loved Ash, the man he had become. And if she survived, Sinjin couldn't have Ash's death on his conscience.

His horse plunged over a ridge of willow and alder, into the open fen. Far across the wet meadows and beyond the tracery of streams meandering toward the river, Sinjin could make out the silhouettes of dogs and the horse bearing his master, racing through the reeds and sedges as if nothing in the world could stop or even slow them.

Arion must be there, ahead of them, but he was beyond Sinjin's sight. Tightening his hands on the reins, Sinjin urged Shaitan into the meadow.

"Sinjin!"

He reined Shaitan in without pausing to think and wheeled the horse about. Pamela sat on a bay mare, elegant in a deep blue habit, her hair slightly undone and catching the light like a field of rippling corn.

"Lady Westlake," he said between his teeth. "I would suggest that you go back to wherever you came from."

She lifted her head, exposing the curve of her delicate swan's neck. "You're after Donnington," she said.

Her directness surprised him. "It's none of your affair," he said, love and loathing roughening his voice.

"Isn't it?" She smiled, so perfect, so lovely. "Would it

surprise you to know that Donnington has told me everything? About Mariah, about Ash and the unearthly place from which he comes?"

Sinjin wasn't surprised. She would have believed his brother if he'd told her that the sun revolved around the earth.

"Of course I already knew some if it," she said in a conversational tone. "Cairbre came to me at Marlborough House. He asked me to help create confusion in the mind of our little Mariah, and I was happy to oblige him."

"What did you do to her?"

She shrugged. "A few rumors here and there."

"You *did* seduce Ash."

"Indeed. That was *my* idea."

"You bitch."

"If you like. But your opinions never mattered to me, Sinjin. Mariah will cease to be a distraction soon enough. And I will have Donnington."

"Are you so certain?"

"Quite." She pulled a small pistol from the skirt of her habit. "Let Donnie have his hunt. It is little enough to ask."

"Put that away, Pamela."

"Not until you have agreed to leave Donnington alone."

He laughed and pretended to relax. "What makes you think I'm in a hurry to help this creature who calls himself Arion?"

"You tried to hold Donnington prisoner in his own house. You have always resented your brother…all the more so now that he has won what you can never have. And you care for Mariah—more than one would think is quite proper."

"*You* speak of propriety—"

"I prefer we not speak further at all." She waved the gun. "Go back to Rothwell, Mr. Ware."

No longer capable of rational thought, Sinjin kicked Shaitan toward her.

She fired.

ARION RAN.

It was a simple matter to keep ahead of the earl and his foolish dogs; whenever Donnington drew close enough to fire his weapon, Arion put on a burst of speed and left him in the dust. He led the hunters away from the Gate, away from the safety of the City of Iron where Mariah was to take shelter. Time was all he needed, time to keep Donnington from thinking about Mariah, or whatever he might have agreed to do for Cairbre.

The human was obsessed. He hardly slowed to rest, pausing only to change from his present mount to the one he had brought as relief. The dogs seemed tireless; they ran as if they knew they would never pursue such game again.

If farmers and fishermen stared as the hunt passed by, they quickly returned to their work. The fancies of the peerage held no lasting interest for them. If they saw Arion at all, it was only to glimpse a flash of light, a glittering shape that was there one moment and gone the next.

Arion plunged through streams and stands of alder and birch, tireless as he led the hounds in ever-widening circles. The sun began to sink toward the western horizon. For the first time the baying stopped; the hounds had finally run themselves into the ground, and not even Donnington's threats could get them moving again.

Arion paused, ears pricked. The sun sank lower, and still there was no sound of pursuit. He dug a deep furrow in the soft earth with one hoof and opened his nostrils wide. It seemed to him that the scents of man and beasts were receding, almost as if Donnington had given up the chase.

But the human was mad. He would not surrender until his prey was dead.

Yet he *had* been thrown off the scent, and Cairbre had yet to be stopped. Arion must return to the Gate very soon or risk allowing the Fane to catch Mariah. Whatever uncertain powers Nola might use to protect Mariah, she had warned him that they were limited.

The fens were wrapped in twilight stillness as Arion carefully retraced his steps, making his way to the last place where he had seen the hunters.

They were not there. Grass had been crushed and earth churned to mud, but the human and his hounds were gone. Arion followed their tracks nearly all the way back to Donbridge, where they simply stopped.

Donnington *had* given up. He would be too late to follow Mariah now.

Rejoicing, Arion set off across the fens at a gallop. He knew now that he would defeat Cairbre; his enemies would fall before him. He would return victorious to his people. Mariah would be free. Free to find another of her own kind to love and to love her in return.

The joy did not last. A burning ache began in Arion's heart, growing heavy as iron. He slowed, the strength draining from his legs.

He would not be free. Already the instinct to survive was dwindling. He would forever be haunted by what he had done to Mariah, what she had suffered because of his lies and selfishness. He would lose her. Not even death itself could be a worse punishment.

If not for the necessity of stopping Cairbre, it would have been better if Donnington had killed him. There was but one reason to go on living.

He resumed his race toward the Gate. The ground rose and grew firmer beneath his hooves as he approached Donbridge and turned to skirt the estate. He barely avoided colliding with the mounted horseman who emerged from behind a stand of beeches.

Donnington. Arion reared and lowered his horn for the charge.

"Ash!"

The voice was broken and low, and it was not the earl's. The man on the horse swayed, leaned over his mount's neck and straightened with obvious effort.

Sinjin. Arion moved closer. The man was bleeding heavily from a wound in his shoulder, which he had tried to bandage with a scrap of cloth. It was clear that he needed healing, but Arion maintained his distance.

"Ash," Sinjin repeated. "I must warn you." He coughed. "Mariah..." He caught his breath. "Mariah has gone through the Gate."

Arion could not speak, or he would have shouted out his despair.

"She's gone to try to reason with Cairbre," Sinjin continued hoarsely. "But he'll never accept any bargain from her now, will he?"

Moaning in his throat, Arion flung his head from side to side.

"I don't know what you can do to save her, but I know you won't let her suffer alone." Sinjin slumped over his horse. "Go. Help her."

Arion gathered his legs to leap away. At the last moment he turned back toward Sinjin, lowered his horn and touched the tip against the bloody bandage across the human's shoulder.

Sinjin flinched, then looked up at Arion, wonder in his eyes.

"It's true, then," he said. "I never quite believed it. You really did heal those people at Marlborough House."

But Arion was already moving again. Desperation pumped fresh strength into his legs, carrying him across meadow and farmland as his hooves struck sparks from the earth. He did not smell the trap until it was too late.

Donnington was waiting beside the Gate, the weapon in his hands aimed precisely at Arion's chest.

"You led us a merry chase, beast," the earl said. "But I knew you would return here eventually."

Arion skidded to a stop. He measured the distance to Donnington, calculating his own speed against the human's skill. Once the iron bullets lodged in his body, he would be poisoned and unable to move at all.

"You can't win, Arion," Donnington said. "I would have liked to kill you on the run, but I will settle for this, and your head mounted on my wall."

There was no hope of reasoning with the man as long as Arion maintained unicorn shape. He changed and dropped to his knees, naked and humble before the human he despised.

"Mariah," he said, finding his voice again. "She is in terrible danger."

Donnington shrugged. "She made her choice long ago," he said. "Her fate is no longer my concern."

Arion howled. He sprang to his feet, moving so suddenly that the bullet only grazed his arm. Donnington aimed again. Arion had gone no more than a few steps when the Gate began to shimmer.

Mariah tumbled out, staggering, feeling before her as if she had gone blind. Arion moved to catch her just as Cairbre followed her through the Gate and seized her arm.

"Ah," Cairbre said with a deadly smile. "I see that we are all gathered together at last."

"Let her go!" Arion roared.

With a cluck of his tongue, Cairbre glanced at Donnington. "I would have thought that such a great hunter would have succeeded in bringing down his prey by now," he said.

The earl's face darkened with fury. "I will kill him."

"Hold your temper, human. Let us enjoy a little amusement first."

Cairbre let go of Mariah and pushed her toward Arion. She took a few steps and stopped, turning her head slowly from side to side.

"Mariah!" Arion moved toward her, watching her with

growing fear. Something was wrong. Very wrong. Her riding habit was torn to the thighs, her hair undone. But it was her face that terrified him. Her expression was blank, slack-jawed, her eyes unfocused.

"Mariah," he said, very softly. "Can you hear me?"

Slowly she looked at him. "Who are you?"

"Ash." He reached out to her. "I am Ash."

Her laughter was wild, like a shriek of pain. "'Ashes, ashes, we all fall down,'" she sang.

Paralysis struck Arion's limbs. "Mariah, come to me. All will be well."

She darted away, still laughing, and spun in a circle with her arms outstretched. "I see you, Mama," she said, whirling and whirling. "Now we can be together." She stopped suddenly, swaying with dizziness, and stared at Donnington. "I know *you,*" she said. Without warning, she flung herself at Donnington, grasped his shoulders and kissed him passionately.

Startled, Donnington nearly dropped his guard. He pushed Mariah away and took aim at Arion once again. Mariah fell onto her hindquarters and burst into fresh laughter, tearing at her hair as if she were trying to remove some kind of animal clawing at her head.

"What have you done to her?" Donnington demanded, his voice not quite steady.

"Don't you know, human?" Cairbre said, watching Mariah with pleasure in his eyes. "There are two things the girl fears above all else. You will fulfill the first when you kill Arion. I have fulfilled the second."

"You've driven her mad."

"She made a foolish attempt to join my enemies. They have won a temporary victory, but my power is still potent enough to punish her as she deserves."

The very earth seemed to freeze under Arion's feet. "You

have lost, Cairbre, or you would not be here," he said. "How long before Oberon strips you of your power again?"

"Too late for your intervention." Cairbre gazed at the girl who sat mumbling on the ground. "I understand that you humans have appropriate habitations for the mad. Perhaps you will enjoy undertaking the task of dealing with her, Donnington."

But the earl's face was as blank as Mariah's. He gave no answer. Arion dropped to his knees beside Mariah and gently turned her toward him.

"Perhaps you will not understand me," he said, stroking her cheek with his fingertips, "but I will say what I should have said long ago. I love you, Mariah. I would have stayed beside you if I could. I would have cared for you until death claimed us both."

Cairbre clapped his hands. "Very touching. Very human. But *your* death will come too soon. She may live another fifty years as she is now."

Arion cradled Mariah's face against his shoulder. "You will find your punishment, Cairbre. Perhaps not for a hundred years. Perhaps not for a thousand. But it will find you."

"I grow weary of this game," Cairbre said. "Donnington, kill this beast."

But still the earl didn't move. Arion changed and laid his horn across Mariah's shoulder.

"You cannot heal her," Cairbre said. "My spell is too strong even for one of your kind."

Arion remained still for a dozen heartbeats, then rose to his feet and faced Donnington.

"Be done with it!" Cairbre snapped.

Donnington held Arion's stare. "I will do what I can for her," the earl said, and raised his rifle. Arion stood ready. The small wood grew silent.

Cairbre laughed.

Arion reared and charged the Fane, his horn incandescent

with his rage. The rifle's report shattered the stillness, sending a flight of screeching birds from the trees. Arion stumbled. Cairbre clutched at his chest, a look of surprise on his face. An instant later, Arion's horn entered his body. Cairbre wrenched himself free, staggered backward and fell through the Gate. Immediately the light went out like a snuffed candle, and the stones became implacably solid.

Trembling, Arion shook the blood from his horn and turned toward Mariah.

"Stay where you are," Donnington said.

Arion stopped. He knew what was to come. He changed and moved away from Mariah, who was still rocking, oblivious, in the dirt.

"It has gone too far," Donnington said. "It must be ended."

"What must be ended?" Arion asked. "Your guilt for what you did to Mariah?"

"*My* guilt?" Donnington's hands shook on his weapon. "Are you any better than I?"

"No." Arion glanced toward the quiescent Gate. "I have betrayed a woman of such purity and courage as neither of us can comprehend. I have used my horn to bring death. My life is over." He met Donnington's gaze. "How do I know that you will care for Mariah?"

There was something like respect in the earl's eyes. "You have my word. My word as Earl of Donnington, backed with the honor of my family name. And because…" He looked down at Mariah. "I would have loved her, if I had been given the chance."

"You wasted your chance, Donnington. As I did."

The earl's expression hardened. "You will have no more time to grieve," he said, and aimed.

But he was not fast enough.

Mariah darted between Arion and Donnington with the speed of one of Cairbre's sprites. She fell as the bullet pierced her chest.

Arion fell with her. He gathered her into his arms. She smiled up at him, the blood already soaking the bodice of her habit.

"I was…rather good, wasn't I?" she whispered. "Cairbre thought he had punished me, but he…wasn't as powerful as he thought."

"Mariah…" Arion laid his cheek against her hair.

"There is no reason…for anyone to fight over me now." She closed her eyes. "Cairbre is finished. Donnington…"

The earl was on his knees, the rifle discarded, his head in his hands.

"Mariah," he croaked. "I never meant…"

"I know," Mariah said. "You won't hurt Arion, will you?"

"No." Donnington began to weep. "No."

"You see?" Mariah tried to lift her hand, but the life was swiftly leaving her body. "It is over. You can go back to Tir-na-Nog. Your people are waiting for you."

Arion felt the tears in his own eyes, tears that marked his humanity but, like so much else, came too late.

"Don't weep, my love," Mariah said. She felt inside the pocket of her torn skirt. "Nola…gave this to me. Keep it. You may need her some day."

She laid the carved sliver of bone on the ground and slumped, exhausted. Death was very near. Arion lifted his head.

"Donnington," he said.

The human didn't seem to hear him.

"Donnington!"

The earl's eyes cleared. "What do you want?"

"There is one way to save her. You must cut off my horn."

"No," Mariah whispered. "Ash…"

"A unicorn's horn may heal, but only its blood can conquer death. You must remove it and spill the blood on her wound."

Donnington stared. "How am I to…remove it?"

"Your iron will crack it. The rest will not be difficult."

"Ash!" Mariah gasped. "It will kill you!"

"No," he lied. He stroked her hair. "I will be well." He set her gently on the ground and rose. "Do it quickly, Donnington."

He changed again and held himself still. Donnington picked up his rifle, rose and tried to raise the weapon. It hung in his hands like a boulder.

"Let her die!"

Lady Westlake entered the clearing, pistol in her hand. She was panting as if she had just run a long distance, and the hem of her riding habit was covered in brambles.

"Pamela!" Donnington cried. "Why are you here?"

"To see that you do not betray me." She walked toward him, her skirts dragging in the dirt. "You promised we would be together. Nothing stands in our way now."

Donnington's hands tightened on the rifle. "What do you mean?"

"Lord Westlake is not long for this world," she said, smiling. "A few more pots of my special tea and I will be a bereaved widow."

"My God," Donnington whispered.

"Perhaps you are concerned about your brother. He will not trouble us again."

"What have you done?"

She examined the pistol in her hand. "What you would not. Should the dowager object to our marriage…well, then she will not be an obstacle for long, either." She seemed to notice Arion for the first time, nothing but cold indifference in her gaze. "Shoot him, and let the girl die."

Donnington raised the rifle. "You bitch," he said.

"You believed I would praise you for killing my brother?"

"He was a weakling." She took another step in his direction. "You are strong, Donnie. Strong and brave. You will do what must be done."

"Yes." Donnington swung his rifle toward Arion and fired. Arion felt his horn crack as the bullet struck and lodged in the ivory spirals. He collapsed under the weight of pain so great that his senses were already leaving him.

But Donnington had not forgotten what he had to do. He threw the rifle down and approached Arion, hands outstretched to take the horn.

He never completed the act. The bullet caught him in the chest, and his face went white with shock.

"Pamela," he grunted.

Lady Westlake dropped her pistol and ran to Donnington's side. "Oh, my love," she said, catching him as he fell. "You do see, don't you? I could not let you betray me."

Arion heard no more. His horn had not broken. He dashed it against the earth, blinded by the agony that shot from the tip down into his skull. Still it would not break.

He stretched his head across the ground beside Mariah, willing her the fading warmth of his body. He, too, was dying. Perhaps not immediately; his horn was badly damaged, but he might survive another few days.

The bone talisman lay where Mariah had dropped it. Arion took it between his teeth.

Nola. Nola, help me.

And she came.

There were deep shadows under her eyes, her once-bright hair hung lifeless around her shoulders, and she moved like an old woman. Her gaze took in the carnage and settled at last on Arion.

Arion heaved himself to his knees. *Save her,* he begged.

Tears streaked her face. "I cannot," she said.

Let me atone. Let her live.

"It will kill you."

I am already dead.

He bowed his head. Nola's hand settled on Mariah's chest. Her breathing was shallow now, almost imperceptible. Cool fingers took hold of Arion's horn.

It required great strength, but Nola had power enough. The horn snapped. Clear blood flowed from Arion's forehead as the life drained from his bones.

Nola worked quickly, allowing the horn's blood to drip onto Mariah's wound. Agonizing moments passed. Mariah's bleeding ceased. She moaned and felt at her chest, at the torn cloth that covered nothing but clean, unmarred skin.

Ash knew little about prayer, but he thanked whatever gods might be listening. He heard a stirring in the shrubbery and a tread he had come to recognize: Sinjin, leading his limping horse. He stopped when he saw Mariah.

"Good God!" he said. "Are you all right, Mariah?"

"Yes," she said, her voice breaking. Her gaze flew to Donnington's body. "I'm so sorry, Sinjin…."

"Donnington!"

The cry of shock and despair echoed through the clearing as Sinjin knelt beside his brother, his hands pressed to the wound in Donnington's chest, while Lady Westlake looked on with a blank and emotionless gaze.

But the earl was already gone. Sinjin straightened and stared at Pamela.

"*You* did this," he said.

She didn't deny his accusation. She didn't answer at all. She merely sat with her legs folded beneath her, maddened by her grief, seemingly unaware that Sinjin had spoken. Sinjin looked at Nola, bitter anger hovering beneath the glaze of anguish

Mariah stirred. With Nola's help, she managed to stand.

"Ash?"

He tried to look at her, tried to meet her gaze. His neck no longer had the strength to lift his head, and blood filled his eyes. Mariah's wordless cry hardly touched his ears.

But she was safe. She was alive.

Tell her goodbye, he said to Nola. *Tell her that I loved her.*

MARIAH KNEW WHAT Ash had done before Nola could explain. She found the broken horn, crawled to Ash's side and tried to push it against the gaping hole in his forehead.

Nola touched her arm. "You can do nothing," she said. "I am sorry."

Her words made no sense. Mariah crouched over Ash, watching the black of his eyes fade to gray.

He was not afraid. He, a creature who should have lived for generations, was prepared to die. He had given up his world, his future, his very life. All for her. She kissed his broad forehead, tasting the blood that soaked his forelock. Then she stood and faced the Gate.

"Unicorns can heal the injured," she said.

"Yes," Nola said. "But there is little chance that they can stop a mortal's death without sacrificing their horns and their lives."

"But Ash isn't mortal!"

"Even if he lived, he could never return to what he was."

"Can you keep him alive? Just for an hour?"

"I don't know."

"Try. Please try."

Mariah continued to the Gate. She spread her hands and focused all her concentration, her will, her love, on the stones before her.

They shimmered, the light beaming into Mariah's face. She stepped through and onto the rich soil of Tir-na-Nog.

The animals were waiting for her, just as before. But they were not alone. The unicorns had gathered by the Gate, snorting and sidling, as if they knew what had occurred on the other side.

"I need your help," Mariah said. "Your king is dying."

Adara stepped away from the rest. She lowered her head to the level of Mariah's eyes.

"I know you're afraid," Mariah said. "Our world was never kind to your people. But you were afraid when you went to fight Cairbre, and you were victorious."

Eyes rolled white. One of the males forcefully touched his horn to the ground.

They knew. They knew what Arion had done to save her.

"I don't ask you to sacrifice your horns," she said. "But with your combined power, surely you can achieve what one unicorn alone never could." She looked from one set of dark eyes to another until she had met every enigmatic gaze. "I ask only that you try."

The male stepped backward, as if he were preparing to run away. Several others seemed ready to follow them. But Adara lifted her head and trumpeted, a call as wild and as stirring as a fanfare. Then she bent to touch Mariah's shoulder with her horn.

"Thank you," Mariah whispered. "Thank you."

The Gate still shimmered behind her. She walked through, trusting that the unicorns would follow.

They did. They stepped into the human world gingerly, ears flattened, nostrils wide to take in the strange half-familiar scents known only to their ancient forebears.

Their hesitation was brief. As Nola moved away from Arion, Adara stepped toward him, moaning softly. Others shied, afraid of the scent of death. But then they began to form a circle around him, a dozen unicorns in hues of gold and silver and bronze and white.

Arion was no longer able to move. His breath came in heaving gusts, growing more shallow by the moment.

"Please," Mariah said, as she crouched beside him. "Save him. Care for him. Take him home."

Adara nibbled at Arion's ear. She bobbed her head as a signal to the others and used her horn to urge Mariah out of the way.

Then the unicorns gathered as close to Arion as was

possible, shoulder to shoulder and flank to flank, and lowered their horns.

As the tip of each horn touched Arion's shoulder, something wonderful happened. His dulled coat began to radiate a multicolored light. The wound in his forehead ceased bleeding and began to close. Little by little his breathing grew more regular, and a ripple ran through his body as if each muscle in turn were coming alive again.

Mariah closed her eyes, bathing in the healing power. Nola, too, was rapt with awe. Sinjin, who still crouched beside his dead brother, lowered his head. There was no sound until the unicorns stepped back, raising their horns as one, and Arion rolled to his knees.

Mariah whispered a prayer of thanks. She longed to run to Arion, but the unicorns had not broken their circle. They surrounded their king like vigilant soldiers, helped him to rise, and herded him toward the Gate.

It was what Mariah had told them to do. Take him back. Let him regain as much of his old life as he could. His people would not reject him. They would welcome him into their healing fold and never let him suffer again.

"He does not remember you now," Nola said, joining Mariah. "He will need much time to recover, and there is no guarantee…" She laid her hand on Mariah's shoulder. "You are choosing to let him go."

"It is necessary," Mariah said, the pain in her heart squeezing the words until they emerged as lifeless, nearly incomprehensible noise. "I think I always knew that he had to return."

"Does he? Is that what he wants?"

"Better that he doesn't remember." Mariah began to back away from the Gate. "He has lost his horn, but he will run again. Cairbre can't threaten him anymore. No one will ever cage him again as long as he lives."

"Mariah," Sinjin said, his own voice broken with sorrow. "I'm sorry."

She smiled through her tears. "You have lost so much today," she said. "Perhaps…perhaps we can help each other."

Sinjin didn't reply. The anger still boiled behind his eyes. He glanced at Pamela. "If they decide she's mad, perhaps they won't hang her for murder."

So much sorrow. Mariah forced herself to watch the unicorns approach the Gate. One by one they walked into the light, until only two remained.

Adara looked back. She bobbed her head…in acknowledgment, in a kind of shared understanding. She rubbed her muzzle against Arion's.

And then he turned. He searched the air with raised head, still glowing, still beautiful. And then his gaze fixed on Mariah. She could feel his thoughts trying to focus, trying to grasp memories that would soon be gone.

"Go," Mariah whispered. "Please…"

He took a step toward her. Adara followed and nudged his flank, trying to turn him back toward the Gate, but he didn't seem to feel her touch. He walked slowly, steadily, toward Mariah.

"Make him go," she begged Nola. "It was always what he wanted."

"Was it?" The red-haired woman brushed Mariah's cheek with her fingertips. "Why are you afraid, Mariah?"

"He'll lose his immortality, won't he? He'll be vulnerable here. Someday he'll…he'll…"

"Is that not his decision to make?"

"I could never live…knowing what he'd given up."

Nola only smiled with that sadness in her gaze. Arion was but a few feet away now, staring into Mariah's eyes.

Remembering. She could not stop him. His hornless head bowed nearly to the ground.

And then he changed, and a naked man stood in his place.

Ash, whose wound was no more than a round scar, hardly darker than his skin.

"Ma-riah," he said, his voice as hesitant as it had been the first time he'd spoken in the folly.

"Yes, Ash," she said. "Mariah."

He smiled, and all the world was in that smile. He held out his hand.

No power on earth could have stopped her from taking it. "You should go back, Arion" she said, the words cracking like brittle porcelain.

"I am *Ash*."

He took one last step and pulled her into his arms, running his hands through her hair, smelling her skin, seeking her mouth with his own. He smothered her protest with his lips and tongue, and when he was done, he held her close.

"I will never go back," he said.

"But, Ash…"

"You said you loved me," he said. "You said you would never let me go. Did you…mean what you said?"

"Yes. Yes." She took a deep breath. "Did you mean what you said when you thought I was mad?"

"Mariah." He cradled her face in his palms. "Yes. I love you."

She wept. She couldn't help it. Ash brushed the tears from her cheeks. And when she looked up, he was weeping, too.

They held each other for an eternity. At last Mariah broke away and looked behind her.

Nola was gone. Sinjin was pulling Pamela to her feet, though she gave no indication that she was aware of him.

"We have to help," Mariah said.

Ash nodded gravely, and held Shaitan steady while Sinjin lifted Pamela onto the stallion's back and climbed up after her.

"Stay with Donnington," Sinjin said quietly. "Just for a little while."

"We will," Mariah said. She and Ash watched as Sinjin

rode toward Donbridge, the woman in his arms gone to some-place far away.

"I am sorry," Ash said, putting his arm around Mariah's shoulders.

"So am I." She took his hand. "Everything has changed, Ash. We still have work to do. Vivian will be grieving deeply. She may lash out. We'll have to be patient, but Sinjin will be on our side."

"Yes."

"We'll have to help both of them."

"I understand."

She turned toward him. "I know you do, Ash. In your own way, you always have."

They kissed. The Gate shimmered one last time, and then the stones were only stones again.

Sinjin returned an hour later with two horses on leads. He and Ash lifted Donnington's body onto one of the horses, while Mariah and Ash took the second.

Ash drew their mount close to the one bearing Giles.

"I forgive," he said to the late Earl of Donnington.

And then the four of them rode out of sorrow and into the light.

EPILOGUE

THE BABY WAS BORN different. Everyone could see it: the wet nurse, the new nanny, the servants, Sinjin, even the dowager.

She was the second to hold him, cradling him in her arms as if he were Donnington reborn.

But Vivian knew he wasn't. Donnington would never come again. He had made many terrible mistakes. But now there was Sinjin, the new earl, with whom she had finally reconciled. He had made Rothwell his wedding gift to his former sister-in-law, though he had grieved over Donnington and had never become more than civil to Ash. And there was Mariah, who had easily forgiven all Vivian's designs against her.

Then there was Ash. When he and Mariah had been married after the requisite year of mourning, Vivian had found it difficult to be in his presence. But gradually, over time, she had learned to accept him, and to find some affection in her heart for the proud but gentle man who always treated her with the utmost respect.

They had named the baby Finnian, after Mariah's maternal grandfather. The boy's hair was as white as his father's, though there was no telling if it would remain so as he grew older. He was strong from birth, his hands grasping long before such an ability was considered normal. His eyes were blue, like Mariah's, with a rim of black. They seemed to look directly into Vivian's soul.

And they found her acceptable.

Vivian rocked him as Ash read, as voraciously as always, and Mariah knitted Finnian a tiny little cap. Vivian was almost content. The old pain flared in her hands, and she did her best to ignore it.

But then Finnian reached out with his pudgy fingers and grasped Vivian's. He smiled. The pain receded and then was gone.

The tears spilled from Vivian's eyes.

"Mother?"

Mariah had come to stand over her chair, her hand on Vivian's shoulder. "Are you all right?"

"Yes," Vivian said. She lifted her hand and demonstrated the easy movement of her fingers. "Finnian is a remarkable child."

"Yes. He is." Mariah knelt beside the chair and ran her finger over Finnian's downy cheek. "He takes after his father."

Ash looked up and met Mariah's gaze, such love in his eyes that Vivian trembled.

There was joy in the house again. Long after she had gone to her final rest, it would remain as it was now. A place of hope. Of magic. And of love.

* * * * *

Turn the page for a
preview of
LORD OF SIN,
Sinjin's story,
coming in September 2009
only from
New York Times *bestselling author*
Susan Krinard
and
HQN Books

THE ROYAL ACADEMY was hot and crowded, even though the Season had scarcely begun. This was supposed to be the private viewing, open only to the best and brightest of Society, but that seemed to include half of London.

St. John Ware, the Earl of Donnington, yawned behind his hand and glanced at the paintings with only the mildest interest. He was far more intrigued by Lady Mandeville's backside. Unfortunately, she was very happily married, unlike a great many of the peerage, and her husband was a rather large man.

Sinjin strolled the hall, seeking more amenable prey. There was Mrs. Laidlaw, whose husband was known to be involved with Lady Winthrop. She was quite acceptable in every way but her hair. It was blond, and that was anathema to him.

Lady Andrew, on the other hand, was dark haired, and her gown was very tight in the bodice, the impressive curve of her bosom all the more accentuated by the severity of her garments. Her husband was a known philanderer, making her ripe for the plucking.

As if she felt his stare, Lady Andrew turned. Her eyes widened as she saw him, and he predicted what was going through her pretty head as she stared at him.

The Earl of Donnington. Wealthy, handsome, possessed of every grace a peer ought to display. Impeccable clothing. The bearing of an Indian prince.

Sinjin laughed to himself. Ah, yes. The very pinnacle of perfection.

And London's most notorious bachelor rake.

He smiled at Lady Andrew. Her lips curved tentatively, and then she turned back to the painting. It was enough. She was interested, and when it wasn't so damned hot, he might pursue the opportunity that had so readily presented itself.

Out of habit, he continued his hunting. And there, across the room…

A mass of curling ginger hair that couldn't quite be contained in the tightly wrapped style of the day, a height neither petite nor tall, a figure neat and fine, a dress so unobtrusive that it made her fiery head all the more striking.

Ginger hair was not fashionable, but it drew Sinjin like a roaring hearth in winter. It collected all the heat in the room and crackled with light.

"Ah. You noticed her, too."

Mr. Leopold Erskine joined Sinjin. He was one of Sinjin's best friends, though not a member of the confirmed-bachelor set of which Sinjin was undisputed leader. "Quite a beauty, isn't she?" Leo commented.

Sinjin chuckled. "How can you tell? All I see is the back of her. And you've left off your spectacles."

Leo began to speak again, but Sinjin's attention had already wandered back to the fire maiden. She had turned slightly, but though her face was still not visible, there was an appealing lightness and grace about her movements as she bent to listen to one of the women standing beside her…a tall, dark-haired woman Sinjin was certain he recognized.

"Is the lady one of those widows I've been hearing about?" Sinjin asked. "The untouchables."

"Ah, yes. I believe they call themselves the 'Widows' Club.'"

"The Witches' Club," or so some apparently liked to call them, Sinjin thought. A half-dozen wealthy, well-bred and eccentric ladies who had vowed never to marry again. He felt a flicker of disappointment.

You may have vowed not to marry again, my dear, he thought, his eyes still on the fire maiden. But that does not preclude a little entertainment on the side.

"What do you know of her, Leo?"

Erskine guessed immediately to whom Sinjin referred. "She is Lady Charles, wife of the late Lord Charles Parkhill. She was completely devoted to him and never left his side during his illness. Even after she was widowed, she remained in the country until this Season."

"She is newly come to London?"

"Yes. The duchess and Lady Oxenham have been introducing her around town, but I understand that she has remained somewhat reclusive." Erskine frowned. "Are you thinking of pursuing her?"

"Have *you* an interest, Erskine?"

"I need not be a member of your Set to decline the pleasure of marriage," Erskine said.

"And you would consider nothing less."

"I am hopelessly old-fashioned, as you have so often reminded me."

Sinjin snorted. "Someday your virtue will take a tumble, my friend."

"And one of these days, old chap, you may find a woman who is your equal."

"If such a creature existed, I would marry her on the spot."

"May I take you at your word, Sin? Shall we make a friendly wager of it?"

"You aren't a gambling man."

"I am merely curious. The study of human nature is one of my favorite occupations."

"I don't know that I wish to be an object of study."

Leo produced his wallet and counted out twenty pounds. "Surely you can afford this much. But if you are afraid…"

"Afraid of a woman?" Sinjin thrust out his hand. "Done."

REQUEST YOUR
FREE BOOKS!

2 FREE NOVELS
FROM THE ROMANCE/SUSPENSE
COLLECTION PLUS 2 FREE GIFTS!

YES! Please send me 2 FREE novels from the Romance/Suspense Collection and my 2 FREE gifts (gifts are worth about $10). After receiving them, if I don't wish to receive any more books, I can return the shipping statement marked "cancel." If I don't cancel, I will receive 4 brand-new novels every month and be billed just $5.49 per book in the U.S. or $5.99 per book in Canada, plus 25¢ shipping and handling per book plus applicable taxes, if any*. That's a savings of at least 20% off the cover price! I understand that accepting the 2 free books and gifts places me under no obligation to buy anything. I can always return a shipment and cancel at any time. Even if I never buy another book from the Reader Service, the two free books and gifts are mine to keep forever.

185 MDN EF5Y 385 MDN EF6C

Name _____ (PLEASE PRINT) _____

Address _____ Apt. # _____

City _____ State/Prov. _____ Zip/Postal Code _____

Signature (if under 18, a parent or guardian must sign)

Mail to **The Reader Service:**
IN U.S.A.: P.O. Box 1867, Buffalo, NY 14240-1867
IN CANADA: P.O. Box 609, Fort Erie, Ontario L2A 5X3

Not valid to current subscribers to the Romance Collection,
the Suspense Collection or the Romance/Suspense Collection.

Want to try two free books from another line?
Call 1-800-873-8635 or visit www.morefreebooks.com.

* Terms and prices subject to change without notice. N.Y. residents add applicable sales tax. Canadian residents will be charged applicable provincial taxes and GST. Offer not valid in Quebec. This offer is limited to one order per household. All orders subject to approval. Credit or debit balances in a customer's account(s) may be offset by any other outstanding balance owed by or to the customer. Please allow 4 to 6 weeks for delivery. Offer available while quantities last.

Your Privacy: Harlequin is committed to protecting your privacy. Our Privacy Policy is available online at www.eHarlequin.com or upon request from the Reader Service. From time to time we make our lists of customers available to reputable third parties who may have a product or service of interest to you. If you would prefer we not share your name and address, please check here. ☐

nocturne™

New York Times Bestselling Author

REBECCA BRANDEWYNE

FROM THE MISTS OF WOLF CREEK

Hallie Muldoon suspects that her grandmother
has special abilities, but her sudden death
forces Hallie to return to Wolf Creek, where
details emerge of a spell cast. Local farmer
Trace Coltrane and the wolf that prowls around
the farmhouse both appear out of nowhere, and
a killer has Hallie in his sights. With no other
choice, Hallie relies on Trace for help,
not knowing if the mysterious Trace is a
mesmerizing friend or a deadly foe....

Available June wherever books are sold.

Susan Krinard

77315	COME THE NIGHT	___ $6.99 U.S.	___ $6.99 CAN.
77258	DARK OF THE MOON	___ $6.99 U.S.	___ $8.50 CAN.
77139	LORD OF THE BEASTS	___ $5.99 U.S.	___ $6.99 CAN.

(limited quantities available)

TOTAL AMOUNT	$ _____
POSTAGE & HANDLING	$ _____
($1.00 FOR 1 BOOK, 50¢ for each additional)	
APPLICABLE TAXES*	$ _____
TOTAL PAYABLE	$ _____

(check or money order—please do not send cash)

To order, complete this form and send it, along with a check or money order for the total above, payable to HQN Books, to: **In the U.S.:** 3010 Walden Avenue, P.O. Box 9077, Buffalo, NY 14269-9077; **In Canada:** P.O. Box 636, Fort Erie, Ontario, L2A 5X3.

Name: _____
Address: _____ City: _____
State/Prov.: _____ Zip/Postal Code: _____
Account Number (if applicable): _____

075 CSAS

*New York residents remit applicable sales taxes.
*Canadian residents remit applicable GST and provincial taxes.

HQN™

We *are* romance™

www.HQNBooks.com

PHSK0409BL